CLASH CITY SHOWDOWN

THE MUSIC, THE MEANING, AND THE LEGACY OF THE CLASH

CHRIS KNOWLES

ACKNOWLEDGMENTS

I'd like to thank the following people for their help and support over the years:

Jeff Dove, Inder Sidhu, Sukwoon Noh, Steve Savage, Teddy B, Eleanor Flicker, BJ Casey, Ralph Heibutzki, John Shipley, Tami Paterson, Jason Stebner, and all the folks who traded with me or sent me gifts during the days of the original Clash City Showdown Website.

Big shout-out to the gang over at Satch's Forums!
(http://boards.gcuber.com/)

This book is dedicated to the Mescaleros- Martin Slattery, Scott Shields, Tymon Dogg, Luke Bullen and Simon Stafford- thank you for all the brilliant, unforgettable nights of chaos and debauchery. Thank you for making Joe's final days so happy and for helping to give the story of the Clash as happy an ending as possible. And thank you for not being too afraid of me.

I can be reached via email at **chris@secretsun.com**

INTRODUCTION 10

CLASH HISTORY <u>18</u>

brief history of clash 19
drugs killed the clash 28
sandinista and combat rock
- not 'real' clash albums either 30
the reissue issue 32
toothless on the terry tour? 35
is there life after the clash? 38
ellen foley 41
did the clash sell out? 44

CLASH MUSIC <u>50</u>

it's all good 51
the clash's greatest record 55
gibsontown and fenderville 56
you're my guitar hero 58
head at the controls 61
the myth of london calling 63
sandinista for beginners 66
one more time 68
shitsville uk 69
westway to the world 71
they wrote the songs 72
who did what 74
you stupid, stupid bastards!!! 78
you're the one that i want (on a sunday) 79
d.i.d 80
the showdown guide to the official releases 81

THE CLASH ON STAGE <u>85</u>

the only good clash is a live clash 86
the essential clash bootleg bible 88
the clash live from here to eternity! 102

COMBAT ROCK CONUNDRUMS 105

combative rock 107
combat rock vs rat patrol 108
combat rock revisited.... 110
a 'beautiful' combat rock 111

CLASH II DOWN IN FLAMES 113

the cut the crap disaster- what really happened? 114
cut the crap track by track 121

BAD 124

the reinvention process 125
bad vibes 127
entering a bad new corporate ride 128
the showdown consumer guide (bad edition) 130

JOE 133

shakespearean strummer 135
joe strummer-celtic shaman 136
joe and the process of reinvention 138
joe's mid term report card 139
a method to his madness? 142
interview with joe strummer 144
the comeback 146
and suddenly, the mescaleros... 156
there goes my hero 159

MUSIC THEORY 164

1981 165
the anti-clash 169
don't kid yourself 170
the showdown guide to punk rock 172

the clash's heirs 174
the clash's legacy 175
the final swindle 177
never mind the pistols 178
i'm so bored with the uk 179

CLASH THEORY **182**

the alchemy of history 183
the chemistry of clash 184
god, fucking, and the clash 185
hands up for hollywood 188
hippies, not punks 190
mythology redux 193
revolution rock? 193
married to the yobs 195
technisonic cinemadelia 197
why the clash rule! 200
cowboys in africa 200

CLASH FANDOM **203**

me and the clash couldn't be pals 205
living in the past 207
grrrls vs. boyz 209
get a life 210
dreamtime 211
post-clash depression 213
the last gang in town 216
the last pilgrammage 218

OUT OF CONTROL 222

AFTERWORD 260

Joe Strummer

WHAT EXACTLY IS CLASH CITY SHOWDOWN?

I'm glad you asked. *Clash City Showdown* was originally a fanzine published in 1994 that soon after became a series of 'dispatches' to fans and subscribers on the Clash/Big Audio Dynamite message board on America Online. These dispatches were collected for a page on Jeff Dove's pioneering *Clash Zone* website before *CCS* became a site of its own. The purpose of the site was never to be any sort of authoritative resource on the Clash. In fact, the subtitle of *Clash City Showdown* was 'A Fan's-Eye View of the Clash.' In other words, it became an outlet for a prolix obsessive-compulsive whose OCD has been focused on the Clash for a couple decades now. Like any fan, I have my own preferences and hobby-horses. In fact, I even have a thesis!

The central thesis of *Clash City Showdown* is that the Clash were not a Rock and Roll band per se, but a Situationalist, multi-media, performance art project posing as a Rock and Roll band - albeit one that just happened to write great Rock and Roll songs. That may sound demeaning, but Rock and Roll bands are a dime a dozen. The Clash were utterly unique. The secondary thesis of *CCS* is that the Clash was a story, specifically a tragedy. The three protagonists of the story- Joe, Mick and Bernie - are tragic heroes in the classical sense. Together, they could've changed the world. But egotism, insecurity, and short-sightedness conspire to shoot them down long before they reach their true potential. In this tragic tale, The Clash make every mistake in the Rock and Roll lexicon, and only the tremendous creative power they possess saves them from being just another *Behind the Music* sob story.

BACK IN THE DAY, EVEN CIRCLES WERE SQUARES...

Clash City Showdown was actually born sometime in 1977, in Mr. Raymond's 7th grade music class at East Junior High School. We had to write a report on a musical topic, so I picked Punk Rock. I hadn't even heard any at this point, but the Sex Pistols were in the papers and *Creem* magazine (my monthly bible) a lot, so I figured it was as good a topic as any. I basically copied a bunch of quotes from the newspapers and probably didn't get a very good grade. But from that point forward, I wrote a school report on Punk Rock whenever I could get away with it. Needless to say, my teachers weren't very impressed, but I had a good time. Especially since there was a radio station in Boston (WBZ-FM 'New Wave Radio') that started playing Punk and New Wave sometime around 1978.

I was bewitched by the Clash before I ever heard their music. I remember seeing a couple articles on them in *Creem* and didn't take much notice, but the review of *Give 'Em Enough Rope* in the Feb. '79 issue of that magazine certainly caught my attention. The Clash were dressed in strange historical outfits: Joe was Jack the Ripper (or something), Mick looked like a 19th Century Royal Marine (or something), Paul was dressed up in an SS costume and Topper was dressed like Bruce Lee. The photo was weird and kind of scary and the review described an album that was militant and extreme. I was a Metal/Prog fan at the time, but I sensed the moment for that music had passed, and I was sick of kids chatting endlessly about their big brothers' records. I was ready for something new. But I hadn't yet taken the plunge because Cheap Trick was taking up most of my time.

Then I read an article in *Rolling Stone* of the Clash's New York debut at the Palladium. The article reinforced my conceptions of the band (extreme, cathartic, intense) but it wasn't the words that grabbed me. It was that famous Bob Gruen photo (which was actually taken at the Harvard Square Theatre) of the Clash on the attack. This is what I wanted to see a Rock band doing - going fucking nuts. I was so sick of hippies and the boring old 70's clichés. Here was a band that looked stripped down, revved up and pissed off. I saw more Gruen pics in my uncle's copy of *New York Rocker* and liked the look— leather, black slacks, baseball bats— it was pure Hollywood. Now all I had to do was actually hear their music.

I got my wish on my 13th birthday. I asked for and received *Give 'Em Enough Rope*. I had spent hours staring at the cover in the record store before ever getting it and wondered what the music inside could possibly sound like. It looked scary and I imagined it sounded pretty scary as well, the aural equivalent of one of the sleazy horror flicks my mother wouldn't let me see. As soon as I put the needle down - well, you know how the album starts. There was a problem, though. It was too intense, too unrelenting for me. I couldn't make heads or tails of it. It took me a few spins to parse the tunes under all the noise.

That set a precedent: every Clash album thereafter took me a few spins to warm up to. When I got the re-release of the first album I was stunned.

Where were the flame-thrower guitars and the hot-wire production? Of course, a couple weeks later I had the entire album memorized. But the Clash stepped back from the edge soon after and got cuddlier and cozier as the 80's progressed. And as much as I loved the mellower sounds and dug the expanding horizons of the band's worldview, I never got those early days out of my head. I could never shake the confrontational and cathartic Clash. The Clash did a lot of things well, but they only did one thing better than anyone else. And that was playing full-tilt, balls-out, crush-your-skull Rock and Roll. I realized I wasn't going to get it on the "official" (read: corporate) albums, so in true Punk fashion, I turned to the DIY Clash underground.

Maybe some of you can't stomach bootlegs. Maybe you can't deal with the coarse, lo-fi sound of most of them. Maybe a lot of you think the Clash were too crazy onstage and prefer the slicker studio work. That's fine with me.

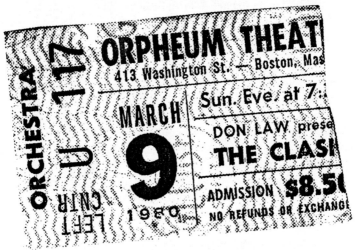

But so much of my experience of the Clash over the years has been bootlegs. You see, I saw the Clash on the *London Calling* tour, most certainly the original band's peak as an ensemble. And I learned first hand what the Clash really were about. And it wasn't the increasingly artificial studio records.

Of course, as the records drifted farther and farther away from the original idea of the band, the Clash became more and more popular. At the same time, the Hardcore movement began, fueled largely by the disgust fans felt with the increasingly commercial stance of the original Punk and New Wave heroes. The Hardcore scene exploded in Boston in the Spring of 1982, just as the Clash were about to release their wimpiest and least inspiring record, *Combat Rock*. All of the Hardcore kids I knew were at the Clash's marathon set of shows in the Boston area in 1982, but few of them were impressed. Due to an unfortunate string of circumstances, I only made it to one show, but it was so underwhelming I wasn't particularly motivated to see any others. As the months dragged on, my fierce loyalty to the band was tested and at some point in 1983, it went into hibernation.

Then the shocker — the announcement that Mick was sacked on September 1, 1983. I was shocked out of my hibernation and thrust into a deep depression. For me, Mick was the 'Rock and Roll' of the band.

I wasconvinced Joe and Paul would turn the Clash into some weird Funk/Dub thing and that would be the end of it. But then they announced that Mick would be replaced by two guitarists. I sat up and took notice. It was hard to imagine them hiring two new axemen if they were going to do a 'Fun Boy Clash' thing. My hopes were raised, but cautiously. One thing I had learned in the past four years is that you could always count on the Clash letting you down in one way or another.

Then the California mini-tour came in January '84 and I was over the moon. Like thousands and thousands of other fans, I had been yearning for the Clash to stop fucking around and go back to what they did best. My experience as a Hardcore scenester had taught me that most Rock critics were weasels, so I was unshaken by some of the negative reviews. But I was angered by them. I had spent the past few years reading the Clash being attacked for all their non-Punk dabbling and for Mick's rock star arrogance. But now that Joe seemed to be following the critics advice, he had become even more of a whipping boy. Of course, most of this was in the British press, and I was too young to realize that most British Rock critics in the early 80's were just a pack of dorks not yet evil enough to make it on Fleet Street. And this was years away from *Q, Mojo, Uncut* and all the rest of the great Brit glossies we have today.

Anyhow, it was open season on the Clash, but the overwhelming power of the new lineup emboldened some journalists to sing their praises, even if they had to slip in the obligatory sniping about "irrelevancy" (read: not beholden to the record Industry's latest prefab trends). So at that point, I beganto fantasize about an alternate source of information for Clash fans.

But - of course- the Clash predictably blew their last chance with the dreadful *Cut the Crap*. And, in the process, they empowered their worst critics. Joe engaged in a lot of revisionism himself about Clash II, claiming he was just along for the ride, but anyone who saw or has heard the Clash in 1984 knows this was nonsense. Joe was never more committed, nor more passionate onstage than he was then. Unfortunately, his plans and hopes for the band were subsumed by his manager's. And without a Mick Jones to back him up and beset by legal problems and personal hardships, Joe's spirit was broken.

I think most of Joe's actions (and music) from *Cut the Crap* until his reinvention with the Mescaleros were those of a broken man. He subordinated himself to Mick in a gesture of repentance with *No. 10, Upping St.* He farmed his talents out to Alex Cox and other Indy filmmakers, with only the *Walker* soundtrack realizing his true musical potential. He labored for the bizarre Class War collective, as if he were ashamed to mount his own tour. He chugged out an uninspired solo LP followed by an uninspired tour. Then he indentured himself to the Pogues, thereby demonstrating a complete lack of self-esteem. When that arrangement predictably crumbled, he vanished. But he did so messily, often promising projects that never materialized, infuriating some of his most zealous partisans in the process.

Mick, of course, soldiered on with Big Audio Dynamite. But he had obviously moved so completely away from what the Clash were about that BAD was simply a pleasant diversion to me. But the Clash's fortunes began to rise again. *The Story of the Clash, Vol. 1*, released in 1988, did well in Britain and the band had a commercial renaissance following the notorious Levi's commercial in 1991. Q had suddenly raised the level of British Rock journalism out of the bog, and there seemed to be a new generation of Rock crits there who were more concerned with music than ideology or record company payola. Even in the "Inkies."

But a new mythology had arisen, one that was probably inspired by the bands corporate custodians. It held that *London Calling* was the apex of the band's output. It held that the Clash did not implode disgracefully, but ended as if their dissolution was preordained. *Cut the Crap* was erased from the discography with a Stalinesque flourish and the new orthodoxy declared that Clash II was a total disaster, despite the excitement and anticipation raised by the 'Out of Control' tour. In some quarters, Joe was made out to be a ungrateful and treacherous passenger on the Clash Express.

This was Corporate Clash; as unacceptable to me as the mindless Clash bashing of the early 80's. This was a Clash tidied up for commercial consumption. So the *Clash City Showdown* 'zine was published in an attempt to counter it. The heart of the 'zine was a in-depth look at the *Cut the Crap* disaster (revised and reprinted in this book) that got the diehards to re-evaluate that era. And the rise of the Internet gave birth to both an active trading network and a free ranging debate on *alt.music.clash* and other message boards.

So much has happened in Clash fandom that it is an entirely different scene than 10 years ago. Joe finally re-emerged from his long slumber, rocked the world and tragically, passed on. Mick seemed to take Joe's place in the shadows as BAD underwent their own implosion. A new generation of fans, who discovered the Clash via the neo-Punk scene, came in bringing their own ideas of what the Clash were about. We've since had Marcus Gray's *Last Gang in Town* books, the *Westway to the World* documentary, the Sony re-issue program, the Rock and Roll Hall of Fame and Grammy award tributes, and countless website and magazine articles. The Clash are a permanent fixture in the Rock Community's consciousness now, not some failed crusade that everyone seemed to be at least slightly embarrassed by.

But the fact that success seemed to destroy the Clash had puzzled me, because they seemed automatically pre-destined for super-stardom. Their rivals and contemporaries, the Police and the Jam, imploded around the same time as the Clash, but both of those bands operated with a far more limited palette and were burdened with the two most bloated egos in modern musical history.

So there was yet another compelling reason for me to continue with the Showdown. To devour every scrap of information I could about the Clash, process it in real time on the Net so that maybe through reaching some critical mass, I could finally figure out why the Clash went so wrong. I needed to analyze the words and actions of the band members, see what made them tick and put to rest the myriad questions I had about the story of the Clash. I do not see the Universe as a conglomeration of random events— I think everything happens for a reason that can be learned and understood. And I needed to understand why things turned out the way they did.

For instance, I needed to understand that the reason the band never patched up their differences and continued was partly because they were terrified of tampering with their mythology. So terrified that the obvious benefits of reforming back when it still mattered were outweighed by the fear that their place in the Rock and Roll Pantheon might be upset. I also needed to understand that the four members were so temperamentally different that only the tumult and excitement of the Punk era could have brought them together and once that rush wore off there wasn't much to keep them together. I will share with you what I've come to understand in the final chapter of this book.

As I said, this book lays no claim to being an objective record of the Clash, in fact, it's the exact opposite. It's the subjective document of a long time passionate fan. A fan who, unlike some others, isn't afraid to hide his devotion to the band, nor hide it behind some cynical pose. This book is a partisan document, but I am not afraid to criticize the band on their numerous short-comings.

The purpose of *Clash City Showdown* was not to be writing about Punk, but Punk writing. It was meant to be confrontational and direct and a little bit obnoxious. So much rubbish had been written about the Clash by 40 year-old clock-punchers, and I wanted to write from the viewpoint of a Punk. Not just as a fan, mind you, not the kind of writing that a 12 year old girl would write about Justin and Britney, but as someone who took the Clash at their word. And what I always strove to do was put the Clash in context and pass on the ideas and ideals they professed.

Music is one of the most important things in my life. It's one of the most powerful forces in our culture, and the most powerful form of communication in the world. The first thing the Nazis banned was "degenerate" music. They knew its power. The Right Wing (and sometimes the Left) in this country has spent millions fighting the music of youth.

Music is a very powerful tool and this country has been changed as a direct result of the ideas and messages that have been communicated through music. When a society would go to war the first thing they would do was write a stirring song to rally the troops. Punk Rock started a process that has changed human society forever.

But, to be a Clash fan is to suffer. The Clash made and then broke a lot of promises, and fell well short of their potential for the usual stupid and prosaic Rock star reasons. They squandered their world-shaking potential on drugs and ego trips. Mick Jones threw his Rock and Roll credibility away for a couple minor hit singles. Joe Strummer surrendered when he should have stood his ground and fought, and then seemed to delight in tormenting his fans in the 90's by announcing projects that never materialized.

I believe that for a period towards the end of the 90's, Joe had literally driven me insane, albeit unintentionally, with this bait and switch routine. And I was already half-crazed with the sheer hell of waiting for him to make his move. But as Fate would have it, just as I had totally given up hope on Joe, he came back and rocked the world for nearly 43 months straight. His frenzied recording and touring schedule came crashing to an end with his premature passing, but the memories of all those brilliant nights and all the music he left behind will last the rest of my life. The Meskies never reached the heights the Clash did, nor were they the thermonuclear force of nature Clash II were, but boy, were they a blast to go see play.

Whatever their failings, the Clash's virtues and achievements far outweigh their short-comings. The Clash showed that the Punk attitude was not a nihilistic and solipsistic dead end, but a new way to engage the world. They also left behind an astonishing corpus of incredible music, both before and after they collapsed. And they also left a wealth of buried treasure for nutcases like myself to dig for. They still continue to attract and inspire new fans, and I hope this book will help to clarify and preserve the band's legacy. Every generation deserves a Clash, and maybe, just maybe, this book will help to inspire a new one. Because the world needs the energy and idealism of the Clash now more than ever.

A BRIEF HISTORY OF CLASH

1976- BACK IN THE GARAGE

The story has been told and retold so many times that even the most casual Clash fan has it memorized. A fledgling practice band asks a pub rock star at the unemployment line to join their outfit, and a legend is born. What is not told is how this improbable outfit was the work of a crazed svengali looking to rival his boss' band, who were in turn put together to sell blue jeans and bondage gear. Mick Jones, Paul Simonon and Mick Jones were three totally different people from one another and even from their fans and contemporaries.

Joe Strummer was born in Ankara, Turkey, the son of a diplomat and his Scottish wife. Mick Jones was the son of a Welsh laborer and a Russian-Jewish woman and Paul Simonon was the scion of Belgian immigrants. The fact that their origins were obscured is not surprising given the nativist sentiments of the English in the mid-70's.

Bernie Rhodes "imagined the Clash" as Joe Strummer put it in the MTV documentary. What is also played down in the official mythography is the control he had over them in the early days. Johnny Thunders went so far as to write a song making fun of the Clash's dependence on Rhodes. In 'London Boys', Thunders sang, quite uncharitably, "You need an escort to take a piss/ he holds your hand and he shakes your dick."

But this band/manager relationship was in the classic British tradition. The Beatles had Brian Epstein, the Stones had Andrew Loog Oldham, the Who had Kit Lambert and Chris Stamp, and Led Zeppelin had Peter Grant. Rhodes' control over the Clash, like McLaren's control over the Sex Pistols, did not mean they did nothing. And the fact that they broke from Rhodes (albeit temporarily) early in their careers shows that they were no man's puppets.

The early Clash numbers were a hodgepodge of London SS numbers and hastily composed Strummer/Jones tunes, strongly reminiscent of 60's mod and garage bands. Jackson Pollock fan Simonon, responsible for much of the Clash's visual style, designed splattered and stenciled outfits that were quite the rage in 1976. The 'bloodshot-and-bulletholes' shirt was a classic. Like the Pistols, the Clash did their learning in public and by the time 1977 rolled around, they showed they had learned their lessons well indeed.

1977- HOPE I GO TO HEAVEN

What can I say about 1977 that hasn't been said before? When most people think of Punk Rock, it's a cinch they will think of 1977. That year, Punk went from being a weird subculture in a few cities to a worldwide media circus. The Clash were a big part of that phenomenon. They burned up the concert circuit all around the UK and Europe, winning many new fans, even stealing them from Punk standard bearers the Sex Pistols. The Sex Pistol's notoriety got them banned in a lot of clubs so the Clash grabbed the spotlight. To see the Clash in 1977 was to see a band on fire. Very few bands have matched the pure catharsis the Clash embodied in their early days. They were a blur onstage, constantly in motion, fueled by their prodigious speed consumption. Strummer performed like the stage was electrified, spitting and shaking and convulsing.

New drummer Topper Headon fit in perfectly, using military sticks to match Chimes' furious anarchic pounding. Chimes left early on in '77, sick of the politicking and head games, but returned to pound the shit of the drums for the sessions for the first album. That LP, instantly hailed as a classic, failed to capture the blistering hurricane that was the Clash on stage, a sad precedent that would plague the Clash throughout their career. the outrageous antics of the Punk movement attracted the attention of Her Majesty's police and the Clash continually found themselves in and out of the dock on a procession of petty charges. This harassment could not stop them, however, and dreary England was treated to an explosion of color and sound from an army of kids sick of the bloated corporate charade that was being passed off as Rock music.

1978 - NOBODY'S KIDDING OR FOOLING AROUND

1978 was a tumultuous year for England, for the Punk Movement and for the Clash. The UK was gripped by political violence, recession, and terrorism. The country's mood had darkened and soured, and the general apocalyptic malaise of the West was particularly acute in the UK. Punk was imploding as the Sex Pistols had traveled to America, had a disastrous tour and broke up. Many of the major bands were releasing disappointing second albums and the "New Wave", the music industry's response to Punk, was softening the impact of the new music. In this maelstrom the Clash soldiered on, polishing and refining their presentation into a more classic Rock and Roll format. Mick had grown out his hair and was looking more and more like Jimmy Page as the year wore on. The Clash began filming *Rude Boy* with Hazan and Mingay and had begun work on *Give 'Em Enough Rope* with Sandy Pearlman   .

Midway through the year, manager Bernie Rhodes was sacked and the Clash hired journalist Caroline Coon to take his place. The Clash continued to run afoul of the law. The famous pigeon shooting incident took place in 1978, as well as the Glasgow Apollo disaster documented in *Rude Boy*. In anticipation of *Give 'Em Enough Rope*, the Clash released three classic singles in 1978. The first was 'Clash City Rockers' b/w 'Jail Guitar Doors', released in February. 'Clash City Rockers' was a further variation on Mick's obsession with the Who's 'Can't Explain'. The single also featured a hijacking of the old British folk tune, 'Bells of St. Rhymney', earlier covered by the Byrds. 'Jail Guitar Doors' was an updated 101'ers track that name-checked Wayne Kramer of MC5, Peter Green of Fleetwood Mac and Keith Richards. 'White Man in Hammersmith Palais', inspired by Joe's experience at an all-night Reggae concert, followed in June backed with 'the Prisoner.' Little needs to be said these great classics, except that they were the first Clash tracks to be self-produced.

In November, the Clash released 'Tommy Gun' b/w 'One Two Crush on You.' 'Crush' was an old London SS tune that the Clash had played in their early days. The song was originally sung by Joe. Bruce Springsteen later borrowed heavily from this song for his 'Ooh-Ooh Crush on You' on his 1980 LP, *The River*. Soon after the release of 'Tommy Gun', the Clash released *Give 'Em Enough Rope*. The album was greeted by a chorus of sniffing from know-it-all critics. Despite the tepid reviews, the LP crystallized the fear, rage and frustration that had London in its grip in the late '70's. The high-tech sheen of Pearlman's production captured the brute force of the Clash's sound, a feat that, sadly, was never duplicated.

The Clash emerged from 1978 as the standard bearers of Punk, a mantle they found quite heavy indeed. A new wave of bands was waiting in the wings, many of the recombinations of first wave acts and the Clash faced 1979 with one imperative: Evolve or die.

1979-80- AT THE GATES OF THE WEST

This is the era that many critics and fans believe to be the Clash's best. It was in this time that the Clash toured America three times (the Pearl Harbor, The Clash Take the Fifth, and Sixteen Tons tours) released the brilliant *Cost of Living EP*, the classic *London Calling* album, the 'Bankrobber' single, and the US only *Black Market Clash* 10" disk. and the *Sandinista* LP. The ratio of quantity to quality of these two years has been surpassed only by the Beatles, and perhaps the Stones, in the '60's. In the eyes of the critics the Clash could do no wrong. The band was touring constantly in support of the *Give 'Em Enough Rope* album, which was released in late '78. The boys visited the US in the winter of '79 making their debut at the Harvard Square Theatre in Massachusetts. The Clash were in hot demand upon their arrival.

The Sex Pistols had broken up the previous year and the Clash were considered the standard bearers of Punk. The concerts were the scathing attacks of fury that had earned the group its reputation as a high-energy concert draw. The band returned to the UK after the tour to begin writing for their new album, to be produced by Guy Stevens who had produced the Clash's demos for Polygram in 1977. So much material had been recorded that the album was set to be a double. The title song was released in advance of the album (the album's working title was *the New Testament*) with the flip side 'Armagideon Time'. That song had been a reggae hit for Jamaican singer Wille Williams in 1978, but the Clash's version was so far superior to the original that it has since become to be associated with the band as their song. The new album was released to generally negative reviews in the UK and to hysterical raving praise in the US. The Clash even scored a top twenty hit in a song that was originally intended to be a *NME* giveaway.

'Train in Vain' helped bring the album into the Top 30 in the US album charts. The Clash visited the US in the Winter of '80 in support of the record. They also appeared on the ABC comedy series *Fridays* and performed four songs from their album. *Rolling Stone* critics named the band and the album the best of the year. The Clash then returned to the UK after a jaunt through Europe to begin work on a so-called 'Singles Campaign'. This new concept was to release a single and then to release another once the previous had fallen from the charts. The first effort from this was the single 'Bankrobber' which CBS initially refused to release. The song garnered attention in the UK as an imported B-side and became their highest charting single in England. Despite this success, CBS, who had their eyes on the lucrative US album market, nixed the singles idea.

The Clash were reported to be extremely upset and threatened to break up. CBS were not impressed and the Clash traveled to New York's Electric Ladyland Studios to record a new LP. Paul Simonon traveled to Canada to shoot a film entitled *Ladies and Gentlemen the Fabulous Stains*. He was replaced in the sessions by Joe Strummer and Norman Watt-Roy of the Blockheads. Many musicians guested on the LP, including Ellen Foley

(Meatloaf), Mickey Dread (who also mixed), Gary Barnacle (the Ruts DC), Ivan Julian (the Voidoids), violinist Tymon Dogg, and Blockhead Mickey Gallagher (who was more or less a Clash member for most of 79-80). Songs from the aborted singles campaign were recorded as well as a number of tunes written in the studio. A prodigious amount of marijuana was reportedly smoked and Topper Headon accelerated his tragic descent into heroin addiction at this time. The end of 1980 saw the release of the 'Call-up'/'Stop the World' single and video. The video was shot in black and white and featured the Clash's first venture into urban guerilla military imagery and clothing.

After the single's release the triple LP, *Sandinista*, was released. There are a number of conflicting stories as to why the Clash saw fit to release a triple-record set. The band was reportedly upset that *London Calling* was only counted as a single LP towards their contractual obligation of ten albums by CBS. Also, the band was said to have had difficulties releasing *London Calling* as a double while CBS released Springsteen's *The River* double LP with little bickering. Other reports have that the Clash were livid at CBS for squelching the singles campaign and foisted *Sandinista* on the company as revenge. Yet another explanation has it that the Clash simply wanted to release everything recorded as an experiment. Whatever the reason, the set was bludgeoned by the British papers and sold poorly in the UK. When the album reached the US in January 1981, however, it was praised lavishly as a bold experiment and a challenge to the Rock Community to explore the rich heritage of Roots and World music styles. *Rolling Stone* went so far as to give the album five stars in a review. The album charted higher and longer than *London Calling*, despite revisionist attempts to paint it as a failure. Despite the filler, *Sandinista* contains many of the Clash's greatest classics and gave rise to the Roots and World

movements of the 80's. I would go so far to say that *Sandinista!* was the Clash's most radical statement and their most influential work. The album blew open the doors and evaporated Rock's self-imposed musical limitations.

1981- LONDON TOWN ON THE BROADWAY

In 1981 the Clash were on the way to becoming major stars in the US. *Sandinista!* got good reviews from US critics even though it was trashed in the UK. The LP charted in the upper 20's in the *Billboard* charts and was probably selling better than that, since *Billboard* didn't use sales from specialty stores where the Clash sold most of their records. The 'Police on My Back' single was getting FM airplay and America was awaiting a major Clash tour. America didn't get one.

Reports of friction in the band were starting to leak out. Topper was having a major drug problem. Paul spent most of the *Sandinista!* sessions filming a movie in Canada and recording a solo LP for Stiff that was never released. Mick and Joe were not on speaking terms and the band did promotional interviews for *Sandinista* separately. In lieu of a tour, Mick had produced LPs for Ian Hunter and Ellen Foley. Finally in May, after a European jaunt the Clash announced a series of dates at Bond's International Casino, a night club in New York's Times Square. The promoter oversold the shows, the Fire Department shut them down, a riot ensued at a canceled show and at a press conference the band committed to more shows to accommodate fans who had been shut out.

The band then made a appearance on Tom Snyder's *Tomorrow Show*, blasting out a searing version of 'Magnificent 7' and debuted a new song entitled 'Radio Clash'. Clash co-hort Don Letts filmed the shows and the boys' walking tour of New York City for a never-released film entitled *Clash on Broadway*. A collaborative video with New York rappers Grandmaster Flash was planned but never produced. The band, after a lengthy break from touring, played a limited tour of London and Paris in late '81 where they premiered such future classics as 'Know Your Rights','Ghetto Defendant', and 'Should I Stay or Should I Go?'. Mick also began sessions with London punk band Theatre of Hate (featuring future Cult guitarist Billy Duffy) A single and video version of 'Radio Clash' was released in late '81, the only new Clash product released that year.

1982- FUNKY INTERNATIONAL ANTHEMS

1982 started off horribly for the Clash. Infighting and drug problems held up the production of their new album, originally entitled *Rat Patrol from Fort Bragg*. Topper Headon was fading into a drug-addled oblivion and Joe and Mick weren't on speaking terms. A tour through Asia often saw the Clash at their worst. Afterwards Joe disappeared to Paris causing the cancellation of a major British tour coinciding with the release of their fifth album *Combat Rock*. That record was praised by British critics as one of their best and shot to

number two on the UK charts. Joe returned, and they kicked out Topper.

Terry Chimes returned and the Clash embarked on an eight-month tour that prduced some great Rock and some not-so-great Rock.

At the end of their lengthy tour, they played six dates with the Who. (the first of that band's many ridiculous farewells)

They also played at a Jamaican festival at the Bob Marley Music Center in the late Autumn. Terry left in early '83, and was replaced by Peter Howard from the London band, Cold Fish. This lineup headlined Steven Wosniak's Us Festival after a few selected gigs in Texas and Arizona. At this festival, the Clash engaged the promoters in numerous battles over charitable distributions of receipts and the lack of black performers invited to perform. The press severely lambasted the Clash for their behavior and Joe's verbal tongue-lashing of the crowd. Despite the controversy, the Clash put in a top-flight performance at the festival. Their set was cut short by the annoyed promoters and Pete and Paul engaged in a brawl with festival security who denied them stage access for a second encore. This was Mick Jones' last show with the band.

1984-85 - TREATED LIKE TRASH

Mick Jones was sacked from the Clash in late '83. Joe, Paul and Pete recruited two new guitarists from a classified ad and began rehearsing for a self-financed tour. Ex-Cortina Nick Sheppard and recent college graduate Vince (Gregory) White were originally supposed to assume full guitar duties but Joe decided he missed playing and the Clash became a three (!) guitar band. The new lineup made their debut in the Santa Monica Civic Center (an event covered by *Entertainment Tonight*). They played several more dates in California before returning to Europe and the UK for a two-month tour. The 'Out of Control' tour, as it was dubbed, was a huge success in Europe and the band traveled to the US for two more months. The group played sports arenas and colleges without financial support from Epic. But daunting legal troubles were on the horizon. Mick had hired attorneys to impound all the band's assets and challenge the use of the name. And the new Clash couldn't make a move without being attacked by hordes of backstabbing journalists.

In December of '84, the band played two concerts in benefit for the Scargill miners strike. Here they performed many new tunes, and announced their album would soon be released. The band entered a studio in Germany in late January of '85. They re-emerged in the spring to play a series of impromptu acoustic shows in train stations, city squares and outside concert halls. They played their last concert in Athens at a festival in July. The British papers reported that Mick Jones' lawyers had the courts forbid the Clash the use of their name in 1985.

In October, the album *Cut the Crap* was released, featuring songs from the tour in radically altered form. Pete Howard and Paul Simonon were MIA, and most of the arrangements heard on tour had been destroyed, and uncredited keyboards by Mickey Gallagher featured prominently in many songs. No explanation was given for the changes and the album was mercilessly savaged by many reviewers. Joe and Paul broke up the band and soon after appeared in Big Audio Dynamite's video for 'Medicine Show'. Despite the incredible performances this conglomeration gave, the sorry end and general misery of the recording sessions and the mess they produced have caused all concerned to look back on this era with shame and regret. Skip the album, get the bootlegs.

DRUGS KILLED THE CLASH
Originally posted Spring 2003

One of the things observers of the Clash speculate on (as have the band members themselves) is why a band that seemed destined for the Pantheon crashed and burned so early in their careers. I think the problem was drugs. All of the ego clashes and musical differences really come down to drugs. Tops had the heroin and coke problem, which took the foundation of the bands sound out from underneath them. I felt vindicated when Tops himself admitted this, especially after all the crap I took on *alt.music.clash* for years for saying this. Tops was an extremely important part of the band's sound and gave the band confidence. The absence of his contribution and the tension from his arrests and problems with dealers drained the will out of the band.

Mick's problems in the late days of the Clash - his arrogance, his self-indulgence and abuse of other band members - seem directly tied into his prof-ligate pot smoking (making him paranoid and indulgent) and his coke habit (which made him imperious and abusive). I know the official story was that Mick quit coke in the late 70's, but I don't know if I believe it. Though never buff, the way he wasted away to a near skeleton in the early 80's - compare Mick in '77 to him in '82 - says big-time coke abuse to me. And Mick seemed to be a gentle, good-natured character in many ways, leading me to believe that his personality issues were chemically induced.

The fact that Paul and Joe were mammoth pot-heads was probably less a factor than the hard drug use of the other two, but Marcus Gray claims in *ROTLGIT* that Paul developed a heroin-sniffing habit as well. But the pot-head ambiance of the band in general really ran counter to their professed ideals and destroyed their espirit-de-corps. But at the same time, both Paul and Joe made a lot of noise that they had quit drugs in '82 interviews, and if that's true, it was certain to have made Mick more uncomfortable.

I know a lot of people dig *Rat Patrol*, but I wince when I listen to it. It really sounds to me like a bunch of drug addicts whacking off in the studio. There was a great article in *Vanity Fair* a few years back about how drugs destroy a band. Viewers of *Behind the Music* will be familiar with the process. The irony is that drugs inspire a band creatively at first, in what the writer called the 'Intoxication' phase. But there's always a big downside once the drugs take over the host. I think it's kind of ironic how quickly this process happened with the Clash. It took the space of two albums, when the process took much longer with other bands.

It's also ironic how the Clash really fell into the trap that every other band has fallen into. I think the Record Industry deserves a lot of blame here. The relentless tour-record schedule that bands were under (especially then) is notorious for encouraging musicians to abuse chemicals just to get through the day. And the fact that none of the Clash members were exactly hardy specimens certainly did little to halt their decline.

With the waning influence of the Multi-Nationals on real Rock culture, it will be interesting to chart the influence of drugs on today's bands. Hopefully, they will learn something from the Clash and other victims of chemical excess.

SANDINISTA AND COMBAT ROCK-
NOT 'REAL' CLASH ALBUMS EITHER
Originally posted Spring 2003

There's been a lot of discussion as to whether *Cut the Crap* is a 'real' Clash album. It wasn't until Ralph Heibutzki published his landmark Clash histories in *Goldmine* and *DISCoveries* magazines that the world understood that *Cut the Crap* was largely the work of Bernie Rhodes and anonymous studio musicians, with the 'new' Clash's frontline called in only for lead vocals and lead guitar. Paul Simonon was absent from the album entirely, his recorded output with that lineup restricted to the b-sides for the 'This is England'12." There has also been a lot of speculation as to why Joe Strummer would tolerate such an arrangement. Why would he allow someone to take charge of the recording process and substitute the members of the Clash with no-name studio hacks? The answer? He was used to it.

The question of the ages to me has always been why doesn't most of *Sandinista* and *Combat Rock* sound like the Clash? Compare the songs on those two albums to their live cousins, or better still, the *Rat Patrol* tracks to the demo versions on the *Hell W10* soundtrack. They don't sound much alike. In fact, in many cases it seems that the actual Clash —— that is Strummer, Jones, Simonon and Headon standing on a stage and playing together - aren't even terribly familiar with the recorded versions of the songs.

This is not the case with any of the songs from the real Clash albums, ie. *the Clash, Give 'Em Enough Rope* and *London Calling*- the albums where the Clash got together and rehearsed a bunch of tunes then went into a studio and recorded them together. There has been some idle speculation that Joe and or Paul don't play on the real Clash albums, but I don't buy it. Play with your balance control on the first LP- Joe's guitar is right there, alone on the left channel (a la the Ramones first LP). Mick may have done some bits here and there, but Joe would play his guitar unplugged when he was doing his vocal takes and I've seen photos and films of the Clash playing in the studio, so chalk that up to revisionism. The live versions on *London Calling* may be more energetic than on record, but that's the nature of the onstage beast.

This integrity all falls apart when we get to *Sandinista*. Paul was absent from the Electric Lady sessions altogether, replaced by Norman Watt-Roy. Mickey Gallagher plays on nearly every track, and Mick even gave up guitar duties on some tracks to Ivan Julian of the Voidoids. Watt-Roy and Gallagher are capable players, but the Blockheads were essentially a bunch of leftover old 'musos' - a wedding band essentially - with a quirky lead singer. The Clash were thrilled to have versatile journeymen at hand to help them develop new ideas, but they paid a price for it. The Blockheads music was tired, cliched and punchless, and they brought this sensibility to Electric Lady with them. The credits list a ton of other studio players, including our pal Tymon Dogg, but its safe to say most of *Sandinista!* was built around Mick, Watt Roy, Gallagher, and the almost-incapacitated Topper Headon.

It has never been really established if the Clash went into the studio with the intention of making a record, or to cut demos. Most of the material

was written in the studio. It was an exciting time for the band and an exciting and ground-breaking album came out of it. But was it a Clash album?

Compared to the first three, no. Not if you describe a Clash album an album played by the four individuals generally understood to be the Clash. Joe played little or no guitar on it, same with Paul on the bass. Taking two out of the four instrumentalists out of the mix and replacing them with studio musicians changes the basic integrity of the group. Neither Joe nor Paul were particularly skillful on their instruments, but both were energetic and enthusiastic, and Strummer's guitar often set the tempo for the band when they were actually playing. In addition, Mick's attention was not on guitar. His guitar generally is heavily treated and very low in the mix, or he is playing a very early synth guitar. The guitar playing that he presented onstage is mostly absent from *Sandinista* and *Combat Rock*. It is, in essence, a dishonest document of the band, which is what an "album" is supposed to be.

This realization stunned me. it's so simple- why don't *Sandinista* and *Combat Rock* sound like the Clash? Because they're not really played by the Clash. They are selected members of the Clash collaborating with other musicians in a very artificial and contrived studio setup. *Combat Rock* started out as a Clash album with the Ear mobile studio sessions (where 'Should I Stay', 'Know Your Rights', 'Long Time Jerk', and 'First Night Back in London' and others were recorded), but once the band returned to Electric Lady, the pattern set on *Sandinista* re-emerged. The bass was handled by Mick, Topper, or one of the studio engineers. Tymon Dogg and the Barnacle Brothers contributed heavily and again the fatal mistake was made - Joe not playing guitar.

Compare the demo of 'Overpowered by Funk' to its slower, vastly inferior 'official' cousin. Of course, the results were skewed by the fact that Mick and Topper were seriously addicted and no real producer was present to provide adult supervision. It's amazing to me that the Clash were able to record anything at all under these conditions, never mind the gobs of Stoner classics that both *Sandinista* and *CR* are lousy with. (I also have serious doubts as to whether the material generally referred as *Rat Patrol* is actually Mick's proposed final mix. He might have been out of his mind on drugs then, but I still think that stuff is half-finished rough mixes- most of those vocal takes don't sound final to me at all).

A couple thoughts emerge here- Mick took control of a band that had prior been a more or less democracy, at least in the studio. He wanted to make what he thought were great records. The irony is that by replacing not-great-but-spirited players with tired, old studio mutts, he robbed the Clash of a lot of their charm and certainly almost all of their energy. He was playing by old rules. As forward as Mick always tried to be, these strategies were corny and dated, straight out of the Brill Building. Slicking up the music and using severely un-Punk Rock retreads like the Blockheads and the Barnacle boys was as old-fashioned as it gets. And let's face it- the decision to do this was probably commercially motivated.

And although we fans love those records, the general consensus is that those are sub-par Clash albums. This may have a lot to do with the fact that both albums are more or less half-filler, but the tired and old-fashioned playing also hampers the esteem both records are held in. And the incredible irony of it all is that they're not really 'Clash' albums either. I just hope that Sony gets wise and releases more live material so the public record can be set straight. As filler-ridden as the last two albums are, there's some great material on them, and it would be nice for the general public to hear them as the Clash actually played them.

THE REISSUE ISSUE

Originally posted 1/20/97

(NOTE: the 2001 reissue program makes this article somewhat moot, but many important points are made about how lax the band was about their legacy for a very long time.)

One of the frequent complaints Clash fans have is the generally low quality of post-Clash reissue material. These reissue efforts more often than not have been slapdash and ill-conceived. For a band that seemed so concerned with "value for money", the avalanche of posthumous cash-ins has been at odds with their Punk philosophy. In other words, with only a couple exceptions, all their reissues are sucky rip-offs   .

The parade of suck started in 1986, when CBS-FOX released *This is Video Clash.* This quickie threw together the Don Letts vids from 'Tommy Gun' to 'Should I Stay or Should I Go' and arranged them chronologically. The 'White Riot' and '1977' videos were nowhere to be seen, nor were the promos for 'I Fought the Law' (taken from *Rude Boy*) or 'Clampdown.' (taken from the same concert as the 'Train in Vain' video) In addition to the flimsy selection, the sound on 'Train' and 'Should' sucks pus. One guesses that this was a record company cash-in, seeing that Mick and Joe were busy with their solo careers, but this is no excuse. *This is Video Clash* is a must for completists but compared to videos put out by other bands, it is a disgrace.

That same year, Epic re-released all the original line-up's records on CD. Aside from *Combat Rock*, there were no lyric sheets or photos in the booklets. This is particularly offensive because all of the original releases had lyric sheets. (with the exception of *Give 'Em Enough Rope*) A whole new generation of Clash fans were doomed to wonder what the hell the band was actually singing about. *Black Market Clash* was not included in the re-issue program, no extra tracks were added to the albums, and the sound on *Combat Rock* was markedly inferior to the vinyl release. "Fuck you, Clash fans" was the message sent by these slapdash reissues.

Next up (following some Aussie/UK scraps here and there) was *the Story of the Clash, Vol.1.* The packaging was handsome, there was a lengthy rant written by Joe (aka Albert Transom) but the sequencing made not a whit of sense. You might expect a record that called itself 'The Story' to be chronological, but this set started off with a truncated version of 'Magnificent Seven', then jumped around to round mostly late-Clash material and then later included earlier material and a measly snippet of the Tony Parsons interview. The sequencing was probably designed to not scare off the curious buyer, and the record rekindled interest in the UK, so who am I to argue? It was obviously for non-committed listeners, so it played it safe. After the Levi's ad, it was re-released and sold thousands more.

CBS licensed some tracks out to indie label Relativity and they put out two collections: one entitled *Crucial Music* and the other *1977 Revisited. Crucial Music* is another Clash-for-the-Masses cash-in, and was released mainly on cassette. (I have yet to see it on CD). *1977* was more notable because it released some rare B-sides and the first-LP US castoffs. I appreciated it for a fresh playing on 'Stop the World', since my single was wearing out. Also included was the live version of 'London's Burning' from the contentious 'Remote Control' single. It is every bit as horrible as the Clash thought it was. The packaging was suitably post-modern and the liner notes were written by has-been Ira Robbins, whose liner notes for the box were rejected by the Clash. This whole package was made redundant by the boxset. You probably guessed right if you thought this was pure record company cash-in.

Somewhere along the line, Australian CBS released a best-of which is notable for including 'This is England.' I can't remember the exact track listing but I remember it seemed more interesting than the other best-ofs I've seen. After the Levi's ad bonanza, there was talk of releasing an UK 45s boxset for

Christmas. This was scrapped and the compromise was the redundant *The Singles* release. Again, the emphasis was on packaging. The cover art was a montage of Pennie Smith photos. The track listing was a straight run-through of the single releases, including the execrable 'Hitsville UK' (why they never scrubbed the Ellen Foley vocals on this, I'll never know). This cash-in flopped and was jeered by the critics.

Next on the docket was *the Clash on Broadway* boxset. There is a lot to be said for this set, not the least of which is the 64-page booklet and the lyric sheet. There's also a lot to bitch about. My first beef with the set was the title. It made sense for the Bond's movie, but why for the boxset? Did they like the title so much they were loathe to let it go to waste? It also seemed to be saying that the Clash's entire career was geared only to gaining success in the States. My other beef was the over-emphasis on early material. Do we really need '48 Hours' and 'Deny' on a boxset? *CCS* followers know I prefer the Clash's 80's material to the 70's stuff, but I don't think anyone can deny there's a lot of deadwood on disk one. Why not the UK album version of 'White Riot' instead of the lame demo? Since dub mixes were a big component of the Clash experience, their absence is also glaring. Why not include the dub mixes of 'Revolution Rock' and 'Rudie Cant Fail' from *Rude Boy*? It was fun hearing 'One Emotion' but what about some of the other early Clash out-takes?

I also have some problems with the third disk. It's good to hear 'Midnight to Stevens' and 'Every Little Bit Hurts' for historical value, even though their out-take status is well deserved. The live version of 'Lightning Strikes' is underwhelming, particularly when you consider the stockpile of live material they have (remember the Shea Stadium live album? Or the Bonds live album? No, well, that's because like the *Rude Boy* soundtrack, they were hyped but never released.) The conspicuous absence of 'Beautiful People' and 'Kill Time' has elicited a fair amount of complaint from Clash fans who wanted good recordings of these unreleased classics, and the inclusion of 'Cool Confusion', the worst song recorded by anyone ever, is inexcusable. The unedited 'Straight to Hell' is inferior to the LP version, and there must be plenty of good live versions of that available. A solid live reading would have been a fitting ending to the set. The hidden track status of 'Street Parade' was welcome, since that song is one of my favorite Clash tunes of all time.

Well, practice makes perfect and the lads got it right for the last reissue to date, Super *Black Market Clash*. This great disk is like a guided tour through the hidden Clash. Great packaging, great liner notes, great selection of numbers. Most of the released dub numbers are present (excepting those dreadful barrel scrapers on the Radio Clash EP), 'Capitol Radio Two' (infinitely superior to the original), 'Long Time Jerk', 'Listen' — this is just a treasure trove. It makes one hopeful that there will be a live set coming executed with the same amount of care.

Tentative, Too Tight, and Toothless on the Terry Tour?

"I don't think, honest to God, we ever played a good gig after (Topper left). Except for one night in New Jersey, we played a good one, but I reckon that was just by the law of averages." -Joe Strummer Uncut *Sept. '99*

One of the things you notice when you read a lot of Joe interviews is that he's a poet, not a journalist. When he reminisces about his past, he doesn't give you a factual recounting, but an emotional impression, a sonnet. Joe's memory has never been what you might call infallible, as any one who's listened to 25 years of forgotten lyrics on bootlegs will tell you. But what Joe says about the 1982 *Combat Rock* Tour (or the 'Terry Tour', for our purposes) has a ring of truth beneath the hyperbole. The Clash played quite a few excellent shows on the Terry Tour in fact, and they never played a Lochem or Sun Plaza-type disaster that tour. But more often than not, they were mediocre by Clash standards. By mediocre, I mean medium, acceptable, fine, pretty good.

1982 sorely tested my fidelity to the Clash and in 1983 my fandom went into hibernation. *Combat Rock* was not the record I wanted to hear, they were over-exposed in the media, the one Terry show I saw was very mediocre, and they were wearing the silliest clothes of their career. My impression of the band is that they had become tamed and toothless. They had been absorbed by the system they were set out to abolish. In hindsight, we now know about the behind-the-scenes turmoil, but I have been mulling over some of the other factors that make some of those '82 boots so oddly unsatisfying.

Some of my favorite boots stem from that era, interestingly enough, including the Asbury Park gigs, Edinburgh, *the Casbah Club* double LP, the St. Paul, MN tape, and the Boston 9/82 soundboards. But even on those shows, the thing that separates them from the rest of the tour was that Mick actually seemed to be awake for the shows. Listening to other shows from '82, say, the Jamaica show and certainly the Who dates, is more telling. Mick seems to be phoning in his playing over the unspectacular playing of Terry, Paul and Joe-the clunkiest rhythm section in Rock. Mick spent most of the tour in his hotel room, smoking himself into oblivion, and his lack of interest on certain shows took the legs out from underneath the band. He, after all, was the musical leader and none of the other three had the capacity to pick up the slack.

I am willing to bet that Mick's withdrawal had a lot to do with Joe's muscling in on Mick's turf. The template for Clash II was evident in the Terry shows. Topper-era shows were wildly divergent, seat-of-the-pants affairs. When they were good, they were the best concerts ever heard, but when they were bad, well, I have one word for you: Lochem Festival. As Mick and ganja became ever more intimate, Joe had decided (I am guessing) to take over as onstage director. I am also guessing that someone suggested to Mick to turn down his onstage volume (which passive-aggressive Mick may have used an excuse to practically turn off). But the slackening of Mick's bludgeoning onstage volume also gave Joe's throat a break, and his singing was much stronger from '82 on, since he didn't have to scream to hear himself over Mick's wall of guitar. (This is probably also where Joe's holding-his-ear move, which persists to this day, came from) The songs were pared down and the "let's-just-wing-it" improv sections of the '81 era were done away with. Some of the drop-out sections and tempo changes that Joe perfected for Clash II showed up on the Terry tour as well.

But I think the problem with the Terry tour was Joe's inexperience and cautiousness as a band leader. I think Terry was a lot better player than he sounds on the *CR* tour, but I believe he was told by Joe to play it tight and LOUD, since Top's playing had gotten so soft in his last days. But playing hard takes away from your tempo, unless you're a big-wristed bruiser like Pete Howard or John Bonham. As the Clash tried to branch away from 12-bar Rock, they were also running in to the brick wall known as Paul's severely limited chops. I think Terry was accommodating his playing so Paul could keep up, since with Mick turned down he could actually hear Paul, a luxury which Topper was spared. On the slower Funk and Reggae material, this strategy worked pretty well, but on the earlier cuts you can hear Terry dragging, and the whole band drags. It's also possible his enthusiasm may have waned as the tour dragged on.

So for the bulk of the tour, you have the unspectacular and un-loose trio of Terry, Paul, and Joe upfront and Mick floating either up front (rarely) or in the background (on most shows). The sound is of three fit but limited players wrestling with their instruments. It's the sound of work, strangely like the

Paul thumbs through Bass for Beginners *while Terry looks on approvingly.*
Hyannis, Ma August 1982

first album. Maybe Joe thought "Right, Terry's back, let's go back to the old pneumatic drill sound." The irony of it is that there were a lot of hopes raised when Terry returned. I didn't know a single Clash fan that didn't want the band to stop dabbling and make iron-hard Rock and Roll again. There was a clique of Quincy boys (including Springa of SSD and Walter of the Outlets) who went down to NYC to catch some of the Bonds shows and they were singularly unimpressed with Topper's playing. They seemed to believe that Terry would bring back the big beat to the Clash. We also had heard a lot of positive feedback from some California kids, who claimed that the old, ferocious Clash was back. I also remember chatting with Mensi from the Angelic Upstarts before a show and he broke the news that Tops was sacked because of his habit and he also seemed to believe that Terry would be a good influence. But I think it was too late for the Clash at that point. Joe and Mick were hardly speaking and the musical gulf was too wide by then.

IS THERE LIFE AFTER THE CLASH?

Unpublished - Originally written for Clash City Showdown #1

The Clash dissolved in late October 1985. Although an official breakup was never announced, Nick Sheppard, Pete Howard and Vince White were dismissed by Joe and Paul, as were Bernie Rhodes and Kosmo Vinyl (who comprised the Clash's management team). Joe announced in this press release (quoted in the BAD *Spin* cover story) that a new single, 'Shouting Street,' (later released on *Earthquake Weather*) would be released soon, and to watch for news of Big Audio Dynamite and Topper Headon for further information. This was never to be, and serious Clash watchers weren't surprised. The album of the new Clash formation was constantly delayed, and when it was released it bore little resemblance to the tunes that fans had heard on the Out of Control tour. Mick Jones' new band, Big Audio Dynamite, released it's debut LP to great critical acclaim and modest commercial success. The Clash were written off by the press as has-beens and fools as the anti-Clash movement that had begun in 1983 ground on. But true Clash diehards persevered. Was there life after the Clash?

The period following the Clash's breakup was a dark one. The Alternative music scene had splintered and reached its creative nadir. On one side was the Thrash movement, a collection of moral twits polluting the world with their atonal, arythmic garbage and newly-found fascist inclinations, and on the other was the legions of neuvo-wavo sellouts playing paint by numbers Dance Pop for art school poseurs across the globe. And bringing up the rear was the 'Flannel Brigades' (dB's, Feelies etc) playing jangly Nerd Rock, destroying any of the glamour and excitement that bands like the Clash and others had worked hard to create in the early 80's. Precious few bands emerged in this period with any interesting musical ideas. 1985 was almost a total washout.

The mid-80's saving grace was bands like the Smiths, the Chameleons and the Cocteau Twins, who had emerged in the early 80's and were building their audiences in the these dark times. Rock critics were celebrating various flavors of the month and assaulting the Clash vehemently whenever the opportunity arose. However in 1987-88 the tide turned. A number of musically interesting bands emerged, particularly Jane's Addiction. Established bands figured out that you don't have to pander to the mainstream to be successful and a number of quality records were released. New musical movements came to the fore, and Hardcore degenerated into bad Heavy Metal and gave up any pretensions of being an alternative movement.

And in this fertile ground, CBS released *the Story of the Clash, Part 1*. This double-LP retrospective made little noise stateside but firmly re-established the Clash as one of the greats in the UK. The LP signaled a re-evaluation of the band among British critics and Joe's Rock Against the Rich tour (where he played a great deal of Clash material) cemented the Renaissance. Joe was stunned by the lavish praise heaped upon him on this tour (the seeds for Joe's return to grace were planted by the release of his brilliant soundtrack to the Alex Cox film *Walker*).

Surprisingly enough, BAD did not benefit from this revival. Their '86 classic, *No. 10 Upping St.*, received a great deal of attention because of the fact that Joe had co-written and co-produced it. But BAD fell into the trap of being yesterday's news in the UK. Their mediocre third LP, *Tighten Up Volume 88*, was poorly received. The bands troubles were further compounded when Mick fell victim to chicken pox and fell into a coma. A tour of Britain and the US was canceled as Mick wandered perilously close to the edge. He spent the rest of '88 in therapy to restore his damaged vocal chords and recuperate from this devastating illness.

Paul at this time was in Los Angeles riding motorcycles with Steve Jones and his cohorts. He was inactive for most of the time following the Clash's implosion, concentrating instead on motorcycling and returning to career as a painter. He met with veteran guitarist Gary Myrick and began work on a new project. Their band, Havana 3am, supported BAD on their 1989 tour and released an LP in 1990. The band had a minor hit with the song 'Reach the Rock', a slick Clash-sounding Rockabilly tune. Havana vocalist Nigel Dixon has since died of cancer.

Topper Headon had various run-ins with the law and according to one report sold his gold records from the Clash to support his heroin habit. He eventually ended up in prison for supplying heroin to a man who died from an overdose. He currently works as a cabdriver. Reports held that Mick Jones tried to interest Headon in taking up the drums again, and sent an employee to purchase a kit for him, apparently to no avail.

In 1989, Joe had a burst of activity. He appeared to great acclaim in the film Mystery Train, directed by Jim Jarmusch. He released an album entitled *Earthquake Weather* to generally positive reviews and set on an autumn tour of the UK and America. Despite the critical acclaim and warm reception Joe received from fans, the LP got zero promotion from CBS and withered for lack of company support, despite the fact that the record contained many Clash-style cuts.

Joe returned to England and some time later renewed his relationship with his drinking buddies, the Pogues. Shane MacGowan, the lead singer of the dismal Pogues, had been a Clash follower since 1976. (his band, the Nipple Erectors, was cited by Mikey Dread in the Clash tune 'Living in Fame' on *Sandinista*) Joe also worked with the band in the Alex Cox stinker, Straight to Hell. In 1987, Joe was called on by the Pogues to fill in on guitar for Phillip Chevron, who was ill and couldn't tour. Joe also produced the Pogues' 1990 LP *Hell's Ditch*. Joe toured with the band as their lead singer, replacing McGowan, who had severely damaged his body through substance abuse. The band was reportedly working on an album with Strummer, but this arrangement did not last and the Pogues' album, *Waiting for Herb*, was released and died on the racks. Reports came in that Strummer was busy producing records and working on unspecified soundtrack work. Rumor has it he is working on a new LP, and even an EP with Bob Dylan, though nothing has been confirmed.

This month marks Joe's return to the scene with his co-writing and performing contributions to Brian Setzer's new album. Mick Jones has continued with his Big Audio Dynamite II concept, temporarily named Big Audio, then back to Big Audio Dynamite. He garnered a pair of modest hits from his

1991 LP, *The Globe.* The LP was originally released as *Kool-Aid* in late 1990 but CBS/Columbia refused to release it in the US. Mick returned to the studio and recut the tracks and scored with his single 'Rush', a lightweight Dance tune that made a splash in the US but was ignored in England. He has toured extensively in support of the LP, first in '91 with the Farm and in '92 with PiL on the MTV *120 Minutes* tour. He later released the oft-delayed *Higher Power* and did a handful of gigs. He left CBS/Sony, then released *F-Punk* on Radioactive, and has not been heard from since, and reportedly has a record that may or not be released in the US.

The last Terry Chimes was heard from, he was practicing homeopathic medicine. After the Clash he played in a variety of Heavy Metal bands, including Hanoi Rocks, The Cherry Bombz, and a very brief stint in Black Sabbath. Nick Sheppard formed the Bristol band Head with money and equipment from the Clash, released a couple of obscure LP's and disappeared. He recently moved to Australia. Pete Howard played in the band Eat for a few years, but they recently disbanded. He has since hooked up with former Wonder Stuff frontman in the band Vent 414, but they haven't made any impact as of yet. Vince White has kept a lower profile, perhaps he is using his biology degree for employment. Micky Gallagher played with Topper Headon's band, and also on *Cut the Crap*, but has not done much of note since the Clash.

ELLEN FOLEY

Originally posted 9.6.97

Some fans often ask me why I am such a big fan of the second, ill-fated incarnation of the Clash. Usually, I answer them with two words: Ellen Foley. They often reply, "come again?", to which I repeat , "Ellen Foley." Or I can make it one word: "Ellenfoley." Or I can make it, "Flellen Flooey." Or "Fa Fa Foo."..no, wait. Wait...OK.

Ellen Foley was the personification of all my fears of just how wrong the Clash could go. I remember dreaming in 1982 that I went to a Clash concert and they were playing show-tunes and having people act out the lyrics. I had another nightmare that the Clash put out a follow-up to *Sandinista* and Ellen Foley had replaced Joe as the lead singer.

Many of you are asking : "Who the hell is Ellen Foley? Are you talking about that little blond lady who played the DA on Night Court?" And I respond, "Yes, the very same." Ellen Foley is also the session vocalist who also screeched on 'Paradise by the Dashboard Light' by Meatloaf. Yes, horrified readers, Meatloaf. She hooked up with Mick sometime in 1980, my guess is through Ian Hunter, and became the Clash's Marianne Faithful (or their Yoko, depending on my mood). She warbled on some tracks when the Clash set up their operation in Electric Ladyland. She sang on tunes like 'Hitsville UK' (or Shitsville UK, as I like to call it) and 'Washington Bullets'. She was surprisingly effective on 'Corner Soul', but I personally think Mick would have been even-more effective. But we can't really blame her for any of this. After all, Mick was in love.

Now I am sure Ellen Foley is a perfectly nice person. I have no beef with her, outside of the fact she had no business within 10 miles of a Clash record. Anyone who has heard a bitching live version of 'Car Jamming' will never again be able to listen to the feeble, half-speed *Combat Rock* version again. Mick's emotions clouded his better judgment, and rumor had it at the time this relationship was the catalyst for another Joe/Mick punch-up (or pun-chout?) after recording of a strange and long out of print chapter in the story of the Clash. Yes, kids; *the Spirit of St. Louis.*

After the *Sandinista* sessions were wrapped, the *Sandinista* band; Mick, Mickie Gallagher, Norman Watt Roy, Topper, Tymon Dogg, and Gary Barnacle went to work on tracks for an Ellen Foley solo album. Joe, Mick, and Tymon wasted...er, wrote a number of new tracks for the project. Tymon followed his own craft-driven muse, but Joe and Mick displayed a new and strange influence: Jacques Brel and other 50's French pop writers.

Accordions, flutes, and strings made their entrance (presumably all played by Tymon), and images of cafes, legionnaires, bicycles, and other European puffery flew about. One particularly awful track -'The Death of the Psychoanalyst of Salvador Dali' (I'm serious) offered up disjointed lyrics in an unpleasant foreshadowing of *Earthquake Weather*. Unfortunately, Joe and Mick were trapped in that mode for awhile after the album- if you don't have *Spirit of St. Louis*, listen to 'Midnight to Stevens' and 'Death is a Star' to get a feel for the sound of it.

Ellen just wasn't up to the material at all. When she isn't screeching, her tone is soft, muffled and deep. It is also utterly bereft of character or dis-tinctiveness. There is a reason she never had a solo career. But Mick didn't help either. His production is blurry and dull, much like Joe's production on the Janie Jones single. The playing is good though. Topper and the *Sandinista* boys are hard to fault here and Mick really stretched himself and came up with some good voicings and licks. I would even go so far to say that this record has some of his best playing. And a handful of songs are really top-flight, albeit ruined by the lousy singing. 'Shuttered Palace' and 'Theatre of Cruelty' would have been good Linda Ronstadt or ABBA songs. Tymon's 'Beautiful Waste of Time' (or in this case, 'Pitiful Waste of Song') would have been a great thing for Dionne Warwick to do in the 60's between Bacharach-David numbers. And two songs. 'Torchlight' and 'MPH' really should have been saved for a Clash record. 'Torchlight' is a classic Joe/Mick call-and-response track that you could just imagine some South American arm of the Spartacist League adopting as their anthem. And 'MPH' would be a great 'Clampdown' like rocker if sung by Joe and Mick. And Ellen's own Siouxsie-like 'Phases of Travel' is well-writ-ten, even though Mick uses too much flange on it.

The Clash were just playing around, trying new toys, but they were horrifying little 15 year-old fans like myself. I was willing to accept the softer, hippified sounds of *Sandinista*, but this was going too far. Not only was this a girl, but it wasn't even a cool girl like Siouxsie or Chrissie Hynde. It was some hack session singer that the Clash were fooling around with. Since I was expecting the Clash to get over all this dabbling and remake *Give 'Em Enough Rope*, *Spirit of St. Louis* made me think maybe they were going sissy on me after all. I remember comparing the record version of 'Radio Clash' unfavorably to the bitchin' version of the tune on Tom Snyder, and thinking the Clash cannot be trusted in the studio.

I was encouraged in '82 by 'Know Your Rights', but I remember when I first heard 'Rock the Casbah' and 'Inoculated City' on college radio and being shocked how incredibly commercial they sounded (the DJ said-"What do you think of the new Clash record? Yeah, me too," in a disgusted tone). '82 was a bad year. The Clash were all over the place, but in a Top-40, un-tough context. All the kids I hated in school were listening to them. I literally was terrified that the band I had invested so much emotion in would fall apart and become a Soft Rock band (and you could make an argument that a lot of *Sandinista* and *Combat Rock* was soft rock). I was plagued by nightmares that they would be playing Barbra Streisand songs on *Solid Gold* or *American Bandstand*. Don't forget this was the heydey of Hardcore, and 'Atom Tan' and 'Car Jamming' were not songs that you wanted to represent your favorite band.

So going from sissy cuts like 'Death is A Star', 'Atom Tan' and Ellen Foley records, can it be any wonder that when Joe was running around the country with a band with three wailing axemen, screaming tunes with titles like 'Are You Ready for War?' and 'Ammunition', back by video monitors showing Mad Max and Clint Eastwood clips, and saving my pals from bouncers that my 17 year-old soul wouldn't fall in line like some modern day Young Pioneer?

DID THE CLASH SELL OUT?

The increasingly toothless Clash at their height of popularity on the 1982 Combat Rock tour

The Clash were accused of selling out at every turn, from the very beginning of their careers until the very end. To ascertain whether the charges were true, one must first define 'selling out." This is a very complex process, since there are number of degrees to compromising with the record business, which is what most people mean by 'selling out'. And one must then realize that compromise itself is a highly subjective verb, and decisions the Clash made to make their music more palatable for the masses weren't always driven by economic incentive. And even when they did clearly compromise their stated ideals, they muddied the waters, both by accident and by design. And one must also question whether they always actually believed in their 'stated ideals' or whether these were received notions or simple hype.

Mark Perry, editor of *Sniffin' Glue*, accused them of selling out first when the band signed to CBS. This accusation was rooted in the complex scene politics of the time. Mark P, a marginally talented musician himself, started a homemade, zero-production-value fanzine and seemed to naively assume that his economic model was viable for a band with the Clash's following. There was a lot of juvenile, Stalinist thinking in 1977 London, a lot of it actively encouraged by the Clash themselves. The Sex Pistols were immune to accusations of sell-out and, in fact, seemed to be amused by them. They were the first to admit that they were a pack of frauds and were in it for as much money as they could squeeze out of the corporate teat. They even wrote songs about it. The Clash's somewhat silly 'street credibility' (none of them were poor street kids) was threatened by any appearance of careerism, but in actuality they were following in the footsteps of their heroes like the Stones and Mott the Hoople. It was the Rock and Roll dream to land a major deal, and the conflict between the Clash's traditionalist roots and their lip service to the Punk ideal caused them grief from the onset. This tension seemed to greatly affect the rest of their career, often compelling them to prove that they weren't selling out as their records got more and more commercial sounding and successful.

The lo-fi sound of the debut LP was possibly a reaction to the purist brickbats. If that was the case, the gambit seemed to work. It seemed to silence the criticism, and the fact that CBS America shit-canned a stateside release only added to their mystique. The Clash cemented their credibility with the astonishing one-two-three punch of their follow-up singles, 'Complete Control', 'Clash City Rockers', and 'White Man in Hammersmith Palais'. However, their next move shattered their untouchable mystique in England forever.

The story goes that CBS insisted that the Clash work with a producer for their second LP, in order to facilitate an American release. The nod was given to Sandy Pearlman, producer of New York proto-Punks Blue Oyster Cult and the Dictators. This seemed to be an acceptable choice. But as fate would have it, Blue Oyster Cult had a hit with 'Don't Fear the Reaper' and suddenly became 'dinosaurs'. So you had the American producer of a AOR band producing the Clash. When *Give 'Em Enough Rope* was released, its professional recording sent many critics into a tizzy. The Clash were accused of courting the American market, ignoring the fact that the high octane Punk of Rope was absolute anathema to American radio. The album went got zero radio play and went nowhere near the Top 40 , putting the lie to 'sellout to the US' accusations.

But the Clash then set their sights on America, and slowly the sentiment in the British press began to rise against them. The Clash seemed unconcerned at first, since American audiences were highly receptive to their music, and had the added bonus of not indulging in the repulsive British habit of gobbing (ie., spitting at the performers.) As the situation in the UK deteriorated and their prospects in America brightened, the band got to work on their next affront to Punk purism.

That the Clash onstage and the Clash in the studio were two separate phenomena is indisputable. Neither *Rope* nor the debut came close to capturing the intensity of the band. But the *London Calling* sessions displayed a Clash that was a totally different animal altogether. I can't think of a single band in Rock history whose records were so unlike their live act. I saw the Clash on the *London Calling* tour and it sounded nothing like the album. It sounded like getting hit by a freight train. But to accuse the Clash of selling out for their cozy, conservative and radio-friendly pose on *London Calling* isn't fair or accurate.

One has to remember that the Clash were fans of Classic Rock and Roll, from Elvis Presley and Chuck Berry to the Stones to the Beatles to Creedence Clearwater Revival and beyond. It's the dream of every bedroom Rocker to make records that sound like their heroes, and the Clash were no different. Mick and Joe were true-blue Rockers from early on, and to add a bit of spice to the mix, Paul had his Reggae roots and Topper his Jazz and R&B. *London Calling* didn't sound like the first two records, nor did it sound like the band sounded playing the same songs live, but it captured the band trying to work out of the dead end of the first blush of Punk by reaching back into their roots. And the fact that the Stonesy, classic Rock sound of the material would better endear them to their new friends in America certainly must have a major factor in the making of the album. In addition, wanting to make music that might appeal to a larger audience is not necessarily "selling out."

What must be remembered was there was nothing like the Independent network of college radio stations and record stores that appeared just a few years later. If you didn't get your records on the radio and in the larger chains, you didn't make any money. And while many of the first wave Punk bands can be faulted for their lack of foresight, they can't all be dismissed as being greedy and opportunist. A band simply couldn't survive by sticking to the underground circuit, or at least, most couldn't. And for a band with big dreams like the Clash, it was impossible. Certainly there was no shortage of bands that betrayed their original mandates, but there were bands like the Clash who struggled to reach the mainstream without abandoning their ideals.

The Clash released *London Calling* as a low-cost double. This again was the 'Punk idealism' coming into play. If *London Calling* was released as a single, it would've been much harder for them to justify as the work of a band who 'stuck to their Punk principles' to their purist critics. The music on *London Calling* was just too commercial-sounding. By releasing a double, they could make a lot of noise about offering 'value for money' and could point to the (somewhat vague) political content of their lyrics and say that they were trying to put across the Punk message in a different way so more people would get the message. There wasn't a single track on *London Calling* that would scare off the curious, and the American single was the radically un-Punk, 'Train in Vain'.

The legend goes that the track was meant for a *NME* giveaway and was left off the track listing because the artwork had already been done. This explanation strains credulity. If the track could be pressed on the vinyl, surely it could have been listed on the sleeve. Perhaps there was a bit of embarrassment involved. The Clash found themselves in a straight jacket of their own making. They sought to distinguish themselves from their rivals the Sex Pistols by presenting themselves as the ideological alternative. They mouthed a lot of rhetoric they probably hadn't even thought over and then were hung out to dry by it when they wanted to pursue their old-fashioned Rock and Roll dream. So with 'Train in Vain', the old Punk gambit took hold- " well, we meant to give the track away, but it fell through." This could help to smooth over Punk feathers ruffled by the band recording such a blatantly commercial love song.

And this thinking seemed to carry over to their next project. The plan was to get back into the top of the British charts by releasing a series of singles. The story this time was that Paul was unavailable for the sessions since he was filming a movie. But his role in *Ladies and Gentlemen, the Fabulous Stains* was essentially a cameo. Couldn't the band have waited until he was done filming? Could this have been a cover story? By sheer coincidence, the band's Punkest musician was replaced by the ultra-slick journeyman Norman Watt Roy and a whole host of polished studio musicians were called in. In another fluke, Joe - the band's second Punkest player - was also sidelined on guitar.

Now, *Sandinista!* is a great album, probably my single favorite in their canon. But the music isn't Punk, in fact, most of it isn't even Rock. The new Clash manifesto of not allowing their music to overshadow their message came into play again. Most of the lyrics are more politically pointed. But the music itself on most of the key tracks was unprecedentedly commercial and non-confrontational. 'Hitsville UK', one of the worst songs in the band's canon, sounded as edgy as the *Three's Company* theme song. The band, in some strange fit of irrationality, released it as a single in the UK. Not only did it bomb, but it caused some to question their sanity. The music on most of the album is unabashedly mellow and slick, aside from a handful of tracks. Now, having come off one of their typically raucous tours, the band was probably tired and wanted to get high, relax and fool around. And with Paul out of the picture, they could try out more listener friendly genres and get some of these damn songs in the charts.

CBS nixed the singles campaign, infuriating the band. The logic of this decision was hard to fault, though. More money could be made on an album in America than a single in the UK. And the record company was probably encouraged that the band had finally calmed down and was producing music that could be played alongside Kenny Loggins and the Doobie Brothers (in fact, tracks off *Sandinista* did just that on Boston's Soft Rock station, WEEI-FM). The creative excitement of recording had probably been extinguished by the singles battle and the band may have suddenly realized that the key *Sandinista* tracks would make for an album that would get the band eaten alive for its commercialism. Was this the reason for a 3-LP release? Many different and contradictory explanations have been proffered at different times. But this one has to be considered. After all, there wasn't even enough material at hand for a 3-LP set, and tracks had to jury-rigged to fill in the gaps. But a 3-LP set would get them noticed. And the band could come across a prolific and prodigious for being able to manage one so quickly after their 2 LP set, which few seemed to notice was itself padded and nowhere near 90 minutes long. And by setting an absurdly low price for it and giving the LP a controversial title, the band's 'integrity' would be seen as being intact.

Now, did all this obscure what began as a 'sellout?' It's hard to say. I am not one of those people who thinks 'commercial' automatically equals 'crap'. Back then there was still a lot of quality music in the charts, and 'commercial' was actually usually perceived as meaning 'popular' and by extension 'good.' I think that the key *Sandinista* tracks were the best songs the band had yet written and even the B-material is pretty damn entertaining. But, most of it didn't sound like the Clash. Most of it wasn't even recorded by what was understood to be the Clash. But the result of all this maneuvering was CBS burying the album and shit-canning a 60 date tour, so the band's 'Punk idealism' blew up in their faces. Even the publicity garnered by the Bonds situation did little to fill their coffers. The next album would have to make money or the Clash would be in serious trouble.

Much speculation has been aroused by the track listing for *Combat Rock*. I myself have been puzzled by the exclusion of 'Radio Clash'. If the Clash were all that concerned about value for money, they wouldn't have forced American fans to fork over $4.99 for the 12" EP of 'Radio Clash', which was simply four versions (two of them unlistenable) of the same song. British fans were forced to pay at least a pound for the single, whereas if it was included on *Combat Rock* it would have cost about 50 cents for fans to hear it among the 11 other tracks. So much for 'value for money'.

The Clash had amassed a strange collection of material for *Combat Rock* with politically abrasive tracks like 'Know Your Rights' and 'Ghetto Defendant' (probably both solo Joe compositions) and 'Red Angel Dragnet' (possibly Paul and Joe), but much of the material was accessible to a fault. Mick wanted *Combat Rock* to be a double LP and everyone else balked at this. There simply was not enough quality material to fill a double. Half the songs were simple jams, without choruses or bridges. But two songs that were in the can were excised and remain unreleased: 'Idle in Kangaroo Court W11' (aka 'Kill Time') and 'Fulham Connection' (aka 'Beautiful People'). Marcus Gray speculated that the songs were too 'left field' for release. This is nonsense. In actuality, they are far too 'New Wave' and commercial sounding. (I also seem to recall a story in *Trouser Press* that reported the excised tracks were slated for an EP release) Again, a strange contortion was made to preserve some semblance of credibility. If the two missing tracks and 'Radio Clash' were included, replacing the many vastly inferior or weird cuts on the record (let's say 'Dragnet' , 'Sean Flynn' and 'Death is a Star'), you would have had an album that would have been stylistically indistinguishable from a Police album. It also might have sold twice as well as it did, and the Clash's treasured 'idealism' and 'credibility' would have been shattered. Cries of sell-out finally would have stuck.

Of course, the Clash didn't need an even more commercial album to succumb to the brickbats. The tour with the Who was indefensible from a Punk standpoint, and the band were ubiquitous on MTV and all the fluffy showbiz programs like *Entertainment Tonight* and *Casey Kasem's Top 40*. Sensing they'd played the game all wrong, management arranged a well publicized tantrum at the Us Festival, in which they accepted a half a million dollars for coming on 2 hours late and insulting the audience. Joe's silly tantrums at what turned out to be Mick's final show didn't come across as righteous and heartfelt; they came across as bizarre, incoherent and contrived. This was what the band had become- a lot of talk and no walk. Strummer justified their appearance by stating that the Clash had to appear in order to represent 'Rebel Rock'. But if he was so concerned about money going to charity, why didn't the band part with a portion of their huge fee? The lesson was finally brought home - you can't be a rebel with a major label contract and expense account. Being truly rebellious will alienate your paymasters. And the band resorted to increasingly contrived rhetorical contortions to obscure the fact that they had been forced to play by someone else's rules just like everyone else. And this tension did little to cohere the band when Mick and Joe's conflicts came to a head.

Having enough of Mick's temper and wanting to stop the slide towards New Wave Dance Pop, Joe went along with Bernie's plan to sack Mick. Joe admitted in interviews that yes, the Clash had made every mistake in the book and been sucked into the machine but now he would set things to right. The Clash toured for nearly five months straight on their own dime, just like a Punk band was supposed to. They surely confused many fans who came to hear the *Combat Rock* Clash, but they did much to repair some of the damage of the previous years with their core fans. But, of course, they almost immediately lost their nerve. Joe, battered by personal crises and deeply uncomfortable with leading a band on his own, acceded control to Bernie, who in turn lost his nerve on his quest to break a 'real Punk' band in America. This is probably why the band was sidelined. I don't believe the boys were hired and put on a marathon tour just to sit on their asses when the album was recorded. The plan was to record quickly in the early autumn. What might well have happened is that Bernie looked at the reviews and the numbers and the charts and decided - yet again - that the Clash would have to compromise 'to get their message across.' Ironically, Bernie walked right in Mick's footsteps, first hiring Watt Roy and Gallagher to rehearse with Joe and Pete and then bringing on some hack to do some lousy programming to replace Pete.

I don't for a minute believe that all these strange moves were done for any reason other than economics. Most of the tour songs were explicitly political but none of the post -tour songs were, so what message were they even trying to convey? They wanted to create a Punk-flavored 1985 Pop record, only they didn't know how to make one. The Clash finally collapsed beneath the weight of their compromises.

If anyone reading this seeks to make a career in music, I think the Clash's mistakes are more instructive than the silly corporate mythology that has sprung up around them. Record Companies are not in the business of advancing music and culture, they are in the business of making themselves disgustingly wealthy. The days of Herb Alpert, John Hammond, Clive Davis and Ahmet Ertegun are long since past. Execs today look at musicians like a rogue tiger shark looks at swimmers. In many ways, Mark Perry was right. But the Clash didn't aspire to be Punk footsoldiers, they wanted to be superstars. They just didn't realize that the times had changed and that the Stones and the Beatles got away with murder in a time when record companies were still relatively minor outfits.

But at the same time, the Clash did in some ways get their message across. No, not their garbled politics, but the Punk message. There was a genuine measure of subversion here. The Clash brought an idea of Punk to precincts that had no concept of it. And surely many fans were converted when they got a dose of real Clash at the concerts. By helping the Clash to reach deep into the American Heartland, the Clash's compromised and watered-down records created a gateway to the real thing. And many of the neo-Punk musicians of the 90's got into the idea of Punk through the Clash. And though self-styled purists continue to scoff at the 1984 Clash, it was mainstream America's first exposure to real Punk Rock, and was vitally important in laying the groundwork for the Punk revolution of a few years later, even more than the dead end of Hardcore. And there's no reason to believe that Clash, or at least Mick, didn't want to make commercial sounding records without any external corporate pressure to do so.

So, did they 'sell out' like Billy Idol, New Order or the Simple Minds sold out? Not really, but no one plays with the Record Industry by their own rules. You play with theirs. Because in that business, he who pays the piper truly calls the tune.

IT'S ALL GOOD
Written sometime in 2000

Back in the first century, the broad and diverse social protest movement that became the institutional religion known as Christianity was full of competing camps, each of whom had a number of ideas on what their nascent religion was about. It came to pass that the narrowest and most restrictive interpretation of Jesus' teachings caught the ear of the power structure of Imperial Rome. And it wasn't long before all those schools of religious thought that weren't in bed with the generals and aristocrats were either forcibly converted, driven underground or simply murdered en masse.

Not to make too tortured an analogy but I sometimes see this pattern repeating itself in modern times. Strange, underground art movements inevitably get institutionalized if they gain success, and certainly Punk Rock has not escaped this fate. Clash fandom also has its orthodoxies that are held tight to the bosoms of the self-appointed guardians of the Clash's legacy, and anyone who dares to question them are held up to ridicule (a new kind of figurative "flame" in contrast to the literal flames the religiously heterodox have faced throughout history).

Back in 1945, a young boy came upon a cave in Egypt and found a pile of old scrolls tucked away in clay jars. It turned out that these jars contained what were known as 'the Gnostic Gospels', the sacred writings of the hetero-dox dissenters of the early Christian era. In the modern age, these scrolls were treasured and studied, not tossed on the pyre as they would have been just a few hundred years before. In my moments of delusional self-inflation, I see the Showdown as a small modern day equivalent to those scrolls. Certainly, the Christian church did not fall when these scriptures were released (the sup-pressed scrolls from the Dead Sea would be more likely to accomplish that) but finally the dissenting view got an airing.

Back in the late 70's and the early 80's, when the Clash began to act according to their own whims and not those of the Music Industry establish-ment, the enforcement arm of the British Music Industry - ie., the Rock critics - went on the attack. People who had no access to a variety of opinion had their attitudes shaped by this concerted attack on the maverick Rock band. In England in 1979, a double LP was very difficult to make money on, and by sheer coincidence, the classic *London Calling* album was attacked by critics. And the triple LP *Sandinista* got an even worse drubbing. Amazingly enough, a profitable, easy-to-market single LP, *Combat Rock*, was praised to the skies by the UK critics, even though most people agree now (and did then) that it was markedly inferior to its predecessors.

There were other factors besides economics in the relentless attack on the Clash. In Britain, they were seen as traitors to British ethno-centrism from the time *Give 'Em Enough Rope* was released. Now, I don't know a single gen-uine Clash fan who doesn't treasure *Give 'Em Enough Rope* as one of the great-est Rock and Roll albums ever made. I know the Clash themselves were dis-appointed with the production process, but you can bet they are dead proud of the music contained on it. But for some reason, I encounter people from time to time who say they are Clash fans and say *Give 'Em Enough Rope* sucks. And then they tell me *Sandinista* sucks. And then they say Pete Howard sucks. And on and on and on...

Now am I advocating some new orthodoxy that says you have to like *Give 'Em Enough Rope*? No, I don't care if you don't, but I feel sorry for you if that's the case. But this brings me to the personal philosophy of *Clash City Showdown* - it's all good.

When I was a kid, I would tell my friends that I liked every note of music the Clash played. Of course, at that point I hadn't heard 'Cool Confusion' yet, but you get the idea. Because I think that 99% of the music that the Clash and afterward, Joe Strummer and Mick Jones, made the a honest document of artists trying their best to accomplish something extraordinary. And their failures were usually the result of trying too hard.

Now I know this point of view gets kind of difficult to defend once you hit the *Combat Rock* period and beyond, but I still say the majority of the music Strummer and Jones have brought forth is at least interesting. And if not success-ful, it is least an honest document of the state of mind of artists whom I hold in high regard. The crappier cuts from the *CR* sessions are interesting (in theory) to me because they document an attempt to try to overcome a personal impasse through artistic over-reaching. 'Cool Confusion' and 'Atom Tan' don't suck because they are lame-ass rewrites of 'White Man' or something, they suck in ways that are far more ambitious. They don't fail modestly, they fail spectacularly.

Longtime readers of *CCS* know I don't like the BAD2 material, but I can at least listen to it on occasion and enjoy the things Mick does well, like melodic structure and natural harmony. And even a record like *Higher Power*, which I see as Mick's artistic nadir, is kind of interesting to me as a document of an artist hitting a creative wall and trying to soldier on. Same with *F-Punk*. It's not successful by most measures, but since I enjoy the sound of Mick making music, I can play it on occasion and pick out the things I like.

Likewise for *When Pigs Fly*. As much as I despise the Pogues and fail to understand why Joe wasted his time working with them, I get a kick of hearing Joe's adorably clumsy compositions played with tin whistle and accordion. The other tracks don't work at all either, but they don't work because Joe was trying to do something way outside of his personal comfort zone, and that type of artistic daring is interesting to me. And even an not-great album like *Earthquake Weather* got plenty of spins round these parts.

I am not saying that I champion this material or even that I listen to it all that much, but I am not going to attack Mick and Joe personally for making it. Even the bete noire of Clash fans, *Cut the Crap*, can be very interesting and intermittently entertaining if you approach it the right way. As Nick Sheppard has said, Bernie wasn't trying to make a bad record and destroy the band, he was trying to reinvent the band for the 80's, only he had no idea how to do it. Bernie can be blamed for using police-state, mind-control tactics on his clients, but in actuality his intentions in making that record were good.

Which brings me back to another of the cornerstones of *Clash City Showdown*, which is to offer a strong and spirited defense of Clash II. Now, nearly all of the true diehards agree with my opinion of Clash II, but I don't deign to personally impugn those who disagree with me simply for disagreeing with me. Some of you might be chortling, but even in the darkest days of the old alt.music.clash flame wars I would always fight on principle and what would seem to be attacks (on whatever topic you can name), I saw as counterattacks. I know some of you out there weren't taken with the idea (and I am only addressing the people who bothered to check out the reality of the situation beyond *Cut the Crap*) of the Clash reinvented as a Hardcore/Punk/ Metal gang, but for fans who came aboard for *Give 'Em Enough Rope*, that was the original intention as we saw it. Now, like it or don't, but even their worst detractors have to admit the whole enterprise was the subject of a vicious and concerted smear campaign, which was quite possibly orchestrated by their record company. Now I don't care if people out there don't like that stuff - and no one seems to emerged from the experience happy about the whole affair - but forgive me if I chortle as I see old Industry propaganda or Rock critic drool recycled in your opinions on it. The fact is that CBS desperately wanted Joe and Mick to patch things up, and perhaps the relentless attacks on concerts that thousands of kids loved written by people whose salaries relied on Record Company advertising were something more than coincidental.

The same holds true for the Mick bashing that pops out from the grittier quarters of our dysfunctional family. I agree that Joe got a raw deal by Mick partisans (or just plain Joe haters) in the press, but now that his star is reascending, is that any reason to bash the man who made you care about Joe in the first place? If not for Mick, Joe would have been that cabdriver who was in that obscure old Pub band, the 101'ers. You know, the band that all the Garage Rock guys would have loved if there had never been a Clash. When you groove on those '84 tapes or Mescaleros gigs, remember who wrote the tunes that bring a lump to your throat. Now that the partisan wars are over and Joe is back on his feet, there's no reason to cut on Mick, no matter what you think of BAD. I know Mick's done some weird shit, but he's had a lot of weird shit done to him, and all of that shit is ancient history anyway.

The greatest thing about this very exciting year for me again was the *Westway* documentary. As I have said before, it laid old ghosts, one's that have been haunting me as well, to rest. No one listened to me when I said that it was Topper's drug addiction that was the catalyst for the Clash's self immolation, but there it was on the screen from the mouth of Mr. Headon himself. And all of that stupid anger I felt towards him evaporated when he spoke those words. And now I feel compassion for him. I can kinda relate to the dilemma of a man who finds out that the only thing he gets any fulfillment from doesn't facilitate the most constructive way of life. But I hope everyone sees that film. I think you will get the same feeling of closure on any number of issues that I did.

I know most of you out there don't live with this stuff like I do, and don't have access to the information I do, and certainly *London Calling* is easier to get a handle on than *Sandinista*, but you know what? It's all good. I guess the ultimate moral of this circular diatribe is a reaction against stupid, arbitrary orthodoxy and some of the bickering that lingers, as well a reaction against the partisan flame wars I am a scarred veteran of. The Internet is a great thing since it allows assholes like me a forum for my meanderings, but it also emboldens people to write things at other people, things they would never say face to face. And though I have roasted Joe's ass over the coals based on some spurious (if not outright deceitful) information and flamed it up with people I should have no quarrel with, I always hated it and did it out of a wrongheaded compulsion to be right and get the last word in. But that's no way to build a future. There's already too much ignorance and aggression out there, and the Clash were about being against those things. I am not asking you to like something you don't but maybe we should all think before we automatically attack people who disagree with us. That's the kind of world people like Pat Buchanan and Pat Robertson want and we should do a lot better. Even in this tiny little backwater of Pop culture.

The Clash's Greatest Record

Originally posted 2/18/00

From time to time we see arguments over what is the greatest Clash record. The focus is usually on *London Calling*, the safe, acceptable pick, or the first record, the choice of the self-appointed orthodoxy. Some diehards weigh in for *Sandinista*, and *Give 'Em Enough Rope* is the perennial favorite of the headbanger contingent, especially those old-liners who were around when it was released.

They're all wrong. When you talk about greatest, you're going beyond essence (and all the above mentioned records are essential to me) into *quintessence*. Quintessence is the result of a process that boils something down to its purest, most concise form. That by definition implies a much smaller quantity. You see, I have a theory that Rock and Roll, real Rock and Roll, died along with the 7″ single. Take a look at the history of Rock since the advent of the CD. OK, how many great Rock and Roll bands have emerged in that time? CD's killed real Rock and Roll for two reasons. First of all, they're too damn long. With a record you had 40 minutes to state your case and you'd best put your absolute best material on. And what's more, the listener was forced to listen to an album in 20-minute portions before he or she had to get up and flip the blessed thing over. This process forced the listener and the musicians to pay more attention. With the advent of 100 CD carousels, music became wallpaper and people became far less demanding of the records they bought. Don't like a certain track? With a click of the thumb you were on the next track or next album. It doesn't matter, it's all just bits and bytes in the endless data stream. La la la.

CD's have also reduced everything to a sterile, risk-free sameness. Cover art is so small and trapped behind a lucite box like a butterfly suffocated behind glass. The disks are glossy, silver, futuristic objects more suited to the clicking and chiming of ones and zeros than to the sounds of metal and wood and sweat. Records were a glorious reflective black, like a hoodlum's jacket. You looked at them and saw your own face through a glossy prism of night. The sleeves were paper and cardboard, which you could cut your fingers on or even clean your stash with. And the size of an album signified the importance that it had in your life. The smallest record was 2 inches bigger than the largest CD, and in this case, size does matter.

If the twenty minute serving of an album side was the expediter of essence, the three minute slab of sound on a single side is the ultimate in quintessence. No Rock and Roll experience is greater than a single side. This is why Punk was so crucial to so many back in the day. The currency of Punk was the single. Albums, more often than not, were anticlimactic. And since the credo of Punk was value for money, the single morphed into the EP, a strange British format of the 60's updated for the skinflint ethos of Punk.

The Clash released one real EP in the course of their career, and they used the occasion to release their most quintessential music. *The Cost of Living EP*, released in the spring of 1979, is the one Clash record that is absolutely bullet-proof, perfect, unimprovable. In comparison, the first album suffers from poor production and a compositional sameness, Rope is too metallic and one-dimensional, *London Calling* is too long and too stuffed with mushy material like 'Lover's Rock' and 'Right Profile' and *Sandinista* is just plain bonkers.

Cost of Living was the Clash as their most crystalline. It has the best ensemble playing of all their records, capturing Topper at his absolute tastiest. Every note sparkles with a sense of urgency and tautness. The cover of 'I Fought the Law' is a summation of the US-UK musical axis, a 400-year musical history. The revamp of 'Capitol Radio' is the Clash at their Punkiest and, simultaneously, their poppiest and funniest. The song explodes from the speakers like nothing they recorded before or since. 'Gates of the West' is Power Pop to the extreme, and the sounds of Badfinger, Big Star, the Raspberries and Cheap Trick resonate in the belly of its sound. And 'Groovy Times' is the Clash at their dystopian height, casting a grim eye on the advent of Thatcherism. Every lyric on *Cost of Living* is perfect, every ooh and ahh impassioned, every riff and drumbeat sparkles with urgency and conviction.

It was the artistic success of that gave the Clash the confidence to take on the world, musically and politically. It captured the excitement of the new geographical vistas promised by America and the growing confidence in their own ability to make new sounds. It was the Clash at their most essential, their most plugged in to the world around them and into the power of Rock and Roll.

Gibsontown and Fenderville
Originally posted 10/4/00

I had a guitar teacher who made a distinction between 'guitarists' and 'guitar players.' He defined a 'guitarist' as a serious player like Steve Howe or Robert Fripp: someone who is versed in the classical tradition of guitar playing and could sight-read and what-not. A 'guitar player', which was how he defined himself, is a player like Keith Richards or John Fogerty, whose playing is simpler and more intuitive. I have a different definition for each of these labels. To me a guitar player is someone who plays guitar as accompaniment, like a singer-player, or likewise uses the guitar as means to some other end. A guitarist is someone who is focused on the guitar itself, on its voice, on its possibilities as a singular mode of personal expression. The kind of guy who always seems to have his instrument on his lap. For some reason, I want to cite James Honeyman Scott as an example of this, but Andy Summers or Jimmy Page will do nicely as well.

At first blush, it may seem that Joe was the guitar player in the Clash, and Mick was the guitarist. But since this is the Clash we're talking about, it's not that cut and dried. I think that Joe was the real guitar enthusiast in the Clash and remains as such today, and Mick saw the guitar as a means to an end.

Looking back over the story of the Clash, I think it's obvious to me that Mick never wanted to be the guitarist, ie; the sideman, but the frontman, which he became with BAD. If the epitaph of the Clash breakup is that Bernie wanted to be Mick, it should also be that Mick wanted to be Joe. Towards the end, Mick spent most of his onstage time playing and singing in tandem with Joe.

The post-Clash discography is more revealing. The guitar on BAD records is mostly decorative, simply another element in the mix. On the whole, the guitar sounds on those records are neither assertive nor particularly creative. Mick wants guitar to be there, but clearly his focus is on the whole production, the singing and the samples and the songwriting. Paul said that he believed that Mick was bored with playing the guitar in the *MOJO* article, and certainly Joe's big beef in his '84 bitch-fests was that Mick "didn't want to play his damn guitar anymore."

I think Mick's interest in the guitar, and therefore his playing, peaked on the *London Calling* record. *London Calling* is the one Clash album I can point to as a guitarist and say that there is some really great playing on. Not the playing on the other records is bad, but it's just not particularly unusual. It's there in service of the song as a whole. There was a tremendous scaleback of his playing on *Sandinista*, but that can chalked up to the fact that he was in the director's chair on the sessions, and had a lot more to worry about. But a real big 'G' Guitarist would make his playing his first priority. That's how I define the term. I think the *Combat Rock* sessions, where Mick was playing a lot Roland synth-guitar, was Mick's last ditch attempt to keep his focus on the instrument. And subsequently, if the playing on *Combat Rock* was minimalist, it was nearly invisible on *This is Big Audio Dynamite*. None of it is bad, there just isn't much of it. Mick's priorities had clearly changed. When asked by an interviewer in 1986 to rate himself as a guitarist, Mick replied, "I'm all right. I never practice."

Now Joe, while certainly not much of a player, is a true guitar aficionado. Don't be fooled; that beat-to-shit Tele is just a stage prop. I doubt he uses it in the studio. In fact, a recent picture of him in the studio had him playing a snazzy looking Les Paul. What strikes me when I listened to *Earthquake Weather* recently is what a guitar album it is. Zander Schloss is a guitar geek of the first order, and the album is an encyclopedia of the sounds you can wring out of a Twin Reverb. And to give credit where it's due, Joe's rhythm playing is top rate. I've said before that Joe's focus on that record was primarily musical and certainly not lyrical. Ultimately though, a song lives or dies on it's melody line, and therefore a lot of songs on the record die, but there's always a coterie of wonks like myself eager to dissect the parts of the corpse and savor them. All of the work Joe did with Schloss (including the *Walker* and *Permanent Record* s/t's) is pure guitarism, often taken to a ludicrous extreme.

Those records are about guitars, they're about sitting in a studio and playing guitars and listening to the sounds that come out. And predictably, all that studio wonkery didn't come off too well onstage. The 'Rock Against the Rich' tour was good, but when Jim Donica, a seasoned pro, was replaced on bass by Lonnie Marshall, an inexperienced guitar geek who seemed unable to play in front of an actual crowd, it was particularly painful to watch.

X-Ray Style is a different case, particularly when you consider that the guys playing guitars are actually keyboardists. There is still the same attention to that warm, crunchy, tube-amp sound but the playing doesn't bowl you over. But Martin Slattery and Antony Genn are real musicians, what they call 'musos' in the UK. They're the kind of guys I hated when I was playing, guys who can quickly learn any instrument and then later kick your ass on it. Slats has reportedly only been playing a couple years, and look for him to improve a lot. I get the feeling Joe is working with those guys first and foremost because he feels a chemistry with them. Neither can touch Schloss or the Clash II guitar-slingers in the chops department, but both probably bring a lot more to the table in other areas.

YOU'RE MY GUITAR HERO

Written sometime in late 1999

Mick's guitar playing has been lost in the sands of time. He had the misfortune of playing his best work at the same time as a number of outstanding innovators and technicians. Mick was neither, but he did a lot of creative work with his instrument.

Mick's primary contribution, in my eyes, is sound. He was adept at manipulating effects to achieve a monstrous live sound from '79 to early '82. From early on, he was using large doses of reverb on his playing, contrary to the spartan image of the early Clash sound. Reverb is what Rock and Roll is all about. The first great Rock guitarist, Scotty Moore, used heavy spring reverb through an Echotone amp, which gave the early Elvis records that haunted feel. From that cheap amp sound (Mick used shitty Hiwatt amps in the early days of the Clash), Mick graduated into using Marshalls in '78 and developed the big rock sound that characterized *Give 'Em Enough Rope*. Playing on top of Strummer, Mick developed a "wet" rock sound, eventually incorporating heavy usage of phase into his setup. A phase unit is a device used heavily in the '70's on records by David Bowie (*Low*, most prominently) and Led Zeppelin (most heavily on *Physical Graffiti*). It also is a trademark on Reggae rhythm playing. If you want on hear a phase in action, listen to the intro of 'Rudie Can't Fail' on *London Calling*. That 'watery' sound on the guitars is phase. Mick used an MXR 100 phaser on nearly every cut on *LC*. Phase is also used to far lesser effect on the WNEW Palladium '79 show. Phase doesn't work well with Punk guitar as it tends to mitigate the power of the sound.

Mick soon began to downplay phase in favor of flange. For an example of flange listen to 'Cheat.' That 'whooshing' sound on the outro is tape flange. A flange unit provides a similar effect, though with a much wider range. Alex Lifeson of Rush used heavy amounts of flange on albums like *Permanent Waves* and *Moving Pictures*. It's an incredibly versatile effect that adds a lot of color to heavy rock guitar. Mick's sound from late '80 on was the result of a combination of Gibson humbucker pickups through flange and delay units fed into a Roland Chorus Echo unit fed into a Mesa Boogie head (over-rated amps that nevertheless do have superior low-range response) and then into two Marshall 4x12 cabinets. If any guitarists out there want to duplicate Mick's live sound (which you will be able to hear clearly when the live record comes out) there is your recipe. I spent years trying to figure out what the essence of his sound was, and the secret of it is super wet effects and good speakers with strong low-end response.

Mick's playing itself was largely Glam derived. He played a lot of Chuck Berry-type licks which he got from Mick Ronson and, to a lesser extent, Keith Richards. Ronson was Mick's strongest influence. Ronson's playing was very melodic and simple, but forceful. Ronson was never a show-off. Instead, he concentrated on moving the song forward. Mick followed this approach and used his guitar as an insistent counterpoint to Joe's electric guitar-like voice. Mick also was technically challenged in relation to shredders like Randy Rhoads and Eddie Van Halen, who were coming to prominence at the same time as the Clash. I believe that one of the reasons that Mick lost interest in playing lead guitar was his feeling that he couldn't compete with these players, and bands like Van Halen were very much on the Clash's mind as they tried to break America. This is a shame, because at the same time that the shredders were coming into prominence, there was a school of far more limited but innovative players such as the Edge who had an equally profound effect on Rock guitar playing. And Mick's live playing, which at most times was superior to his latter recorded work, fit in perfectly with this new generation of British guitarists. Jones' most impressive work as far as lead guitar is concerned is on *Rope* and *London Calling*. He was experimenting to interesting runs and melodic devices that more than compensated for his technical limitations. His playing was far more sparse on *Sandinista* and *Combat Rock*. This may be partly because of the immense amount of material they were recording at the time, but it may also be because Mick was intimidated by the new metal players. Mick did do a lot of interesting textural work on *Sandinista*. Songs like 'Mag 7' and 'Crooked Beat' have interesting rhythm figures and there's also interesting use of long delay on songs like 'Charlie Don't Surf' and use of flange on 'One More Time'. Mick was trying to emulate the texture of Reggae and Funk players, but his limitations prevented him from achieving true forgeries. But at the same time the creative work within the parameters of his playing made for some innovative playing.

I recommend the Ellen Foley/Clash record, *Spirit of St Louis*, for one reason: Mick's playing is a lot better on it than on *Sandinista* and *Combat Rock*. I am mystified why Mick saved some of his best playing for such a strange venture, but I enjoy it nonetheless. I think Mick was trying to create a more mainstream sound for Foley and perhaps was a bit more rigorous in his playing. Or maybe it was love.

On *Combat Rock*, his playing was hampered by Headon's disintegration as well as the type of material they were playing. As Headon and Jones tried to reassert their primacy in the band, they took it upon themselves to develop the material without Joe, which robbed the tracks of the propulsion his rhythm playing provided. Mick's work is extremely sparse on the record and much of his playing is through the Roland synth-guitar. But all that being said, there are quite a few musical gems on *Combat*. His use of double delay gives 'Sean Flynn' that haunted, tropical feeling. The solo on 'Know Your Rights' is, in my opinion, one of the greatest Rock guitar solos in history. The pitch-shifted synth-guitar work on 'Death is a Star' is the only thing about that wispy nothing of a song that I find interesting. I am also quite fond of Mick's playing on 'Beautiful People', but in true Clash tradition, the song with his best playing from those sessions was left off the album. But most of the other stuff on the record is feeble, albeit often texturally interesting.

To me, Jones best work was saved for the stage. His solos were often sloppy blurs, but that's not what the crux of Mick's playing is about to me. Mick's playing was geared towards ensemble, textural syncopations. Mick went back to Bowie to borrow Carlos Alomar's rhythm-as-lead style (best heard on 'Look Back in Anger' off of *Lodger*) and gave songs like 'the Call Up' and 'One More Time' added punch (see *Down at the Casbah Club* and the Bonds radio broadcast for examples of this approach). In late '82 he took most of the meat out of his sound, but he also became subtler in his playing. But seeing that he spent a lot of time singing in tandem with Joe, there was also a lot less playing in '82/'83 than there had been previously.

Mick's post-Clash guitar? Not much to talk about. Mick seemed to lose interest in pursuing the guitar as craft with BAD. Not that he hasn't done some interesting work. I think his best post-Clash playing is on *No 10, Upping St*. I'm especially fond of the serpentine solo on the original version of 'Hollywood Boulevard'. I think he has done some interesting bits here and there, but it's obvious that his focus has not been on guitar for much of his tenure with BAD. He did a lot of lead work live when I saw him with BAD 2, but much of it was school-boy pentatonic stuff. But he does have this uncanny knack of wringing out strange harmonies out of standard barre chords using delay, and I have by no means given up on Mick-as-guitarist. Guitars exude a strange magic and once bitten, they got you for life. Mick's best work could lie ahead.

HEAD AT THE CONTROLS
Written sometime in 2000

The Clash's records seem to be divided in two: There's the first three, which everyone seems to like, and then *Sandinista* and *Combat Rock,* which a lot of people don't like (there's also *Cut the Crap* — which everyone hates, but it doesn't count in this discussion). Why is there this division between the two? Well, the difference is in my opinion, production.

Production is poorly understood. A lot of people confuse it with engineering, which is how well a piece of music is technically recorded. Engineering does play a big part in production, and it's nearly impossible to for a poorly-engineered record to be well-produced, but production is a much more complex animal. Look at it this way: a lot of people look at George Martin as being the fifth Beatle. This is absurd. He's really the first Beatle. He got them signed and he got their act together and made them the legends they became. He often wrote the parts the band would play, he arranged all their songs and he conducted the session musicians who played on their records. It was his technical mastery that allowed the Beatles to really become 'the Beatles'. And if you need proof of how important he was to their sound, listen to most of Lennon and McCartney's post Beatle work. With the exception of *Band on the Run* , there is little that equals a Beatles record.

Another example to be looked at is U2. U2 are talented musicians, but look at what happens when they don't have a strong or sympathetic producer at the helm. Their first single, produced by Matin Hannett, went nowhere. It was Steve Lillywhite, the penultimate early 80's producer, who gave them their big, cavernous sound. And it was Brian Eno who made them the superstars they became. U2's last record was not produced by Eno, and it was a commercial and artistic disaster. Unsurprisingly, they are using Eno for their next record. Or listen to *Nevermind*, produced by real producer Butch Vig, compared to *In Utero*, produced by a hipster charlatan.

I bring up Eno and Martin because they are the strongest examples of what a great producer brings to the table. A great producer helps a band select material, helps them arrange it, helps them create the sonic landscapes for their songs to inhabit. A great producer coaches a band how to play and, like a great conductor, wrings the best possible performances out their artists. The Clash never really worked with a great producer. They worked with a very good one, Sandy Pearlman, and hated every minute of it. Why? Because when they would blow a take, they had to re-record it. They had to do numerous overdubs, because that's what it takes to make a polished-sounding heavy Rock record.

After they worked with Pearlman, they worked with Guy Stevens. Stevens apparently didn't do much but create a wacky, anarchic mood while Bill Price, another very good producer, did most of the heavy lifting. On their first three records, the Clash were fresh and eager and excited to make great Rock and Roll records and perhaps the producer was almost incidental to the process. But with *Sandinista*, it seemed that the Clash wanted mostly to get really high and play with some very expensive toys. *Sandinista* and *Combat Rock* are not good Rock and Roll albums at all. The playing is rarely exciting, the sound is weak and watery and the energy that the songs displayed live is sorely lacking. But both records were recorded during hectic times for the band, and they probably saw studio time as an opportunity to relax and experiment. So if those records aren't good Rock albums, what are they?

They are great Stoner records, almost mystical in their attenuation to the brainwaves of Heads and Stoners the world over. Mick was at the helm for these two records in large part, and the communal, THC-damaged headspace the Clash were lost in is virtually audible in the grooves. The Clash were enamored of serious Dub Reggae, which in reality is ritual music for a Caribbean drug cult. The Clash in this time period reminded me of the crew in the 1984 version of *the Bounty* - tough, disciplined British fighting men who are seduced by the carnal and psychic power of the tropics and 'go native'. They at the same time adopted the political sympathies of the Tropics. You can almost feel the sunlight and smell the foliage in the grooves of those records.

And that Stoner vibe has its own power. Just last night, I dreamt my usual dream of finding that elusive bootleg of lost Clash classics (last night it was a 5-record set!) and most of the tunes have that *Sandi/Combat* tropical-funk vibe. I don't fault the Clash for going off in that direction per se, I just fault them for being so sloppy in their execution. I fully understand the allure that the hot and sensual Third World has for lads from cold, grey England. But the Clash were quick to record their latest fixations before they fully understood them or fully understood how to operate the studio. Both Joe and Mick are OK co-producers, but neither have demonstrated the discipline required to fully put their musical gifts on record. Unlike a lot of other fans, I look forward to their future work. Art is an evolutionary process and true artists never stop trying.

Readers of the Showdown are probably mystified as to how I can be seemingly of two minds about the Clash's work, about how I can alternately praise and condemn their later work. Well, I look at it from two different viewpoints. On one hand I deplore their abandonment of their core identity, but at the same time I know the power of the forces they were seduced by. Fletcher Christian's mutineers came to a sorry end, and the Clash did as well. The Clash may have seen strong producers as Captain Blighs, but in reality a strong skipper could have steered the Clash home.

THE MYTH OF LONDON CALLING
Originally posted Apr 15, 2000

At some point in time, and I'm not sure when, *London Calling* became elevated to fetish status. That is, it became an unassailable cult item possessing of some innate power beyond the music it contains. Come to think of it, it was probably when *Rolling Stone* named it the Number One album of the 80's in late 1989. Since then, Sony has had a mythical "great work" to market the Clash with. I would argue that, in no way, does *London Calling* contain better material than the other Clash records. I've always seen *LC* as the Clash's mainstream move, which is probably why it has become such an object of veneration. No one can deny that *LC* contains the Clash's safest and least challenging music, albeit alongside some of their best songs.

Let's backtrack to 1979. Punk was then just another fading 70's fad, not the institution it later became. The Clash at the time were seen as Hardcore Punks, the serious face of an movement that was often frivolous and self-effacing. The Sex Pistols' demise had placed the burden of leadership on the Clash's shoulders, and subsequently had made them a target. Sniveling, spineless critics and fake fans had attacked (and continue to attack) *Give 'Em Enough Rope* as a failed and strident record. All true Clash fans recognize *Rope* as a masterpiece, but the album's principal transgression was perfectly capturing the mood of a very troubled and troubling time. Writers who didn't bother to learn the lyrics assumed 'Guns on the Roof' was about Topper and Paul's BB-gun arrest, ignoring the fact that the song was a protest against superpower conflict and totalitarian excess. Wags assumed that 'Last Gang in Town' was about the Clash, not a bitter satire about the pointless gang violence rocking England at the time.

Britain was burdened at the time with the most obnoxious and vicious critics in the history of media (Burchill, Bushell, etc.), but the Clash paid an inordinate amount of attention to what these desperately jealous hacks had to say. They were also concerned with the adulation coming in from the opposite side of the Atlantic. The US press was in the waning days of the Golden Age of Rock writing and people like Bangs, Christgau and Greil Marcus still had important things to say. US critics were seen by the Clash as their most important allies stateside, and the Clash saw that their only chance for long-term survival was breaking the States. This was a natural progression for them, and Joe had surely seen how important critics had been in the success of one of his role models, Bruce Springsteen.

1979 was another bad year for England, with Margaret Thatcher taking power and the ascendancy of Fascist gangs being fueled by record unemployment. Having purged their need for catharsis with *Rope*, the Clash were showing a distinct trend towards Rock classicism with the brilliant *Cost of Living EP*. Their cover of 'I Fought the Law' also got them a smattering of US airplay, so the way forward must have seemed clear. The Clash would reinvent themselves as the latest incarnation of the Great British Rock band, just like their idols, the Rolling Stones. They would toss in elements borrowed from the Who 'Clampdown') the Kinks ('Lost in the Supermarket'), and the Beatles (Mick would play the McCartney co-lead role more aggressively). The Clash also raided the celestial jukebox: by roping in Guy Stevens to 'produce', borrowing production ideas from Phil Spector on 'the Card Cheat', finding lost bluebeat classics like 'Wrong Em Boyo' and 'Revolution Rock' and even a English Rockabilly gem that sounded instantly familiar to American ears.

But the Stones were the main touchstone for *London Calling*. The guitar thunder was radically toned down and heavy use of phase was introduced, eerily duplicating the guitar sound on *Some Girls*. Big band horns were thrown into the mix just like *Exile on Main Street*, Big City Blues tracks like 'Jimmy Jazz' and 'the Right Profile' sounded like Stones covers and the double LP format itself was another nod to *Exile*. Just like Springsteen had made *Born to Run* to be an instant classic, so were the Clash doing with *London Calling*. The more overt politics of the first two albums were toned down to emphasize 'personal politics' and the Clash even modified their shock-tactics method of dressing in favor of what Marcus Gray referred to as the 'Hollywood Rock and Roll' look.

A preview airing of the *London Calling* material in the late summer of '79 met with extreme disfavor by Garry Bushell, one of the few Inkie wags who liked Hard Rock. Undaunted, the Clash took the show on the road with their 'Clash Take the Fifth' tour, the 'Fifth' being Blockhead Mickey Gallagher. They played the new material with the guitar firepower left over from Rope fully intact, so the transitions were relatively seamless. After the tour, the Clash returned home and awaited the release of the double album. UK reviews were mixed, with many critics sniffing out the Stones moves right away. Nevertheless, the title single charted at #11 and the album did well on the charts. The following month, *London Calling* was released in the US and was greeted with hysterical, raving critical praise unseen since the days of the Beatles. 'Train In Vain', a last minute addition, made the US top 40 and the album got the attention of educated Rock fans who had previously written them off as Punk ranters.

It's clear that the Clash intended to make a 'classic' Rock and Roll album and raided the past to construct it. But is it representative of the Clash as whole? I would argue that *London Calling* is an aberration. It is a very conservative record, overly concerned, in my opinion, with the history books. I don't even think that it contains a disproportionate amount of great songs in comparison to the other Clash records. 'LC', 'Cadillac', 'Rudy', 'Spanish Bombs', 'Supermarket', 'Clampdown', 'Brixton', 'Death' and 'Train' are all top-flight songs by any measure, but to me tracks like 'the Right Profile', 'Jimmy Jazz', 'Koka Kola', 'Lover's Rock', 'Four Horsemen' and 'I'm Not Down' are glorified B-sides. Square in the mold of quality 70's Clash B-sides, but 'B' material nonetheless. Truth be told, it wasn't until the *Rolling Stone* poll that I started hearing people talk about *London Calling* in the glowing terms we've heard since. Previously, it was generally accepted that the first album was the 'classic' Clash record, both by fans and in the press. I think a lot of the impetus for this is company driven as well. The success of *Story of the Clash* in the late 80's necessitated a 'holy book' for the Clash, and the first two records were too brutal and the last two were too whacked out, so *London Calling* won by default. When I was a kid, I never took the Clash fans whose collection began with *LC* and ended with *Combat Rock* seriously.

I've always felt that the Clash's best songs were contained on *Sandinista* and *Combat Rock*, although they were either surrounded by filler or poorly performed on their recorded versions. The best tracks on *Sandinista* to me are both more challenging and more interesting melodically than their counterparts on *London Calling*. I think if the Clash weren't so whacked on drugs when they made *Combat Rock*, it would have eclipsed their prior records. Live versions of tracks like 'Car Jamming', 'Know Your Rights' and 'Ghetto Defendant' are much more representative of what the Clash were actually about than most of the cuts on *LC*. But Rock and Roll is a business as well as an art form, and the myth of *London Calling* is much more effective in making the cash registers jingle.

Sandinista! FOR BEGINNERS
Written sometime in 2000

From time to time there are anguished cries raised on the net by bewildered fans who bought *Sandinista* only to find themselves suddenly in the middle of 2+ hours of very strange and un-Clash-like music. So for my monthly mitzvah I write this guide on how to listen to *Sandinista* properly.

• The most important step is your first: accept that this is a very strange record that doesn't fit into the popular conception of what Punk Rock is. The Clash defined Punk as no rules, and that's what this album is all about. Sort of.

• Second verse same as the first; Open your mind and be willing to listen to new and different types of music. This is the sound of a band exploring and experimenting.

.

• Third: Remember that this album is as controversial within the Clash camp as without. Joe Strummer adamantly believed it should have been a single, Kosmo thought it should have been a double and it was Mick's idea to make it a triple.

OK, there are your first three rules. More may be coming if I can think of them, so read carefully.

Now let's get to the record itself. It would be easier if you have the vinyl. For those that do, listen to the second LP (sides 3 and 4) and then work in the rest as you see fit. Considering that *Sandinista* came out less than a year after *London Calling*, it's a nice single LP to chew on. Pretend the other two records don't exist and then make believe you stumbled across a bootleg double record set of out-takes (LPs 1 and 3).

OK, set your CD player to program. First of all, skip the first four tracks ('Mag 7', 'Shitsville UK', 'Junco' and 'Ivan'). Many Clash fans love them dearly, but they are the sound of the Clash being very silly. Your first song off the album will be 'the Leader', but don't enter it as your first track in the program. Start with song #10, 'Somebody Got Murdered', a nice, almost traditional Clash song with loud guitars and stuff. You probably heard it on *Clash On Broadway* or the *Story of*, so you're familiar with it. The next track, 'One More Time', is a nice follow-up. Very similar to 'Guns Of Brixton', in fact probably written by Mick and Joe as their answer to that tune, seeing that they were probably jealous that they didn't write it themselves. OK, you can skip the dub if you want, but it's pretty killer. Now go back to song #5, 'the Leader', another song on the box. Nice trad Rockabilly number, kind of like 'Brand New Cadillac' with funny lyrics and a 1957 mix. Then, if you're brave, go to song #6, 'Something About England', another *London Calling* kind of number. It's a little strange, but this is *Sandinista*, remember. OK, there's your first four tunes, out of twelve on the original LP. We skipped 'Rebel Waltz' for now, 'Look Here' and 'Crooked Beat'. 'Look Here' is like the version of 'Junco', a silly and essentially guitar-less New Orleans cover. 'Rebel Waltz' you can go back to. It's a nice song that sort of presages the Pogues' later and immeasurably inferior work. 'Crooked Beat' is good for the reggae fans and it's optional with your introductory program. I recommend you skip 'Mag 7' and replace it with the dance/dub version from Super Black Market if you are going to do this all on tape. OK, next track is lucky 13, 'Lightning Strikes'. Possibly the first Rock/Rap fusion ever, rather than a Rap knockoff. Lots of energy and aggression and fantastic lyrics. Then go next to 'Up in Heaven',another *London Calling*-ish track. Actually play out the side. 'Corner Soul' is a nice Springsteen-ish urban ballad, 'Let's Go Crazy' is a jumpy Ska/Calypso fusion, and you're probably ready for the dub poetry of 'If Music Could Talk'. Then finish off disk one with 'Sound of the Sinners', which is a fun Gospel parody with very Punk Rock vocals and, again, great lyrics. Whew. That's 9 songs out of 18. Again, add any optional numbers into the program as you see fit. But don't bite off more than you can chew.

Right, disk 2. OK, 'Police on My Back' is easy enough. Go ahead to 'Midnight Log', another Politicobilly number. OK, now it gets difficult. Skip 'Equaliser' if you don't love really spacy Dub. 'Call-Up' might be familiar, but again you might be better off listening to the *SBMC* dub, which has a superior mix. 'Washington Bullets' will throw the Punks for a loop, as will 'Broadway'.

But they are both great tunes, so be open-minded for once in your life, will you, Sid? OK, as soon as 'Broadway' stops, skip right away to 'Charlie Don't Surf'. If you hear Maria Gallagher mangle 'Guns of Brixton' it could ruin everything. Go to 'Charlie Don't Surf'. Skip 'Lose this Skin', it has violins on it. And, oh yeah, it's not really a Clash song, just a song Joe's old buddy Tymon Dogg wrote and had Mick and Topper play back up on. Right, where were we? All right, 'Charlie'. Lot like 'Bullets' and 'Broadway', mellow but very cool. OK, you've been patient, so go to 'Kingston Advice'. It's a straight-ahead Rock... well, kinda Rock and Dub....OK, it's not very straight ahead but it has loud guitars on it. Well, actually has a couple power chords thrown in on the choruses. OK, feeling better now? Well, next comes 'Street Parade', another mellow atmospheric thing that is also very cool. Listen and enjoy.

Then... well, you're kinda screwed for the rest of the record. There's only one real song on side 6, er...the last six songs, and it ain't exactly 'Complete Control'. Then they make dubs of some of the weirder songs from earlier on. Don't get excited - that version of 'Career Opportunities' is a Karaoke-for-kids version. And 'Shepherd's Delight' is a slow-motion jam of the Junior Murvin version of 'Police and Thieves' with some sheep noises added on. But we managed to squeeze eight tracks out of this disk, added to the 9 from the first disk, which is still a lot of music. You can sample some of the other things now and then, but I recommend you do it slowly and carefully. If adverse effects continue after seven days, have a dose of *Give 'Em Enough Rope* and email me in the morning.

ONE MORE TIME
originally posted 1/25/97

While we're on the topic of *Sandinista* , I thought I would talk a little about one of my all-time favorite songs, 'One More Time' ('OMT'). For some bizarre reason, this track has been left off of all the posthumous comps, despite the fact it is perhaps the Clash's most successful attempt at making a new music form out of Punk and Dub. In addition, 'OMT' was a concert highlight from '81 to the new Clash in '84. I had always thought that *the Story of the Clash* should have taken it's track listing from a typical Eighties live set list, an approach that would have ensured 'OMT's inclusion. But I will go to my grave not understanding the Clash's irrational artistic decisions, and I have a feeling that they probably will too.

The recorded version of 'OMT' is like a hurtling cab-ride through a urban hell. Strummer's lyric summons up a palpable sense of brooding menace, and the music has the breathy percussiveness that Tricky has made his own. As the heavily-reverbed snare snaps like gunshots, a flanged guitar and high-hat build up a terrifying cinematic momentum. Joe punctuates his lead vocal with shouted gospel-style proclamations in the background. In place of a guitar solo, Mikey Dread enters the fray like a Jamaican Isaiah shouting down the sins of Babylon. That move would prefigure Don Letts role in BAD.

And as if all this urban terror was not enough, the dub track follows hot on it's heels and the listener is submerged in a PCP daze and forced to relive the nightmare. These two tracks demonstrate Mick's genius for intuitive production, as well as Mikey's immense contribution to the *Sandinista* vibe.

There are tons of great live versions of this track out there, but I thought I would point out my two absolute favorites. The first is the version from the *Casbah Club* set. The song, already perfect, is further enhanced by Terry's sledgehammer drumming, and Mick takes MXR fueled feedback to a new realm. The brassy slickness of the LP version becomes a head-throbbing pounding. Equally impressive is the Clash II version from the Miner's benefits at the Brixton Academy. Joe's feeling about the song is illustrated by it's use as an opener on both nights. The song starts out with Nick playing a riff based on the chord sequence and Vince joins in with all that wacky harmonics stuff he utilized in the Spring. Then the drums join in and finally after 5 minutes the song roars full-on with bass and vocals. Joe even drops in a few lines from former opening act Lee Dorsey's 'Working in A Coal Mine'. Both versions are must haves for a true diehard's collection.

Shitsville UK
Originally posted 2/15/00

One of the great things about the Clash was their ability to fail spectacularly. No pussyfooting with this bunch. *Cut the Crap*, 'Cool Confusion', Lochem Festival- they put as much energy into being lousy as they did being great. I am reminded of this as I read through George Gimarc's brilliant *Post-Punk Diary*. Here is an excerpt dated Jan 15, 1981 concerning the single release of '(S)hitsville UK.'

"Sounds *follows along the same thread writing that it is...'horrendous, horrendous, horrendous. This is like watching your best friend die in a singularly acid-headed nightmare. If Alfred Hitchcock had written pop tunes instead of making films and someone had ordered him to write a song that sounded like the Clash in their most extreme stages of character disorientation or personality crisis, it would sound like Hitsville UK. This is mad.'* "

Mad? No, not 'mad'. Nauseating, treasonous, unlistenable, and terminally inept maybe, but not mad.

The backing track isn't the problem here. That is, if you ignore the fact that the guitar sounds like it was being played by a hamster. No, the problems with this 3 minute piece of aural dogshit go far deeper than that. First off are Joe's embarrassing lyrics. He seems content to reel off the names of a bunch of UK Indie labels he never listened to in a feeble attempt to equate them with Motown. Then it gets crazy worse with the introduction of one Miss Ellen Foley.

Foley makes 'Hitsville' even worse than it already was with a soft focus vocal that sounded like she had just been handed the lyrics. Mick sounds like he phoned in his vocals from a sick bed. Perhaps they phoned in their vocal takes while ensconced in their hotel room. Judging from the feeble levels, I'd say its a good bet.

WESTWAY TO THE WORLD ISN'T ABOUT THE CLASH, WESTWAY TO THE WORLD IS THE CLASH!

1999 is the year of the Clash. For the long-suffering diehards who have endured this largely Clash-less decade, your patience is being rewarded. Certainly there has been little to talk about since the release of Super *Black Market Clash*. BAD has been sidelined due to grievous misdeeds by their record company, and Joe had reportedly been staring down Sony in an effort to free himself from his contract. But all of a sudden, there is a lot to be excited about. Joe toured fairly extensively in the Summer and dates have just been announced for the second leg of his Lazaraus-style re-emergence. Mick and Bill Price have been hard at work on the live album, now on track for the 19th of October. The buzz on this project has been overwhelmingly positive and being familiar with the sources for the songs used I can guarantee the diehards will be satisfied. Hot on the heels of the live album will be Joe's first new record in 10 years, *Rock Art, and the X-Ray Style*. A rough mix has been circulating on this record and as Showdown fans know, it's a killer. Several British magazines have been running comprehensive articles on the Clash including last month's *Uncut*, this month's *MOJO* and next month's *Q*. Word has it also that VH1 is planning a *Behind the Music* on the Clash. Let's see: Tour, tour, and album, new Clash live record, VHI show...what else have I forgotten? Oh, yes...

The coup de gras of this orgy of Clash-y goodness is *Westway to the World*, a film made by one of the many 'Fifth Clash-'ers' Don Letts. This is the ultimate testament to the Clash's grandeur, as well as a fitting epitaph. This documentary is as important as any album or concert the Clash have ever done, and hopefully a home video version of it will be available stateside very soon. This film is important also because it puts the band's legacy to rest at last and will quiet the calls for reunion once and for all.

Only Letts could have made this brilliant film. Only he has the skill and the insight to deliver this project. Letts is also the personification of the UK/Jamaica collision that defined the Clash and distinguished their legacy. It was Letts who as DJ in the Roxy nightclub introduced the young, first generation Punks to the power and drama of Reggae and Dub. And it was Letts who was the minister of visual propaganda for the multimedia political theater group known as the Clash.

In the film, the Clash discuss their lives from the beginning and many pictures from their childhoods are shown. They discuss their influences, their up-bringings and the records that changed their lives. There is some extremely rare footage from the 101'ers, as well as priceless footage of the Clash in 1976, including a hilarious clip of the band practicing with Mick on the drums.

Letts favors interviews of the band shot against a black backdrop over all else. There is a huge wealth of documentary and live footage but the band's testimony makes up the meat of the film. All the members look older and wiser, but leaven their memories with generous doses of humor. The charm and chama of the Clash is evident even now, putting current Rock "stars" to shame.

Most of the film dwells on the '76-'77 era, as is to be expected. The *Give 'Em Enough Rope* and *London Calling* eras are touched upon briefly, but the next act of the film centers on the *Sandinista*/Bonds era. Letts draws extensively on late-era Clash for incidental music and songs like 'Sean Flynn', 'Justice Tonight', 'One More Dub' and even 'Mensforth Hill' waft around the footage. The chaotic creative frenzy that created *Sandinista* is explored in-depth and the Clash are unapologetic about defending their misunderstood masterpiece. Special attention is given to the Bonds residency and there is some priceless footage shown from the aborted *Clash on Broadway* film.

From then on, the story gets difficult. A ravaged Topper appears for the first time in more than a decade and he is much the worse for wear. His addiction is explored in ways that are surprisingly candid. He admits that it was his addiction that tore the chemistry of the band asunder, but also admits that he would probably do the same again if given the chance. Joe is very blunt that the level of drug usage Tops was indulging in destroyed his ability to continue as the Clash drummer. Paul states that he was pleased that Joe invited Bernie back despite the grief it caused. Bernie is given his props throughout and the band seems to make it clear that their own inter-personal difficulties were more responsible for the end.

But there should be no regrets, in my view. As the band come forth to tell their side of the story, the arc becomes clearer and more inevitable. The Clash were a great story and once the dragon was slain, there was nothing left for the band to accomplish. The story ended before it got silly, though not before it got ugly. As we hear their voices on the history old ghosts are laid to rest and the past loosens its grip. They all have a lot to be proud of and their legacy only continues to grow. It's so refreshing for this diehard to get the real story rather than the corporate whitewash of the reissue days or the BritCrit sniping of the *Last Gang in Town*. Meanwhile we are being our given long-over-due reward for keeping the flame burning. Joe is back and ready to attack, Paul paints, Mick is recharging his batteries and hopefully Tops will shake away the demons that have tormented him for the past two decades.

THEY WROTE THE SONGS
Originally posted 9/25/00

Even though the set-up always seems to be doomed to eventual failure and dissolution, I think the two songwriter setup is always best. Every band needs a strong songwriting team, even if they don't always work within the straight lyricist-composer framework.

Contrary to popular opinion, John Lennon and Paul McCartney didn't really collaborate much, but their relationship was important in another way. If Paul or John were ever stuck for a bridge or an intro, one of them could come in and help and help the other. And often the difference between a good song and a bad one is a decent bridge. Look at a writer like Phil Collins, who never seems to know what the hell to do in the middle of a song. Whatever the quality of the Clash's tunes, the structure was usually solid, and you can bet that having two capable songwriters on board made the difference there.

Joe and Mick both have different strengths and weakness as songwriters, much like Lennon and McCartney. Like Lennon, Joe tends to over-simplicity and has problems with transitions. And like McCartney, Mick has a tendency towards cutesy-ness and weightlessness in his writing. I think like the Beatles, Joe and Mick also competed with one another, though a more apt analogy in this case might be Jagger-Richards. Post-Clash, Mick usually seemed to structure a tune without much trouble, but the issue is often: need he have bothered? Joe is usually more meaty in his musical and thematic ideas, but he often gets lost somewhere in the middle. 'Generations' is a perfect example of this. The song has a great groove, a great verse melody and a great refrain, but the chorus is leaden and lacks drama. It's still a good song, but this structural difficulty keeps it out of the Clash's league. Joe has written plenty of good songs himself, but technically has always had a lower batting average than Mick. Mick oozes melody and structure, but often doesn't seem to have much on his mind.

I also think that Joe was not the Dylanesque wordsmith people take him to have been. I think he was at least as focused on the musical component of a song. After all, this is a guy who composed a fairly considerable amount of instrumental music for films. Joe's topical songwriting was limited to the Clash and the songs he wrote for *No 10 Upping St.* Even in the Clash, the tendency towards stream of consciousness wordplay had almost taken over by the time of *Combat Rock*. The tightly metered lyrics to the Clash II numbers were a result of his taking over the musical component of the songwriting, and the lyrics were subservient to the gut punching melodies Joe had developed. From *Permanent Record* all the way to the end, most of Joe's lyrics were dreamy, non-linear, Beat-inspired musings. I think the main weakness of *Earthquake Weather* is that the lyrics were a total afterthought for Joe. He had just finished two mostly instrumental soundtracks and he was stuck in that frame of mind. Hence the album is a frustrating mix of tightly constructed backing tracks and melodies and carelessly slapped together lyrics. The Clash style vocal presentation of the lyrics does nothing but highlight the erratic meter and utter meaninglessness of the lyrics.

I have no idea what Don Letts did writing-wise for BAD so I can't comment on that, but Joe's relationship with Anthony Genn bears some analysis. Genn seems to be pretty solid on his fundamentals, but since he and Joe have done very little writing so far, that analysis must wait. I do think that Joe worked well with Norris on the *X-Ray Style* songs, but who did what exactly, I can't say. The bassline on 'Yalla' sounds a lot like Joe's doing to me, in that it reminds me of some of his Clash II musical ideas - 'This is England', to name one. And getting back to Genn, I must say that the two-chord structure of 'Willesden to Cricklewood', like 'Yalla', is typical of Joe. Joe is a more capable songsmith than he gives himself credit for, but he usually needs a second hand to help him organize his ideas.

In the end result, it will be the songs Joe and Mick did together that last, and I would count the songs they wrote on their own as part of their collaboration as well. Like most songwriting teams, their muses pulled them apart but the music lives on.

WHO DID WHAT?
Originally written sometime in 2000

One of the great past-times of serious Clash obsessives is guess who was responsible for what on Clash records. The official story is this - Joe wrote the words, Mick wrote the music, Paul 'played bass' and Topper hit things. The Clash were never particularly comprehensive in their liner notes, so there are some blanks to be filled there.

Most of the early songs were written by Joe and Mick together. But 'Janie Jones' and 'Protex Blue' were both London SS leftovers, as were many of the songs that didn't make the record like 'Mark Me Absent' and 'I Don't Know What You Want to Know about Me', or what ever the hell all those cheesy Kinks knock-offs are called. Paul was too busy learning to play at this point, so it's probably safe to say that his musical input was basically nil. Tops didn't come on board until after the album was finished so it's safe to say he didn't put in anything there either.

'Strummer/Jones' was a publishing arrangement rather than a description of songwriting. Lennon and McCartney co-wrote very few songs together- that credit was strictly a business arrangement. But Strummer/Jones is more analogous to Jagger/Richard here. Both teams co-wrote, but they also wrote their own songs in their entirety. 'Complete Control' was written by Mick, both lyrics and music. This is instructive for us obsessives because we can see the differences between Joe and Mick's writing styles. Mick tended to introduce an idea in the first stanza and then elaborate on it. He also wouldn't cram as much esoteric references in his lyrics either. I would hazard to guess that the post-bridge ranting ad-libs in 'Control' are Joe's alone. I can't imagine Mick writing "You gotta blega onarega onarega andnoga/ That means YOU!"

The next interesting number is 'Jail Guitar Doors', a reversal of the Strummer/Jones arrangement. Mick wrote new lyrics for the verses over a tune that Joe had written for the 101'ers ('Jail' is also one of my favorite unheralded Clash numbers). Some of the early singles feature some new twists on instrumentation, including harmonica on 'White Man' (probably Mick) and piano on 'Clash City Rockers' (probably Joe). These twists would become much more important in later records.

Give 'Em Enough Rope has some uncredited barrell-house piano (on 'Julie') which is neither Mick nor Joe, and saxophone on 'Drug Stabbing Time'. Most of these songs are credited to Strummer/Jones, with the exception of 'Guns on the Roof', which is probably a nod to the pigeon shooting incident that inspired the title. 'Stay Free', of course, is Mick's lyrics, a buddy song written in tribute to Robin Banks/Crocker. According to Marcus Gray, Joe wrote 'Tommy Gun' in its entirety, which makes sense since he played it on his '99 comeback tour. If Joe wrote anything himself on this album, which is unlikely, I would imagine it was 'Cheapskates', which is E minor, which is typical for Joe numbers, but not for Mick's. A review of Mick's songwriting career shows that he rarely used minor keys. Moving along, '1-2 Crush on You' was another London SS tune (one that Joe had sung in the early days) so Mick does a turn on the lyrics. 'Pressure Drop' is the only other B-side from *Rope*, and there's a bit of piano in there somewhere, which is probably Joe again.

Next up is the 'London Calling' single, which is ripe for obsessive speculating. It's another E minor song with a 1/4 note rhythm, both of which are Joe trademarks. My guess is that Joe came up with the verses and if anything, Mick probably contributed on the choruses. 'LC' is too Joe-y to be a tune that Mick originated. The flip 'Armagideon Time' has organ, which is probably Micky Gallagher, and some piano which is probably Joe.

The album has juicy bits for trainspotting as well. First off, the organ playing is Gallagher, and the horns are played by the Irish Horns. Paul wrote 'Guns of Brixton' and Topper isn't credited with anything. Again, my guess is that Joe wrote most of 'LC', and reportedly he wrote the music for 'Rudie' as well. After that it gets tricky. I would guess he might have also written 'Four Horsemen', since there's that 1/4 note motif and a bit of transitional awkwardness. My guess is that 'Clampdown' is a 'Day in the Life' deal. The verses and chorus are in A minor and the intro and bridge are in E major. Neither one is known for key-jumping, so I would guess that Joe had the verses in G (in keeping with Joe's habit of sticking to the frets with the dots on them) and

Mick came in a did the other parts to finish the song. Mick wrote 'Train in Vain' as we know, and probably wrote 'I'm Not Down', which has some lyrical bits that I couldn't imagine Joe ever writing. I am going to go out on a limb and say that Mick probably wrote the words and music to most of 'Card Cheat' as well. It has that A/B-A/hanging-B meter that we see on 'I'm Not Down', and I can't imagine Joe ever writing a line like "There's a solitary man cryin' hold me/ It's only because he's lonely." Joe sees himself as too butch for a line like that. Marcus Gray credits Joe with the lyric, but I'm not too sure of that. He also credits Joe with the music for "Spanish Bombs' 'The Right Profile' and 'Death or Glory'. I'm going back out on that limb and saying 'I doubt it' on 'Spanish Bombs' and 'Death or Glory', Mick claimed in a 1986 interview that 'Spanish Bombs' was one of the best songs they wrote together and 'Death or Glory' may have originated with Joe, but I smell Mick all over it. I believe the claim on 'Right Profile' (not that that's much to brag about) and add one that could have been Joe's: 'Koka Kola'. Like 'Right Profile' and 'Four Horseman' there are stilted stabbing chords and weird transitions on 'Koka Kola'. And it was a staple for many Clash II shows, which spells Joe to me.

The next single is 'Bank Robber', which Joe wrote the words and music for. But, I think there was a lot of input on it from Mick and from Mikey Dread, as well as from Gallagher. 'The Call Up' is definitely Strummer/Jones, and although VoidOids guitarist Ivan Julian plays on it, what exactly he's doing I don't know. I would guess he's doing the serpentine fills at the end. Joe wrote the music for the flip by accident when he was trying to figure out 'Green Onions', which tells you a lot about Joe's keyboard playing abilities.

Sandinista! is a nightmare or a gold mine for obsessives, depending on what variety of mental illness you suffer from. We know that a lot of the tracks were cut with Micky Gallagher and Norman Watt-Roy while Paul was in Canada basking in a nubile Diane Lane's divine presence during the making of that *Fabulous Stains* film. Marcus Gray claims that Paul overdubbed a lot of Watt-Roy's basslines in London after the Electric Lady sessions were completed, but I can't imagine he did all that much. Let me say that that there is no way in hell that Paul is playing on the following cuts: 'Mag 7', 'Hitsville', 'Junco', 'Look Here', 'One More Time' and 'Lose this Skin'. The rest are open to argument but I stand my ground on those cuts. 'Mag 7' is credited to Clash but it should be credited to Clash/Blockheads. Watt-Roy came up with the bassline that is the only distinguishing musical component that you would put on a piece of sheet music. For those of you who don't know that's Tymon Dogg singing on 'Lose This Skin', Topper on 'Ivan', and Mikey Dread on 'Living in Fame'.

Topper wrote the music for 'Ivan meets GI Joe', and I've been told that Julian plays guitar on this number as well, though I can't begin to imagine where. Mick apparently wrote the lyrics for 'Up In Heaven', one of my favorite Clash songs, and that 'hanging B' thing again gives that fact away. I'd also credit him with the lyrics to 'Street Parade' as well. I don't know if Joe wrote any music on this set, but given the free-for-all of the sessions, it's certainly possible. My only guesses on solo Joe compositions would be 'Midnight Log', since it has that two chord motif Joe has used on a lot of his songs and possibly 'One More Time'. Suffice it to say that a lot of songs on *Sandinista!* were written on the fly in the studio, so I can't imagine a lot of it can be pinned down for credit, though a great deal of the songs could be straight up Strummer/Jones. Joe has been credited (more accurately blamed) for the lyrics on '(S)hitsville UK', a song I blamed on Mick for years. Neither one I am sure would be too keen to take credit for that mess today   .

We have the mixes of 'Mag 7' and 'Call-Up' which Gray credits to Mick and which are credited to Paul, Joe and Bernie in the Super *Black Market Clash* liner notes. My vote is for the latter. The Unidos name shows up on *Cut the Crap* and 'Pepe' is Spanish for Paul. I can't imagine Bernie would borrow a Mick pseudonym for his own later. Mick was also doing a lot of outside production work at the time, so that seals it for me.

'Radio Clash' was the only post-*Sandinista* single, credited to Clash, but should be more accurately credited to Clash/Queen. Mick straight-out lifted 'Another One Bites the Dust', and then changed it around when called on the lift. It's still a great song, and a lot more interesting than it's source due in large part to the lyrics and arrangement. Who plays the synths and sax on the track? Probably the Barnacle brothers.

Combat Rock is next. The Clash were getting a little better in the credit department by this time, so we know who played what, mostly. 'Casbah' was written by Topper and Joe, not by Topper alone, which too many people believe. This brings up a pet peeve of mine here: Topper simply laid down a piano riff he'd been toying with for years and the song was spliced together in the studio. Sources have claimed that he did not play the bass as reported, that it was actually played by one of the engineers. Not to diminish what Topper did but it's as much Joe's song as Topper's. I think a lot of guilt on Joe's part has inflated Top's actual role in the writing of this song. Any how, my guess is that Joe wrote most of 'Know Your Rights', due to that 1/4 note thing and the bizarre Ab minor key. Mick wrote 'SISOSIG', but this is actually a brazen lift of 'Little Latin Lupe-de-Lu'. Mick loves his lifts. I would venture to guess that Mick wrote 'Inoculated City' in its entirety as well. The lyrics are much too coherent to be Joe-circa-'82 lyrics. I know Joe sang this in '81 when the song was first premiered, but that's probably because Mick needed to concentrate on the riff. Joe wrote the lyrics for 'Red Angel Dragnet', but I am not sure if Paul wrote the music. It sounds like Mick's other stabs at Funk/Reggae riffs and maybe Paul was given the song to foster that one-for-all vibe. There is a lot of synth on *Combat Rock* but a lot of it is probably Mick on the Roland synthaxe. Tymon Dogg shows up on piano on the last tune, 'Death is A Star.'

Then everything went kerplooey and we have *Cut the Crap*. The songs are credited to Strummer/Rhodes and the production (sic) to Jose Unidos. OK, let's get the production out of the way. Everyone agrees that it was produced by Bernie and that the 'Jose' was added to Unidos so Bernie could shift blame to Joe. Strummer was livid at that and also livid that Bernie claimed co-writer credit. Here's what we know: Joe wrote a large number of songs for Clash II and some of them were vetoed by Bernie for reasons unknown (Sheppard claimed that the songs cut were insufficiently political). Clash II played about 12 new songs live in '84, eight of which ended up on the album and four of which ('Sex Mad', 'Pouring Rain' [re-written by the entire band in soundchecks], 'Ammunition' and 'Glue Zombie') were cut. That leaves four which were written when the band was off the road.

I would say that 'We Are' and 'Dirty Punk' were Rhodes-influenced, at least. I would also say that when 'Sex Mad War' became 'Sex Mad Roar' that that was Bernie's input as well. For some reason, there seemed to be a conspiracy to cut 'War' out of the titles. 'Are You Ready for War?' was rechristened 'Are You Red..y.' 'Movers and Shakers' is definitely Rhodesian as is 'Cool Under Heat' and 'Play to Win'. And Rhodes definitely was the one who decided to strip the songs down compositionally and tart up the arrangements. So if you were Bernie Rhodes, you would think it well within your rights to claim credit. And as I have stated in other dispatches, the bulk of the music was played by Gallagher, Watt-Roy and Michael Fayne, and according to an 2000 interview with Joe in *Record Collector*, the rhythm guitars were played by none other than Mr. Bernard Rhodes himself! Why am I not surprised?

YOU STUPID, STUPID BASTARDS!!!

Originally posted Jan 9, 1997

Yeah that's right, ex-Clash members, I'm talking to you. Why did you do it? What were you thinking of? I mean of all the cockamamie hare-brained schemes I've ever heard, this one takes the cake. I mean, whose idea was it to not to make a record with Pete Howard?

Oh, and all you Mick groupies out there, stop acting so smug. Even if Mick had recorded the sixth Clash album, do you think he would've used Pete? Mick has yet to make a BAD album with real drums, so what makes you think he would have used a drummer on a Clash record?

In my opinion, Pete was the best Punk drummer ever. Can you imagine if Joe and Mick used their best songs on *CTC* and *TIBAD* on a Clash record with Powerhouse Pete? People would be saying "London What"? If any of you purist yobbos still don't get it, why don't you get your filthy paws on some '83 shows and hear the Clash with a proper drummer. Pete was like a combination of John Bonham with that seismic kick-snare combo, and also had the Stewart Copeland lightning-fast wrists. Even in some of the later Clash II shows when it was obvious the frontline wasn't rehearsing enough, Powerhouse Pete is flawless. My favorite Pete moment ever is the Arizona '83 boot (all-time killer Clash show) when they do 'Car Jamming', and Pete sounds like every great unsung New Orleans session drummer rolled into one.

Pete got a very rough shake in the Clash. He replaced Terry Chimes in early '83, stuck with Joe through the big divorce, took some very nasty verbal abuse from Joe, Bernie and Kosmo and was rewarded for his loyalty and hard work by being shut out of the *Crap* sessions. And then, to add insult to injury, he was listed in the *Crap* credits anyway. This is a perfect illustration of just how sick and Stalinist the Clash had become in those final days. Pete was left with an extremely nasty taste from all this, and only recalled the '83 and '85 mini-tours with any degree of fondness.

Pete has stayed busy, despite it all. He played with the band Eat, then played in Miles Hunt's short-lived band Vent 414 and is now slamming the skins for the British Goth Punk outfit, Queen Adreena.

YOU'RE THE ONE THAT I WANT (ON A SUNDAY)
Originally posted 10/21/00

I was driving down the highway not so long ago and I had WCBS-FM, the NYC Oldies station on. They played a number from the cultural phenomenon known as *Grease* entitled 'You're the One That I Want.'" For those of you who don't remember, that's the bouncy little number at the end of the film when Olivia Newton John finds her inner slut and gives John Travolta enough of a woody to send his voice up a couple of octaves. I had the bass on extra loud on my car stereo for some reason and I was struck by the bassline. Where did I hear it before? Then it hit me like a ton of bricks- Mick lifted that bassline for 'The Leader!' The irony of this struck me because this wasn't the first time that treacly number made its present felt in Clash City. You'll all remember Joe yeLPing "I'm the One that I Want!" at the fade of 'Capitol Radio.' I was laughing to myself, wondering what lifts I've yet to discover on Clash records. I also got a chuckle out of the fact that it was crap like *Grease* that made me a Punk in the first place.

Mick was shameless about his lifts, like any self-respecting songwriter. Just imagine how different Clash history would be if Sandy Pearlman allowed Mick to keep the riff he stole from Sammy Hagar's 'I've Done

Everything For You' on 'Safe European Home!' (some of you might remember that riff from Rick Springfield's version of the Hagar the Horrible tune)

Joe's a tougher one to spot lifts on. It may have a lot to do with his somewhat shambolic method of songwriting. His tunes could be full of lifts for all we know, but once they filter through his head they come out all Strummerized. I'm pretty sure the riff for 'Trash City' comes from somewhere, but I can't for the life of me remember where.

D.I.D.
Originally posted 9/18/00

Not that anyone ever asked me, but if I could only have one Clash CD, it would be Super *Black Market Clash*. No contest. Why? I'm glad you asked.

Since I feel that the Clash was a story, first and foremost, I find that no one of the studio records tells that story well enough. The first two are too Punk, the last two are two weird and *London Calling* is too conservative and transitional. *Cut the Crap*... you're kidding, right?

One thing that must be said is that all of the Clash singles, up to and including the 'London Calling' single (with the possible exception of the 'Tommy Gun' single), were double A-side singles. For my money, all of those early B-sides are as good, if not better, than the A-Sides. And the only reason the later singles didn't have strong B-sides is that the Clash were releasing pretty much everything they recorded on the albums. And the mixes on the later singles were important because they, like the album mixes of those tracks, were statements of intent. It wasn't until *Combat Rock*, when the Clash were gasping for creative air, that the B-sides really sounded like B-sides. (Ironic that Mick wanted those tracks on *Rat Patrol*!) In fact I always look at *Combat Rock* as six singles (say 'Rights', 'Stay', 'Casbah', 'Hell', 'Ghetto' and 'I.City') with the balance of the album as the B-sides. You could probably do the same split with *Sandinista* (especially so, since those tracks were recorded as the basis of a singles campaign) and the second record of *London Calling* was originally intended to be a bonus EP. So in essence it wasn't that the Clash ran out of B material, it was that they were putting all the B material on their albums. But I digress...

I can always tell a reviewer is a Clash novice (or just a plain twiddlehead) when he dismisses the songs on *BMC* and later, *SBMC*, as merely B-Sides or leftovers. 'Jail Guitar Doors' and 'the Prisoner' were set-list staples up until mid-1979. 'Pressure Drop' was in the setlist from '77-'85, more than can be said for a lot of tracks on *Story Of*. 'Groovy Times' and 'Gates of the West' were on the *Cost of Living EP*, intended as a singular piece of work. 'Capitol Radio' is an all-time classic that just fell between the cracks. And all the dub mixes are as interesting as the original cuts ('Mustapha', 'Justice Tonight') or much more interesting ('Mag Dance',' Cool Out').

I think *SBMC* is a much more representative document of the Clash because A., it's chronological and B., it's a warts and all telling of the story. You have the early tracks which demonstrate the Clash's ferocious energy, the *Cost of Living* era stuff which shows that energy maturing, the Dub/Funk stuff showing artistic adventurousness and the dismal *Combat Rock* stuff showing creative collapse. When you listen to tracks like 'First Night Back in London' you can practically hear the strain between the members of the band. I think the album holds together really well, despite all the different sessions and eras included. I hate purism in all its manifestations, but especially the purism that says a record is only good if it was recorded in one place at one time. *Physical Graffiti* is essentially a compilation and that is one of the greatest records of all time. So if you ask, Super *Black Market Clash* would be my first choice for Desert Island Disk.

BELABORING THE OBVIOUS
The Showdown guide to the official releases

I was tempted not to include this section in the book, since it is my belief that any reading this book would have all of albums on this list. But some people might be expecting a record review section, so I thought I would take this opportunity to indulge myself and offer random musings that might not fit elsewhere in the book. I'm not going to rate them, it's unnecessary. The first four albums (and I'm counting *Black Market*) are untouchable classics and are obvious A's and the last three need to be looked at carefully. I've separated the records into separate sections based starting with...

THE CANON

THE CLASH (US version) - I'm not going to prattle on in this section about all the better live versions I've heard of all these songs. This is a classic album, purism be damned. By contrast, the original UK version is too short and one dimensional. 'Clash City Rockers', 'Complete Control', 'White Man...', '...Law', and 'Jail Guitar Doors' are infinitely better than the tracks they replaced. The only off note here is the incongruous inclusion of 'I Fought the Law,' included because Epic needed an album to launch the single version from. I got this when it first came out and had the lyric sheet, so I had a great advantage on my friends who didn't know the lyrics to any of the songs. Every single kid I knew in the Hardcore scene would get wistful when they heard this album, whether or not they had thought the Clash had 'sold out' or not. If you possibly can, get this on vinyl, because the early CD version sounds like shit and I hate the way these tracks were remastered.

GIVE 'EM ENOUGH ROPE - Forget everything you've heard about this album. Forget all the foolish intra-scene politicking that gave this album a bad reputation. Forget all the bad notices pencil-neck critics foisted upon it. This is a classic Rock and Roll album, start to finish. To me, it's the only Clash album that is perfect, complete, and unimprovable. It may not contain the band's best songs, but it captures their best performances back before the drugs played havoc on Mick and Topper's chops. One of my favorite pastimes is snickering at so-called 'Clash fans' who say they don't like this album.

LONDON CALLING - As irritated as I get by how inflated *London Calling*'s reputation is, the album itself is great. Sure, there's plenty of B material, and sure those watery, phased guitars wear out their welcome long before its all over, but it ruled my life when I was 13, and that alone is praise enough. It's also The Clash's last gasp as a coherent recording ensemble, and the last album they made where they actually rehearsed all of the songs before they recorded them. I still think its slightly too conservative and self-conscious, but is there a better album to drink beer to? I think not.

BLACK MARKET CLASH - Because I was 14 years old when this came out, I am best qualified to declare its inclusion into the Clash canon. Like *Cheap Trick at Budokan*, *Black Market* was the landmark that separated the Clash's essential recording era from their difficult years. For all of the different material included here- first LP castoffs, a *Rope* B-side, and dub tracks- this holds together quite well as a singular work. Every track is absolutely crucial and the second side suite of 'Bank Robber' and 'Armagideon Time' and their dubs puts the *Sandinista* efforts in that vein in the shade. The later Super *Black Market Clash* is great, but doesn't serve the same purpose the original does. Though we didn't know it at the time, *Black Market Clash* marked the end of the Clash's glory days on record. Interestingly enough, this was reissued on CD in the UK, but not in the US.

THE DIFFICULT YEARS

After the untouchable perfection of the first three LPs and various singles, the Clash lost the plot in the recording studio. Or they did so when it came to track selection. I know I'm tough on the Clash's production skills, but the real problem was the preponderance of filler on the last two LPs by the original band. So in lieu of reviews of these records (which you can find anywhere else) I'll share with you my DIY solution to the Clash's filler problem.

SANDINISTA! - I hated this album when I first heard it in early December 1980. Where was the real Clash? Then a few short weeks later I drove my family crazy by playing it nonstop. I continued to do so for the next year, at least. As much as I love the entire record, I think there's a monumentally great single CD here, even without any remixing. As I've said elsewhere, the best way to look at this album is in light of the aborted 'Singles Campaign'. *Sandinista* is rough half-killer, half-filler, ie., half A-sides and half B-sides. Since you can easily fit any 17 (my lucky number) tracks on a single CDR, I think what I will do (once I finish this fucking book, I mean) is make my own *Sandinista*. I'll print out a label and then scan the art in and futz around with it to make my own booklet. The only question is what tracks do I include? I think what I would do is put them on the CD in the original order they appear, and of course omit the tracks I don't think make the A list. Hmmm, let's see. OK, I'll do 'Mag 7', 'the Leader', 'Something About England', 'Somebody Got Murdered', and 'One More Time' from the old first LP and 'Charlie Don't Surf', 'Kingston Advice' and 'Street Parade' from the third. That's 8 tracks so I have nine to choose from the 2nd Lp (which has the highest ratio of quality cuts).

OK, 'Lightning Strikes', 'Up In Heaven', 'Let's Go Crazy', 'Sound of the Sinners' (gotta love Joe's vocals on that one), 'Police on My Back', 'Midnight Log', 'Call Up', and 'Washington Bullets' will fill the balance. I'll bump 'Broadway' since I liked it better live and it's too down-beat. 'The Street Parade' is a nice closer. Damn, if you ask me, that's a pretty fucking amazing batch of songs. Diverse and eclectic, but also a lot more coherent without some of the more whacked out experimental and genre stuff. I'll pretend that this was the real *Sandinista* and the official one was some director's cut collectors edition thingamajig. Of course, every single person reading this will quibble and pick their own favorites, and if I was truly rigorous, I'd bump it down to 12 cuts. In that case bump 'Midnight', 'Kingston', 'Sinners', 'England' and.... oh shit. Can I make it a bakers dozen?

COMBAT ROCK- I'm sort of at the point where I think that if you don't already have *Combat Rock*, you needn't bother getting it. Most of the crucial tracks are available elsewhere. But then again, 'Know Your Rights' is only on the *Singles* CD and 'Sean Flynn' is a pretty crucial cut. Hmm. OK , I changed my mind- if you don't already have it, get it. But be prepared- *Combat Rock* is the weakest album by the original band and the wimpiest of all their records. If you hate it, don't worry: Joe did too.

But thanks to the combined miracles of the Internet and I Tunes, I was recently able to compile a 'dream' version of the *Combat*-era material. The recent *Essential Clash* DVD included a number of demo versions of the *Combat Rock* songs so I was able to replace some of the lame-ass album and B-side cuts with superior (albeit instrumental) versions. *Combat Rock* was not only a weak album in and of itself, it wasn't even the best tracks on hand from that era. So I gathered my personal best of late period Clash and entitled it *Wombat Rock*. I'm less excited about this batch of songs now than I was when I first assembled them, but I think it's still a pretty solid set of late Clash weirdness. My filler free *Sandinista* is a hell of a lot better than this aggregation, but this bunch also reminds me of the type of material I would hear on those weird out-takes bootlegs that I found in those recurring dreams of mine. The weird and druggy flavor of these cuts is pretty dreamlike in an of itself. Granted, there is still some filler here, but it's fun filler. Some of you may not be so impressed with my selection, but it works for me. Anyhow, here's the track list with added comments.

Know Your Rights (*Combat Rock*) - None of the out takes can measure up to the final.
Know Your Rights (*Hell W10 s/t*)- Nice to hear all the guitars flying around without the vocals to distract.
Mustapha Dance - Because I am sick to death of 'Casbah'.
Red Angel Dragnet (*HW10*) - Very nice instrumental track. The vocals kill it on the album.
Straight to Hell (*CR*) - see comments on 'Know your Rights.'
Overpowered by Funk (*HW10*) - Topper and Mick must have done the album version after a quaalude party. Stick with this Ear demo. Great rhythm playing by Joe on it, too.
Atom Tan (*HW10*) - kicks ass on the album.

Sean Flynn & Ghetto Defendant *(CR)* - plus the *HW10* demo of 'Ghetto'
Inoculated City *(Rat Patrol)* - This song needs the coda, the *CR* version
makes no sense.
Long Time (full version from Casbah 7") & Long Time demo *(HW10)*
Fulham Connection aka B. People *(RP)*
Idle in Kangaroo Court W11 aka Kill Time *(RP)*
Radio Clash (pt 2)- *(SBMC)*
Cool Confusion *(HW10)*-Rock version, death forever to the B-side version
First Night Back in London *(SBMC)* First Night demo— *(HW10)*
Torchlight *(Ellen Foley)* - If Shitsville counts as a Clash song, why not this?
Theatre of Cruelty *(Ellen Foley)*- I REALLY wish I had a instro of it. Great
backing track.

THE POST-SCRIPT

CUT THE CRAP- I know I 've a lot of time bashing *Cut the Crap*, but it was
such a crushing disappointment to me when it came out that my feelings are
forever ambivalent about it. When I first played it, I was literally nauseous
with panic. But, I didn't like any Clash record when I first heard it, and my
expectations for Crap were impossibly high. And I certainly have spent a lot
of time listening to it. I just saw the new version of *England's Dreaming* by Jon
Savage and he passionately defends it, so that got me to thinking: if you separate the backstory and the controversies from the album itself, it really is a
pretty good record. There are some glaring problems with it- 'Dictator' is
ruined by the synths, 'We Are the Clash' is too slow, and 'Play To Win' is a
headache inducer, but the balance of the tracks aren't bad at all. Is it on par
with the best of the Clash? Certainly not, but how bad can an album with Joe's
singing and loud guitars on it be? And I must say, I am certainly glad the Clash
catalog ends with Joe screaming and yelling over blaring guitars on 'Life is
Wild' then with the sound of a bunch of drug-addicted talent-wasters nodding
off on the worthless *Combat Rock* snoozer 'Death is A Star'. Buy it and listen
without prejudice. The battles are over, so we should enjoy it for what it is.

Or not.

The CLASH On STAGE

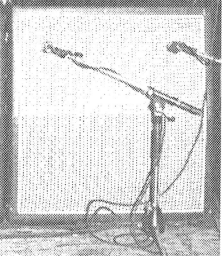

THE ONLY GOOD CLASH IS A LIVE CLASH!

When I was a freshman in high school, I remember hanging out in the attic room of Gang Green's original drummer, Mike Dean. His brother was one of the first Punk Rockers in Braintree and Mike inherited a lot of great stuff from him. One of the things he got was the original *Capitol Crisis*, the double LP boot of the all-killer Passaic, NJ 3/8/80 show. Mike had a killer stereo (probably his brother's as well) and he would crank that puppy. Even though it was an audience recording, I remember being totally amazed by how much more powerful the songs were than their officially recorded cousins.

There's something fundamentally wrong with the way most Rock records are made. No matter how slick or overdubbed they are, they are essentially artificial. And when you start fooling with crap like sequencers and drum machines, the problem gets even worse. I got the Moby album *Play* and really enjoyed it. But I stopped listening to it awhile ago, and every time I think to put it on I invariably change my mind. It's a great record, but something just bothers me about it. There are certain styles of music like House or Industrial where this artificiality is part and parcel of the experience, but with Rock and Roll, something dies with every overdub.

There are a lot of artists who specialize in making great Rock and Roll recordings. It's an arcane science, but they pull it off. But in the end, is it really Rock and Roll or is it just ear candy? I think that what Rock and Roll is, in its purest manifestation, is music played in front of a very excited and engaged audience. I don't think it's possible to play great Rock in front of an apathetic audience. And Clash audiences were very rarely apathetic.

When I saw the Clash in 1980, the entire crowd was on their feet the entire show. It was in a theater, with big, plush seats, but everyone stood and danced. The music forced you to. It compelled you. It was like a physical force that picked you up and shook you. The Clash never put that force on an album. I don't think they ever could. It was too huge.

One of the reasons I actually prefer audience-taped shows is that I can hear the rafters shake. I hear the metal seats reverberate. I can hear the feet stomping. It's not the real thing, but it's a lot closer than the soundboard stuff. The soundboard stuff is great, and a good soundboard show is a treasure rarer than platinum, but I don't feel like I'm there.

The ideal Rock and Roll record is a live album. Think of how more vital *Live at Leeds* is than the Who's studio records. Cheap Trick is another great live record act, and their recent *Music for Hangovers* is even better than the more tarted-up *At Budokan* (also a great record.) The audience is part of the experience, and their energy feeds into the energy of the musicians. The second-best type of Rock and Roll record is a record where the band essentially plays the music live in the studio. This is how records used to be made, before the days of multi-track recording. Most classical recordings are the sound of an orchestra playing the music all at once, in real time. A lot of the classic Jazz albums were made this way as well. Rock and Roll is a different animal, since you usually have smaller combos with less expert players, but if a band can't pull off their material in a take, they haven't rehearsed it enough.

I've spent some time in recording studios and I hated every minute of it. It's a boring, tedious process and most bands tend to rehearse only enough to be familiar enough with their material to put down the basic takes, then they do take after take of overdubbing. This often squeezes the life out of a song, since you are in the strange position of sitting there with a set of big, puffy headphones on, and everything is too close to your head and sounds like shit. You tend to be too careful and the energy level lags. I hear this all over Clash records. With any artist, don't ever wonder when a record isn't as good as those live recordings or those demos you heard are. Be amazed when the record is any good at all.

It's funny, because you see a tendency in other entertainment media developing. On TV, you have a choice between over-produced dramas or sit-coms, usually done on stage and this new crop of reality shows. In movies, the only thing people want to see are millions upon millions of dollars on the screen. In music, you have the phony spectacle of the boy bands and the singing sluts and the WWF-type Rock such as Limp Bizkit or the grittier Rappers and the remaining Punk and Grunge bands. It seems like people want total spectacle or reality. This is because we are over-mediated and have con-sumed too much artifice. We either want steak or cotton candy.

I think Rock and Roll records should be documents of a well-rehearsed band playing their music together at the same time, preferably in front of an audience. Some overdubbing is cool, since its the equivalent of post-production on a reality show. But if you want to add strings of whatever, do it the way Phil Spector or Berry Gordy would, all at the same session. Fuck separation or whatever, that's just phony. Remixes are tired and played out. Other music doesn't have to be made this way, but other music isn't about the same thing Rock and Roll is.

My experience of the Clash's music has been mostly live recordings, usually when they weren't aware they were being taped. They always held back a little when the tape was running, unless cameras were running too (they loved playing to cameras). The stage was where the Clash played their best. Of course, as time went on and drugs crept in, they were usually more hit or miss, but when they hit, they slammed.

I remember fretting in late '84 and early '85 waiting for the Clash II record and being upbraided by a friend who said "What the hell do you need an album for? You already have the songs the way they're meant to be played." He was referring to the bootlegs that I had, like the Brixton 3/9/84 tape and the *Five Alive* LPs. I thought he was giving me a hard time, but his dad was a Jazz musician and he understood this stuff better than me. In hind-sight, I realized that my real Clash II album was *Five Alive*, and I had it in 1984 when I really needed it. What's so official about *Cut the Crap* when you think of it? It's a document of the rotting of the corpse of a band.

From all the tapes I have from the different bands I played in, my favorite is this series of live- in-the-studio things with my first real band. We had practiced our material for about 9 months without a drummer and then we got a guy who was really good and really hyper. (all of our songs gained about 20 bpm with him!) Before we got sick of each other, we would tape our rehearsals. We were all so damned excited and well practiced (I even had my solos down) that the stuff just smokes. There are magical moments that crop up- a furious riff here, a superhuman drum fill there, a soaring vocal aside- that could never be reproduced in a studio setting. I mean, we were in a studio, but we were playing all together, sharing the same experience. That's Rock and Roll. The rest of it is one kind of candy or another.

THE ESSENTIAL CLASH BOOTLEG BIBLE

You can go on the web and find any number of complete Clash bootleg discographies. That is not my intention here. What I set out to do here was to provide the curious with what I think is a meaningful representation of the evolution of the live Clash, ie., the real Clash. The emphasis here is on recording quality or historically significance. There are any number of excellent shows available in the tape traders' network, and if you get bitten by the bootboy bug, you can waste a great deal of time hunting them down. My emphasis, as always, in on the 80's shows. Part of what fueled my bootleg obsession back in my youth was my need to hear material from *Sandinista* and *Combat Rock* played by the Clash, not by Mick, Topper and a bunch of studio hacks. I've also listed a number of Clash II shows, since the actual band's entire recorded output consists of two hastily recorded B-sides.

However, as long as you can stomach the recording quality, I also recommend any show the Clash did. Particularly recommended are any 1977 gigs, when the Clash's firepower was in its first full bloom. The intensity of those shows is unparalleled. But the shows I've listed are the ones that either are the most widely circulated or those I feel are most musically powerful or historically important.

09/05/76 - **Chalk Farm Roundhouse-London, England**
Available on: 5 Go Mad In the Roundhouse (CD), Going to the Disco (LP), traders' copies
Deny/ 1-2 Crush on You/ I Know What to Think About You/ I Never Did It/ How Can I Understand the Flies/ Protex Blue/ Janie Jones/ Mark Me Absent/ Deadly Serious/ 48 Hours/ I'm So Bored with You/ Sitting At My Party/ London's Burning/ What's My Name/ 1977

This is an invaluable snapshot of the early five-man Clash: Strummer, Jones, Simonon, Chimes and the soon-to-be-departing Keith Levene. Haven't heard the non-LP tracks listed above? Don't worry about it. Most of them are pretty feeble variations on old Kinks and Who tracks, lacking the fury of the later material. However, 'Flies' has some interesting drumming from Chimes - a drummer who was rarely accused of as being interesting - and 'Mark Me Absent' is a great Garage rocker that you should get your band to cover. The band is remarkably tight, especially when you consider just how sloppy the Clash could be, especially in their drug days. But the guitars sound cheap and nasty and an observer could be forgiven for not recognizing the embryonic Clash as future world beaters. While the band struggles to tune up, a pre-Cockney Joe berates the audience for being lame. The sound is a remarkably OK audience recording.

05/13/77 - De Montfort Hall-Leicester, England
Available on: Cardiff '77 (LP), Live in Cardiff '77(CD) , Super Golden Radio Shows (CD) , traders' copies
I'm So Bored With the USA/ Hate and War/ 48 Hours/ Deny/ Police and Thieves/ Cheat/ Capital Radio/ What's My Name/ Protex Blue/ Remote Control/ Garageland/ 1977

Taken from a BBC radio broadcast, this set is a wonderful example of the Clash in full first bloom. The sound is more or less the sound of the first LP, only faster, crisper and more aggressive. Topper Headon is on the kit, and his snappy playing gives the songs greater dimension than the Chimes sessions displayed. This is a great white-knuckle run-through the early material, punctuated by snaggle-toothed Strummer-isms like "Let's Kiss! To the latest Clash love song" at the beginning of 'Deny.' Put away your UK version of the first LP and spin this instead.

12/28/78 The Lyceum-London, England
Available on: Sony Promotional cassettes, traders' copies, Flash Bastards CD
Safe European Home/ I Fought the Law/ Jail Guitar Doors/ Drug Stabbing Time/ City Of the Dead/ Clash City Rockers/ Tommy Gun/ White Man In Hammersmith Palais/ English Civil War/ Stay Free/ Cheapskates/ Julie's In the Drug Squad/ Police and Thieves/ Capital Radio/ Janie Jones/ Garageland/ Complete Control/ London's Burning/ White Riot

The source for this was CBS pro recordings, a couple of which have been released on the live album and boxset. Pretty amazing show, particularly if you are a *Give 'Em Enough Rope* fan like me. The band is really at a peak here. However, the sound is not the steely rush of some of the earlier shows. Mick had begun to experiment with effects pedals at this point and there's a lot watery Phaser all over the place here. Probably the single best example of '78 Clash, particularly if you get your mitts on a low-generation copy of the Sony promo cassettes containing this show.

02/14/79 -The Agora-Cleveland, Ohio
Available on: Police and Firemen on My Back (LP), Agora (LP), traders' copies
I'm So Bored with the USA/ Drug Stabbing Time/ Jail Guitar Doors/ Tommy Gun/ City Of the Dead/ White Man In Hammersmith Palais/ Hate and War/ Safe European Home/ Stay Free/ English Civil War/ Guns On the Roof/ Police and Thieves/ Capital Radio/ Jane Jones/ Garageland/ Julie's In the Drug Squad/ London's Burning/ White Riot/ Complete Control/ What's My Name

If the Lyceum shows are the Clash playing it relatively safe for posterity, this show is the Clash at their most frenetic and confrontational. Their usual Pearl Harbor tour opener, 'Bored with the USA', sets the tone: a hopelessly out-of-tune, gnarly, infuriated Clash playing at Hardcore speed and intensity. Again, Mick's phased guitar makes the guitars sound worse than they should, but niceties like guitar sounds and properly tuned instruments are completely beside the point here. Four of the tracks from this set were broadcast on the old *King Biscuit Flower Hour*. One can only imagine the reaction of America's drug-addled youth, innocently waiting to hear the latest jams from Kansas or REO Speedwagon, to this volley of sonic hatred.

09/21/79 - Palladium-New York, New York

Available on: Klashing with the Klash, Clampdown USA , Pearl Harbor '79, Bronx City Rockers (CD), Guns Of Brixton (CD), Money Made Us Flexible (CD), New York City Rockers (CD), Live USA (CD), traders' copies
Safe European Home/ I'm So Bored with the USA/ Complete Control/ London Calling/ White Man In Hammersmith Palais/ Koka Kola/ I Fought the Law/ Jail Guitar Doors/ The Guns Of Brixton/ English Civil War/ Clash City Rockers/ Stay Free/ Clampdown/ Police and Thieves/ Capital Radio/ Tommy Gun/ Wrong 'Em Boyo/ Janie Jones/ Garageland/ Armagideon Time/ Career Opportunities/ What's My Name/ White Riot

Unfortunately, this is the most widely circulated Clash bootleg. Why 'unfortunately?' Well, it's not a particularly good show to listen to. I am sure it was fabulous to be there, but Mick's monster guitar blows Joe's voice away on many of the tracks, and the playing seems to be hurried and unfocused. That being said, there is plenty to love here. The sound is hot (at least on the LP version I have) and the opening salvo of 'Safe', 'USA' and 'Control' is astonishing. The version of 'Capitol Radio' is absolutely tooth-gnashing, despite Mick's fuckups on the breaks. Beware: many of the CD transfers I have heard are markedly inferior sound-wise.

12/27/79 - Hammersmith Odeon-London, England

Available on: 16 Tracks (LP), Dispatches from Clash Zone (LP), traders' copies
Clash City Rockers/ Brand New Cadillac/ Safe European Home/ Jimmy Jazz/ Clampdown/ The Guns Of Brixton/ Train In Vain/ Wrong 'Em Boyo/ Koka Kola/ White Man In Hammersmith Palais/ Stay Free/ Bankrobber/ Janie Jones/ Complete Control/ Armagideon Time/ London Calling

Probably one of the best performances the classic lineup ever gave. This was part of a series of benefits for the People of Kampuchea (Cambodia) were just liberated from the horror of Pol Pot's genocidal Khmer Rouge. The Clash were playing with the cream of British Rock and were inspired to show their stuff. Although I'm not particularly a huge fan of the Clash's conservative 'Classic Rock' era of '79-'80, I can't recommend this show highly enough. Most of the highlights from *London Calling* get a run-through here and Joe's early version of 'Bankrobber', featuring Mick on slide guitar, also gets an airing. Look for *16 Tracks* on Ebay. Like most of the shows in this section, it is best experienced on vinyl.

03/08/80 - Capitol Theatre-Passaic, New Jersey

*Available on: bootleg video, Capital Crisis (LP, CD), For F*CKS Sake! (CD), Capital Radio 1980 (CD), traders' copies*
Clash City Rockers/ Brand New Cadillac/ Safe European Home/ Jimmy Jazz/ London Calling/ The Guns Of Brixton/ Train In Vain/ White Man In

Hammersmith Palais/ Koka Kola/ I Fought the Law/ Spanish Bombs/
Police and Thieves/ Stay Free/ Julie's In the Drug Squad/ Wrong 'Em Boyo/
Clampdown/ Janie Jones/ Complete Control/ Armagideon Time/ English
Civil War/ Garageland/ Bankrobber/ Tommy Gun

The best way to experience the 'Classic Rock' Clash is on the wide-
ly-bootlegged video of this show. This is a superlative example of the Clash's
'16 Tons' tour. The band is at a peak here, even with a hobbled Topper
Headon. Mickey Gallagher's organ playing added a lot of dimension to the
band's sound, especially on the *London Calling* numbers, and the band is
tight and together. Mick's guitar sound is particularly impressive here.

03/09/80 - Orpheum Theatre-Boston, Massachusetts
Available on: trader's copies
Clash City Rockers/ Brand New Cadillac/ Safe European Home/ Jimmy
Jazz/ London Calling/ The Guns Of Brixton/ Train In Vain/ Protex Blue/
White Man In Hammersmith Palais/ Koka Kola/ I Fought the Law/ Spanish
Bombs/ Rudie Can't Fail/ Hit the Road Jack/ Police and Thieves/ Stay
Free/ Wrong 'Em Boyo/ Clampdown/ Janie Jones/ Complete Control/
Armagideon Time/ English Civil War/ Garageland/ Tommy Gun/ London's
Burning

This show is not very widely circulated, but I was at this concert, so I have
to put in the word for it. Hearing recordings of the Clash will never impart just how
loud they were: it was a level of volume that seemed to have an overwhelming
physical mass. This show is essential to me, although maybe not to you. But there
is a nice drums and voice version of 'Hit the Road, Jack' that is eerie and goofy all
at once. So it has that to recommend it, as well as the fantastic overall performance.

6/17/80 Hammersmith Palais-London, England
Available on: Clash Songbooks, traders' copies
Clash City Rockers/ Brand New Cadillac/ Safe European Home/
Jimmy Jazz/ Revolution Rock/ Julie's In the Drug Squad/ The Guns Of
Brixton/Train In Vain/ London Calling/ Spanish Bombs/ White Man In
Hammersmith Palais/ Somebody Got Murdered/ Koka Kola/ I Fought the
Law/ Jail Guitar Doors/ Police and Thieves/ Wrong 'Em Boyo/
Clampdown/ Stay Free/ English Civil War/ I'm So Bored with the
USA/Complete Control/Armagideon Time/ Rocker's Galore/ Bankrobber/
Tommy Gun/ Capital Radio/ London's Burning/ Janie Jones/ What's My
Name/ Garageland

The Clash late into their '16 Tons' tour and already showing a transition to
their *Sandinista* phase. Early versions of 'Somebody Got Murdered' and
'Charlie Don't Surf' show up, but 'Charlie' is nothing like the album version.
This version is a hypnotic, dubbed-out chant with no chord changes. Very
much a radical departure from the Clash's usual modus operandi. There's a
great run-through of the rarely played 'Revolution Rock' and a healthy dose of
other *London Calling* material as well as several Rope cuts. However, my

favorite cut from this show is a lethal new version of 'Rockers Galore' with Mikey Dread on vocals. This is true Punk Reggae; sharp, stabbing and anchored on a fantastic riff. Unfortunately, Topper's playing is already starting to stiffen up on the faster material, a problem that would worsen over time.

In my musings, I often think of the Clash in 1981 as the band at their Clash-iest. With the return of Bernie Rhodes, the band got their conceptual and visual acts back together, and the *Sandinista*! material played live is a lot edgier than the safe, Stones-y *London Calling* tracks. Although the '81 performances are generally not as tight as the '80 ones, they are more interesting and atmospheric. '81 is definitely my favorite year for Clash bootlegs.

05/10/81 Jaap Ede Hal-Amsterdam, The Netherlands
Available on: Londonderry (LP), traders copies
London Calling / White Man In Hammersmith Palais / Lightning Strikes/ The Magnificent Seven / Bankrobber / One More Time / I Fought the Law

This is an eight-song sampler from Dutch radio, and the sound quality is top-notch and so's the playing. There's apparently a soundboard floating around out there of this gig, but the mint sound is a real treat. The Clash were such a great Rock and Roll band in 1981 and this is a great example of the band at a peak. Three tunes off of *Sandinista* get the full electrical shockers treatment, leaving you to wonder why it all would go so wrong by the end of the year.

05/21/81 Velodromo Vigorelli-Milan, Italy
Available on: traders copies, *New Speedway* LP
London Calling/ Safe European Home/ White Man In Hammersmith Palais/ Train In Vain/ Lightning Strikes/ Junco Partner/ The Guns Of Brixton/ This Is Radio Clash/ Complete Control/ The Call Up/ Ivan Meets GI Joe/ The Leader/ Charlie Don't Surf/ The Magnificent Seven/ Bankrobber/ Wrong 'Em Boyo/ Somebody Got Murdered/ Career Opportunities/ Clampdown/ One More Time/ Brand New Cadillac/ Janie Jones/ Armagideon Time/ I Fought the Law/ London's Burning/ Jimmy Jazz/ White Riot

This show is a good snapshot of the Clash in a transitional phase from their conservative 1980 gigs to the looser, more hippified late '81 shows. There are 11 *Sandinista*!-era songs here, and the combination of funky rhythms and red-hot Rock guitar would later be incalculably influential. I could get on my hobby horse about what a shame it is the Clash didn't never got that sound on record, but I needn't bother. There are enough great shows available from this period. Look for the LP on Ebay.

Joe Strummer, onstage in 1981

06/09/81 Bond's International Casino-New York, New York

Available on: S.O.S. (LP), Trick Or Treat (CD), Pier Pressure (CD), trader's copies
London Calling/ Safe European Home/ The Leader/ Train In Vain/ White
Man In Hammersmith Palais/ This Is Radio Clash/ Corner Soul/ The Guns
Of Brixton/ The Call Up/ Bankrobber/ Complete Control/ Lightning
Strikes/ Ivan Meets GI Joe/ Charlie Don't Surf/ The Magnificent Seven/
Broadway/ Somebody Got Murdered/ Police and Thieves/ Clampdown/
One More Time/ Brand New Cadillac/ The Street Parade/ Janie Jones/
Washington Bullets

Another well circulated but underwhelming show from New York.
There are many versions of this: some taken from a radio broadcast, others
taken from cleaned-up CBS tapes. And when I say 'underwhelming' I mean
the performances are inferior to many of the other gigs from the same period. But that's relative: it is still a crucial part of any fan's collection. This is
high-octane Rock and Roll from start to finish. And what the band lacks in
finesse, they more than make up for in spirit. Mick's guitar is red-hot, and
Joe and Paul's fuck-ups and tuning problems are cleaned up in the CBS versions. It's also fascinating to hear the Clash, rather than the Electric Lady
band, play tracks off of *Sandinista!* Find out what version is available before
you pick this up. The CBS/Sony one is the best and the most complete.

09/24/81 Theatre Mogador-Paris, France

Available on: traders' copies
Broadway/ One More Time/ This Is Radio Clash/ Should I Stay Or Should I
Go?/ The Guns Of Brixton/ White Man In Hammersmith Palais/ The
Magnificent Seven/ Train In Vain/ Ivan Meets GI Joe/ Clash City Rockers/
Koka Kola/ Bankrobber/ The Leader/ Graffiti Rap/ Washington Bullets/
Ghetto Defendant/ Complete Control/ Clampdown/ Somebody Got
Murdered/ London Calling/ Lightning Strikes - Overpowered By Funk/
Armagideon Time/ Safe European Home/ Inoculated City/ Brand New
Cadillac/ Spanish Bombs/ Know Your Rights/ Straight to Hell/ Janie Jones/
Pressure Drop/ Garageland

The Clash reached a superlative level before it all went kerblooey. At the
time of their seven night residency in Paris, they had synthesized a new Rock and
Roll - spacious but aggressive, diverse but unified, traditional yet forward looking.
But of course since we are talking about the Clash here, it goes without saying they
never put this music on record. No matter: check out any of the shows from
Autumn '81. I pick this one more or less at random— there are plenty of others just
like it, mostly available on cassette. There was a 3 LP bootleg from this era called
Hits, but good luck trying to find it (or afford it if you do find it, for that matter).
Reggae and Funk were the backbone of the Clash's new Rock, and
they informed every other song the band played. Mick's guitar sound was like
a Tyrannosaurus trapped in a vast cavern and the rest of the band was equally impressive. These shows were long and jammed out by Clash standards,
with the band often settling into a groove while Mick went wild with his
effects. The *Sandinista* tracks benefit greatly from the road testing, and those

numbers are far stronger in the Fall '81 shows than the Spring. Trippy, Dubby, and Punky all at the same time, these boots capture the Clash at their conceptual peak. It would all come crashing down very soon.

10-22-81 London Lyceum-London, England
Available on: traders' copies
One More Time/ Broadway/ Know Your Rights/ Should I Stay Or Should I Go?/ The Guns Of Brixton/ Train In Vain / The Magnificent Seven/ White Man In Hammersmith Palais/ Clash City Rockers/ Koka Kola/ Ivan Meets GI Joe/ Junco Partner / Charlie Don't Surf/ The Leader/ I Fought the Law/ Ghetto Defendant/ Somebody Got Murdered/ London Calling / Clampdown/ This Is Radio Clash/ Safe European Home / Bankrobber/ Revolution Rock/ Career Opportunities/ Armagideon Time/ Graffiti Rap/ Complete Control/Brand New Cadillac/ London's Burning/ Janie Jones

The best Clash concert ever. There's a paradoxically laid-back urgency in the playing. It's as if the Clash understood the power they were capable of wielding and didn't feel the need to play quite so frenetically. There's a seductive, atmospheric charge to this show as well. The Clash sounded huge and mysterious in late '81. I picked this show as their best for a several reasons. First of all, the playing is razor sharp and hard as nails. Second, the set list is incredible. They open with 'One More Time', one of my top five Clash tracks (and one that has been inexplicably left of the posthumous comps) A bizarre prototype of 'Know Your Rights' gets an airing. It's not as cathartic as the *Hits* version, but certainly as strange. It reminds me of the prototype for 'Charlie Don't Surf' heard during a Swedish show from June of the previous year. Both songs are strange chants with repetitive riffs, unlike anything the band ever record. There's a nice version of the early 'Ghetto Defendant', but the real surprise is a vicious, minor key revamp of 'Revolution Rock'. Topper is at the top of his form on this track and works the top-kit like a demon. This is also a nice long set with a whopping 29 cuts and an emphasis on the *Sandinista* material. Not a great recording, but their greatest show.

01/24/82 - Shibuya Kohkaido-Tokyo, Japan
Available on: traders' copies
Should I Stay Or Should I Go?/ One More Time/ Safe European Home/ Know Your Rights/ Train In Vain/ White Man In Hammersmith Palais/ The Magnificent Seven/ The Guns Of Brixton/ Charlie Don't Surf/ The Leader/ Ivan Meets GI Joe/ Junco Partner/ Broadway/ Stay Free/ London Calling/ Janie Jones/ Somebody Got Murdered/ Clampdown/ This Is Radio Clash/ Brand New Cadillac/ Armagideon Time/ London's Burning

Another one of the greatest shows the Clash ever played. Considering the turmoil in the camp at the time as well as the poor quality of some of the subsequent shows, that's a pretty remarkable statement. This show has everything: great set list, incredible performances, anarchic energy, fantastic lead guitar and classic Joe-babble. For some bizarre reason, it's only available on tape or MP3. There are fuckups galore on this, but you won't care. The last stand from the original lineup.

02/01/82 - Sun Plaza Hall-Tokyo, Japan

*Available on: White Riot (LP), White Riot in Tokyo (CD), Yellow Riot (CD), Rockin'
the Red Point (CD), This is Live Clash (CD), traders' copies*
London Calling/ Safe European Home/ White Man In Hammersmith
Palais/ Brand New Cadillac/ Charlie Don't Surf/ Clampdown/ This Is
Radio Clash/ Armagideon Time/ Jimmy Jazz/ Tommy Gun/ Fujiyama
Mama/ Police On My Back/ White Riot/ Train In Vain/ Washington
Bullets/ Ivan Meets GI Joe/ Career Opportunities/ Janie Jones/ Clash City
Rockers/ London's Burning

And then there's Sun Plaza. The recording on this show (from a Japanese TV concert) is pristine, so in true, idiot-bootlegger logic, it's one of the
three most bootlegged shows. However, pristine recording is all this show has
to offer. Though not as bad as the Lochem Festival, this is still the Clash at their
weakest. The playing is scattered and disunited, Paul's rubbery bass is inexplicably high in the mix and Joe's voice is shredded. Topper makes a big show
for the TV cameras, but can't seem to take his sticks off the snare. The bottom
had somehow dropped out of the band's playing and in place of passion was
desperation. Get it if you must, but don't blame me if you hate it too.

05/20/82 - The Lochem Festival Lochem, Holland

*Available on: Summer of '82 (LP), Lochem Festival (LP), Garageland (LP), Live
(LP), Into the 80s (CD), partial show with 2/1/82 as Che Guevara (CD), Police and
Thieves (CD), traders' copies*
London Calling/ Safe European Home/ The Guns of Brixton/ Train In Vain/
Clash City Rockers/ Know Your Rights/ The Magnificent Seven/ Ghetto
Defendant/ Should I Stay or Should I Go?/ Police and Thieves/ Brand New
Cadillac/ Bankrobber/ Complete Control/ Career Opportunities/ Clampdown

Topper's last show. That pretty much sums it up, but I'll elaborate.
To the untrained ear, this show might be acceptable, but to those of us who
have heard the Clash when they were on and when they were off and know
the difference between the two, this show is painful. I sold my CD of this
ages ago. Fuckups and general rustiness abound, but the heartbreak on this
show is to hear the band play as if they were phoning in their performance
from four separate locations. Topper's once impeccable meter is all over the
map, and poor Paul's rudimentary skills are taxed to the limit as he struggles
to keep up. There were hints of this from the beginning of the previous year,
but this was truly the end. Topper's playing had been wildly inconsistent for
nearly two years, but this show is the sound of him finally hitting the wall.
And the conservatism that would mark much of the *Combat Rock* tour is
sadly in evidence here, despite the airings of 'Rights' and 'Ghetto.'

07/11/82 - Brixton Fair Deal-London, England

Available on: Down At the Casbah Club (2LP, incomplete show), traders' copies
London Calling/ Clash City Rockers/ Know Your Rights/ Spanish Bombs/
Complete Control/ The Guns Of Brixton/ Somebody Got Murdered/ White
Man In Hammersmith Palais/ Career Opportunities/ The Magnificent

Seven/ Train In Vain/ One More Time/ This Is Radio Clash/ Rock the
Casbah/ Police On My Back/ Brand New Cadillac/ Clampdown/
Bankrobber/ Armagideon Time/ Should I Stay or Should I Go?/ I Fought
the Law/ Straight to Hell/ Stay Free/ Garageland

Yet another one of my favorite Clash shows, even though I've only
heard a truncated version. And everyone complains about the recording
quality here, but I think its fine. With steady Terry Chimes behind the kit and
the band back on home turf, the Clash launched one of their fiercest salvos
ever here. It was one of those nights when everything went right, and what
Joe called 'the X factor' kicked in. The playing was that much more intense,
the singing just that much more passionate, and the songs seemed to take on
a life of their own apart from any previous airings. The LP opens with a
flame-throwing version of 'Guns of Brixton', highlighted by Terry's note-for-
note cop of the intro to 'She Drives Funny Cars' (by the Clash's spiritual forebears, the Jefferson Airplane). The stomp-you-to-death version of 'One More
Time' is a must hear as well. I'll tell you what, get a good pair of earphones
and fuck the recording quality. This is one of the Clash's top 5 performances.

08/11/82 -Civic Center-St. Paul, Minnesota, USA
Available on: traders' copies
London Calling/ White Man In Hammersmith Palais/ Know Your Rights/
Spanish Bombs/ The Guns Of Brixton/ Somebody Got Murdered/ Rock the
Casbah/ Ghetto Defendant/ The Magnificent Seven/ Police On My Back/
Charlie Don't Surf/ The Leader/ Car Jamming/ Train In Vain/ The Call Up/
English Civil War/ Garageland/ Police and Thieves/ Armagideon Time/ Should
I Stay or Should I Go?/ I Fought the Law/ Straight to Hell/ Pressure Drop

Jeez- another insanely great show, and again from the generally mid-
dling *Combat Rock* tour. This show is the spiritual cousin of the Shibuya
Kohkaido set from January. Both shows were tour openers, but both shows have
the same intensity and scope in common as well. Mick's guitar here is stultify-
ingly powerful and the six tracks from *Combat Rock* get the stoolie-in-the-show-
ers treatment, rendering then nearly unrecognizable to those familiar with the
spineless album versions. 'Ghetto Defendant' is particularly impressive, but 'Car
Jamming' has to be heard to be believed. Imagine the Clash from 1977 getting in
a time machine, kicking the fuck out of the 1982 Clash and you have a pretty
good idea what this tooth-gnashing playing of 'Jamming' sounds like. Another
absolute must-have, particularly for those fans let down by *Combat Rock*.

11/27/82 Jamaican Music Festival-Kingston, Jamaica
Available on: Jamaican Affair (CD), Jamaica (CD), From London to Jamaica (CD)
London Calling/ Police On My Back/ The Guns Of Brixton/ The
Magnificent Seven/ Armagideon Time/ The Magnificent Seven (reprise)/
Junco Partner/ Spanish Bombs/ One More Time/ Train In Vain/
Bankrobber/ This Is Radio Clash/ Clampdown/ Should I Stay or Should I
Go?/ Rock the Casbah/ Straight to Hell/ I Fought the Law

This show sounds like what the Clash were threatening to become in '82. I can't quite put my finger on it, and I can't quite tell you what other shows (well, aside from the Who shows) were like it, so Jamaica will have to do for now. A lot was made of the fact that there were a lot Reggae songs in the set, but this is actually a pretty conservative 1982 show. Mick's guitar is almost identical to his early BAD sound, and believe me when I tell you that that sound was all wrong for Joe's voice. This isn't a bad show by any means, just not a particularly good one. The place to get this show is in the *From London To Jamaica* CD, which has almost painfully clear sound.

05/28/83 -The US Festival II-San Bernadino County, California, USA
Available on: Clash Calling (CD), This Is TV Clash (LP)
London Calling/ This Is Radio Clash/ Somebody Got Murdered/ Rock the Casbah/ The Guns Of Brixton/ Know Your Rights/ Koka Kola/ Hate and War/ Armagideon Time/ Sound of the Sinners/ Safe European Home/ Police on My Back/ Brand New Cadillac/ I Fought the Law/ I'm So Bored with the USA/ Train In Vain/ The Magnificent Seven/ Straight to Hell/ Should I Stay or Should I Go?/ Clampdown

The Clash did a number of warm-up gigs with Peter Howard in preparation for the US Fest, and most of them are better than the actual concert they were in anticipation of, but the US Fest remains the landmark from this era. Mick's guitar seems stuck in sort of a no-mans land between his Clash and his later BAD sounds, but that's my only complaint about this show. It's a high-energy show, even if the Clash seem lost on the enormous stage. Joe has some sort of bug up his ass (and actually makes reference to just that), but that just makes his performance all the more entertaining. Pete Howard's drumming is flawless and blends the power of Terry with the finesse of Tops at his best. And when you factor in that this is Mick's last show with the band, I needn't remind you of its "must-have" status.

02/17/84 The Isastadion-Stockholm, Sweden
Available on: Five Alive (2LP), Out of Control (CD), Mutable Punks (2CD)
London Calling/ Safe European Home/ Know Your Rights/ Are You Ready for War?/ Rock the Casbah/ Sex Mad War/ Clampdown/ The Guns Of Brixton/ The Dictator/ Complete Control/ White Man In Hammersmith Palais/ This Is England/ Police and Thieves/ Three Card Trick/ Garageland/ This Is Radio Clash/ Janie Jones/ I Fought the Law/ Glue Zombie/ Tommy Gun/ We Are the Clash/ Brand New Cadillac/ Armagideon Time/ I'm So Bored with the USA/ English Civil War/ White Riot

This is one of the two most widely bootlegged Clash II shows. When compared to sets from a few days before it took place, it's astonishing how quickly this lineup came together. They cover the ground the original lineup trod quite nicely and add some nice touches of their own. This show is also invaluable for the seven Clash II originals that get aired, all of which are immeasurably superior to anything heard on *Cut the Crap*. 'Are You Ready for War' is a pounding slab of Punk Funk, 'Sex Mad War' is raving psychobilly, 'The Dictator' is a lost *Give 'Em Enough Rope* outtake, and 'This is England' is a cousin to 'White Man,' which it follows in the set. 'Three Card Trick' is played here as high impact Punk Rock, not Ska like the album version, and 'Glue Zombie' and the original 'We Are the Clash' make use of weird syncopations that 80's era drum machines were incapable of simulating. This is a great set for those curious about this ill-starred lineup and a nice rejoinder to those who say they were inept musicians. Ignore Gray's silly comments on this show in *Return of the Last Gang in Town*.

03/01/84 - Espace Ballard-Paris, France
Available on: Live in Paris 1984 (LP), CD-R, traders' copies
London Calling/ Safe European Home/ Are You Ready for War?/ Rock the Casbah/ The Dictator/ The Magnificent Seven/ The Guns Of Brixton/ Ammunition/ Clampdown/ Sex Mad War/ I'm So Bored with the USA/ This Is England/ Tommy Gun/ Three Card Trick/ Janie Jones/ I Fought the Law/ Brand New Cadillac/ Complete Control/ Armagideon Time/ White Man In Hammersmith Palais/ Career Opportunities/ Garageland

Pound for pound this is the crucial Clash II document. *Give 'Em Enough Dope* has better sound and performances, but this has a much broader setlist and more Clash II tracks. The recording is a nice fiery soundboard, unlike Stockholm, which is dry and compressed. You also get the added bonus of Joe's stumbling attempts at French. The playing here is raunchy and thuggish— the sound of black leather. Every song is played with the intensity of a runaway freight train barreling towards a tour bus filled with pensioners. There was an LP culled from this set, but go on the Internet and get someone to give you a CD of the same show. If for nothing else, this show is a must have for the soundboard recording of 'Ammunition', Clash II's most frenetic tantrum.

04/14/84 - Hofstra University-Long Island, New York, USA
Available on: traders' copies
London Calling/ Safe European Home/ Know Your Rights/ Rock the Casbah/ Are You Ready for War?/ Spanish Bombs/ Three Card Trick/ The Guns Of Brixton/ Ammunition/ The Magnificent Seven/ In the Pouring Rain/ Clampdown/ Armagideon Time/ Sex Mad War/ Police On My Back/ Janie Jones/ I Fought the Law/ Police and Thieves/ Brand New Cadillac/ Tommy Gun/ Career Opportunities/ I'm So Bored with the USA/ White Riot

This show is on cassette only, but you'll never hear a more intense Clash concert in your life. The show was delayed because of the usual Fire marshal hassles but Joe and his boys came out swinging and didn't let up until they had barreled through the entire set like a rocket-fueled Sherman tank. Pete Howard's drumming can be heard literally shaking the rafters of the gymnasium this show was played in, and Joe's shamanic frenzy almost takes on a life of its own. The show is so short (70-something mins.) because every song was played at nearly double speed. This is the sound of pure adrenaline. 'Career' has to be heard to be believed.

Give Em Enough Dope CD

Sun Plaza Hall, Tokyo, Japan, 1 February 1982
Train In Vain/Washington Bullets/ Ivan Meets G.l. Joe/ Career
Opportunities/Janie Jones/ Clash City Rockers/ London's Burning
Seattle, Washington, USA, 30 May 1984
Are You Ready For War?/ Complete Control/ In The Pouring, Pouring
Rain/Clampdown
Eugene, Oregon, USA, 29 May 1984
Sex Mad War/ Janie Jones/ Straight To Hell/ Brand New Cadillac
Chicago, Illinois, USA, 17 May 1984
Clash City Rockers/ Three Card Trick/ Safe European Home/White Riot

There is a curious story behind this CD. Sometime in 1988, three EP's
showed up that contained what sound very much like professionally recorded
versions of Clash I and II songs, cut from the 1984 tour. The cover art was a
melange of candid shots of the band, from both lineups. Included was a pristine
run-through of the last great Clash song, the unreleased 'In the Pouring, Pouring
Rain'. And Clash-fan heads have been scratched ever since. Rumors circulated
that the tracks were released by castoff guitarist Nick Sheppard, but no proof of
that has ever been offered. Other speculation abounded that they were the work
of one Kosmo Vinyl, who was preparing to move to the US from England at the
time. However, no one has come forth and claimed responsibility   .

What is remarkable about these tracks is not only do they sound professionally recorded, they sound professionally mixed. There seems to be stereo
separation, the drums are soaked in reverb (something you wouldn't hear on a
soundboard recording) and the levels were high and clean. And the CD gives
you a nice contrast between Clash II and the dismal Sun Plaza gig, effectively
making the case for the second lineup's existence. If anyone reading this has
access to the full recordings, please email me.

12/06/84 - Brixton Academy London, England
Available on: traders' copies, One More Time (LP)
One More Time/ London's Burning/ Complete Control/ This Is Radio
Clash/ Spanish Bombs/ Rock the Casbah/ North and South/ Are You Ready
for War?/ Fingerpoppin'/ What's My Name/ The Dictator/ Capital Radio/
Broadway/ Tommy Gun/ We Are the Clash/ Career Opportunities/
Bankrobber/ Three Card Trick/ Garageland/ Dirty Punk/ Ammunition/
This Is England/ White Riot

The Clash existed in name only by the time this show was played. Joe
was tending to his terminally ill mom, Paul was off doing God-knows-what
and the three hirelings were sitting in a rehearsal room, numbly staring at each
other as they tried to puzzle out Joe's new "songs" (actually random chords
backed by a drum machine). But this is a pretty great show. The band is rusty
from all the time off, but the playing is lively and spirited. The radically different versions of the *Crap* material are the obvious highlights, but the radical

reworkings of 'One More Time' and 'Spanish Bombs' are the hidden treasures.
Avoid the vastly inferior 12/7 show. If you can't tell the setlists apart, just remember that the good show is the one with 'Fingerpoppin'. A super-crisp soundboard of the first half of this show was culled for the *One More Time* LP and that will do you just fine.

05/11/85 - Gateshead Subway Station Sunderland, England
Available on: Back to Basics (LP) , Acoustic Daze (CD), traders' copies
Movers and Shakers/ Cool Under Heat/ The Guns Of Brixton/ Spanish Bombs/ Police On My Back/ Jimmy Jazz/ White Man In Hammersmith Palais/ Straight to Hell/ Clash City Rockers/ I Fought the Law/ Brand New Cadillac/ White Riot/ Bankrobber/ Stepping Stone

Their spirits broken by the miserable *Cut the Crap* sessions, the Clash made one last stab to come together as a real band. Joe , Nick and Kosmo set up the now-infamous 'Busking' tour and the Clash took off for Northern Britain in a flatbed truck, with a handful of beat up accoustic guitars and some drumkits as their only gear. Interestingly enough, they had a fabulous time, despite being deprived of the company of one Bernard Rhodes. This show is the essential document. Two more tracks sacrificed at the altar of the *Cut the Crap* get played for those making their own alternate *CTC* comp and the rest is pure silliness and high camp. It sounds like they were having a ball. Too bad it all fell apart immediately after.

06/29/85 -Roskilde Festival Denmark
Available on: traders' copies
Complete Control/ London Calling/ Janie Jones/ Safe European Home/ Hate and War/ Garageland/ Armagideon Time/ The Magnificent Seven/ Rock the Casbah/ Three Card Trick/ Pressure Drop/ Police On My Back/ What's My Name/ Spanish Bombs/ Clash City Rockers/ London's Burning/ Clampdown/ Bankrobber/ Broadway/ Brand New Cadillac/ I'm So Bored with the USA/ Tommy Gun/ I Fought the Law/ White Riot/ Garageland

The band was broke and on its very last legs, but the spirit of the Clash came through for what was the last great Clash concert. Just as the original band seemed on the cusp of a startling new kind of Rock and Roll before it all went south, here too the second lineup was in danger of creating a new and unique sound. The dub and funk elements were back in full force, and were played with as much, if not more, finesse as the original band. All those solitary hours of practice had paid off for the three hirelings, and they obviously spent a good deal of that time just jamming. Joe's hatred for Bernie is reflected in the Mick-penned opener and Mick's shadow seems to hang heavy over the proceedings. But the sound is tough, tight and bouncy and even Paul's savage annihilation of 'What's My Name' can't damper the proceedings. The jamdowns on the 'Arma/Mag 7/Casbah' triptych are spacy , funky and tasty- easily the equal of anything the '81 band pulled off. The Clash did a couple more gigs after this one, but this is the capper to an amazing stage career for the Only Band that Mattered.

THE CLASH - LIVE FROM HERE TO ETERNITY!

I was very tempted to leave this review out of the final draft of this book. I was disappointed by **From Here to Eternity**, *but I felt at the time that I needed to write a positive review of it. The writing in this article is dry and uninspired for the most part, because that's exactly how the album left me feeling. It's a great record, but at the same time it was a terrible disappointment. But for many fans it may well be their only experience of live Clash, so I felt it necessary to include it for their benefit. In addition there is an important message for those in the Clash camp at the end of this article. I hope that those reading this will try to get some of the bootlegs I discussed earlier. Most of them are superior to the official live release.*

'**Complete Control**' (*NYC Bonds 6/81*)- I have heard this version before, on a soundboard tape and on an audience tape (on the Japanese triple LP *Hits*). It's a great opener, one of the better playings of the song I have heard, especially of this recording quality. The sound is hot and the live presence is very solid. And in a bit of studio alchemy that runs throughout the entire record the track runs straight into...

'**London's Burning**' (*Victoria Park 5/78*)- Never one of my favorite songs, this version is from the gigantic 'Rock Against Racism' rally featured in *Rude Boy*. The playing is fairly solid for '78 Clash, but the sound is a bit thin compared to the tracks that surround it. Unsure why this track was picked, but it certainly does no harm to the set.

'What's My Name' (*5/78, Music Machine*)- Great run-through of this classic track. Like most playings, the intro is dropped and the band launch straight into the main riff. The guitar sounds great and Joe garbles the lyrics as best he can. Not my favorite playing of the track, but very tight and extremely rocking.

'Clash City Rockers' (*Boston Orpheum Theatre 9/82*)- This one's a bit of a head scratcher-why is Joe's guitar louder than Mick's? I have heard tapes from this show and this is not one of the songs I would have picked. That being said, it could have been better but I think most people will enjoy it.

'Career Opportunities' (*Shea Stadium 10/82*)- This is the video version from the opening slot for the Who. This mix is a lot better than the one from the video. A bit slower than some of the earlier playings but a lot more coherent. Like most of the album, it's a great song to drink beer to.

'White Man In Hammersmith Palais' (*Boston 9/82*)- Nice, solid playing of this classic, though, again, Mick's guitar is not loud enough. But on this track it doesn't matter, in fact, it gives the track a nice authentic feel. Terry plays a mean cowbell.

'Capital Radio' (*Lewisham Odeon 2/80*)- A great, great version of this song, probably the best live version I have heard. This is the first real surprise of the set and one of the highlights.

'The City Of The Dead' (*Lyceum 1/79*)- Some people question this song's inclusion, but being a real *Black Market Clash* fanatic, I am overjoyed by its inclusion. I love Mick's vocal harmonies on the live playings of this song and it helps remove my memories of Zander Schloss raping it in 1989.

'I Fought The Law' (*Lyceum 1/79*)- Old favorite from *Rude Boy* and the boxset. Probably the best playing of the track I have heard on a pro recording, so I have no complaints about the redundancy.

'London Calling' (*Boston 9/82*)- Good choice from the Boston shows. I actually prefer the Bonds playing of it, but this playing has some nice lead guitar work, as does most of the Boston stuff. Terry is a bit leaden here. You can see him in videos trying to beat his snare to death, which isn't a good way to swing.

'Armagideon Time' (*Lewisham 2/80, with Mikey Dread*)- Really fantastic version. The Clash with Mickey Gallagher sound like the Wailers and Mikey Dread's toasting adds a lot of authenticity. This is a great example of the Clash at their peak. They really should have held onto Gallagher. He filled out the sound.

'Train In Vain (Stand By Me)' (*Bonds 6/81*)- Stop groaning, you loved this song the first couple of thousand times you heard it. This is a nice version from Bonds. Topper is playing that 'oompah' beat but Mick adds some great guitar work. It rocks, so don't worry about it.

'Guns Of Brixton' (*Bonds 6/81*)- Another Bonds play. I actually like Terry's 'marauding Hun' intro better than Topper's 'hoofbeats-on-the-distant-horizon' intro but this a great playing. You can just see Mick in the studio getting his knuckles rapped by Bill Price every time he tried to bring down the guitar. I could never figure out why Mick was always so timid about guitar volume in the studio but would always try to deafen his band-mates on stage.

'The Magnificent Seven' (*Boston 9/82*)- Again, I would have preferred the Bonds version, but this one is more faithful to the original. Joe's ad-libs are very comical.

'Know Your Rights' (*Boston 9/82*)- It's really a shame they couldn't get the multi-tracks from the US Festival for this song, because this version can't hold a candle to that Pete Howard-powered burst of musical hate. Nothing to be ashamed about, but unfortunately for me this album is competing against a backlog of superior material.

'Should I Stay Or Should I Go' (*Boston 9/82*)- Don't skip this one, you'll miss some great full-tilt rockin'. Thankfully, they didn't use that dreadful version from the video. This is one one of the surprises on the record- a version of 'Should I Stay' that I can stand to listen to.

'Straight To Hell' (Boston 9/82)- This goes really well until they forget to edit out Joe's meanderings towards the end of the track. Listen to Joe free-associate badly kind of detracts from the mood of the song especially during the bridge.

So, what do I really think? I think it's a worthy document, a nice sampler. It's sure to be a crowd-pleaser. I really enjoy how the songs all mesh together so it sounds like one concert, despite the different time periods and sources. Mick and Bill deserve a round of applause for their studio wizardry.

But...but... it's not nearly enough. One crummy CD from all the shows they have on multi-track? I don't think so, Charlie. I really hope this sells well so all involved will get all the other material out in front of us. This stuff isn't meant to make the charts, it's meant for the hardcore fans. Most other bands of the Clash's stature have a lot, and I mean a lot, more live material out there. King Crimson seems to put out a live boxset on a weekly basis. I think that old Clash studio timidity kicked in again here. It's time to clear the vaults and get this material to the people. I really don't think the Clash need to be so precious about it all. I mean, *Eternity* is good as a representative document, kind of a message to the world outside, but there is so much material, so many other great tracks that we should be hearing. I mean no 'Stay Free'? No 'Police and Thieves'? No 'Bank Robber'? No 'Rock the Casbah', even?

I say to the boys, great start. You've really gotten off on the right foot. But let's keep it coming. Listen to some of the material that the Who and Led Zeppelin have put out. It's by no means perfect, but it's for the fans. The stuff is recorded, bought and paid for. Put it out. Keep the revenue stream coming. People will buy it. The Clash's recorded output thus far is woefully incomplete. And since we won't be hearing any more new material, bring out the live stuff. Remember *Clash City Showdown*'s motto: 'The only good Clash is a live Clash!'

SHOWDOWN ON 8TH STREET!

JOLTIN' JOE STRUMMER vs. MIGHTY MICK JONES

Combat Rock has always been a conundrum for me. I've never been able to get a handle on it. Do I love it or hate it? I've listened to it plenty (most often when I was young and dissolute), but I've done so in the hopes that it would get better, or that somehow I would figure out what they were trying to accomplish on it. Was there some message I was missing? Is there a proper way to listen to it that I haven't tried yet? Part of my obsession with it ties into my general OCD personality. I've heard it said that OCD rituals stem from trauma, and that they become a way for sufferers to process the trauma in a way that helps them to gain control over it. *Combat Rock* was traumatic to me in that it was such an immense disappointment on many levels and was looked at on with deep scorn by many of my circle of acquaintances (I often felt like I was being blamed for it cause I was the "Clash guy"), and to top it all off, this was the last record the original lineup left us with. 'Death is a Star' was a pretty shitty way for a and that entered the world with 'White Riot' to exit with. But at the same time, there was obviously a much better album buried beneath the weak, scattered grooves of Rock, and the story behind the album fascinated me. So here are a few of the dispatches where I worked out my *Combat Rock* trauma...

COMBATIVE ROCK
Originally posted 11/5/95

The Clash were exhausted physically and creatively by the time they entered the studio for *Combat Rock* in late '81. The Bond's fiasco had occurred in the spring, *Sandinista* had seriously damaged their relationship with CBS, Topper Headon was at this point a hopeless junkie, and Bernie Rhodes was playing his warped mind games on the band. Mick and Joe usually settled their creative differences with fights and were exchanging songwriting ideas through intermediaries. In addition, putting out a three-record set that explored almost every possible musical direction had left them unsure how to proceed. In spite of this, they had written a new batch of superior material that was premiered in Europe and the UK on their fall tour. The new songs heard in the fall of 81 were; 'Know Your Rights', Should I Stay...?', 'Radio Clash', 'Overpowered by Funk', 'Inoculated City', and 'Ghetto Defendant'. These are generally the songs considered the strongest of this period with the exception of 'Rock the Casbah' and 'Straight to Hell', which were written in the studio. Little is known about 'Beautiful People', but my guess is that is was not written in the studio, simply because it's too complex. So with the exception of 'Casbah', which again was more or less pre-written by Headon and 'Straight to Hell', the strongest songs were premiered on tour in '81.

That leaves 'Car Jamming', 'Red Angel Dragnet', 'Atom Tan', 'Sean Fly', 'Death is a Star', 'Kill Time', 'First Night Back in London', 'Long Time Jerk', and 'Cool Confusion' as songs that were, in all likelihood, written in the studio. The one thread that ties these songs together is their incompleteness. These are half-written songs, all characterized by a somewhat static riff played unenergetically, and topped with stream of consciousness lyrics and lazy melodies. These songs are the product of a band trying to write songs on the spot with little inspiration. Jones added layers of studio gloss on each of these songs to cover their inadequacy, but for intents and purposes they are B-sides (albeit in Sean Flynn's case, a killer B-sides. Marcus Gray reports that 'Sean Flynn' was recorded during the same sessions as 'Radio Clash' so maybe it was the intended B-sides).

After writing the 30 odd songs for the *Sandinista* sessions, tunes for the Ellen Foley project, and various other side ventures in addition to the usual grueling touring schedule (and writing the afore mentioned songs for it), no one can blame the Clash for running out of ideas. And the restrictive contract they were under required them to make a new album whether they had the songs or not.

But, wait: it gets worse.

Mick and Joe hated each other at this point, and Bernie Rhodes' re-entry simply aggravated the conflict. Joe spoke of how the situation had deteriorated to the point that they were begging Mick to come out of his hotel room. Mick told the band that if *Combat Rock* was not recorded in New York, the Clash would have to record it without them. Jones was enamored of the burgeoning Hip-Hop scene and was trying to incorporate Hip-Hop into the Clash's music (which there is surprisingly little of on *Combat Rock*).

Joe was reportedly disgusted with the Ellen Foley record and apparently made no secret of it.

After the Foley sessions, Joe flew back to London and told several reporters the Clash were finished. Mick was perhaps humbled by the failure of the Foley record (and the Ian Hunter record he worked on) and the Clash got back to work in late summer. Following the European tour, the Clash flew to New York and continued the *Combat Rock* sessions, which were started in London using the Rolling Stones mobile studio. The listless playing on *Combat Rock* is clearly an indicator of the atmosphere in the studio. The sessions dragged on and the plan was to release CR (then titled *Rat Patrol from Fort Bragg*) as a double set, since the Dub-heavy songs were all well over five minutes long. The recording was apparently finished but the record was unmixed and a planned Asian tour was nigh. The band toured Australia and the Far East and attempted to mix the record after gigs. Mick Jones apparently took over mixing and submitted what Joe called a 'home movie mix' to CBS.

Needless to say, everyone hated it. Bernie Rhodes then arranged to have veteran producer Glyn Johns come aboard and clean up the mess. Joe OK'd the deal and shattered his already stormy relationship with Mick, who liked his own mix (which was atrocious, as anyone who has heard the 'Outtakes' boots can attest to). After some unexplained delay, the record was released in late spring of '82. The UK press went ga-ga and the LP shot to number two on the charts. The Clash then played a show in Holland with a painfully inept Headon. Fed up, Joe ran off to Paris without telling anyone where he was off to. Kosmo Vinyl hired a private eye to find him and he returned to London. And interestingly enough, a group meeting was called in Paul's apartment and Headon was sacked.

Terry Chimes was summoned from his gig as a clerk in a paint store (or so the story went) and the Clash resumed their tour. The band's sound was much different, as Joe had reportedly taken control of the band and Chimes' drumming was much heavier and far more steady. And strangely enough, the *Combat Rock* material was down-played on the tour, especially in comparison with previous albums tours. Whereas at least half of *London Calling* and a third of *Sandinista* got aired on tours supporting them, only 'Know Your Rights' Should I Stay' 'Casbah' and 'Straight to Hell' were played regularly in '82. 'Ghetto Defendant' and a vastly improved and rocked-up 'Car Jamming' were occasionally aired, but none of the other tracks got played in '82. Which perhaps illustrates the band's opinion of the *Combat Rock* material.

Combat Rock vs Rat Patrol
Originally posted 12/29/96

Joe vs Mick. Or better yet, the Cinematheque vs the discotheque.

Sometime in 1980, Mick had made up his mind that the Clash were a Dance band. The sound he had in mind for the Clash was the sound he has pursued single-mindedly with Big Audio Dynamite. Strummer gave lip service to this new concept in interviews in the early Eighties, but his proclamations were unconvincing, and according to Marcus Gray, insincere. But despite Joe's frontman status, Mick ran the Clash with his own iron fist after Bernie Rhodes was fired. Disregarding the band's sound, Mick began to create a fiction-al artefact of the Clash in the studio. He began a gradual turning down of the band's signature guitar fire for *London Calling* until the guitars were barely audi-ble on the *Rat Patrol* mixes. In effect, the Clash on record were a separate entity from who the Clash in rehearsals and onstage. In other words, the Clash on record were not the Clash at all, but a fictional construct. This concept reached it's apex in 1982 when the Clash were transformed from a rough and ready Rock band into a Downtown New York style Dance band, a la ESG or Liquid Liquid.

Mick pursued the 'Big Audio Clash' concept in earnest in '81/'82 and the Funk and Reggae tinged Hard Rock songs the Clash had previewed in Europe in the Autumn became Funk and Reggae tinged Pop songs, ready-made for the Manhattan clubs where Mick was spending most of his evenings. Perhaps seeking to make a final break with the original Clash following, *Rat Patrol* took shape under Mick's oversight. According to Gray, the Clash were presented with the mix-down of a two record set before the Asian tour which they rejected out of hand. Of course, that mix was leaked and Clash fans now have an comparison to make.

First of all, the *Rat Patrol* mix is exactly the 'home movie mix' Joe complained about in '84. The fades and dropouts throughout the tracks are gimmicky, a nod to the nascent Hip Hop scene taking shape in New York at the time. Joe's vocals are dreadful on many tracks, including 'Know Your Rights' and 'Death is a Star', and Mick's are even worse on 'Should I Stay...'. And followers of the *CCS* know my opinion of 'Cool Confusion' and 'Atom Tan'. The latter is tolerable in the *RP* mix and format, but the the former is the worst pile of crap ever recorded, and the Clash should all receive a hearty broken-ribs beating for daring to commit it to tape. Now that an earlier Rock and Roll instrumental version of the track has been released on the *Essential Clash* DVD, the B-Side version is even more unforgivable. But given the choice, I think *Rat Patrol* is in many ways a better record.

The main weakness with *Combat Rock* is it's disunity. It's too scatter-shot for a single LP, and just seems like sides 7 and 8 of *Sandinista*. Side one hangs together OK, but side two is where it falls apart. Track one is a bad Disco song, track two is a half-assed Stones song, track three is a brooding sound-track piece, track four is a Dub track, track five is a Beatlesque pop track, and track six is a non-song that threatens to evaporate before your ears. Awhile back I posted my fictional CR, which would borrow 'Radio Clash' for the lead-off track, bring back 'Kill Time' and 'Beautiful People', delete 'Atom Tan' and 'Death is Star' and possibly 'Car Jamming' and restore 'Inoculated City' to it's original length. I would keep the Johns mix, and rock it up even more. This, in my opinion, would be better than both Mick and Joe's versions.

Mick's record benefits from the relative integrity of concept. This was the record he made, the Clash were basically his sidemen (like the various BAD's) at that point, and hence it works as a whole more than *CR*. Weaker songs like 'First Night Back in London' benefit from the thematic ambiance (again, the demo of this song, heard on *Hell W10*, is far superior), stronger songs like 'Beautiful People' stay on, and a song like 'Inoculated City' works better with it's coda. After listening to *Rat Patrol*, it seems like a single piece of work. A single work with a shitty mix and bad vocals, but a single piece of work, nonetheless. It's interesting to note that Mick determined the shape of his future career during these sessions and has pursued it relentlessly ever since.

Of course, Joe's version went on to sell a couple million worldwide and establish the band as major stars after Mick's *Sandinista* nearly destroyed them. The success of CR must have been devastating to Mick coupled with *Sandinista*'s commercial failure, and this success swelled Joe's head to Napoleonic proportions, resulting in Mick's expulsion the following year. This was, in hindsight, inevitable. To paraphrase Donny and Marie, Mick is a little bit Disco, and Joe is a little bit Rock and Roll. As we have seen recently, Strummer's foray into Dance music ended with him scrapping an album made at a very expensive studio, and Mick's attempt to go back to his Punk roots resulted in a remake of *Cut the Crap*. Rumor has it Joe is making Punk songs again and Mick is trying to reverse-engineer the BAD concept.

Ca plus change, I guess.

Combat Rock Revisited.....
Originally posted 9/27/00

I was listening to *Combat Rock* the other day. Even though all of the songs don't hold up, it always keeps my attention on a textural level. After it ended, I thought I'd listen to something else in the same vein. But I was soon stumped, because there isn't anything in the same vein. You could suggest *This is BAD* or *X-Ray Style*, but the guitar playing on those records isn't nearly as interesting. There's something about all those scratchy, psychedelic guitars on CR that is just so darn satisfying, even when the song writing isn't. I was going to chalk all this up to Mick, but since the sounds are not nearly as interesting on *Rat Patrol* (and on some tracks the guitar is so far down in the mix, it's hardly there at all), I have to say it's a combination of Mick, Joe and Glyn Johns.

As has been discussed here on *CCS* and elsewhere, the mix for CR was taken away from Mick and eventually handled by Joe and Glyn Johns. If we use *Rat Patrol* as a guide, Joe went in and recorded a lot of extra guitar. This is most obvious on 'Know Your Rights', 'Car Jamming' and 'Should I Stay', but I'd imagine that Joe put a lot of guitar on 'Overpowered by Funk' as well. It's been said that Joe didn't do a lot of playing on the last two albums, and I think that this is a major factor in the lessening of the energy level on those records. Joe wasn't a guitarist per se, but a weird kind of per-cussionist and it's obvious how his playing set the tempo on the songs live.

To be sure, Mick had laid a lot of interesting textures down on the CR material, but the *Rat Patrol* demos show how insubstantial they sounded with-out a grungier counterpoint. Just like salt can bring out the sweetness of sugar, Joe's clicking and grinding gives Mick's playing that much more depth and complexity. I've heard that Mick and Topper laid down the basic tracks for the album without Joe and Paul, and that might be one of the reasons that the album lacks energy. This lack of vigorous rhythm playing also robs a lot of the

Sandinista tracks, especially the Watt-Roy/Gallagher session material, of texture and energy as well. But Mick was smitten with the weird, sparse sound of the New York Funk Underground of the early 80's (bands like Tom Tom Club, Liquid Liquid and ESG) and assertive guitar was definitely not the idea. But I think Joe and Johns did the right thing by trying to Rock the material up. And I think in the final analysis, Mick would agree as well. Just another illustration of the Taoist nature of Mick and Joe's relationship.

Finally, though I once was smitten with Mick's echoed-out live guitar in '81/'82 (which one guy I knew described as the 'Hey, I just got a Memory Man' style of playing), I've got to admit that the more shows I hear with it, the less impressed I am. I much prefer the shows when he played it straighter (like my beloved St. Paul, Mn '82). His playing was a lot more complex with out all those repeats, and since delay takes a lot of bottom end out of a signal, the band's sound thinned considerably with all those effects on Mick's guitar, which after all, was the most important element of the band's sound.

Except for a few shows on the '83 tour, he didn't try to get that more complex *CR* studio sound onstage. His playing in the studio incorporated a lot of right-hand muting, and that's really hard to do when you're flopping around back and forth onstage. It's also hard to do when you're really stoned and when you want to sing co-leads on every number.

Maybe when the avalanche of bands emerges set to take up my Mongrel Rock crusade, they can further explore this type of point-counterpoint guitar playing. *Clash City Showdown* is on a mission, kids. That mission is to point out all the amazing and over-looked elements of the Clash's career and Mick's late-period guitar playing bears more scrutiny.

A 'Beautiful' Combat Rock
Originally posted 3/16/96

'Beautiful People' was an uptempo Samba-flavored rock tune that inexplicably got cut from *Combat Rock*. The lads were all bummed out when the record was being made and I guess they wanted to make room for the more dirge-y type material, so they could sit around and mope and stare at each other. A shame. They probably lost the master tapes to 'Beautiful People' and 'Kill Time', the other lost CR tune, so that's why they didn't show up on the boxset. (a side note - my favorite description of 'Midnight to Stevens' was by a reviewer who wrote that is was a song that Joe didn't remember recording, and you won't remember hearing.)
Here's my dream *Combat Rock* track list, in sequence.

side one
1. **Know Your Rights** - Keep it as opener, boost the guitars in the mix
2. **Radio Clash** - Big mistake not putting this on an album
3. **Should I Stay...** - Of course.
4. **Beautiful People** - Mix down the synths
5. **Inoculated City** - The full dub version, and soak it in bright reverb
6. **Overpowered by Funk** - Use the faster original demo playing

<u>side two</u>
7. **Rock the Casbah** - I mean, *Rock the Casbah*. Wouldn't it be a great side opener?
8. **Red Angel Dragnet** - The unreleased version with Ranking Roger, scrap Kosmo's pitiful Travis Bickle impression.
9. **Ghetto Defendant** - One of my all-time faves. Perfect. Great live, too.
10. **Sean Flynn** - Great bong-hit song.
11. **Kill Time** - Cut it by a minute. And scrap that farting synth for God's sake.
12. **Straight to Hell** - Would have been a great closer

This would have been the album the Clash wanted to make. It would have been tougher, more up-tempo, more consistent, less like sides 7 and 8 of *Sandinista*. The Clash would be seen as a tough, focused dance-rock band. 'Ghetto', 'Sean' and 'Hell' would have given the LP pacing.

Now to the songs that I would bounce....

Car Jamming - Badly fucked in the studio. This was supposed to be a Bo Diddley number, then it became all lazy and tropical in the MJ mix and then became an inert pop song on *CR*. I have heard some live versions of this that rock the fucking house when Terry gets his pissed-off, ham-fisted hands on it.
Atom Tan - What is this song supposed to be? It sure as hell ain't Rock and Roll. The rife would have worked if played a lot faster, but then the lousy lyrics would have been impossible to sing. I hate this song.
Death is a Star - Snooze. Four-minute borefest. Nice lyrics, I guess, but the music is a wimpy mess.
Cool Confusion -The worst piece of music the Clash ever made. Hell, one of the worst pieces of music ever made by anyone.
Long Time Jerk -This song is a lot of fun, but like the other B-Sides, it was just a riff, not a real song.
First Night Back in London - B-side material. Would have worked well on a double LP.

I might add that none of the bounced tunes make me think of Combat. They make me think of gardening.

THE CUT THE CRAP DISASTER-
WHAT REALLY HAPPENED?

Photos in this section by Jeff Slate
©1984, 2003 Jeff Slate

In October 1985, the last album to bear the Clash's name was released. Entitled *Cut the Crap* , it was soon followed by the band's dissolution. Clash-haters snickered and gloated. The album was widely attacked (even though it received some positive reviews), and the band's breakup ensured it's failure in the marketplace. But Clash fans, particularly the real fans who had seen them on the 'Out of Control' tour were mystified. The songs on *Crap* bore little resemblance to way they were performed live. Whole sections were stripped away, and all the solos and leads were absent. Peter Howard's drumming, perhaps the most important factor in the improvement of the band's live sound, was replaced by a poorly programmed drum machine. The vocals were buried in the mix and loud, annoying 'Oi!' choruses entered in on every song.

What happened? No one really cared. The alternative scene had moved onto paint-by-numbers R.E.M. clones. Cookie-cutter, reactionary Hardcore was all the rage in Punk circles, and corporate MTV rock was cluttering up the airwaves. In the Rock and Roll wasteland of 1985, where a feeble piece of trash like the *Little Creatures* LP by the Talking Heads was considered the top album of the year in the *Village Voice* 'Pazz and Jop' Critics Poll, a great Clash album would most likely have been buried, like a gem in a trash-heap. For those who cared, however, troubling questions remain. How could a band that was so great live make such an awful album?

Careful research reveals that *Crap* was the result of a bitter power struggle, which, coupled with crippling litigation, destroyed the Clash for good and tarnished their credibility.

On Sept. 1, 1983, a press release had informed the world that Mick Jones was no longer a member of the Clash. Remaining original members Joe Strummer and Paul Simonon stated that Jones had "strayed from the original idea of the Clash." Open auditions were soon-after held for what a classified advert referred to as a "loud, wild guitarist." In November it was announced that Nick Sheppard, former guitarist of the Cortinas, And Vince (Gregory) White, a student from Finsbury Park, were chosen as Jones' replacements. The two 24-year old guitarists would free Strummer from rhythm guitar duty, allowing him to concentrate on vocals. A tour was announced for January. Dubbed the 'Out of Control' tour, it would start in mid-sized cities in California, go to Europe and the UK, and make its way back to the US in April.

The opening night at the Long Beach Arena brought great press attention. Entertainment Tonight ran a report on the concert. Critic Cary Darling echoed the general sentiment by stating the concert displayed "an urgency and passion that had been missing from the Clash for awhile." Darling also described the new Clash's sound as a "virtual explosion", and declared, "now, let's wait for the record." Not all reviews were positive, however. One critic bemoaned that the Clash were too fast and too loud! The tour moved up the West Coast before making its way to Europe for a stadium tour.

The Clash then returned to the UK, where Strummer gave a series of interviews to the British weeklies. Jones, he said, refused to tour, "wouldn't play his damn guitar", and had told Strummer that any decisions made by the Clash would have to be cleared by his lawyer. Strummer said he told Jones "to go and write songs with his damn lawyer." Jones, in response to this public dirty laundry airing, went on holiday and had his lawyer freeze the Clash's assets, including the royalties from the 1.5 million selling "*Combat Rock.*" He also publicly challenged the Clash's right to the name, though he denied filing suit to prevent them from touring.

Strummer and co. went on despite this, and the UK tour was described by *NME* as a "lightning sellout." A series of concerts at their home venue, the Brixton Academy, showed that the Clash still enjoyed rabid support, with or without Jones. Critical opinion was mixed. *Record Mirrror* stated that the new lineup was "thrilling" and a "dynamic spectacle", but that the Clash had "lost meaning." *NME* continued their 5 year old anti-Clash backlash and declared them to be "Jail Guitar Bores." Sounds approved of the shows, stating they were still the "World's Greatest Rock and Roll" band. *ZigZag* declared that the new lineup's shows were "easily as good as the old Clash."

In general, however, press reaction was hostile to the band. Not musically, mind you, since most journalists were forced to admit the new lineup put on a great show. The common theme in most of the hit pieces was that the Clash were no longer 'relevant', ie, they were no longer following the trends dictated to artists by the record companies who controlled the British music press. UK critics were then totally enthralled with corporate, pre-fab acts like Frankie Goes to Hollywood and Bananarama, and the Clash's violent new sound and look clearly did not suit the tenor of the times. The fact that the band was acting in open defiance of their record company obviously did little to help their case with the press. The irony is that the talent-free, SynthPop poseurs who were allegedly the future of Rock were seen as corny and passé only a couple years later, and the look and style of Clash II would be profoundly influential in next decade.

The Clash set their sights back on the US in April. The US tour did not enjoy the same success as the UK and European tour, but a lack of record company support and no album to promote made that impossible. A full tilt 'back-Clash' was in full swing among the self-appointed Rock elite, who were currently touting the 'New American Rock'. This ephemeral phenomenon was the invention of promoters and writers who were seeking a hip, Heartland musical equivalent to Ronald Reagan's 'Morning in America' re-election campaign (and also were trying to refute the previous years 'New British Invasion').

What also served as a detriment to the Clash's success was the renewed interest in Top 40 pop, both by the record-buying Public and critics seeking to legitimize a popular fad. Cyndi Lauper, Duran Duran, and Huey Lewis were dominating the charts with their sunny pop and the blowtorch Punk of the new Clash was decidedly out of touch with the times in the US as well. However, the only real judges of the new Clash, the army of kids who loved them, gave the tour their whole hearted approval. The band returned the favor by keeping the kids from being roughed by security goons. When a kid was attacked by bouncers for stagediving, Strummer bellowed, "One day people will be treated like human beings when they go to a concert, even in this fascist country!"

The concerts on the tour were usually more than an hour and a half and included a number of new songs, as well as a large helping of Clash classics. What was remarkable about the shows was the number of songs from the *London Calling* and *Sandinista* collections. despite the apparent intent of the band to move back towards a more classic Punk sound. 'Magnificent Seven', 'Spanish Bombs', and even 'Broadway' were staples of the new setlists, as well as more dance-oriented tunes like 'Rock the Casbah' and 'Radio Clash'. But the songs were performed as high-energy Rock, and played with greater clarity and tightness than the original lineup ever seemed capable of. The new songs

received an encouraging reception and the real fans seemed to agree that the Clash were back in full swing. Another remarkable aspect of the tour was the band's invitation to the fans to visit them backstage after the shows for conversation and autographs. Many favorable notices in the press followed and the future looked bright. The tour stretched out until June and the Clash played sporadic benefits upon their return to Europe.

Various contradictory reports began to surface concerning the band entering the studio to begin work on the next album. Many reports had the album coming out in the autumn. Lisa Robinson reported that the Clash had entered the studio in October. The silence was broken in December as the band played a benefit for the striking Welsh Coal Miners. Strummer announced to the crowd that "we have a record" and that it would be released in the new year, after "some things go by." The band proceeded to play 10 new songs, again totally unlike the songs that had appeared on *Crap*. Then, more silence. An article in *Spin* magazine on Mick Jones announced the release of the new Clash record in May, coinciding with the release of Jones' new band, Big Audio Dynamite's single. More silence. *Spin* then heaped praise(!) on 'This is England', the unreleased new single by the Clash, in June. Still, more silence.

Finally in October, Big Audio Dynamite's first LP was released. It was soon followed by the new Clash collection entitled *Cut the Crap*. The album showcased 8 of the songs that the Clash had played live, but in radically altered, almost unrecognizable form. And to make matters worse, the album did not include two songs that were centerpieces of the tour, 'Sex Mad War' and 'Ammunition' ('Sex Mad War' showed up as 'Sex Mad Roar' on the B-side of the 'This is England' 12"). Soon after, the Clash announced that White, Howard and Sheppard were being dismissed.

In the time between the tour and the release of *Crap*, a number of things were occurring. Manager Bernard Rhodes, who was reportedly responsible for Jones' ouster, had taken control of the recording sessions according to Strummer. Strummer was apparently on the emotional ropes after the tour. His father had died during the UK leg, and when he returned from the US, his mom was diagnosed with terminal cancer. Subsequent interviews with Mick Jones had revealed Jones' belief that Strummer had fallen under Rhodes influence. When Mick was asked his opinion of *Crap*, he stated, "That's not their album. It's their managers album."

That it was. Premier Clash historian Ralph Heibutzki dug into this mess, interviewing many of the principals involved and got many revealing answers. According to Nick Sheppard, the general feeling was that despite the success on tour, the new lineup had not jelled into a real band. When the tour was over, the new members were kept in the dark, fed only rudimentary chord structures to practice on their own. At one point, they were told they would not be used on the album at all. Session stalwarts Norman Watt-Roy and Mickey Gallagher were called in to rehearse with Strummer and Howard, but that idea was scrapped. The whittling process eventually got to Howard, and the abysmal drum programming was done by the talentless Michael Fayne.

Strummer has said little of this period, so we have no idea what on Earth he was thinking about. The band was so tight, the album could have been done live. Here, Rhodes' shadow hangs heavy. According to Sheppard, Rhodes was in complete control of the entire process. The album was made according to his specifications, and Strummer's role was apparently reduced to be Rhodes' sideman. It's entirely possible that it had been decided that a Punk Rock album wouldn't sell as is, but would have to be tarted up with a dungheap of synthesizer and drum machine noise so it would more closely resemble the crap on the charts at the time.

The sessions ground on and Sheppard tried to make the best of it. Watt-Roy and Gallagher stuck around, putting down the bass and keyboards, which left Simonon relegated to only a couple of B-sides.

©1984, 2003 Jeff Slate

©1984, 2003 Jeff Slate

Sheppard and White put lead guitar tracks down incrementally after most of the work had been done on the album. When the whole mess was over, the lads decided to strike out on the road. They grabbed some acoustic guitars and went on a mad busking tour in the north of England and into Scotland, playing anywhere and everywhere, day or night. This jaunt proved to be therapeutic, and the new Clash were finally a real band. This euphoria was not to last. Rhodes took off with the tapes from the *Crap* sessions, leaving Joe no indication where he was going.

In the summer, the band reassembled to do some money-making shows in Europe. Sheppard told Heibutski that on the tour bus, Joe glared at Bernie, and it was obvious to Sheppard that "Joe just hated Bernie." In September, Joe, in a move of desperation, flew to the Bahamas to track down Mick and asked him to rejoin the Clash. Although the two patched up their differences, Mick remained committed to his new band. Finally, Joe called the boys together and told them he was breaking up the band. Bernie tried to pick up the pieces and began auditioning new singers (!), but the jig was up. CBS released the whole mess and the rest is history.

Strummer has stated that he regrets the entire episode, going so far as to state that the Clash died the night they sacked Topper. He has often said that once the synergy of the classic lineup was broken, the elusive spirit of the band died. I don't know how true this is. Certainly some of their shows with Terry in '82 were as good as, if not better, than many shows with Topper. And he offered these insights during occasions when he was trying to put the original Clash back together, so a grain of salt is required. And even writers who disliked the '84 shows have pointed out how good the band sounded and how possessed Joe seemed on stage.

But, *Cut the Crap* remains. A god-awful record by anyone's standard, *Crap* is like the malformed child of a couple who go on having children long after it is wise to do so. In Rhodes' defense, however, the problem with *Cut the Crap* is not the ideas or even the songs. Many of the ideas on *Crap* have been utilized by many of today's top bands. The idea of Musique Concrete, the mixture of punk guitars and dance rhythms and shouted mob choruses have surfaced in records by bands like Ministry and Nine Inch Nails.The problem is that you can't take rowdy drinking songs meant to be played by a real band and try to fit them into a dancey format. Rhodes' downfall was his hubris. He was way out of his depth in the studio, and *Crap* remains as a monument to his technical incompetence. And the album to have done all this conceptual fiddling with was the second Clash II album . They had enough on their hands just trying to establish the band in the first place. It is perhaps no accident that he has not been heard from since, outside of a few quotes in articles on the Clash.

So, who cares? Well, Clash fans should. The 'new' Clash had great potential that was destroyed by politics and ineptitude. Strummer was castigated by the press and 'fans' who never heard how the band actually sounded. White,Howard and Sheppard, three worthy musicians, never got their shot at the big time. Revisionists have written off the entire affair as an artistic failure solely on the basis of *Crap*. The amount of sheer nonsense written about the band has been staggering, even by people who should know better. There has not only been an avalanche of misinformed opinion about the band, but an astonishing degree of revisionism and outright lying from journalists, some of whom I once respected. In following the story of Clash II, I discovered that journalists like to construct narratives that hew to their own biases (*shock horror*). They also hate loose ends, because loose ends call their authority into question.

©1984, 2003 *Jeff Slate*

A number of unofficial recordings are available from the Out of Control tour. Particularly recommended is the *Five Alive* double LP set and the *Give 'Em Enough Dope* CD. As a rule the UK and US shows in the Spring were stronger than the rest, and any recordings from that time are a good bet. The outside world may never know or care about this incident, but real Clash fans should know the 'new' Clash were not the disaster Crap would make them out to be, but were the victim of overwhelming adversity and manipulation.

But, as they say, Life goes on.

CUT THE CRAP TRACK BY TRACK
Originally posted Dec 30, 1996

In a previous *CCS* dispatch, we discussed the battle between the two Clash camps over the final 'classic' Clash record. Lurking somewhere in the distance was the figure of one Bernard Rhodes. After the breakup of the Clash, Joe mentioned that the clash of the titans within the Clash was Mick vs. Bernie. Contrary to *alt.music.clash* mythology, Bernie was as much of a founder of the Clash as was Mick. Bernie recruited Joe, and got them a place to rehearse and created their identity. Joe re-recruited Bernie to help him with his struggles with Mick, who was calling the shots with the bands' musical direction in 1980. We all know what happened in '83, and we all have suffered through the final fruits of September 1983. Bernie was the Clash's alpha and omega, their creator and destroyer. In all likelihood, Joe would have never thrown out Mick without Bernie whispering in his ear like a devil's advocate. But he also would have been unable to bridge the growing chasm between himself and his partner.

Cut the Crap was by no means a Clash record, it was a Bernie Rhodes record. Of the original Clash, only Joe Strummer is present on all the tracks. Paul played on two B-sides ('Do it Now' and 'Sex Mad Roar'), but not on the album. Most of the foundation of the music on the record was created by the untalented Michael Fayne, Mickey Gallagher (according to Nick Sheppard, though Gray disputes this in *Last Gang*- I'll stick with Nick) and Norman Watt-Roy of the Blockheads. The godawful guitar noise was created by overdubbing multiple layers of distorted guitar, which breaks rule number one of recording hard rock. The layers of guitar cancel each other out, and the harmonics of the various tracks overlap to create a cacophony. The annoying massed choruses were the result of recording a crowd of drunken non-singers in a single session. The blips and bleeps and squonks that litter the grooves are often louder than the lead vocals, and the few solos are all soaked in a pitch shifter. The CD remaster does much to clean up the sonic confusion of the vinyl version, but what is really called for is a remixing of the entire record.

Looking back at the tour, one notices that not one of the very tightly arranged songs played live was recorded intact. Whole sections of the songs, including solos and bridges, are removed almost at random, and certainly without any regard to their integrity to the composition. And most of the songs that were unheard on tour are the worst songs the Clash had produced since the all-time lows of 'Cool Confusion' or 'Atom Tan'. These 'new' songs were most likely the songs that Bernie Rhodes had co-written, or perhaps written entirely.

Here's a track by track evaluation of the damage...

The Dictator - One of the earliest songs played live. Nick Sheppard maintained that all of the songs on tour were Joe's songs, and most of them were arranged by the band. Live, the song had a half-time bridge with a military march and twang guitar. All of these elements were stripped and atonal synth bursts were added. A terrible lead-off track.

Dirty Punk - A Bernie song? The lyrics on 'Punk' are simplistic and border on the moronic, and the arrangement is dull. Played live at the Brixton shows, but sounded extremely unrehearsed. Definitely written after the tour. Of course, we now know that after the tour Joe was spending his time with his terminally ill mother, so this track has Bernie written all over it to me.

We Are the Clash - Possibly written in response to Mick's lawsuit, but most probably written at Bernie's behest. Slowed down considerably on record, with the bridge amended to an intro, and the call and response chorus heard in the spring was also removed. The *CTC* solo is a feeble echo of the live one. This song earned the 'new' Clash a lot of heat, but I've heard some killer live versions of it.

Are You Red..y - Unforgivable butchery of an all-time great Clash song. The main riff of the song is buried in the outro, the lead guitars are all stripped, the vocals are inaudible. I cannot adequately express my rage at what was done to this track. What were they thinking?

Cool Under Heat - Another post-tour song. Could be a Bernie number, but unlikely since it was played on the busking tour. The *CTC* version is a case study in bad production. There's a Glitter Rock-inspired tune buried beneath all the aural garbage.

Movers and Shakers - Half-hearted Joe number, but a could've been. The one song where *Cut the Crap* threatens to build up a head of steam. I can only picture Joe writing lyrics this trite while Bernie was holding a gun to his head. Another one played on the 'Busking' tour.

This is England - For all the hoopla made about the *CTC* version, it pales in comparison to a good live playing. The live version had a lot of tempo changes, a melodic lead guitar line and a lot of dynamic breaks. Despite the hype, the *CTC* version is just a one-dimensional reggae rock thing.

Three Card Trick- Somewhere along the line this became a ska song, which was a big mistake. This originally was a killer, balls-out, mother-fucking rock song with a great, drum-driven bridge. Of course, it was decided that Pete

Howard, the most technically proficient of the Clash drummers, was not to play on *CTC*, so 'Three Card Trick' had to be reformatted. The Ska version was played out in '85 and it seemed perfunctory. And doesn't this sound suspiciously like a BAD song? The remix of 'This is England' from the Dutch 12" does so as well.

<u>**Play to Win**</u>- This crap has Bernie written all over it. A sound effects sampler gone awry, broken up by unintelligible chanting and an inaudible talking verse. If 'Cool Confusion' did not exist this would be the all-time worst Clash song.

<u>**Fingerpoppin'**</u> -This must've been an attempt to cash in on the Casbah vibe, and strangely enough, it has the best production on the album. Straight Funk Rock, this has echoes of the Frankie Goes to Hollywood and the Chili Peppers. The only time I have heard this live was at the Brixton 12/6/84 show, where it was a strange, hopping Rock track that was obviously just invented. I can't say that version is much of anything, but you may wanna hear it.

<u>**North and South**</u> - Another butcher job. The hideous production on this track cripples its potential as a power ballad. Of all the post-Out of Control songs, the original version of this is the only really good song, which makes me suspect it was written earlier.

<u>**Life is Wild**</u>- I must admit a perverse fondness for this song. The way it descends into madness at the end and then cuts is fun, and I think it has a good rhythm. Of course, the Oi chorus nearly obliterates it but hey, what the hell, right? This song was never played live, and I can't tell what influence Bernie had on it, aside from the musique concrete stuff at the end.

Let me close in saying, that my disdain for *Cut the Crap* is based upon comparisons to the live performances of the songs and the enormous potential of Clash II. The album was a disaster, but only in light if what it could have been. I think that every Clash fan should own it, and I actually enjoy it if I take it for what it is. It is certainly no worse than most of the crap that was released in 1985, and can be quite entertaining when played very LOUDLY.

Jon Savage continues to champion it in the new edition of *England's Dreaming*, but I am willing to bet he didn't see the band live. I am tempted to do likewise, but the miserable backstory behind prevents me from doing so. This album broke everyone's heart who made it, even Bernie's. I gave quite a few defiant airings when Joe passed away, but I am afraid I have to list the album in the tragic 'could-have-beens' file.

THE REINVENTION PROCESS
Originally posted 9/12/1997

We are nearing the 14th anniversary of Mick Jones' ouster from the Clash. It seems so far away now, doesn't it? And as I write this, it seems that the Clash reunion we have all wished so hard for is not only unlikely, but also uncalled for.

It just occurred to me that Mick Jones is not really Mick Jones of the Clash anymore, or even 'Mick Jones, ex-Clash member'. He's Mick Jones of Big Audio Dynamite, a Mick Jones light years away from his previous incarnation. He's Mick Jones of the sunny beat and the smiling face, not the glowering, sulking axeman from the street-fighting Clash. To many kids, he was Mick Jones of *120 Minutes* house band BAD, or of 'Should I Stay' fame (tied with 'Train in Vain' as the most uncharacteristic Clash songs ever) and only later did they discover there even was a Clash. Forced out of the band he started by the man he started the band with, he reinvented himself so completely, and so long ago, that it's inconceivable to see him back as the old Punk. And that's why the Clash reunion will most likely never happen. And when you have run your own show so completely, for so long, how do you go back to being one among equals? And could you see it as anything but burlesque?

You see, Mick has been able to do with BAD what Bernie Rhodes was unable to do with the Clash, create a band that is solely focused on his personality, with a endlessly revolving cast of anonymous musicians almost completely irrelevant to BAD's viability and music. Mick ridiculed Bernie for tampering with the Clash's lineup, but in the context of today, we can see another, more subtle motivation: ridiculing him not for his gall perhaps, but for his ineptitude.

There were three main components to the Clash. What we think of as the superficial signifiers of the Clash: the slogans, the anger, the style, the visual thrust - that's all Bernie Rhodes. No one can deny that. Joe was a Hippie Pub singer, Mick was a Mick Ronson wanna-be, and Paul was a painter. Anyone who has heard the early Clash material: the London SS leftovers with trite lyrics and borrowed riffs, hardly sees the making of a revolution there. Bernie gave the Clash everything except their native talent.

Mick was the Pop in the Clash, in a classic English sense. Mick did with the Clash what he does with BAD, tune into what is happening on the city streets, interpret it and give it a smiling visage. Despite the vitriol of many of the early Clash numbers, there's a humor and openness that gave the Clash it's appeal. Contrast those numbers with Joe's pissed-off Clash II songs. Those later songs have no knowing wink to them, no peak behind the curtain, just a feeling that the person singing them is about to punch you in the face.

If Bernie was the packaging man, and Mick was the tunesmith, Joe was the 'clash' in the Clash. Then, he was a naturally pugnacious and obstinate little man, determined to stare down the world. A gnarly, throaty howl and a clicking, grinding Telecaster used as weapons against all the schoolyard bullies who were now ensconced in the boardrooms of the world. Joe's response to the slick 70's was the squatter proto-Punk sounds of the 101'ers. His response to the 101'ers was the even gnarlier Clash. His response to the punk Clash was the Yippie sounds of *Sandinista!* and *Combat Rock*. His response to the success of *Combat Rock* was the blowtorch of hatred on the Clash II 'Out of Control' tour. His response to Bernie's synth-Punk agenda of the *Cut the Crap* sessions was an acoustic busking tour in the depressed north of Britain. His response to Bernie at the end of it all was to go and work for Mick on a BAD album. His response to Mick's synth-mania was a Latin jazz record made with a orchestra. His response to the even slicker late 80's was a neo-Pub record made in a 16 track studio and a home movie video. And to honor a Punk compilation that asked him to cut a track, he gave them a *Combat Rock* - style Calypso number, replete with '82 vintage synth guitar. As I struggle to understand the real motivations of the Clash split, another layer becomes evident. Mick was willing to sign an armistice with the world outside, and Joe wanted to keep on fighting.

What are the results of this? Mick, willing to go along to get along, had enjoyed 12 years of modest success with his own band, and Joe was dropped by his label. We are going on 8 years of near-total silence from the House of Mellor. A recent interview with Clash partisan Bill Flanagan did not leave me with much optimism that we will blessed with product from Joe anytime in the near future. And my feeling is that Joe has not yet figured out who he really is.

I just reread for the millionth time the breakup chapter in *Last Gang in Town*, trying maniacally to find something in-between the lines. I started *Clash City Showdown* primarily to do two things: to redefine the real meaning and importance of the Clash, and to clear the name of the second Clash, which had been buried under a pile of lies and revisionism unseen since Stalin. With the publication of *Last Gang* and Ralph Heitbutzki's brilliant articles in *Goldmine* and *DISCoveries*, and finally the *CCS* zine, that mission faded into the background. My present obsession is to understand the real story of the Clash - how a band who seemed to be primed to be the biggest Rock and Roll band in the world fell apart at the height of their popularity. I can't think of too many other bands who that happened to, if there indeed are any. This is a really interesting story, one of the most interesting stories in Rock and Roll history.

This is a process of realization, where murky facts become clear and then strike you like a thunderbolt with their clarity. Having grown up with Mick as a guitarist in the Clash, it had yet to become real to me that Mick had changed at some point in time, probably at some time in his tenure in the Clash. The image of Mick in my mind is not with a blood-splattered shirt, or with a leather jacket, but with a white dungaree jacket and Puma cap, or with a white lab coat and oversized horn-rim glasses. I really can't imagine Mick singing 'Protex Blue' or the 'the Prisoner' anymore, with sweaty, greased back hair and black engineer boots. It's just inconceivable.

Mick reinvented himself, a process that was most likely precipitated by necessity. I don't see Mick with a scowl but with a smile. He has been in BAD (or more accurately, has *been* BAD) for 13 years now. This may seem ridiculously obvious, but to many people it isn't. I think a lot of problems that people have had with BAD, as well as Joe solo stuff, is that it is not the Clash. The Clash was a time, a place and a concept.

Look, Joe went down to the Bahamas and humiliated himself begging Mick to return to the Clash. Mick refused, and by doing so, denied himself his shot at being in the Rock and Roll upper echelon for the rest of his life. He must have had a pretty compelling reason to do so. And I think that reason is that he had just changed and was no longer Mick Jones of the Clash , but Mick Jones of Big Audio Dynamite.

BAD VIBES
Originally posted 1/2/97

I must admit I am not terribly heartened by Mick continuing with the BAD concept. I think it's passé, and judging by the jump-start tactics he is utilizing on *Entering A New Ride BAD*, I would posit he himself has lost interest in it. The fact is that the past three BAD records (I am including the hits comp) have bombed badly, and on top of that, BAD has never had a bonafide US hit record, unlike their clones EMF and Jesus Jones. The revolving door at No. 10, Upping St. is certainly another indication of internal crisis. Having said all that, I think Mick could potentially climb back yet again if he made the kind of record that only he could make.

The best BAD songs ('E=MC2', 'Beyond the Pale', 'V13', 'Just Play Music', 'Everybody Needs a Holiday', 'Innocent Child') harken back beyond all the dance nonsense to the kind of McCartney-esque pop he brought to the table with the Clash, and further back to the Beatles and Kinks records he devoured as a kid. This is his strength, and I think the annoyance I feel about the BAD beatbox party is how contrived it is, compared to the records he could be making. Mick's true niche is Pop in it's best sense, in the Beatles/Kinks/T-Rex sense, not in the No Doubt/Celine Dion/whoever-the-hell-else sense.

I was just listening to the first BAD album and I was stunned by how old and dated it sounded. It sounded more like an '82 record (Tom Tom Club seems to be a big influence) than an '85 record, whereas *Combat Rock* - which actually *is* an '82 record - sounded a lot more contemporary. The latest technology may make a record hot and current at the time, but it also dates it. I would love to hear a Mick record that has no drum machines or synths, no 16th-note beats, no samples. Drums, bass, piano, organ, guitars, real instruments. I would love to hear a Mick record that wasn't arch or ironic, but warm and honest. I would love to hear a Mick record that is varied and rewarding, that has him singing about things he really thinks about, not about what he thinks BAD should be singing about. And I bet a lot of other people would love to hear that record, too.

ENTERING A BAD NEW CORPORATE RIDE
Originally posted late 1999

There has never been a worse time to be a Major Label recording act. Record companies don't even bother with the pretense that their acts are independent artists pursuing their own careers. To be on a Major Label is to be a slave, pure and simple. You are told what to record, when to record it, how to record it and how to promote it. Michelle Shocked went so far as to sue her record company on 14th Amendment (which outlawed slavery) grounds. Established acts are being dropped by the bucketful, popular performers are being dictated to by their overlords, and many stars are finding themselves without a home or with a record held in limbo. The latter is the current fate of Mick Jones.

Mick is on his his 4th or 5th permutation of Big Audio Dynamite and has recorded an album entitled *Entering A New Ride BAD*. It is somewhat of a departure for the BAD sound. It dispenses with the found samples and beatboxes, pumps up the guitars and dumps the sing-songy tunes of the past few records in favor of melodic toasting and rapping. It is very much the formula I would have recommended to Mick if he had ever asked. The record has been making the rounds on the 'grey' market (apparently on CD-R in Europe) and I have had the good fortune to have heard it. It's a tragedy that this record will probably never be officially released, though Mick is hoping to put it on MP3 on the BAD World website.

There are a lot of great tracks on this record. A highlight for me is the Spector-ish 'BAD and the Nighttime Ride'. This galloping rocker has hooks and melody to spare, and harkens back to the similarly inspired 'Card Cheat'. The only official release off the record was 'Sunday Best', a dance rocker built on a simple riff that recalls songs like 'C'Mon Every Beatbox'. The song briefly made the rounds in dance clubs where it apparently was quite well received, but its success didn't help the album's cause with the MCA suits.

The predominance of Rock and Roll guitar on the album was probably particularly confusing to folks in the Dance division. Mick probably does more guitar work on *New Ride* than on several previous BAD albums combined. Another excellent cut is 'Sound of the BAD' (Bo Diddley-ite titles and lyrical self references are particularly strong on this record). The sound is built on a sample of the 'Train in Vain 'drum riff and on a typically Kinks-y power chord riff. A loping, melodic bass line propels the song and a killer House piano riff enters in towards the coda. The interesting thing about this album is that even though most of the vocals are chanted, the musical beds are extremely melodic. Mick still has that uncanny knack for hummable riffs and retains

his alchemic ability to squeeze harmonic overtones from simple barre chords. His lead guitar work is tasteful and very much in the 60's British Invasion tradition.

Reggae, missing since the first couple of records, also makes a comeback on this album. 'Bang Ice Geezer' and 'Nice and Easy' are built on Dub basslines and feature Ranking Roger on some hard to hear toasts. Many of the cuts boast fast Rock tempos like the propulsive 'Get High', a tune highly reminiscent of the early Pop Will Eat Itself (a band directly influenced by the original BAD).

There are a couple weak spots - a cover of an old Disco song entitled 'Must Be the Music' falls flat. It's certainly listenable, but superfluous. Some of the rapping by the new members can get monotonous ("Check one -two's" ad infinitum) and their voices aren't nearly as appealing as Mick's. But on the whole, this is an immensely satisfying record. The playing is tough and tight and the production is a lot rockier that any BAD record since *No. 10 Upping St.*

Where does this leave Mick? Hopefully he will take the bull by the horns and release his own material. The giant corporations don't care about music, and care less about veteran rockers like Mick. His fans are savvy enough to track down his music wherever he chooses to release it. The next logical step for the BAD concept would be to go online, since BAD has always been about utilizing the latest technology to advance the Westway sound.

THE SHOWDOWN CONSUMER GUIDE
(BAD EDITION)

I'm not sure at this point what BAD records are still in print. It's strange to say that because they were a pretty big deal on the Alternative scene in the 80's. Columbia backed them to the hilt, and every BAD record up until *Higher Power* received the kind of promotional full court press the Clash didn't get until *Combat Rock*. They were practically the house band on MTV's *120 Minutes*, and in fact, actually became the *120 Minutes* house band when they headlined that show's 1992 package tour. As many have noted, the biggest problem with BAD's records is that they were produced to sound contemporary, which means they are now hopelessly outdated, production wise. However, there is still plenty of good music in the BAD catalog. Mick was blessed with the gift of melody, and BAD's records are worthwhile to hear Mick coax rich and inventive melodies out of the simplest song structures. On the downside, the material is often twee and the lyrics are underwhelming, to put it mildly. But every Clash diehard should at least check these records out, if for nothing else to hear where Mick's muse took him after leaving the band. I am going to focus on the studio records here. There are a couple BAD comps out there, and they are obviously recommended, especially if your patience for the BAD concept is limited.

THIS IS BIG AUDIO DYNAMITE - The template for this entire record (and in some respects, for BAD in general) can be clearly heard on the unedited 'Inoculated City' from the *Rat Patrol* mixes. BAD also owes an incalculable debt to Cabaret Voltaire, and to *My Life in the Bush of Ghosts* by David Byrne and Brian Eno. BAD also cribbed ideas from the Art of Noise and other arty dance bands of that time. That being said, there is still much to enjoy on this record. The first four tracks are all sparklers, even if most could have benefitted from a bit of editing. 'E=MC2' is a flat-out classic, and is probably the best song in the bands entire catalog. The second half of the record is a bit more problematic. 'A Party' buries a solid tune under a huge layer of flab, as does album closer 'Bad'. Both tracks frustrate, because they both could have been so much better. However, 'Stone Thames' and 'Sudden Impact 'are terrible tracks, with absolutely nothing to recommend them. They're not even fun to hate like 'Hitsville UK' or 'Cool Confusion'. OVERALL GRADE : **B**

NUMBER 10, UPPING ST.- This is the legendary album co-written and co-produced by Joe Strummer. From the first note of 'C'mon Every Beatbox' you can hear Joe's influence. The beats are harder, the guitars are sharper, the lyrics more pointed and the songs more concise than the first BAD LP. Having Joe there to handle some of the chores inspired Mick to focus more on his strengths, and the melodies and guitar playing are exceptional. Joe wrote lyrics for five tunes, or at least is credited as such. I have a strong suspicion that he also wrote most of the lyrics for 'Sambadrome' and 'Hollywood Boulevard', but perhaps dodged credit out of modesty or because of contractual issues. This is the closest we will ever get to a Clash reunion LP, so it's worth picking up for that reason alone. (Note: Mick remixed some of the tracks for the CD

and those versions are vastly inferior to the original LP mixes. Go on Bay and get this one on vinyl.)
OVERALL GRADE: **A-**

TIGHTEN UP, Volume 88 - For whatever reason, Mick's heart was clearly not in this album. There is little to recommend here, outside of the great lost Paul McCartney single analog 'Just Play Music.' Mick seemed to be back-tracking a bit here towards basic Rock, but the playing and production are so weak that the songs seem to evaporate into the ether as they are being played. You can get 'Just Play Music' elsewhere, so do yourself a favor and skip this one.
OVERALL GRADE: **C +**

MEGATOP PHOENIX- What a difference a year makes. After a near fatal bout with chicken pox, Mick tapped into the rich, late-80's Dance scene for this set, and his excitement is palpable. The songs are sharp and concise and deliriously entertaining aural collages bridge the individual tracks. The melodies are rich and ingratiating and old fogies like me will appreciate the snapshot-in-time nostalgic value of the record on the whole. The only bum notes for me are, ironically, the two singles 'Contact' and 'James Brown'. The former is hopelessly twee and contrived and the latter just flat out sucks. That being said, they go by without much harm done.
OVERALL GRADE: **A-**

After the record and tour for *Megatop*, Mick faced his second band mutiny in six years. Feeling under appreciated for their contributions, the entire band quit and reformed as Screaming Targets. Their album was conceptually identical to BAD, but lacked Mick's drawing power. Mick reformed BAD with a pack of far lesser talents and set his sights on the mainstream. It would turn out to be a Faustian bargain...

KOOL AID/THE GLOBE - *Kool Aid* was a limited UK release of tracks that would go on to comprise *the Globe*. I hate both records. The songs are facile (excepting 'Beautiful Child'), the playing is dinky and the production is thin. But *the Globe* was a big hit on the strength of 'Rush' (called 'Change of Atmosphere' on *Kool Aid*). 'Rush' broke big on college radio when it was adopted as an unofficial theme song for Rush Week and went on from there. It also was the opening video on *120 Minutes* several weeks in a row. Interestingly enough, Mick's original gambit— placing 'Rush' on the b-side of the 'Should I Stay' single (which went to #1 in England) didn't seem to do much for BAD in the UK. The band had been a commercial non-entity in their home country after the first LP. Mick had clearly not learned his lesson about the fickleness of the Pop audience from that experience. The failure to do so would come back to haunt very shortly.
OVERALL GRADE: **C**

Mick took almost two years off after the *120 Minutes* tour and then changed the band's moniker again, shortening it to Big Audio.

HIGHER POWER- Though BAD's mission from the onset was to be commercially cuddly and non threatening, Higher Power was naked in its pursuit of a mainstream pop audience. 'Looking for a Song' was the single here and it is cutesy to the point of being nauseating. We're talking 'Care Bears' cutesy. The album sounds exactly like what Joe was warning us about in his 1984 ravings. Mick's pop instincts had clearly failed him. With the charts ruled by AlternaRock and Grunge Lite, and with Gangster Rap dominating the Underground Dance scene, the album was several years too late. Mick was playing footsie with an audience that no longer existed. Sensing this, he got to work on the next LP.
OVERALL GRADE: **D**

F-PUNK - With Green Day and the Offspring bringing Punk Rock to America's strip Malls, Mick seemed to believe it was time to show the upstarts who had blazed the trail. But this gambit simply resulted in Mick's second major blunder in a row. Recorded on the cheap, the album is all over the map stylistically. Though there's little actual Punk Rock here, even the schmaltzy love songs are buried in cheesy, faux Punk guitar. Mick's bout with chicken pox had badly damaged his vocal cords, severely limiting his ability to wail like the material demands. The single, 'I Turned Out a Punk,' is insanely bad and insanely badly produced. The album's *London Calling* style graphics do nothing but add to the sense of half-hearted cash-in. The bitter irony here is that this album is nothing like *London Calling*, but is conceptually identical to *Cut the Crap*. All that being said, there are some decent melodies buried beneath all the failure.
OVERALL GRADE: **C-**

ENTERING A NEW RIDE BAD (unreleased) - Mick had learned his lessons about the Record Industry and the Pop audience the hard way. He had also learned something about sticking to your guns and following your passion. How do I know this? The proof is in the pudding. I've reviewed this record elsewhere in the book, but suffice it to say that *New Ride* was Mick's best record since *Megatop*. It's also a damn shame his record company couldn't even be bothered to release it, but fans have it and Mick has the dignity of knowing that he made the kind of record he wanted to make. If BAD went down, at least they went down swinging.
OVERALL GRADE: **A-**

SHAKESPEAREAN STRUMMER

Originally posted 12/28/96

You all must remember reading *Julius Caesar* in high school. It certainly made a big impression on me, as did *Hamlet* and *MacBeth*. But in my musings, I connected a couple of dots and came up with this revelation: Joe Strummer is Brutus!

Like Brutus, Joe Strummer is an impassioned idealist. Like Brutus, he is brave and hearty, and like Brutus, he was undone by a naiveté that was fueled by narcissism. In this scenario, Mick Jones is both Caesar and Mark Antony, and Bernie is Cassius, the wily schemer who seduces Brutus into his plot to assassinate Caesar for the good of Rome. So like Caesar, Mick is 'slain' by being thrown out of the Clash, where he then transmogrifies into Mark Antony. Joe Strummer, like Brutus, addresses Rome and tells the multitudes why Jones was power-mad, a threat to the Clash, and temporarily wins over the crowds with the Out of Control tour.

But Jones, in his new incarnation as Antony, addresses the throng with *This is Big Audio Dynamite* , which seems like something new in the shallow, novelty-obsessed 80's, and turns the tide against Strummer. Like Cassius and Brutus, allied with their army, Strummer and Rhodes march back with *Cut the Crap*, which becomes Phillipi, where Cassius and Brutus made their last stand against Antony. In Shakespeare, Brutus was haunted by Caesar's ghost before Phillipi, which is analogous to Strummer's trip to the Bahamas to try and re-recruit Jones. Like Phillipi, *This is BAD* vs. *Cut the Crap* was a rout in the marketplace, even though both records are eerily similar in many ways (did Rhodes have a spy in Jones' camp?)

But, let's look in history to Antony's fate. Although Antony was at first triumphant, and married both Octavia and Cleopatra, his fortunes soon turned and he was then defeated by Octavian (later Augustus) at Actium. This ignoble defeat recalls *F-Punk*, wherein Jones inexplicably decides to remake *Cut the Crap* almost exactly, from the crappy mix to the shoddy songs to the drowned out vocals to the filthy, over-distorted guitars. Antony retreated to Egypt, and Jones has retreated to London.

Antony, of course, committed suicide in Egypt, and Radioactive is having BAD commit commercial suicide by insisting on a UK-only release for his new record. History repeats...

JOE STRUMMER-CELTIC SHAMAN?
Originally posted 9/16/97

When I read the new GQ article on Joe, I was struck by a certain passage. Bill Flanagan mentioned how he sent a writer off to interview Joe. The writer came back with tales of Joe leading a midnight dance about a fire at the WOMAD festival and other strange behavior. Reading this passage, I experienced one of those 'A-ha' moments when a long-held theory crystallizes, namely my theory of Strummer as shaman. I understood why the Clash were so powerful in their time and why Joe has been so unable to get his act together since. I also realized Joe's numerous affinities with Johnny Rotten.

Both Rotten and Strummer share common traits. Both are of Celtic extraction, and both came of age at the end of the 'Swinging London' era of the 60's and the beginning of the Great English Malaise of the 70's. And both were shamans, not in the puerile, neo-Pagan sense, but in the eternal archetypal sense. Both were possessed of a burning charisma that made one overlook their glaring musical inadequacies. Both embraced the shamanic tradition of Reggae in reaction to the suffocating conformity of late 70's Corporate Rock.

Joe was perceived as the leader of the Clash even though Mick held the reins in between Bernie's stints as capo. But Joe was what made the Clash unique. In pursuit of his elusive 'X-Factor' or Ultimate Wipeout', Joe would inspire an atavistic frenzy in audiences. Like Rotten, he sought chaos, even

though chaos never fit into his public philosophy. Joe loved violence and romanticized it. In a classic case of Freudian approach-avoidance syndrome, he gave lip-service to anti-violence, but this was nonsense. The very name 'the Clash' implies violence. This may also explain why Mick was sacked. It was very difficult for a million-selling pop act to appear controversial. The contrived 'militant' theatrics of the Us Festival proved this. The Clash seemed like petulant brats, not revolutionaries. There is a limit to shamanic power, and it's hard to inspire your audience into a frenzy when you appear as a dot on a distance stage, or an image on a 50 ft. video screen.

When Joe spoke of that elusive X-Factor, he was referring to transcendence, to ecstasy. His garbled attempt to explain the 'burn' on the MTV documentary made this clear. He blamed the rupture of the chemistry, but the real problem was scale. The Clash were playing larger and larger halls and festivals. You can't 'burn' when the crowd is peppered with curious dilettantes and uncommitted believers. The Clash were not about Rock and Roll, they were about ritual, in actuality the Pre-Christian shamanic rites of violent ecstasy.

JOE AND THE PROCESS OF REINVENTION
Originally posted 9/16/97

Since Joe was so much the real essence of what made the Clash distinctive and powerful, reinvention has been a daunting task. Part of this dilemma stems from the fact that Joe is now seen as the Clash, seen as the personification of the Clash. This must be frustrating for Joe, considering the fact that in his time in the Clash he was never in control. Rather, he was subject to the often inscrutable whims of both Mick Jones and Bernie Rhodes, and subject to the entropy and disorganization that typified the Clash. The Clash seemed to be constantly on the brink of disaster when they strode the Earth, and to remain to be chained to the Clash is to still be subject to that almost metaphysical disorder.

I believe that Joe is not really a Punk, but a sort of Beatnik/Hippie. He has no time for any of the crassness and artifice that typify Punk. Joe himself is painfully earnest, hopeful, genuine to a fault, idealist, Romantic. Joe's favorite hang-out is the annual WOMAD festival, the annual 'World Music' Mecca for British Crusties, Hippies, radicals and dreamers. Jah Wobble also hangs out there. Wobble, one of the very first British Punks, is no longer the knife-wielding, junkie thug of the Punk days, but a blissed-out, visionary, World Music mystic.

I think that musically Joe has a clear sense of where he is personally, but still doesn't have a sense of where he is in the public eye. A good example of this is the 'Generations' track. Here you have a Punk compilation with one-trick ponies like Green Day and Pansy Division and Pennywise, and Joe assembles a 'Punk supergroup' with himself, the bassist from the Ruts, and the drummer from the Damned. And what do they record? A Calypso track strongly reminiscent of *Combat Rock* out-takes 'Kill Time' and 'Beautiful People'. Nothing wrong with that - in fact it's a killer tune - but I bet there are a bunch of little Punks out there scratching their heads at it.

Punk has become a religion, as dogmatic as any other Fundamentalism. When people put on a Punk record, they know what they are supposed to expect. And with the avalanche of Ska-Punk taking the Fundamentalism into other musical territories, the infection is spreading. And since the revisionism has cast the Clash as the 'Punk Gods' (who just happened to make all those other non-Punk records, but forget them, right?), people are naturally going to expect Joe -the Clash - to make Punk records, something he is not interested in doing. In fact, for all the Punk posturing of the '84 Clash, Joe only wrote a couple tracks for them you could really call Punk Rock, most of the others were Punkabilly, Punk Reggae, Punk Funk, etc.

Joe is something more primal and more resonant than a Punk - he is a genuine shaman. In his finest moments, Joe acted to pull himself and the audience into a purer dimension, an ecstasy that healed. For all the anger and aggression of a Clash concert, fans would leave feeling happy and relieved. This is the result of catharsis and ecstatic transcendence. The shamanic tradition is old as Man. Ever since people started banging on logs and bellowing about the hunt, we have had shamans. The shaman is usually a troubled visionary, who uses his pain and takes on the pain of others and releases it in ritual settings. Look at the best Clash footage -you see Joe as a man possessed, out of his head, using his shamanic power to deliver the young, frustrated audiences from a place of vulnerability to a place of power. The closest parallel I can think of for what Joe at his best could do is Jim Morrison. At his best, Morrison would transform concerts into atavistic rituals that would transcend their settings. To see Jim Morrison at his best is to see a man possessed. You see this also with Jimi Hendrix. This comes from the Blues tradition. Hollering, broken men singing sad songs that made their audiences feel better. You see this also with reggae elder statesmen like Prince Far I and Burning Spear.

Unlike Jim and Jimi, I think (I hope) that Joe has not dispersed his shamanic power by burying it with drugs. And I also think that if Joe can realize his power, we may be at the cusp of a new era of Joe Strummer. Joe was born to be 45. Unlike the wizened, Dr. Phibes lookalikes in the Rolling Stones, Joe still looks like a guy who can rock with some credibility. And he has always sought to write songs that are timeless, and always sought to model his career after legends like BB King. Will he be able to pull it off? Time will tell.

JOE'S MID TERM REPORT CARD
Originally posted 1/10/97

Now that Joe is about to break his nearly eight year silence, I thought it was an appropriate time to review the solo work he has done to date. Since there is so little of it, it is a relatively easy task. We'll do this in chronological order.

Love Kills - I don't like this song much. It sounds very clunky and awkward, and I think the lyrics really suck and have nothing to do with Sid Vicious. This is for all intents and purposes a Clash song, however, since it was written, produced and performed by Jones and Strummer, but the Clash made bad songs sometimes, too. **(C)**

DumDum Club- This song is a lot more interesting than 'Love Kills', and is also a Clash song of sorts. The lyrics are very "*Combat Rock*," as is the music. But still, I think it's just an average song in this incarnation. It was a hell of a lot more exciting when I saw Joe perform it live at the Palladium in '89, when it was one of the evening's highlights. **(B-)**

Evil Darling (*Straight to Hell*) - Interesting to listen to, but not much of a tune. Of course, I don't really expect much from a *Straight to Hell* track since the movie itself is a joke. **(C+)**

Ambush at Hanging Rock (*STH*)-Ennio Morricone punk. Driving rhythm and all, but again, this sounds like Joe made it up as he went along. **(C)**

WALKER **soundtrack** - This is one of my favorite records of all time, and it was one of the few records that redeemed the otherwise dismal year of 1987. A track-by-track evaluation would be pointless, since the record really stands as a single piece of work. The first side is steamy Latin Jazz a la Joe, expertly embellished by top-flight musicians. The second side is Folk and Bluegrass with three great songs sung by Joe, including 'Tennessee Rain', a song that you would swear is an old standard written by Steven Foster or someone. For an artist to go from barnstorming Punk to this in the space of two years is really an remarkable achievement. Of course, this record was completely ignored, in large part because the film was such a bomb. (**A+**)

PERMANENT RECORD **soundtrack** - Joe recorded 12 songs for this film, but only five were used, probably because he was still in Latin Rockabilly mode. Which was fine, but wholly inappropriate to this Keanu Reeves vehicle. One of the out-takes, 'Cholo Vest' showed up on the Island Hopping 12". The music is very retro and has a nice raw, warm production. (**B**)

(Note: the other 7 tracks have recently surfaced and are nothing to write home about.)

Trash City - Basically a one-riff wonder, with Joe spouting the nonsense lyrics he was so enamored of in the late 80's. It's a bad single, but effective in the context of the record. The one thing that is good about this track is the very Clash-like sound. Warm, raw and atmospheric, with great trash can percussion. (**B-**)
Baby the Trans - Great Strummabilly number. A hook to end all hooks, and hilarious backup vocals. The nonsense lyrics work for this song, and the guitar work is great. (**A**)
Neferitti Rock - OK song, but again, the five songs listened to together are much more than the sum of their parts. Sounds like a 101'ers out-take. (**B-**)
Nothing about Nothing - Trademark quarter-note Strummer rhythm, and a nice chorus. Seems to be the track where Joe gets the gets the biggest head of steam going. Very Clash-like. (**B**)
Theme from Permanent Record - Very simple but effective instrumental, with some nice work by Schloss. When I saw the movie in an empty theater, I was impressed by the foreboding aura the song lent to the film. (**B**)

Burning Lights/Afro Cuban Be Bop - Taken from the film *So I Hired a Contact Killer*, these two cuts are reminiscent of Bruce Springsteen's Nebraska album. Joe accompanies himself on guitar and an uncredited bongo player bongs along. Both songs are solid Strummer tunes, but are also impossibly sad. (**B+**)

GANGSTERVILLE 12"- When I got home and slapped this record on, it gave me exactly the same thrill a new Clash record did in the old days. It's a shame the album wasn't as good (but believe me, mister, I listened to that plenty when it came out. I remember when I saw Joe at City Gardens, Jack Irons kept staring at me in amazement because I knew all the words to the new songs). I will stick my neck out and say that these four songs are as good as most Clash tunes. (**A**)

Gangsterville - Zydeco rock with a Reggae bridge and a Carousel solo. The lyrics are iffy, but the playing is zealous, and Joe's vocals are top-drawer. Great song to jump around to. This was great live and the Palladium when it was played double-time. (**A**)
Jewelers and Bums- Again, iffy lyrics, but this track was the most Clash-like number on *Earthquake Weather*. Great power chord riff, really good chorus, great playing, good production. (**A**)
Punk Rock Blues - Which, of course, is a Country track. This should have been on the record, since it is immeasurably superior to a lot of cuts, not the least of

which is 'Boogie with your Children'. Beautiful guitar, crystalline production, great melody, and surprise, surprise, good lyrics. Would have been a classic if it was on a Clash record. (**A+**)

Don't Tango with Django - You know, Joe has put out a few clunkers in his day, but the man can then turn around a put out an instant classic. 'Don't Tango with Django' is an absolute masterpiece. The sound is warm, rich and clear, with guitars ringing like bells. When you hear this track you cant believe it wasn't a Ventures or Shadows standard. (**A+**)

EARTHQUAKE WEATHER

The only solo album to date by Joe Strummer was released nearly eight years ago. Joe had stated in some interviews that he did it because he was 'skint'. Maybe this was a defensive reaction to the cool reception it received. The main problem with this record is that the lyrics just seem like throwaways, after-thoughts. And often they are so badly written that they tarnish the very well-constructed music that accompanies them. Joe was bumming around LA at the time, and probably didn't have much on his mind, so he kind of just rambles on. Zander Schloss is an extraordinarily accomplished guitarist, but a lot of folks didn't think his playing was appropriate. The bass playing is underwhelming, a totally incongruous slap-style that farts along regardless of the style of the actual song. The drumming is fairly hot, provided by Latino-Rockabilly War drummer Willy McNeil and present Pearl Jam drummer Jack Irons.

The album bombed big, partly due to Epic's utter lack of promotion and partly due to it's inappropriateness to the contemporary music scene of 1989. Epic then put the kibosh on Joe's follow-up and told him not to bother making any more records, because they wouldn't release them. Mick was CBS' boy after the Clash broke up, and was the recipient of enormous amounts of money for promotion, videos, and advertising (including TV ads)— money which, unfortunately, never translated into the big sales CBS obviously had in mind.

Gangsterville - Joe is trying to make a statement equating corporate and criminal behavior (a la 'Midnight Log') but can't seem to get his point across. The music is still great, however.
Lyrics: **C** Song: **A**

King of the Bayou - More beatnik stream of consciousness - as if this record needed more. Understanding the lyrics is as frustrating as trying to read Kerouac's later material, and the meter is all over the map. Energetic playing is further hampered by prosaic chord sequence.
Lyrics: **C** Song: **B-**

Island Hopping - I think these are the only cogent lyrics on the record. Strongly reminiscent of the second side of *Walker*, musically speaking. This was a single, but really shouldn't have been.
Lyrics: **B** Song: **A**

Slant Six - Clash-style rocker with nice slide work by Zander. Nice meaty riff, energetic guitar work by Joe,and halfway decent lyrics.
Lyrics: **B** Song: **A**

Dizzy's Goatee - Horrible title, like many other tracks on this record. Is it just me, or does this song sound a lot like Dire Straits? Moody and cinematic, but hobbled by lyrics that don't seem to be about anything. ("Headlights and sluice"?)
Lyrics: **D** Song: **B-**

Shouting Street - Clash III leftover. This track should have been the leadoff single. Great Beatle-esque melody, great riff, great guitar playing. But again, what's this song about?
Lyrics: **B-** Song: **A+**

Boogie with your Children - Awful, awful song. Up there with 'Cool Confusion' and 'I Turned Out a Punk' as the absolute worst Clash-related song ever.
Lyrics: **F** Song: **F-**

Leopardskin Limousines - This one goes in the 'good idea, but...' file. Joe's piano playing seems to defy all logic and meter, and Zander adds some nice guitar accents. But, the lyrics? Don't ask.
Lyrics: **C** Song: **B+**

Sikorsky Parts - Nice funk vamp, smoking Jeff Beck-style guitar work, and I am no longer going to comment on the lyrics. (*"Doing a dance called the Robocop/This gesture means I love you"*)
Lyrics: **D** Song: **B**

Jewelers and Bums - See earlier review.

Highway One Zero Street - Very Seventies sounding, almost like a BTO track. Typical Joe tempo changes and dynamics. Good to drive to.
Lyrics: **C-** Song: **B+**

Ride Your Donkey - Great Reggae cover, fantastic guitar work, lots of fun all around.
Song: **A**

Passport to Detroit - Quintessential Joe track, with the stabbing quarter-note rhythm that dates back to 'London Calling' and 'Know Your Rights'. Would be a classic if it had proper lyrics.
Lyrics: **C+** Song: **A**

Sleepwalk - Beautiful melody, very wistful. Zander contributes some wonderful Latin accents , and the band rises to the occasion. Good one, Joe.
Song: **A**

A METHOD TO HIS MADNESS?
Originally posted 12/18/97

Back on the 'Why doesn't Joe release anything anymore' tip, I had another interesting thought. I buy lots of records and used to go to concerts. There are plenty of records that I like and plenty of bands that I like quite a bit. But nothing that really lights me up. I went Christmas shopping last night at Borders and I thought, Jesus, there's just too much of everything. Everything is too available. You can get box-sets and reissues of everything. Any band that lasted more than a couple of years has tons of product that you can find easily enough. We live in an age of constant media bombardment. The Internet makes information cheap and available, but it also cheapens information. Nobody is really excited about anything. Back in the days of Elvis, kids were so electrified by Rock and Roll that adults thought that they would be rioting in the streets. Can you imagine that now? I went to see Nirvana in 1994, and kids were milling around, chatting in the hallways, looking bored while the band played. The mosh pit started off strong and steadily shrunk as the concert went on.

Ten years earlier, I saw the Clash and kids were tearing up seats, taking pot shots at bouncers, and rushing the stage to the point that the concert was stopped before the last encore. The minute the first chord was struck, kids were on their feet and didn't sit down until they were back in their cars. If the Clash had played 'White Riot' there probably wouldn't have been a Providence Civic Center left.

All across the land, has-been New Wavers try to resurrect their careers, using the most sophisticated graphic artists and promotional people to make them seem relevant again. Alas, to no avail. Ten years ago, David Byrne was on the cover of *Time* magazine. But his latest album went nowhere near the Top 100. Ads were placed on MTV, in magazines, puff pieces were done in Rock rags, all for nothing. The Cure are on tour this year. Did you realize that? Seven years ago, they played Giants Stadium. This year, they played Irving Plaza, a 1000 capacity club. Duran Duran can't get arrested. One-time superstar Michael Hutchence was reportedly so distraught over his band's slide that he hung himself. Why is all this happening?

Audiences are fickle. They make you a star and then spit you out. Critics are even worse. They are so busy taking their own temperatures and trying to impress each other, that most of them have no idea what to write anymore. Joe got a full dose of this disease in the Clash. From '79 on he was attacked constantly by the press for not staying true to Punk (contrary to popular opinion, the Clash were not 'press darlings' in the 80's). He couldn't open a paper without being attacked for not making Punk records anymore (nobody usually thought to blame Mick, who had complete control over the recording and composition process. Joe was mistakenly perceived as the leader of the Clash). So Joe reforms the band, plays Punk songs and is then attacked for being too Retro! The critics never took into account that the kids loved every minute of it.

In any event, people's attachment to Pop Stars is a lot like a schoolboy crush. We love these stars who seem so above us, so beyond us. If only they would notice us! If only we could possess them or a piece of them. But just like a schoolboy when he finds out that that girl likes him back, when these stars become too available, too ubiquitous, we don't want them anymore. Today, celebrities are our stand-ins for deities. If they come down to our level, they can't be any good, can they? It's the sense of distance, the sense of unavailability that makes them so god-like to us.

Joe has been unavailable to us for this entire decade. This year he bombarded us with three songs, that you had to pay 40 dollars for three different records if you wanted to hear them. He teases us by dropping hints of various projects. They usually don't materialize. But in all fairness, it's not always his fault. For instance, Joe put together a little band purely to record some tracks for *Grosse Pointe Blank* and *Generations*, and the story goes out that Joe is ready to reemerge with a new band. Joe's fault in this is that he communicates this stuff badly, and is in need of a PR person. But in the event that Joe decides to release something, this newsgroup will become electrified like it was 1980 all over again. The Clash blew everyone away in the old days, because they were something so different, so novel, so unavailable. They weren't like everything else the corporations were shoving down our throats. Today, there is really nothing Joe could do musically that would have that impact. Everyone has heard everything all before. But what he will have as his ace in the hole is himself.

Critics and know-nothings were rabid and relentless in their campaign to blame everything that was wrong with the Clash on Joe. Part of this was poetic justice, because Joe was so nasty and unfair in his attacks on Mick in '84, but none of Joe's mea culpas or explanations of what went wrong with Clash II were given as wide a airing as Joe's mistakes. Joe became the scapegoat for everything that went wrong with the Clash and Punk Rock. Joe was blamed for *Cut the Crap*, a record whose perceived evils were wildly inflated in this drive to attack Joe personally, although the record was the handiwork of Bernie Rhodes. His record company gave up on him in 1983 and made no secret of it. But I think the tide is turning. Lots of kids are discovering the Clash today, kids who aren't concerned with the ideological battles or the progressivist pretensions of the past. They just want to hear the music. There are plenty of websites out there that tell the whole story of the Clash, not just the Joe-haters version. Even Marcus Gray's book manages to tell a qualified version of the truth of Joe's role in the Clash. Mick has shown for 12 years now that he was serious about moving beyond the Clash and Punk for good. And Joe has begun to reinvent himself in the UK, as a Rock and Roll wise man. If my theory is correct, that Joe has been loathe to re-emerge because of the crap he has suffered from morons for his supposed sins in the Clash, perhaps the forecast is beginning to clear for a Joe comeback.

"INTERVIEW" WITH JOE STRUMMER

In the late 90's, Joe Strummer had not only not released several projects that had been announced (including a Clash reunion album) he had taken to spending most of his time in the company of London scenesters, the most egregious being the insanely talentless Shaun Ryder. This was like rubbing salt in my wounds. I am hard pressed to name an artist as completely devoid of natural talent than Ryder. We're talking a Shaggs level of untalent. Ryder is certainly the least talented musician in history to reach his level of success. To see Joe following this man around like a groupie was tantamount to Prince bumming around with Wesley Willis. Maybe he did it simply for the drugs. In any event, I was so disgusted with this (at that this point I was extremely disgusted with Joe in general) that I wrote this little satire...

Q: So, Joe, what have you been up to lately?
Joe Strummer: Well, I have been keeping busy looking after Shaun. Doing His laundry, darning His socks, backrubs when He's stressed out, you know. It's a full-time job in it's own right.
Q: We've been seeing you in the press a lot.
JS: Well, only if Shaun says it's all right. We did the *Raygun* interview, little bits here and there. Shaun only allows me to be interviewed or photographed if it's backstage at a Black Grape show. And whatever Shaun says goes, to

paraphrase one of my old numbers.

Q: What about your Strummerville record?

JS: Oh, that. Well, Shaun thought it would compete with the Black Grape record so He told me to can it. However, He is letting me do a number with him for the English football team, and maybe He'll let me play maracas or tambourine on his next record if He doesn't OD before then.

Q: What about the Clash reunion?

JS: What? Are you kidding? Shaun would never approve of that! Besides, as I have said, we'll only do it if Topper does it!

Q: But Topper doesn't even have a drum kit. And he'd never make it into the States with his prison record.

JS: (blank stare)

Q: Alright, let's change the subject. You played piano on a Levellers record and then you wrote some songs on a Brian Setzer album.

JS: Yeah, but Shaun told me I was overexposing myself and He had Brian take most of the songs off his record.

Q: (sarcastically) Boy, don't burn yourself out.

JS: (oblivious) Yes, aren't I wonderful? I need a bit of a rest.

Q: So, what's next for Joe Strummer?

JS: Well, Shaun gave me a to-do list for today. He wants me to fetch him some fish and chips, and a six pack of Newcastle. Then, I have to pick up His methadone from the clinic. Then, He wants me to tidy up his flat, which is a real chore because He is such a slob!

Q: Why do you keep referring to Shaun as 'Him'. Isn't that a designation reserved for Jesus Christ?

JS: Oh, don't be silly! Shaun is much more important than Jesus!

THE COMEBACK

Originally posted July 1, 1999

Never in the darkest days of my Strummer withdrawal could I have imagined a night like Wednesday. For a man who spends a lot of time pining for the good old days I certainly got a nice taste of them, and on the day before my 33rd birthday to boot! Let me start from the beginning...

By phone and e-mail we agreed to convene at Pete's Tavern on Irving Place, the 'oldest bar in Manhattan'. An appropriate venue for a night so fraught with the weight of history. I got there and only Magnificent Matt Baier was there. We sat down at the bar and unloaded our weekly woes and started the flow of cold beer into our gullets. Next in was the enchanting Elgrrl, aka Eleanor, who introduced herself and immediately seemed like an old friend. She regaled Matt and I with tales of New York City in the glory days of Rock. Her devotion to the Clash was truly extraordinary. Then came in Bob Fitz, all smiles and handshakes. The trickle turned into a flood as Showdown loyalist Alex Casti (aka 'Johnny Rock and Roll') arrived, then my bud BJ and his homeboy Gary, and finally my boy Jeff brought his pals, Lance and Thomas. Copious amounts of alcohol were then consumed and stories of shared obsession with the only band that matters were flying about, followed by a painful shout-along of the first few stanzas of 'White Man in Hammersmith Palais'. Other diehards were attracted to this gathering like moths to the flame, and the excitement level built as showtime approached. We bathed that place in the warm glow of fellowship and fidelity to a Great Lost Cause - the tragic heroes known as the Clash.

We marched to Irving Plaza like Vandals towards the gates of Rome, and then split as half the contingent craved victuals. Like the Donner Party, we wandered aimlessly in search of manna, finally discovering a deli on Third Ave. where my mates were treated to a Knowlesian display of drunken obnoxiety. Having satiated their hunger pangs, the lads followed Matthew and I to our hour of destiny, like flagellants to Fatima. Outside the venue we met a poor soul who resembled Clint Howard, whom I accosted, reminding all and sundry that Ron Howard had hosted *SNL* the night of the Clash's appearance. The chap must get this a lot and he brusquely stated that yes, he was in fact Clint Howard. For those of you wanting to know how packed this show was - outside, scalpers were *asking* people for tickets!

We then made our way into the venue, which that night was a cathedral, opening its bosom to the long suffering faithful. Instantly, I was reminded of my first live encounter with the Clash, at the Boston Orpheum (or temple of Orpheus, the Greek god of music). The Orpheum, like Irving Plaza, is a grand old theater converted to a temple of Rock. I inhaled deeply to soak in the vibes, letting the precious nostalgia flow in like nectar. Then we stampeded like wild boar to the main hall. Tasty sounds of Jamaica thundered in the background. Being in a stand up venue such as that reminded me of the show at the Cape Cod Colisseum, where I met my high school girlfriend. The ale acted like an Alchemists solvent, helping to summon great moments from the from the calcified depths of my memory.

Soon the Slackers stormed onstage. There were about of thousand of them , and they serenaded the few who had sauntered in from the city's publick houses with sounds of the Isles, in this case, the isles of Jamaica, Brittania, and New Amsterdam. We wondered if someone was actually playing a record and the Slackers were not miming to it, a la Milli Vanilli. That is to say, they were tighter than an Olsen twin. The '82 vibe was sustained, as I remembered that the great Boston Ska band, 007, opened for the Clash at Hyannis. And of course, every single little recollection was shouted in the ears of all my companions. Being in the throes of Dionysius as we were, the lads and I decided to dance heartily to the troubadours' sounds, which surely the surrounding patrons confused with the spastic lurchings of the demonically possessed, and they therefore gazed upon us with a mixture of pity and terror. After the Slackers long outwore their welcome, a motion picture screen descended from the ceiling and various roadies scurried about, preparing the dais for the event of the year.

The house lights went down and a veritable army of Britishers took the stage. The man walked to center stage and the hall erupted in the type of cheering that only those who have been deprived of their hero for many years can muster.

I instantly got a flash of the grand days of 1984 as I saw that four man - three guitars and bass -front line. The band was tight and the new songs played were very lively. The scene was set and I am afraid that the recurrent events are a bit of a blur. Let me paint in broader strokes. I shall reconstruct the show using the set list, courtesy of Eleanor, with some minor revisions by yours truly...

<u>**Diggin' the New**</u> - This tune was mid-tempo with a strong Carib feel. Unfortunately, the sound was not great, but the crowd gave not a whit. I don't remember much about this tune, as I hadn't sweat out the alcohol yet, but I do remember liking it.

<u>**London Calling**</u> - Joe started this off with his guitar, which sounds as crummy as ever. The band was extraordinarily tight and the new drummer is yet another one in a long line of Clash/Joe drummers who play nothing like Topper Headon. That is to say the beat was hard and solid. Joe then introduced the band, all of whom are young Britons, and mostly not from London. No chops fiends from Orange County or schmucky studio hacks from Culver City were to be found onstage. All of Manhattan breathed a sigh of relief. Joe's band intros brought me back to 1984, especially when he introduced Pablo Cook 'on the back of the kit.' Pablo is surely actually named Paul, but one drumming Paul Cook was apparently enough in Joe's eyes.

Next up-

<u>**X-Ray Style**</u>- This was a slow brooding number that Joe stopped midway to indulge in a rant about Guiliani's New York. After Joe let some steam (inspired by a sleepless night of visa troubles at JFK), the tune began and Joe wailed and mourned this number, which blended old Rock and Roll with island rhythms. Very tasty indeed.

<u>**White Man In Hammersmith Palais**</u> - Joe surprised everyone by starting this tune without the crashing intro, instead lurching in the first verse straightaway. Instantly every voice in the hall rose up to accompany him. It was an awe-inspiring moment. And as an added bonus, Joe remembered all the words to this and all the other Clash songs. Dark whispers of senility instantly dissipated.

<u>**Tony Adams**</u>- I love this new tune. Firmly in the camp of Clash-style Hard Reggae, this number was presaged by a Joe-rant about soccer. The audience was implored to shout out 'Chelsea, Chelsea' in honor of Joe's beloved footballers. Lost on the crowd was the fact that Tony Adams plays for Arsenal. A top-flight song.

Somewhere during the set, Joe was threatening to punch someone down front in the mouth. Don't know what presaged this little outburst, but I got a kick out of it.Hopefully, it was a Rock critic. Feisty as ever, that Joe is. The main problem with the show was the mix. The guitars, which according to Showdown sources were crisp and crunchy in Washington, were hard to hear both with Joe and with the opening band.

<u>Straight To Hell</u>- Another perfect rendition that went on a long time as Joe ad-libbed over the outro, impressing upon the audience the virtue of walking your talk. Again the audience sang every word. Newcomer Anthony Genn played some very Mick Jones circa-1982-like guitar.

<u>Rock the Casbah</u>- The low point of the night. No one seemed to be too excited about playing this hoary old chestnut and no one seemed too excited to hear it either. The band seemed to sense the audience's lack of enthusiasm and it was quickly dispatched. It was dedicated to Topper as has been Joe's wont on this tour. Touching and ironic, both at the same time.

<u>Yalla Yalla</u>- Here's where it got interesting. I loved this song and couldn't believe how cool it was. Kind of like Joe singing on an old PiL track. Very hypnotic, very intense. The PA problems were addressed during this song and the room was instantly by an impossibly deep dub bassline.

<u>Brand New Cadillac</u>- Joe introduced this as one of two great British Rock and Roll songs. The other was 'Hippy-Hippy Shakes.' Never one of my favorites, 'Cadillac' was nonetheless played very well.

<u>I Fought the Law</u>- Another tune the Clash made their own. A solid rendition, but I would have preferred this Clash slot to be filled by a Strummer/Jones tune. But the crowd sure loved it. Not everyone lives with this stuff like I do, so no one quibbled.

1st Encore:

<u>Techno D-Day</u>- This tune was introduced with a Joe-Rant about a police crackdown on a rave he was DJ ing at Omaha Beach in France. Brilliant, punny title and a nice, tough World-Punker .

<u>Forbidden City</u>- Very tuneful mid-tempo rocker inspired by the Tienammen Square massacre. Strongly in the mold of Joe's better ballads, this tune was dedicated to those resisting tyranny in China and Tibet. Earlier Joe gave shouts to the Beastie Boys, who were in the house copping ideas for their next record.

<u>Bankrobber</u>- Another crowd singalong. Lots of fun. Great version. Great idea for Joe to hook in Martin Slattery who plays a mean keyboard, as well as guitar and wailing sax. MVP of the Mescaleros.

2nd Encore:

<u>Junco Partner</u>- Joe played this solo for the first few verses and did it 101'ers style, not in the Clash Reggae style. Another Clash cover, just like in '89. Again, I would have preferred another Strummer/Jones composition, but this was not a night for hair-splitting.

<u>Tommy Gun</u>- The grand finale. The sound problems of earlier in the night were solved as if by magic and all three guitars were crisp and crunchy. The version was letter perfect and was the perfect release of energy after a set of slower material.

So what does this all mean? Ironies abounded. All I could think was that Joe was calling this band 'Mescaleros' because it was Spanish for 'Clash 3'. That's really what it is. Joe's doing late-Clash music his way, with big guitars and drums. But this is fitting because despite Joe's old protestations, he was the eclecticist in the Clash. It was Joe who was fixated on Caribbean sounds and genre-hopping, a fact made plain in his subsequent solo work. He seems to want to 'boil it down to one music' with this new outfit, and the augurs are encouraging thus far. I am personally taking this one step at a time, because I know all too well what its like to have high hopes dashed. But Joe looks great, and is in fine form. Soon enough the tapes will start circulating, so all of you who didn't get a chance to see him can at least get a chance to hear him. And for those who missed him, Joe will probably mount a full-scale tour when the record is released. I still pine for that great Joe Strummer record and maybe it's on its way.

JOE IN NEW YORK AND PHILADELPHIA
Originally posted November 28th, 1999

The night started as it should have, with a good meal at a Thai restaurant on 56th street. Midtown was hopping with a panoply of humanity which just enhanced the festive vibe of the evening. Then we hopped into a Mexican bar for a couple of Coronas, further enhancing the multi-culti vibe of the evening. After the last sip had been taken, we ventured forth to Roseland, an old ballroom from the Big Band days. Then I met up up with Matt 'Hairboy' Baier, BJ 'the Bear' Casey and two of his homeboys. Hairboy told me Elgrrrl was up front but a search for her was unsuccessful. The Pietasters were running through their 9th generation Bosstones clonery and I instantly missed the Slackers.

After an eternity, they left the stage and the heavy, heavy Dub kicked in. I was playing 'Stump BJ' as each track began, and he held his own. Joe's sound guy came up to me and complimented me on my 101'ers shirt in a nearly indecipherable Cockney brogue. We watched as the HBO guys got everything ready for the *Reverb* taping. And then that crazy Afro-Creole jam kicked in and I sped up to as close to the front as I could get. The Meskies took the stage and the show began....

DIGGIN' THE NEW- Nice version, the guitars were pumped and primed at Roseland that night. Joe was very animated but not as chatty as he's been on other dates. Unfortunately, like for most of the other non-Clash tunes, no one seemed to be familiar with this great track. 95% of the crowd was there for Clash songs and merely listened politely as Joe aired his solo stuff.

NOTHING 'BOUT NOTHING- Nice old chestnut that also fell on deaf ears. Good version though, it brought back memories of Latino Rockabilly shows. But when will Joe realize that 'Baby the Trans' is the best song off of *Permanent Record*? The Mescaleros were certainly more high-impact for this show then they were at Irving Plaza.

X-RAY STYLE- Joe didn't seem to be too enthusiastic on this tune. The crowd didn't want to hear it either. This is a great tune for a small club, but not for a big venue like Roseland. It just got lost.

ROCK THE CASBAH- Another perfunctory playing, but it got folks moving. Smiley doesn't groove on this track and the tempo lagged a bit. But at least it woke up the punters.

ISHEN - This was a fantastic version of a not-very fantastic song. This was the Mescaleros at their best, and Genn weighed in some very tasty dubbed-out guitar noise. Genn is a great keyboardist, but hasn't found his voice on the guitar. But on the Ragga jams, his impressionist licks really added a nice atmosphere.

BRAND NEW CADILLAC - Again, a perfunctory Clash run-through that got people moving. I guess Joe really loves this song, but the Mesc's don't know what to do with it. Slattery tried some lead work that fell flat. Why not come in with a smoking sax solo? That would have driven people nuts.

TONY ADAMS - Great, tough version of this great track. Nice long jam which points to an exciting territory for this band to explore. The Mescaleros are a Reggae band, not a Rock band. I loved the extended jam session, even if some of the folks around me didn't.

TRASH CITY - This tune kicked in with some serious guitar firepower, which made the monotonous riff a lot more palatable. It also was the first non-Clash number to get the junior high crowd up front moving and shaking. I was dreading hearing this track since it fell flat during the '89 shows, but it seriously rocked here.

NITCOMB - This song doesn't work live at all for me. But it demonstrated that Pablo is a much more interesting drummer than Smiley. The Brit-Pop vibe of this X-Ray style gem 'clashed' with the Rootsier sound of the songs around it. Great album track, weak live number.

ROAD TO ROCK & ROLL - Another clunker for me. Not dynamic enough for a live number. This kind of trotted along with almost zero reaction from the crowd.

WHITE MAN IN HAMMERSMITH PALAIS - This track got off to a strong but ultimately false start. Joe was complaining about something or someone who was throwing off his meter and they started it from the top. Then Joe was trying to rescue some crowd surfers from security and left the Mesc's to sing the final verse. The crowd didn't care and the band sounded great. I got a laugh as Joe started ranting on about crowd surfing being banned. It added to the anarchic vibe of the second half of the show.

SAFE EUROPEAN HOME - Then they blasted into this number and all of sudden I was fourteen again. Reserves of energy I didn't know I had animated my poor old frame. A real smoker, even if Genn and Slattery lacked that full-on Clash firepower.

YALLA YALLA - Another tune that showed the Mescaleros in their element. Genn dropped some outrageous dub noise of this track and the bassline was shaking the walls. Again the live playing of this track leaves the album version in the dust. Only live does the true magnificence of this number reveal itself.

RUDIE CAN'T FAIL - Nice playing of this great old tune, but it missed Slattery on the organ. Any tune with any Jamaica in it at all needs Martin tickling the keys.

LONDON CALLING - This tune has picked up since the Spring shows. Slattery weighed in with some Jonesian riffs and the run-through wasn't the wan retread I expected.

PRESSURE DROP - Same deal with Rudy, definitely a nod to the neo-Ska fans in the crowd. I think Joe was more of a Ska fan than was Mick, which probably explains why the Clash dropped the form after *LC* and why Joe recorded two Ska tracks with Clash II.

TOMMY GUN - Nice end to the set, but made me yearn for the Clash II bullet train version of this tune. As good as this playing was, you can't help but notice how much the band needs a real guitarist.

TECHNO D-DAY - This was the first tune of the encore and it started with a very tasty Afro-Cuban percussion jam. Very rocking version of a tune no one watching seemed to know.

STRAIGHT TO HELL - They played this slower than usual and longer. There was a tremendous extended power chord and percussion jam at the coda that was something to behold. This song was made for the stage. I have heard very few playings of this track that weren't great.

I FOUGHT THE LAW - They brought the fireworks in for the intro and then played the tune almost Ska style. Again, not my first choice but it rocked and got the people moving.

BANKROBBER - Another great Mescalero playing of this tune. It's funny because I always saw this as somewhat of a set-killer back in the Clash days, but the more authentic Ragga sound gives it more of a punch. Slattery impressed again on keys.

At this point in the show Joe held up his fingers in a 'W' formation and I knew that 'White Riot' was next. I started yelling to everyone around they were going to play 'White Riot' next and I was greeted with blank stares. But of course they then blasted into...

WHITE RIOT - They obviously just picked this track up. There were mistakes galore, but no one cared. It was just the palette cleanser needed to end the show. Everyone went nuts and no one noticed the innumerable fuckups. Great way to end the night.

Well, I got home at about 3 am and needless to say I was trashed the next day. I signed on only to read a missive from Clash priestess Elgrrrl. She hooked me up with Clash fan supreme John T. who had traveled from sunny San Diego to catch the East Coast leg of the tour. John graciously hooked me up with a backstage pass for the Philly show. I immediately got to work and printed out transfers for the 'Joe Has Risen' and 'Joe Lays Down the Law' Showdown tees. I got them onto shirts and got ready for the show. Of course, getting ready mostly meant taking a nap. Anyhow, me and Mrs. Gnolls left the boys with a sitter and trekked down to the City of Brotherly Love. I was grooving because Philly reminded me a lot of Boston. I felt like I was heading to the Orpheum to sit down and let Joe serenade me. In any event, I got my pass and then Mrs. Gnolls and I strolled down bustling South Street. There were young hipsters and boutiques everywhere. We found a Mexican/Indian restaurant and sat down for a much-needed meal. The place was a hole in the wall, but served a heavenly Tandoori and Biryani. The two blokes in front of us were chatting and I heard a thick Liverpudlian accent. So I chatted with these other diners and it turned out they were Joe's roadies and they shared some amusing tales of the tour. They told us of a raging aftershow in NYC that lasted into the wee hours. This of course followed a near riot the night before that many lucky Bostonians will not soon forget. I felt a twinge of apprehension: will the boys be too tired to Rock?

In any event, we finished our supper and made our way to the venue, secure in the knowledge that Pietasters were safely away from our eardrums. Much to my chagrin however I soon learned that the 'Theatre of Living Arts' was no such thing, but a small, dumpy, insufferably hot standup venue. The Mrs. and I went upstairs where there were both a couple of electric fans and a wet bar. As the night proceeded it got more and more crowded and subsequently more and more stifling. It soon became apparent to me that the show was drastically oversold and the 700-capacity room was holding far more than that. All my various OCD anxieties kicked in and I kept picturing myself being trampled on or burnt alive. The TLA had a lot of strikes against it already.

Anyhow, Joe came on and began hammering out a rhythm, then began howling "Down on the corner/ End of the Railway.." and the band launched into a smashing Rocksteady jam of 'Shouting Street.' It was pure genius and set the stage for a night heavy with mellow jams. And the synchronicity of Joe chanting 'Biryani/Biryani' was not lost on me after our meal. I won't run through the setlist again but I will tell you some of the highlights, in no particular order.

'Shouting Street' was a revelation but there more to come. 'Ishen' again impressed and 'Yalla Yalla' was played as straight-out Kingston Riddim sound. Slattery played some Ragga organ on the tune that was straight out of Studio One. Later on, Joe played a jazzy jam of 'Island Hopping' with some nice piano work and twelve bar walking bass. 'Junco Partner' got a similar treatment, starting with Joe solo and joined by the Mescaleros. Joe also did some stream of consciousness ad-libs, asking the crowd for some fresh socks. Joe was in high spirits and good humor, but he was clearly ready for the tour to be over. The manic energy of the night before was gone, but Joe was more relaxed and friendly. At times, he seemed like an old Vaudevillian with a sharp tongue and quick wit and a natural stage presence. I knew Philly would be a better show musically without the cameras and Joe certainly didn't disappoint. In fact, the only setback to the show was the fact that I couldn't sit back and groove to the jams. It was definitely a easy-skanking show, except of course for the old Clash numbers. Again the tunes that fell flat the night before didn't improve all that much. All in all, it was a fun night, hampered only by the heat and the lack of a seat.

The crowd refused to leave after a stronger playing of 'White Riot' and it took awhile for the club to clear. Feet were stomped and hands were clapped in a vain effort to bring the main man back to the stage, but alas the house lights went up. Me and the Mrs. then ventured to the stage door and chatted with other diehards as the Rockers finally drifted off.

Anyhow, after an eternity we were let into the funhouse maze leading to the dressing room. After climbing several narrow staircases, we were confronted by Pablo Cook. I shook his hand complimented him on a fine performance. I then ran into the aptly-named Smiley, who spoke of the mayhem at the Boston Roxy gig. Hell of a nice guy. Various British scruffbags wandered around. Lucinda, Joe's wife came out next. She looked so damn familiar, but I couldn't place her. Two of the diehards with us told us that Lucinda gave them passes for tonight's show out of nowhere. She seemed like a sweet person and I credit her with Joe's new mindset. It seems she has been a very good influence on Joe. We spied Joe a few feet ahead and he looked very happy. I was reminded of that fabulous night in '84, and saw a bit of symmetry with those glorious days (which I won't belabor you with).

In any event, we were soon in the presence. Joe was taking some pictures with some muckety-muck's kids and he turned his attention back to the

line. He looked at me and asked me who my wife was. I introduced myself as the guy from *Clash City Showdown* and that this was my wife. This went right over Joe's head and he told me to hand beers out to the people in line in back of me. My heart sank. He then started talking to me and the Mrs. about the source for the art on the album cover, which he was wearing on his shirt. He was amazed at the figure holding up the didgeredoo, explaining that they were very heavy. He said the art was 100,000 years old. It was strange talking to Joe like he was just some guy we ran into on the street. And he looks you straight in the eye when he's talking to you, which intimidated a hopeless fan like me.

Joe turned his attention back to the kids and told one of them, "just remember if you don't want to work for a living, join a Rock and Roll band." I sensed an opening and blurted out, "or be a cartoonist!" This caught Joe's ear and he he turned to me and said "Yeah! Are you a cartoonist then?" I nodded and pulled out the shirts.

I had him! Joe immediately started laughing. He was reading the head-stones on the 'Joe has Risen' shirt and he called out "Oi Lucy, come have a look at this then!" Lucinda was downstairs and Joe turned to Antony and Shields and was showing them the shirts. He laughed out loud at the 'Billy Idol's Career' headstone. He also seemed very impressed that I had put 'Ocean of Dreams' on the tablets. I was kind of out of my body at this point, but Mrs. Gnolls tells me that Joe asked if he could keep the shirts, said he was going to frame them and put them up at the house. At one point he said he wanted to be a cartoonist, but couldn't hack it. I told him that I enjoyed the cartoons on his site and said they betrayed a bit of training and he laughed and shrugged it off.

But he couldn't take his eyes off the shirts. He asked me what I had to be signed and I gave him the Julian Yewdall book. I told him to autograph his favorite photo and he yelled out in mock protest ,"I hate them all!" He really has a quick wit. He signed the title page and then leaned over and signed my 101'ers shirt. My wife laughed and told him, "Now he can't wear that shirt anymore!" Joe returned to the T's and said, "these are really great, what can I do to repay you?" A guy in back of me shouted out, "Wear one of 'em on Conan O'Brien!" I reddened in embarrassment and laughed out "Yeah, wear one of him on Conan!" The guy in back walked up and Joe saw his '86 vintage BAD hat and Joe exclaimed 'You've got a real Roots hat there!' The guy gave it to Joe to sign, and there was a Mick autograph already. Anyhow, my fanboy instincts kicked in and I made a stupid comment about putting 'Pouring Rain' on the next album. I could tell Joe wasn't thrilled by the reference to his lost years, but politely said, "Yeah, but we'd have to give it a Hip Hop beat." He said that that was one of those songs lost in the grave. Wishing to leave before I further ruined the vibe with my OCD drooling, me and the Mrs. said our goodbyes and turned to go. Joe shook my hand and called to me as we left the room. "Thanks for the shirts, really. They're mega!" I think only a personalized blessing from the Pope or the Dalai Lama would have been more amazing.

I can only affirm what a lot of the people who've encountered him this year have said: Joe is an amazing guy. He seems like a man utterly at peace with himself and a person lacking in pretense. That old egotistical bluster is long gone and the impression of confusion you can get from his garbled syntax in print vanishes when you meet the man. His eyes burn with a restless intelligence you wouldn't expect from a hard-living 47 year-old. It's no wonder so many interviewers come away from him spouting such praise.

In 2000, Joe embarked on a tour supporting the Who, bringing to mind memories from 1982

AND SUDDENLY, THE MESCALEROS...

There were two groups of musicians known as the Mescaleros. The first was a collection of sidemen. The second was a band.

The first lineup - Antony Genn, Martin Slattery, Scott Shields, Pablo Cook and Smiley - was assembled fairly quickly by Antony Genn when work began on what became *Rock Art and the X-Ray Style*. This lineup was capable, but was utterly lacking in chemistry. I talked a lot on the *CCS* site about the underwhelming feeling most of the shows this band played instilled in me.

Certainly all of the Autumn/Winter '99 shows left me strangely empty, as if I had seen an animatronic version of a band, or had watched a bar band doing Clash covers, with Joe sitting in just for a lark. Joe's body language for these shows was telling. He rarely moved from his spot at stage center, and rarely lifted his hands from his guitar. This was Joe's tell-tale cue that he was uncomfortable with the people he was playing with. You saw it in a lot of '82/'83 Clash gigs, the second half of the Roskilde gig (when Joe suddenly seemed to realize not bringing his guitar wasn't such a great idea after all) and during the '89 tour. Joe only let loose when he was fully comfortable with the people backing him up.

Shortly before a support tour with the Who, Antony Genn dropped out of the Meskies. Smiley and Pablo Cook soon followed. Strummer fans were panicking - was it all over before it began? I was unfazed. Neither Genn nor Smiley were up to the job and Cook's contribution always seemed superfluous to me. Genn is to be commended for plucking Joe out of his premature retirement, but his songwriting skills were negligible and his guitar playing never gelled. Then came the shocker: Tymon Dogg was tapped to replace Genn. This was a stroke of genius on Joe's part. First of all, replacing a guitarist with a fiddler was the kind of perverse gambit Joe was famous for. Secondly, Dogg was not only an amazing fiddler, but a crackerjack guitarist, keyboardist and songwriter. In addition, he was one of Joe's oldest friends and an uninhibited showman. His presence was what Joe needed to loosen his feet from the marks and break out of the shackles onstage. *Global a Go-Go* showed that Shields and Slattery could make an album nearly all by themselves and Dogg's influence gave it the kind of exotic flair Joe had been seeking.

photo: Eleanor Flicker

Two other changes sealed the deal. The addition of powerhouse drummer Luke Bullen completely changed the dynamic of the sound. Luke was what Smiley wasn't - a real Rock and Rock drummer. Simon Stafford, late of the Long Pigs, came in on bass and freed up Shields to focus on guitar (Stafford also blows a mean trombone). Shields was no Stevie Ray Vaughn either, but he played with a lot more energy than Genn seemed capable of.

This was the *real* Mescaleros. I first saw them at the Virgin Megastore (their US debut) show in July '01 and saw them four more times after that. Although they never were the Clash, they certainly stopped my pining for a Clash reunion. I had the opportunity to talk with Joe at Virgin, and my boy BJ and I drunkenly raved about how he should dump all the boring Clash leftovers like 'London Calling' and 'Rock the Casbah', and dig deeper in to the catalog. We also raved that he should play more Reggae numbers live. We were gratified when he did just that. The October 2001 show we saw at the Theatre of Living Arts in Philadelphia was a fantastic show— one of the best concerts I can remember seeing. The Irving Plaza show the following week was less impressive, but still amazing. (I was a lot drunker at that show, so really - who knows if it was better or not?)

The last two shows I saw were at St. Anne's Warehouse in Brooklyn. This was Joe's stab at recreating the Bond's vibe. The two shows I saw were even better than the ones I saw in October, the April 5 show being particularly impressive. The vibe seemed to be drifting away from the World Music feel of *Global A Go-Go* and back towards Hard Rock, so I was very encouraged by that as well. Earlier in the week, I had the pleasure of being on the receiving end of a patented Mick Jones snub as well, so my experience was complete!

But as the year wore on, troubling portents appeared. Joe seemed to be ill a lot, and it seemed his voice was going. The summer shows in California and the *Bringing it All Back Home* tour displayed a Joe that finally seemed to be showing his age. The band, which only months before had been taut and fiery, seemed flabby and unfocused. The new material wasn't bowling me over either.

I still think that somehow, someway, Joe sensed the end was nearing. But I think he was genuinely happy with this band. I think they were a real band and that Joe was ushered from this world to the next in fine company. Thanks guys, for all the great shows and good laughs.

THERE GOES MY HERO...
JOE STRUMMER 1952-2002

It all makes a kind of strange and terrible sense. Five weeks after sharing the stage with his old partner-in-crime Mick Jones for the first time in 19 years, our hero sat down in his kitchen and never woke up.

It had been a heady time for Joe Strummer. His endless tour-recording binge was nearing its fourth year. It seemed as if he would never stop. With the Mescaleros, Joe seemed determined to play as many shows as the Clash ever had. And if his ticket and album sales were never what they were with the Clash, it was more than made up for by the tremendous love and affection that he seemed to receive from nearly everyone. Once an irritant and thorn in the side to the supercilious twits of the British press and Record Industry of the 80's, Joe received adulation from journalists who had been baptized in the sweat and fire of the Clash's revelatory concerts. And if the music and the shows never quite matched the pure catharsis of the Clash, they were certainly a damn sight better than nearly anything else out there.

photo: Eleanor Flicker

In addition, Joe had eased himself into the role of Rock Elder Statesman, but still was able to retain the credibility that most of his contemporaries and predecessors would never be able to buy with their cash-in 'best-ofs' and $500 a seat ticket prices. One look need no further than Sting, Joe's old rival, to see just how far a star could fall into total irrelevancy and fatuousness to appreciate how tightly Joe clung to his principles.

Joe was almost universally recognized as a major influence on what has followed him and his company was prized by many of today's top artists. His effortless charisma, grace, and easy-going manner were prized by fan and star alike. Just before he passed, he was working with no less than a superstar than Bono, on a number for no less a luminary than Nelson Mandela.

Joe was hard at work on an album with the Mescaleros, following a year of guerilla raid touring. For those of us who have watched Joe closely over the years, there were worrisome signs on the recent 'Bringing it All Back Home' tour. Photos of Joe showed him looking pale and haggard, and his mighty bellow was weak and thin on many of the recordings I've heard. If you were in the crowd, this was probably un-noticeable. Joe and the stage are a magical combination, and I found it impossible to look at him onstage and think he was a minute older than he was in the early 80's.

If Joe's solo work hadn't the instant classic feel of the Clash, it was certainly enormously entertaining and satisfying taken on its own terms. And it was impossible to sign on the Internet while he was touring without being bombarded by testimonials about 'how great Joe was when I met him'. Having written a few of those myself, I can corroborate them. Joe was an artist but he was also a tremendous fan of music.

I had the pleasure and honor of meeting the man many times. The time that sticks out most in my mind was in '99 at the tour-ending show in Philadelphia. I had made two T-shirts for him, using cartoons from the *Clash City Showdown* site. I'll never forget the look on his face when I gave them to him. Sheer delight and surprise and even - dare I say it - admiration. Joe was also a fan of cartooning and he really seemed to enjoy seeing himself the subject of a cartoon.

The second time was at the Virgin Megastore in-store appearance the day *Global a Go Go* was released. Having hunted down an advance promo, I and my cohort-in -Clashery, BJ aka Sonny Burnit, knew all the songs by heart. Having read a report on the London in-store, I also knew then-new drummer Luke's name. BJ, Matt and I were seriously inebriated by the time we entered the store, and we spotted Luke setting up his kit and inaugurated the now customary 'LUUUUUUUUUKE' chant. He later told us we scared the shit out of him.

BJ and I spent the entire show screaming out the lyrics with Joe and then drunkenly shouting out nonsense between the songs. When we met Joe, I was honored to find he remembered me from Philadelphia and he was shocked to realize that we already had memorized all the new numbers. We alternately scared and amused the assembled Mescaleros with lunatic, drunken raving, but Joe was obviously pleased and flattered. He made a point to say goodbye to me by name and we ascended the escalator screaming and hollering his praises. He later christened BJ and I the 'Decibel Twins'.

Being able to see Joe eight times in the past three years, as well as the two solid sets he released in that time easily made up for the Dark Ages of Joe fandom, which essentially began the minute the Out of Control tour ended and were evaporated only the night before my 33rd birthday on 17 Irving Place in the great city of New York. Joe's wilderness were emotional torture for this obsessive-compulsive fan, and I ran the entire gamut of responses as the interminable waiting of the 90's wore on.

There were wonderful surprises in these dark times, as Joe floundered to recover from the epiphany that was the Clash. There were the indisputable triumphs of *No. 10 Upping Street*, his collaboration with Mick Jones and BAD, the brilliant *Walker* soundtrack, his appearance in *Mystery Train*, the killer *Gangsterville* 12" EP and various re-release projects, but it wasn't until the 1-2-3 punch of the *Westway to the World* film, the live *From Here to Eternity* CD, and the Mescaleros summer mini-tour that all the bad feeling and disappointment and the endless waiting were swept away and forgotten.

Following those events, I had launched the *Clash City Showdown* site, which had been enormously successful in my eyes for the 2 years it was really cranking. Events conspired to end its original run, but the primary purpose of the site had been fulfilled and there were any number of Joe Strummer sites to take on the next phase of the story. As much as I enjoyed what Joe was doing, the focus for me was always the Clash: that peculiar multi-media collision of vision and Zeitgeist that created something that far exceeded the sum of its parts. Joe's new collaborators were outstanding musicians but Joe always worked best for me with Mick's incessant melodicism, Paul's glamour and Bernie's lunatic subversiveness.

In a strange way, I felt something coming to an end recently but I had no idea it would be Joe's brilliant life. I was content to let Joe carry on, feeling that my contribution to the cause had been completed. He seemed happy and content, and that was enough for me. I do regret that some of the shenanigans of a few of his professed fans had soured my enthusiasm for Joe at the end. But all it took was a glance at some old videos to relight the flame all over again. That's what makes a classic a classic- it does the trick for you time and again.

But now he's gone forever in body, but here forever in spirit. Having begun this year losing my best friend and former musical collaborator to cancer and then ending losing my all time musical idol, I am learning how to cope with loss.Perhaps I can offer some comfort to people who like me, are suffering from this seemingly senseless loss. First of all, Joe went out peacefully and with dignity, in his home near people he loved.

photo: Eleanor Flicker

Second, Joe died with his boots on, having just returned from the studio where was working on his almost-completed third album with the Mescaleros, following a mad dash across the Island that culminated in him sharing the stage with his brother in arms, Mick Jones, for the first time in two decades. Joe had been in the public eye like never before, through involvement with high profile charities, a pilot on MTV2 and his occasional show on the BBC World Service.

Joe had two speeds- fast and off. Having spent nearly a decade in the 'off' position, Joe was making up for lost time since the turn of the Millennium. His notorious appetite for hard work and hard partying probably hastened his demise, but would he have it any other way? He pursued everything he did with abandon and gusto. That's what made him Joe Strummer. He lived life more fully than any ten normal men. And he left an amazing legacy.

Joe was a man, just like any other. He wasn't perfect, wasn't divine, wasn't faultless. But knowing that just makes his achievements all the more remarkable. Is there an intelligent and creative person between the ages of 35 and 45 that wasn't influenced by him? The Clash were the dividing line between the old and the new back in their heyday. Before the hits you really knew where someone stood when they said they were a Clash fan.

Human mortality is a mystery. Joe lost both of his parents back in the Clash days, and his brother long before. Maybe Joe came back in '99 and was so eager to live his life to the absolute fullest because something in him knew there was a deadline approaching, and better to go down singing and shouting and rocking than playing snooker. Joe got a pretty good second run at his career, a career that had been pretty remarkable to begin with. And even if he didn't experience the same level of success, I am reasonably certain he enjoyed himself quite a bit more this time around.

So what am I going to do? I'm going to remember Joe the way I think he wants to be remembered, and I am going to continue to take inspiration from his courage and his honesty. Back in the Prog-Rock days, no one would have bet on some sandpaper-throated chord banger to change the world. But he did so because he dared. I take inspiration from that and from his willingness to put it all on the table with every hand. Again, look at other artists from Joe's heyday to see what dishonesty, compromise and fatuousness a careerist musician is capable of. Whatever you think of Joe's body of work, it was always from the heart. And that is exactly why so many people still care about him.

And I can never forget seeing the Clash and huge they were onstage in their prime. That's the kind of thing that never leaves you. Nor all the great nights- famous nights- I had out at Meskie gigs. Or all the great people I've met because of a shared interest in the Clash. And the music and all the boots live forever. And his kindness, open-heartedness and enthusiasm.

Don't mourn Joe—-celebrate him.

December 23, 2002

1981

Originally posted May 8, 1997

The last year the Clash existed as a fully functioning band was also one of the most exciting years in the History of Rock and Roll. The true importance of 1981 may not be realized for some time to come, given the intractable and reactionary nature of popular music in the 90's. But 1981 was a pivotal year and many of the important innovations made in Rock music flowered in this brilliant year. For those such as myself who were conditioned to expect non-stop excitement in popular culture, many of the years since have been bitter disappointments.

In fact, 1981 was so great,it actually started in late 1980. Many of the records released in late '80 were to dominate the Rock community's consciousness (when such a thing existed) in the first half of 1981. Within weeks of each other, David Bowie's *Scary Monsters*, U2's *Boy*, Blondie's *AutoAmerican*, Talking Heads' *Remain in Light*, the B-52's *Wild Planet*, the Clash's *Sandinista!* and the first of the Buzzcocks '1-2-3' singles, and Siouxsie and the Banshees definitive single, 'Israel' were released.

This was an astonishing barrage of immeasurably influential music. Bowie's *Scary Monsters* is thought by many to be his greatest record, and the musicians of 1983's 'New British Invasion' owe a mammoth debt to it. Blondie brought rap to mainstream America with 'Rapture'. The Heads' album and *Sandinista!* essentially created the World Music movement by refocusing New Wave's outlook to the Third World in general, the Caribbean and Africa in particular. Siouxsie's 'Israel' single-handedly created the template for an entire subset of British Post-Punk, namely the Goth movement. And all of this was taking place while the focus of the British Establishment was still focused on the dreary, ephemeral New Romantic movement!

These records set the tone for '81, in many ways raising the goal for their rivals and admirers. It's hard to believe now, but once musicians believed that they were obliged to something new and innovative, rather than just rehash ideas found in their older siblings' record collections. And once the gauntlet was thrown, the floodgates roared open.

The Psychedelic Furs entered the fray with their all-time classic, *Talk Talk Talk,* produced by the then-very busy Steve Lillywhite. Although the Furs were to go on to considerable success as a arty Pop band, this album was a pounding Rock assault, clattering and clanging with FX-drenched guitars and sax. The Furs were once a six man band, and each player seemed determined to make more of a racket than the other. American post-Punk archetypes Mission of Burma released their *Signals Calls and Marches* EP which contained the classic 'That's When I Reach for My Revolver'. Gang of Four released their second LP in the Spring, the classic *Solid Gold*. On that great LP, the Gang dropped the last Punk Rock vestiges in their sound and created a violent, disjointed post-Funk assault. You can practically hear sweaty hands striking their instruments with blunt force on songs like 'Outside the Trains Don't Run on Time.' The music drew on antecedents like Captain Beefheart and Pere Ubu, but was utterly unique.

Even more unique was Public Image Ltd's *Flowers of Romance*. Having fired their thug/genius bass player Jah Wobble for nicking *Metal Box* backing tapes, PiL decided not to replace him. Working with drummer Martin Atkins, PiL recorded track upon track of vicious percussion, and then dubbed all sorts of sounds from eerie synths to clockwork toys. Levene recorded only two tracks worth of his landmark guitar playing. Over this din, Johnny howled, at the top of his lungs, lyrics filled with bizarre nightmare imagery. Also working in a percussive nightmare vein were Industrial-Metal godfathers Killing Joke. Their '81 release *What's This For?* basically created the template that bands like Ministry and NIN would later follow: Distorted vocals, flame-thrower guitar, thudding funk bass and bellicose synths. Every sound on this album was percussive and assaultive, even the vocals. Every song was a nightmare vision of Hell on Earth.

Not to miss out on all the gloomy fun, Siouxsie and the Banshees released their black magic masterpiece, *Juju*. Combining Siouxsie's howling, much-imitated vocals with some of the best musicianship of the era, *Juju* created the sound that artists from the Cocteau Twins to Sinead O'Connor and nearly every Goth band would try to make their own. But no one could match Siouxsie's twisted lyrical vision. *Juju* conjures visions of Hammer horror, black magic rituals and snuff films in both words and music, as the Banshees' brilliant playing is as disturbing as the lyrics. *Juju* is also noted for having a song with one of Rock's most twisted choruses, 'Fuck the Mothers/Kill the Others/ Fuck the Others/Kill the Mothers.'

Where Siouxsie turned her rage out at the world, Banshee's sister band the Cure turned it inward and created some classic Mope-Rock. The Cure released one of their most beautiful records in '81, *Faith*. This was the opposite of many records of the era, inward, mournful and desolate. A pinnacle of sorts was reached with the classic 'Drowning Man'. And just to complete this black-mascara'ed tableau, Bauhaus released their best album *Mask*, which contained the classics 'Passion of Lovers' and 'Kick in the Eye' as well as the terrifying title track.

In the midst of all this gloom and anger, U2 made a splash with *Boy* and later in '81, *October*. Drawing upon many of the same musical ideas as their angrier contemporaries, U2 brightened the mix with their boyish optimism and Christian mysticism. It's hard to remember a time when U2 were not constantly admiring and analyzing themselves, but in '81 they were a breath of fresh air and he band most likely to. Two other bands drawn from the Joy Division well shone in '81 also. Echo and the Bunnymen deepened and broadened their sound with *Heaven Up Here*, a heavily Doors-influenced set of soulful post-Punk. Echo were also to go on to considerable mainstream success, especially in the UK. And Sheffield's finest, the woefully under-appreciated Comsat Angels, released the brooding, atmospheric classic, *Sleep No More*.

It boggles the mind to think that this creative frenzy was almost completely ignored by mainstream America. FM radio was still stuck dead in the mid-70's, forcing one poodle-haired, Cock Rock band after another down the throats of radio listeners. But the musical ferment broke through to America's consciousness through another medium, the 6 O' Clock news. In May, the Clash created a media feeding frenzy when the Bond's season started. Denied touring funds by their record company, the Clash booked a week of gigs at a New York nightspot. The gigs were typically oversold, the Fire Dept. shut them all down, and a riot ensued in Times Square. Newly reinstalled Clash manager Bernie Rhodes exploited this furor to full advantage by holding press conferences. The Clash were the center of attention in Manhattan, and news of the riot made the national news which then set the stage for the Clash's brief rise to stardom. An incendiary performance on the Tomorrow show further cemented this coup.

Porn-Punks the Plasmatics also garnered national news attention when singer Wendy O. Williams was put on trial for obscenity and public lewdness. In the midst of this, The Plasmatics made a hilarious appearance on ABC's Fridays program. Performing their Retard-Rock classic 'Butcher Baby' (chorus-'Ooh yeah now, oh no/ Ooh yeah now oh no') Williams chain sawed a guitar in half and then brought the light scaffolding down with a shotgun. Around the same time, Public Image Ltd. decided to join in the anarchic fun and caused a riot at New York's Ritz where they 'performed' behind video screens and insulted the audience (Lydon-'You're all a bunch of hippies!').

A far more serious Punk-related news story developed in England that summer with the so-called Southall Riots, which soon spread throughout the country. Perhaps seeking to provoke local residents, a skinhead 'Oi!' concert was put on in an Asian community in south London. The volatile mix of racist skins and a community tired of harassment erupted into riots that spread throughout London then spread north. The fighting thrust the embryonic skinhead Oi! scene into the nations consciousness, and tied in with the media frenzy concerning the violent LA skinhead scene. The media coverage on the US hardcore scene lapsed into cartoonishness when idiot prime-time dramas like *Quincy ME* and *CHiPs* did 'exposes' on the hardcore scene. US coverage of the riots on ABC's *20/20* centered on the Specials' mid-riot TV performance of their anti-violence anthem 'Ghost Town.' Ironically, all of this coverage was the catalyst for the US Hardcore movement, for by summer's end, every major US city had an active Hardcore scene.

In the midst of all this excitement, many of the heroes of the late 70's were beginning to either fall apart or show their true colors as frauds and band-wagon jumpers. Put Squeeze, Elvis Costello and Joe Jackson in the latter column. These aging Pub Rockers gave up the pretense of being cutting edge in '81 and showed what boring old Vaudevillians they really were. Squeeze released the dull MOR of *East Side Story* and had a hit with the Doobie Brothers soundalike, 'Tempted'. Elvis produced that mess, and released his own mess, *Trust*, an album of half good Rock and half-Harry Chapin rejects like 'Shot with His Own Gun' and 'Different Finger.' *Trust* bridged the yawning gap between cool old Elvis and the old fart he became. Also in '81, Elvis released the dreadful country covers album, *Almost Blue*. When it came to alienating his fan base, Costello would spare no expense. Elvis clone Joe Jackson opted out altogether with the totally irrelevant be-bop flop *Jumping Jive*. Former next-big-things The Boomtown Rats churned out the pointless *Mondo Bongo* and began their rapid descent into un-stardom. Gary Numan faded from view and Devo hit the charts but ran out of ideas with *New Traditionalists*.

The Ramones started to drift away from their original idea with the radio-friendly *Pleasant Dreams*. 1981 Ska hitmakers the Specials, the Beat and the Selecter all released disappointing follow-up LPs, even though the Specials still had one more great single and the Beat one more great album left to go. And Blondie marked their creative demise with a 'Best-of' set.

In contrast to the doom and gore of the earlier part of the year, the second half of '81 gave birth to the Synth Pop and Dance Rock movements, two genres that would soon dominate 80's Alternative Rock. Depeche Mode emerged with 'Just Can't Get Enough' and 'Dreaming of Me.' The Human League released the classic synth-pop statement *Dare*. Soft Cell slithered out of their holes and unleashed *Non-Stop Erotic Cabaret*. Heaven 17 burst onto the scene with their singles 'Fascist Groove Thang' and 'Let Me Go'. Tina Weymouth and Chris Frantz enlisted some Heads side-people for the fun Tom Tom Club LP which featured 'Genius of Love' and 'Wordy Rappinghood.' The Police utilized both synths and dance rhythms for their late '81 release, *Ghost in the Machine*, their only filler-free record. Not to be outdone, the Clash entered the fray with the 'Radio Clash' 12", which featured remixes by Kid Creole mastermind August Darnell. (The Clash had scuttled a planned collaboration with Grandmaster and the Furious Five.)

As if 1981 was not momentous enough, MTV, an all-music cable station, signed on at the end of the year. Soon the telegenic armies of the New Wave would burst into the public consciousness and the early 80's as people remember them would begin. Here the legacy of '81 would end. Passion became fashion and the luminaries of the Post-Punk movement would all queue up for their share of the booty.

You see, as great as so many '81 records were, they sold for shit. The public wanted happy sounds on the radio and the soon to emerge New British Invasion was all to happy to provide them. And a band like the Clash, who thrived in the turmoil of the previous years, would find themselves seriously out of their element in the go-fun 80's. Although they made a much more accessible record, and toned down their aura of menace, they could not cover up their essential gnarliness, and they were soon eclipsed by serious crowd-pleasers like the Police and U2. The 80's steam-rollered any sense of idealism or artistry, and Joe Strummer's quixotic quest to stare down the new consensus later in the decade failed miserably. Video killed a lot more than the radio star.

THE ANTI-CLASH
Originally posted May 23, 1997

I just saw a picture in the Post today of PiL's legendary appearance of Tom Snyder's show way back when. The picture showed Johnny glaring at Snyder with Keith Levene smirking at the floor and I had another 'a-ha!' moment. Joe recently complained about Johnny's incessant needling of him in the *BAM* interview, but perhaps Joe doesn't realize how deep Rotten's obsession is with him.

When the Pistols evaporated, the Clash took up the Punk throne immediately. Johnny was instantly a has-been, and Joe Strummer was Punk's new king. This must have seared Rotten's brain, being usurped by some bloody Pub Rock singer. Now, here's my theory: in a fit of pique, Rotten hunts down Levene, former Clash guitarist, and recruits him for his new group. Levene, never a workhorse, was last heard guesting on the Cowboys International LP (who also featured ex-Clash drummer Terry Chimes- did Rotten try to recruit him too?). Rotten now has his own Mick Jones. The first PiL album is Punk done Rotten's way, all arty and dissonant. Untouched by this, the Clash continue to dominate and now become the object of a lot of American attention. The Clash then start to explore Reggae in the context of Rock and Roll. Rotten says the hell with Rock and Roll and explores Reggae in the context of Art-Noise on the LP *Metal Box*. The UK critics go ga-ga, and blast the Clash for *London Calling*, but the Clash go to the US and start winning fans and appear on TV and stuff. In answer, Rotten brings his anti-Clash over to the States and in a fit of conceptual brilliance, appears on Dick Clark's vapid American Bandstand, hilariously miming to their non-hits 'Poptones' and 'Careering'.

The Clash, stung by this artistic coup, go arty and experimental on *Sandinista!*, which displays a not-insignificant PiL influence. The Clash also release a three-record set, but these records play at 33 rpm, not 45. PiL one-up the Clash by producing the anti-music classic, *The Flowers of Romance*, storming into territory where the Clash cannot possibly go. PiL the stage their own mini-riot with their Situationist appearance at the Ritz and the Clash, not to be outdone, make the national news with a riot of their own uptown at Bonds. The Clash then make another record, this time with unmistakable PiL-like elements, and hit the US platinum jackpot. They then tour in '82 without their drummer and rake in megabucks. In response, PiL tour America without their bassist, albeit on a far smaller scale. They announce that they will make an album entitled *You Are Now Entering a Commercial Zone*, which in it's original form was not all that different from some of the music the Clash had hit the jackpot with. Was the title a swipe at the Clash's new-found acceptability? They record a tune called 'This is Not a Love Song', filled with sarcastic lyrics about selling out. Another swipe at Strummer's rationale of the Clash's commerciality? (Joe said that they didn't sell out because they didn't play love songs) PiL releases this single and scores a hit. Soon after, Strummer fires Mick from the Clash, and replaces him with anonymous sidemen.

Parrying that strange stroke, Lydon fires Levene and then Atkins (he probably didn't want to miss out on the wacky fun drummer-firing provides). In a situationalist parody of the Clash's new lineup, Lydon recruits a Holiday Inn band ('The Penquins') and cranks out a quickie Tokyo live album. He then sets to work demolishing the *Commercial Zone* sessions and creates the template the Clash would follow for *Cut the Crap*. But Johnny gets his new PiL LP *This is You Want This is What you Get* out more than a year before *Cut the Crap*. Both records will set new lows for the Punk movement.

After the Clash breakup and Joe goes into exile, Johnny gives up any artistic pretense and turns PiL from a conceptual art band into a pseudo-Rock joke. But not before he appears in BAD video that also features Joe and Paul. He does this simply so he can machine gun his rivals in the hopelessly lame 'Medicine Show' video. With Joe out of the picture, BAD and PiL (notice both are three-letter acronyms) slug it out for the pre-Nirvana *120 Minutes* audience. But the Clash then rise from the grave for a Levi's commercial and reap an astounding post-houmous reissue bonanza that allows Joe to continue to gaze at his navel and become the beloved scenester he always yearned to be. Johnny stung by this, records an ad for Mountain Dew, but no similar Pistols chart frenzy occurs. The Clash then set the Rock world abuzz with rumors they will headline Lollapalooza in '95. No such reunion occurs, but the hullabaloo is enough to inspire Rotten to revive the Pistols and launch the anticlimactic *Filthy Lucre* tour. And so it goes. One can almost picture Rotten and Strummer in the same retirement home slugging it out for the pureed bananas...

DON'T KID YOURSELF
Originally posted 02/01/98

My last dispatch dealt with the corporate strangulation of Rock and Roll. This state of affairs is the result of 40 years of creeping co-option by Multi-Nationals who control the distribution and manufacturing of 80% or more of recorded music in the world. They also control the radio stations and have an enormous influence on the music press, largely through multi-billion dollar advertising budgets. This is nothing new, except in the totality of the control.

Wags who drone on about musical 'progress' are in actuality unwitting pawns for the PR machine which seeks to constantly replace troublesome established artists with new, more malleable ones. There is no 'new' musical movement out there, and in actuality most of the musical forms popularized in the past ten or fifteen years are simply new packagings of older musical ideas, most dating back to the 60's. The only 'evolution' is not conceptual but a question of packaging and recombination.

Lest we forget, the Clash themselves made a pact with the very same multinationals in order to further their own interests. 'Indie' purists eternally condemn them for this, but the Clash would have not made nearly the impact they did if they had been tucked away in some indie label with limited distribution. Indie music has never really presented a threat to the majors. On the contrary, they are seen as farm teams for the majors, a good way to do some on the spot R&D for future trends. Artists have to eat, and most (but not all) musicians can only make a living above subsistence level on a major label.

New variations on established genres continue to emerge, but the non-stop parade of new bands and performers only serves to dilute the impact of other artists, and devalues the currency of music. This is the logical result of the DIY ethic, but it also only serves to strengthen the hand of the major labels, not of the artists. A troublesome artist can be replaced quickly by a dozen others, no matter how inferior the replacements may be to the original. And as long as music is a secondary concern to young people's lives, no new style can rectify this. Pearl Jam tried to use their multi-platinum status to try and upset the corporate apple cart, only to find themselves struggling to be even a gold band.

So all you aging hipsters, stuck in their outdated rhetoric of 'musical progress' and 'diversity', you're fighting yesterday's battles. People will listen to what they want to, no matter what mud you think they are stuck in. Last year, in the midst of the corporate sponsored bonanza of hype for Techno music and all its sub-genres, the Rolling Stones and Fleetwood Mac were the top money makers, and the charts continued to be dominated by utter disposable crap that no one will remember or care about in 5 years.

If you want to really defy the consensus, you won't go chasing the latest frippery in an embarrassing quest to stay current, but instead focus on real talent. In this age of promiscuous 'diversity', a true counter-culture would focus on craft and excellence and fidelity. What artists out there display these attributes? Well, there aren't many. But I myself am much more interested in those few artists who have a body of work that spans a certain period of time that withstands the test of time. Anyone can make a good record or two, but how many can raise themselves from a decade-long artistic death like Bowie has done? Who has made as many lasting innovations to the way popular music is made as Brian Eno? And for my money, Jack Dangers still blows away his contemporaries with Meat Beat Manifesto, and he's been around since the mid-80's.

I think that craft is due for a big comeback. I think people are getting tired of generic music, and want to hear something special. This is counter to the 'Punk ethos' to be sure, but the 'Punk ethos' is more than 20 years old, and doesn't really have much to do with life in the late 90's.

THE SHOWDOWN GUIDE
TO PUNK ROCK

I get a lot of mail from confused young Punks who wonder why I am so dismissive of modern Punk Rock. They howl in dismay as I dismiss most of today's acts as Punk-flavored Pop. They email me and ask what I would recommend instead. Well, since I care deeply for my young readers and their developing pallettes, I am offering this somewhat truncated consumer guide of what I consider to be essential Punk Rock LPs. Every record listed here is invaluable for it's historic and artistic significance and are listed in no particular order. Every band here, though all comfortably fitting in the Fast/Loud category, has an strong identity and sound, and no two of these bands are alike, whether in concept, sound or image. I consider every band on this list to be trailblazers and pioneers, and all of these records to be essential documents of a time and place. So if you want to know what my personal experience of Punk was like, buy these records, research these bands and ponder what the difference is between them and the modern acts that call themselves Punk Rock.

RAMONES-ROCKET TO RUSSIA - Though some would argue for the first album on grounds of purity, Showdown readers know I have no time for purity. Rocket is faster and funnier, and boasts as many stupid classics as any Ramones album does. Note to neophytes - avoid any Ramones album made after 1979.

SEX PISTOLS - NEVER MIND THE BOLLOCKS -There is no excuse for not owning this album. Go out and buy it now before your friends find out you don't have it. Simply the grandest expression of righteous rage ever recorded by four total poseurs.

MISSION OF BURMA - VS. - American Punks could be as arty as their British cousins. Not sure if the full Rykodisc comp (entitled *Mission of Burma*) is still available , but if it isn't, *Vs.* is a wonderful consolation prize. One of the greatest bands of any era, MOB deconstruct Punk and Hardcore and make almost everyone else sound ordinary.

DEAD KENNEDYS - FRESH FRUIT FOR ROTTING VEGETABLES - Before they went political, the DK's were a sick joke band. And *Fresh Fruit* contains their sickest and catchiest jokes. Interesting to hear real musicians playing Punk this early. I don't have much time for their later, more strident material.

WIRE- PINK FLAG - Art school Punk. They play a great riff over and over until they get bored and go onto the next one. Every song is a Punk classic, and *Pink Flag* 's short and fast formula set the stage for Hardcore. Wire would soon get much artier and earn the nickname Punk Floyd.

KILLING JOKE - KJ set the stage for other elements to find their way into Punk, like dance and Heavy Metal. Essentially a template for Industrial Metal, this album avoids that genre's wretched excesses by embracing the Punk ethic whole-heartedly. Every song here is a classic.

<u>X-RAY SPEX- GERM-FREE ADOLESCENTS</u> - The first wave of Punk was much more egalitarian than later eras. Hence you had lots of great bands with female lead singers like X-Ray Spex. And X-Ray Spex boasted a sound as tough and gnarly as any boy band. The CD includes the classic single 'Oh Bondage, Up Yours!'

<u>DISCHARGE- WHY</u> - This Second Wave UK act essentially created Hardcore. Every song they performed was short, brutal and explicit. Fanatical in their anti-war politics, Discharge sought to shake listeners out of their apathy by illustrating the horrors of war with their blistering sonic assault. Sample lyric 'Horrific disturbing visions of war fill my eyes/ Among the maimed and slaughtered my body lies'

<u>CRASS- STATIONS OF THE CRASS</u> - The Punkest band ever. Hardcore anarchists who walked every single syllable they talked. Every album came with a book's worth of propaganda and art on the fold-out sleeves. Their music was as strange and ugly as anything ever heard. Hated the Clash and delighted in ridiculing them for their hypocrisy.

<u>CIRCLE JERKS- GROUP SEX</u> - This album epitomized the Cali Hardcore mentality circa '80. Fast, short blasts of humor and nihilism. Performed a civic duty by fully illustrating the vapid moral emptiness of Me Generation Southern California. The Jerks never made another worthwhile record. Joe's former guitar slinger Zander Schloss played bass in a later Jerks lineup.

<u>BAD BRAINS- ROIR cassette</u>- Like ever other band on this list, the Bad Brains peaked early. This cassette (also issued on CD) showcases the BB's at their furious peak, and every single note on this record is classic. The Brains flawlessly shift between revved-up Punk and spaced -out Dub. Indispensable.

<u>BLACK FLAG- THE FIRST FOUR YEARS</u> - I always laugh when I see Rock crits listing *Damaged* as a great Punk record. Because as any old-school Punk will tell you, Black Flag was over by the time Rollins joined the band. This comp has most of the great Keith Morris/Ron Reyes/ Dez Cadena material, though 'Police Story,' the best BF song ever, is strangely AWOL.

<u>BLITZ - WARRIORS</u> - For some strange reason, I bought a lot of Oi records back in the early 80's. With the exception of a few singles here and there, it was as wretched as anything ever made. Except for Blitz. Although hampered by wretched production for most of their short career, Blitz was, hands down, the most vital and exciting Oi! band of their time.

<u>BUZZCOCKS- SINGLES GOING STEADY</u> - These old codgers are still around, though without the rhythm section and producer that made them so special. This is the classic lineup with the incomparable John Maher on drums and the indispensable Martin Rushent behind the glass. Rushent gave these silly pop tunes a futuristic sheen that is inseparable from their essence. Green Day should pay them intellectual property royalties.

STIFF LITTLE FINGERS - INFLAMMABLE MATERIAL - Incendiary politi-Punk from occupied Ireland. SLF loses a few points for having their manager write the lyrics, but he wrote good ones. One of the few bands on this list who made good music past their first record. Adored and emulated the Clash. Imitated by many American fifth-wave acts.

SIOUXSIE AND THE BANSHEES - ONCE UPON A TIME - This comp captures the Banshees in their early thrash days as well as the later, more refined material. The Banshees were Pistols groupies who started their own thing and distilled the Weimar decadence that was so important to early Punk. 'Love in A Void' is as essential as any Punk Rock single ever made, and sounds more like '77 than anything else currently available.

UNDERTONES - Early Punk pop from Derry, Ireland. The Undertones were angry young men who formed a band to avoid joining the IRA like all their mates. Dealt with the 'Troubles' by ignoring them in their music. Made two great records. Toured with the Clash in '79, and played their tune 'Casbah Rock' to a very interested Joe Strummer. Fast, fun, now and wow.

WIPERS - YOUTH OF AMERICA - Punks who could play. Greg Sage is revered by people like Nirvana and Pearl Jam, but don't hold that against him. Took American Punk to new places it was loathe to go. Title track is an eight minute fever dream that recalls the music of another favorite son of Seattle, Jimi Hendrix.

DEVO - ARE WE NOT MEN? -Punk's real cradle is the Midwest. Anyone with a brain in Rust Belt nowheres like Akron and Detroit couldn't help but be a little crazy and rebellious. Devo were doing since the early 70's and *Are We not Men?* Captures the essence of the concept. Devo were so inventive with guitars that's it a shame they discovered synths. Became a bad joke soon after.

I'm sure there are a few stragglers I'm missing, but this pretty much captures the major Punk records of my mis-spent youth. You probably have heard of most of these bands, which is a testament to their enduring power. And just by the fact that you are on this site shows you have advanced skills of discernment and taste. For all you old-schoolers, I am sure you have your own picks, but I would bet that any number of these records are on your personal best of Punk lists as well.

THE CLASH'S HEIRS
Originally posted 8/31/96

There has been an endless parade of Clash imitators in the past 18 years from Stiff Little Fingers to the Red Rockers to the Alarm to the Looters to Midnight Oil to the Manic Street Preachers to SMASH to Green Day (more in look than sound) to Elastica to Rancid and thousands of lesser known bands in-between. The Clash in my mind have influenced other bands in other ways more than any other band since Led Zeppelin.

But to me, the inheritors of the Clash's mantle are bands who owe a spiritual debt to the Clash, but have followed their own muse. Many of these bands have explicitly acknowledged the Clash as their major influence, but don't parrot them. The bands who give me the same charge as the Clash did are bands who explore the world of music and sound with a mongrel spirit and individuality. I thought I would recommend some of them to you...

BEASTIE BOYS - *Check Your Head and Ill Communication* -I'm sure many of you have these records but to me the Beasties are the only major band that kept the SPIRIT of Punk intact by restlessly exploring other grooves. The prime American contender to the Clash throne.

MEAT BEAT MANIFESTO - *Satyricon*- These noise-terrorists acknowledge the Clash as a major influence in the liner notes of this amazing record. This record has the same sprawling feel as *Sandinista* and *Combat Rock* but is much more focused. They also realize that the ultimate struggle is the struggle for consciousness.

RENEGADE SOUNDWAVE - *SoundClash*- The title says it all. Every track is killer on this landmark album. Again, squarely in the mold of a tightly focused *Sandinista*. They sample the Clash ('White Riot') on the song 'Phantom' and on their '94 record, *How You Doing*, they sample the Drum beat from 'Bankrobber' on the best song, 'Blast Em Out.' My friend BJ tells me their new record, *The Next Chapter of Dub*, is an absolute killer.

TRICKY - *Maxinquaye*- Massive Attack rapper on his own. Hiphop, Punk and reggae blend with some of the sexiest female vocals on the planet. Iconoclastic, lush and danceable. Check out the killer remake of Public Enemy's 'Black Steel in the Hour of Chaos' done Clash-style.

MASSIVE ATTACK - *Protection* - Bristol's trip-hoppers mix it all in into a luscious stew. Everything But the Girl's Tracy Thorn sings the languid title track. Dub-Hop for the 21st Century.

JAH WOBBLE - *Rising Above Bedlam, Without Judgment, Take Me to God* - Former PiL bassist and original EastEnd Punk has been blowing out the doors for 15 years now. His last three record's have been very Clash-like in spirit, mixing in all sorts of World musics anchored by his huge dub bass. His next CD is a collaboration with living legend Brian Eno.

THE CLASH'S LEGACY
Posted sometime in 1998

I saw a picture of Joe Strummer in the new *Rolling Stone*. It was taken when he helped dedicate something or other in honor of the Mighty Mighty Bosstones. Joe looked like one of the guys I used to see down at Connolly's Pub after Sunday mass. He must have come across as a familiar and comforting figure to Dicky Barrett. Dicky was reportedly touched to the point of tears. I was a bit puzzled by this, since having known Dicky back in the early 80's, I never knew him to be a Clash fan. Dicky's great love back then was Madness. But I believe his love is genuine, since imitation is the sincerest form of flattery. The Clash are to the MMB's what the Stones were to the J.Geils Band who were the 70's analog to Dicky's merry men. This tableau seemed to beg the assumption that the Clash's legacy was still strong. But, is there still a legacy? At this point in time when all of Rock and Roll is on the ropes, where does the Clash even fit in the cultural mosaic?

After Nirvana sounded the death knell for a viable Rock counter-culture, it wasn't long until Rock and Roll was next. Since the early 60's, Rock has been periodically rejuvenated by 'Underground' movements, most of them originating in England. It is said that the English invent nothing, but improve upon everything. This pattern followed from the Beatles' hijacking of old time R&B, to the British Blues boom that birthed Clapton and ultimately nurtured Hendrix, to the Glitter movement which repackaged bar-rell-house rhythms and coated them in sequins and mascara, and finally to Punk, which gave three-chord American garage sludge a political conscious-ness and is still the last great Youthquake identity. But when the Seattle boom annihilated the demand for English underground Rock and replaced it with a reactionary homegrown analog, English audiences embraced the empty, mindless dance movement and much of the music emanating from the UK this decade has been depersonalized brainwashing foolishness that American audiences have wisely avoided. But without that energy that was traditionally generated in a tripartite axis between LA, NY and London, Rock has withered and the charts are ruled by a Logan's Run-like landscape of 15-minute rap acts and dull, glossy divas.

There is still plenty of music happening in various basements and cor-ner clubs, but there is no unity of consciousness or purpose there. College radio is spinning dry, academic Fugazi clones in heavy rotation and calling it 'Emo-core'. There is still a small cult of Punk and Hardcore fans, but the emphasis seems to be on ideological purity rather than interesting music. The first album Clash template is still being utilized, but in the sunny late 90's it is clearly out of place. MIDI technology has allowed anyone to make a record, usually a dance record. Desperately seeking to separate themselves from the hordes of other marginal talents, musicians will compose a track with just the slightest variation of thousands of previously heard tracks and declare the birthing of a new genre. There was a time when older Rock stars like U2 and Johnny Lydon tried to jump on this bandwagon, feeling that a remix by the Chemical Brothers or someone would make their tired old schtick seem rele-vant again, but those days are mercifully gone.

Those of us lucky to live in an area with a good alternative radio sta-tion don't have to suffer through this. It is my good fortune of being in the broadcast area of WFMU, a free form radio station which plays a nearly bewil-dering selection of music, most of it interesting (available on the web at wfmu.org). Fans of *Sandinista* will find FMU's crazy quilt familiar.

Anyhow, I don't know if there is any Clash influence on the culture at large anymore. The Punk revival is over and the Ska revival is following close behind. There is a certain sartorial and attitudinal Clash influence (plus the Setzer connection) in the Swing revival, but the less said about that tired, pre-fab, marketing ploy the better. The Clash's legacy is tied to the viability of a counter-culture, and there can't really be a counter-culture when there's no real culture out there. Things are happening too quickly, and we are too heavily mediated for any culture to develop. Cultures grow best out of the glare of television lights. Even Disco grew out of the public eye, in gay basement clubs and black and Hispanic dance halls. The smallest inkling of a culture will rear its head nowadays and instantly be appropriated for a soda commercial.

The energy of counter-cultures was the frustration marginal characters felt by being shut out of the conversation. But with the Internet, even the most depraved crank can have a bitchin' web page and most of them do. And America's abused step-children, namely racial and sexual minorities, have become ever more insular and self-sustaining, so that tension is also lost. In the past, a closeted gay or a gifted black artist would enter the culture and subvert it, creating new variations on cultural verities. Today, no identifiable group is uncatered to with its own magazine and website.

The real problem though is on the demand side. Kids aren't bored anymore. A billion-dollar industry ensures that every moment of a child's leisure time is filled with videogames, the Internet, paintguns, soccer leagues, special interest magazines and theme parks and restaurants. I would dare say that even in London, kids are not lacking for entertainment at any moment of the day. Songs like 'London's Burning' and '48 Hours' seem quaint now. What can a kid bitch about now - the re-sale prices at Funcoland?

So, I think the Clash's influence is on the wane again. But the music remains, and maybe one day the Clash will get around to treating us all to that long-promised live album and video. Maybe Joe will gather up the courage to actually release more than one tune a year. Maybe Mick will stop chasing the approval of the London Disco Gestapo and make a Rock and Roll record. Maybe Paul will... uh, put out a monograph of his paintings or something. And maybe I will spout gills and take to the seas like a dayglo, typewriting tunafish.

THE FINAL SWINDLE
Originally posted 03/19/96

I think the Pistols, when they reform, should really suck. They should play completely different songs at the same time, or play songs backwards with detuned instruments. They should be really atrocious so they can perpetrate the final swindle. All these dopey kids who think a bunch of old has-beens are gonna to recreate 1977 will realize that the Pistols, for all their former magnificence, were a band tossed together to advertise bondage gear for a twisted little pervert named Malcolm McLaren.

The other good thing is that this insures that the Clash will never reform, for fear of being copy-cats. Joe can go back to hanging out with his rockstar friends, Mick can do his BAD stuff, Paul can paint and Topper can, well, God knows what the fuck Topper is doing. (Is he still alive?) Anyhow, they can all go about their business and collect royalty checks. Face it, reunions might be a great way for bands to get a paycheck, but they are almost always mystique-destroying artistic disasters.

NEVER MIND THE PISTOLS
Originally posted 1/18/97

Last night, The Learning Channel showed the Punk episode of the *History of Rock and Roll* series. I am sure you lot have all enjoyed this show and the lavish attention the Clash receive. It was interesting to see the contrast made between the Clash and the Pistols then and now. Punk history has it that the Pistols were the real thing, the originators, and that the Clash were phony band-wagon jumpers. The absurdity of this view was fully revealed last summer, when the aging Pistols humiliated themselves by jumping on the neo-Punk bandwagon two years too late.

Further revealing the Pistols as a campy burlesque (or as Henry Rollins referred to them 'corny poseurs') was the footage on this special. The Pistols live were a joke, then and now, a static, lifeless display of posing and preening. And I wanted to kick my TV set in every time Malcolm or Johnny did their worst lip-pursing, Malcolm McDowell riffs. They both seemed to be auditioning for the latest English bad-guy role in a Saturday morning cartoon.

Sure, the Pistols were exciting in the late 70's when nothing else but Disco was going on, but that was then. Now, they seem so mannered and unthreatening. Johnny unfortunately did not follow Neil Young's advice and burn out. We have all watched and winced as he has rusted year after year. PiL were revolutionary once, but after Wobble and Keith Levene left PiL became a brand name for toothless, semi-commercial pseudo-Rock. Wobble's solo work has carried on the original PiL mission, leading one to speculate on how much input Lydon really had on the early sound. McLaren lost the plot soon after Duck Rock and he has unleashed one half-baked concept after another in the interim.

Contrast McLaren and Lydon's campy cheese and the Pistols' inert stagecraft with Joe's salt-of-the-Earth honesty and the Clash's blistering assaults on the TLC show. Joe spoke plainly and modestly, often struggling with emotions still extant. And the Electric Circus clip shown was a pure charge of raw hate, and the 'London Calling' performance from Bond's showed the Clash at a peak of streamlined impact. The producers were wise enough to give Joe the last word, and to replay the *London Calling* clip during the credits.

I'M SO BORED WITH THE UK

Originally posted April 13, 2000

Oasis just put out a new record and it's already fallen off the US album charts. BJ swears that it's a good album, but the stuff I heard off it doesn't interest me. Oasis are superstars in Britain and can't even chart here. Something is dreadfully wrong and I blame the Jam.

Most of the so-called 'Britpop' of the past decade has drawn exclusively on UK ethnic idioms, popularized by the Jam, but developed by other acts like XTC, the Kinks and other Limey songsters. There is a large segment of folks in the UK that resent the US' cultural dominance and have sought to develop a home-grown counterweight. The only problem is that very little of it has translated outside of Britain. The Jam couldn't get arrested here, outside of various Anglophile pockets on the coasts, and Paul Weller has expressed constant scorn for America and American audiences. He waited until leaving the Jam and forming the wretched Style Council before shamelessly aping American musical forms. He failed at that as well, as has his subsequent solo career, since most of his songwriting has consisted of what Joe has termed "lock, stock and barrel lifts."

The Jam were a decent band in their later days, but their tendency to whip up jingoistic chauvinism had a corrosive effect on an entire generation of British, and to some extent Irish, performers. The British Invasion's incredible success sprang from what amounted to a conversation between America and England. Musical giants like the Beatles, Stones, Led Zeppelin and the Clash immersed themselves in American music and send it back adding a uniquely English perspective to the music. This formula revolutionized the culture of the World and established a cross-cultural pipeline that flourished for more than 20 years.

There were dissenters of course- the early Who, the Kinks and the early Move and David Bowie records were also essentially ethnic navel gazing. But the cross-oceanic exchange kept music fresh and the culture alive. The Jam openly scorned this exchange and thus were unheard except by the usual Anglophiliac fetish crowd here. But they planted poisonous seed that took root in the bitter soil of Thatcher's England. The Smiths took up the nativist gauntlet once the Jam imploded, which was ironic for a band composed entirely of first and second generation Irish immigrants. As pre-fab bands dominated the UK charts in the Thatcher years and the underground was largely manned by arty Goth-type bands, a growing anti-British sentiment took hold in the US alt-Rock community, and the infection was worsened by the provincial and willfully ignorant mindset of Hardcore and Indy.

However, inspired by BAD's attempts at fusing American dance music and Rock, there was a brief renaissance signified by the success of BAD imitators like Jesus Jones and EMF, as well as the growing popularity of veteran acts like the Cult, the Cure and Depeche Mode. There was a 'Prague Spring' of cross-Atlantic Rock in the early 90's. But the sour mood of the Bush years and the growing backlash against Black musics like Hip Hop and House fueled the Seattle Grunge phenomenon, a reactionary backlash disguised as a progressive movement. Grunge for all its 'Punk' pretensions, was a movement based on early 70's Rock like Grand Funk and Black Sabbath, only dumber, uglier and whiter.

UK acts were flushed off the charts in the tidal wave, and the record companies scoured the American bar scene for Nirvana imitators. The UK response to this nativist explosion was surprise - more nativism. Overnight, inconsequential, monosyllabically named bands like Suede, Blur, Ash, and Pulp burst onto the scene and played to the hometown crowd. Just like the Jam did. Paul Weller re-emerged from the deserved exile he earned from the last few Style Council records and doubtlessly whispered anti-American rhetoric into the ears of young British musicians. Blur, whose music is unlistenable, raised the Union Jack and attacked bands like Bush for appeasing the Americans. After a string of abysmal failures on the US charts, Blur aped the Grunge sound and achieved permanent one-hit wonder status in the US.

The problem is that Rock died in the UK sometime in the late 80's. Britpop was just the twitching of the corpse. Raves and psychotropic chemicals forever changed the cultural landscape in the UK. Britons, in large numbers, came not to be interested in music for its own inherent value but as a backdrop for nightlife. Hence, there's a lot of British music (like BAD spinoff Dreadzone) that sounds great but wilts under anything more than casual attention.

Now UK acts don't really have a prayer here anymore. British culture is now as foreign to American kids as Swedish or German culture. You may see some novelty crossover now and again, but British music has blown it, badly. It probably doesn't matter anymore, though. Rock is finally dead now, and no amount of self-interested protestation by critics or musicians can change that. Most modern bands are becoming like professional wrestlers, selling a toxic brew of stupidity, costumery and violence that makes Kiss look like the Beatles by comparison. British kids who once would be learning their Chuck Berry licks are probably learning how to write code, or planning their move to the sizable English film colony in LA. But when I hear unbridled dogshit like Gay Dad it makes me pine for happier days when London was calling and actually had something to say.

Clash THEORY

Der Alkemismus Rhodes

THE ALCHEMY OF HISTORY

Originally posted sometime in 1996

Anyone who has been in a band will tell you: it's like a marriage with no sex. You get all the bullshit and head games and drama that a marriage could provide, but you usually don't get to kiss and make up (well, usually). The most fragile element of a band is its chemistry. When it's on, playing and writing can be magical. When it's not, well, have you listened to *Cut the Crap* lately?

The Clash started at a disadvantage. Unlike many long-lasting bands, the Clash were not a group of mates who got together when they were young and learned to play together. The Clash were assembled by a very strange man, Bernie Rhodes, for the expressed intention of creating a rival to his former boss' band. That two radically different people like Joe and Mick even had anything to discuss is a mystery. Mick came out of the Glam Rock movement and Joe out of it's polar opposite, the Squat Rock movement. Paul was a skinhead painter with no musical experience and Topper was an over-qualified, wristy jazz-guy. No wonder this aggregation lasted only a few years.

But the vinyl evidence showed that this volatile blend of musical elements created a explosive musical mix. I need not remind any of you of that. Also in the mix were Situationist provocateurs Rhodes and Kosmo Vinyl. Another important element was the tumult of the times, certainly the UK's most chaotic period since the Second World War. To understand the Clash, one must be holistic. (see the article on 1981 for further elaboration) That is, one must add together the personalities of the people involved and the political and musical environment.

The bit players in the Clash drama were obviously mismatched. The journeymen that played with the band at various times were too stable to fit in with the hyperkinetic Clash. Terry was entirely conventional. Unconcerned with the trappings of Punk, Terry was only there to play drums. This made him a target for the newly-converted true believers of the Clash. I believe his return added nothing to the Clash chemistry. He simply came back at a time when the Clash were beyond the pale. Mickey Gallagher was the prototypical wage-man musician. Peter Frampton, Ian Dury, the Clash... it was all just a paycheck for Mickey. He had a family to support and couldn't be bothered with these yobs. The Clash II hirelings were simply too young to begin to relate to the Clash veterans. Pete Howard was too Heavy Metal, and White was too Punk to the older Joe and Paul. Sheppard seemed to be able to relate best, having slugged it out in Punk's first campaign with the Cortinas. But as Pete Howard said, he simply wasn't in the same league as Mick Jones. Take a listen to Nick's post-Clash band Head for confirmation of this. He formed the band and only co-wrote one of the songs on their first LP.

Although the Clash remain on friendly terms, it is evident that they travel in different circles today. I think the need for a band like the Clash brought them together. The Alchemy of History created the Clash, and once History no longer needed them, it spit them back out. Ronald Reagan's America had no room for a Clash, and Thatcher's Britain had long since shown it wouldn't tolerate the nonsense Callaghan's Britain had   .

CHEMISTRY CLASH
Originally posted 03/05/1996

I was sitting around a table the other night with my editor and my artist discussing the plotting of a comic book that I am writing. As we hashed out ideas, it occurred to me, that even though I was coming up with most of the ideas, the chemistry of three people sitting around bouncing ideas off one another was the true author of the ideas. The give-and-take and the role competition plays is an important partner in the creative process. I noticed this a lot from my band days, too. The whole was always greater than the sum of the parts, even though I could have written all the various parts of a song myself.

This is what Joe was talking about with the Clash. The Clash's music was written by process, a process that Bernie and even Kosmo were active participants in. When Topper fucked it up and was tossed, that process was disrupted. The chemistry that was unique to the classic Clash was gone. The reason Clash II was so brilliant live and so terrible in the studio was also because of chemistry. When the band was on stage, all the players shaped the sound of the band, and many of the arrangements were worked out in sound checks. In the studio, Bernie Rhodes took control of the process and dictated to the band how the music should be played. And that is why all the studio recordings, including the EP B-sides, are dreadful. The reason Joe chucked the whole thing was that that chemistry of the Clash couldn't be reproduced with three newcomers, and to Joe, chemistry is everything.

To me, the genius of the Mick-Joe synergy is most clearly evident in my favorite Clash song, 'Gates of the West'. Die-hards will know that 'Gates' first incarnation was as 'Oh, Baby, Oh', a featherweight piece of fluff that was demoed for *Give 'Em Enough Rope*. 'Oh Baby' suffered from vacuous subject matter and the simplistic A-B rhyming couplets familiar to fans from some of BAD's lyrics. By contrast, 'Gates of the West' has the expansive, cinematic thrust characteristic of Joe's lyrics, and the visionary words seemed to inspire Mick to lay down his best ever vocal. It is three minutes of pure Power Pop brilliance.

London Calling is the result of the full chemistry of the Clash focused like a laser beam on a common goal. *Sandinista* is the product of that chemistry becoming unstable, but still retaining enough power to create an immense amount of music, all of it good, some of it great. *Combat Rock* is the sound of that chemistry coming unglued.

What will probably end being seen as the great BAD album, *No 10 Upping Street* was the last by-product of that chemistry, the last reverberation of a chemical explosion.

GOD, FUCKING, AND THE CLASH
Originally posted 3/11/96

I ran to Compact Disc World the other day to buy the new album by Bel Canto, a Swedish band I am a big fan of. Their sound (up until this new album) could best be described as Neo-Gothic Europop, with a heavy debt to the Cocteau Twins. Like the Twins, they boast a supernaturally gifted female singer, Anneli Drecker, whose vocals absolutely drip with eroticism. The eroticism is not the vulgar and crass "naughtiness" of Madonna and her ilk, however, but of the nature-loving Scandinavian variety. Unlike American eroticism, which is tinged with guilt, the attitude of the Scandinavians is like, "Hey, you like it, I like it, let's fuck." And unlike leering American singers, Anneli can sing about utter foolishness and you know she really means, "Let's fuck."

However, this new record was a different animal, musically. It is of the World-House-Funk variety that is currently the vogue in Europe. Indian and Arab influences drift about and the disco beat is relentless. I scanned the lyric sheet, and mixed in with the broken-English foolishness (sample: "Oh, there's a crocodile beneath the mud/ and it wants a little snack/Oh, there's a crocodile beneath the mud/it is a little bit too excited") is neo-mystic frippery like "It's about a rumor/ it's about God in me/ So, if you talk about a rumor/ you talk about a higher love." As I listened to the record and read the lyrics about Bombay and jungles and God and fucking , I said to myself: "Shit, this sounds like Jah Wobble!" And sure enough, as I scanned through the credits, there he was playing bass and producing a couple of tracks. And then a thought burst into my head; I said ,"Damn, I wonder if Jah is fucking Anneli Drecker!"

Jah Wobble is best known for his ground-breaking bass work on the first two PiL albums. His influence is impossible to underestimate, and the history of the ultra-deep bass so prevalent in House can be traced to his nimble fingers. Along with the Basement 5 (Leo 'EZ-kill' Williams' alma mater) and New Age Steppers, Jah Wobble laid down the law on Punk Dub on his early solo records. Along with the Clash and Talking Heads, PiL were the vanguard of Artsy Punk-types raiding the Third World for inspiration. Unlike the Heads and the Clash, Jah Wobble extracted something of vital importance from the Third World, namely explicit Mysticism and explicit Eroticism.

The history of Rock and Roll is traced to when the first African slaves came to the British colonies and collided with the original American slaves, namely white, indentured servants from the British Isles. Both of these groups had one thing in common: lusty, rhythmic music that their overlords looked down on as 'Devil Music.'

The pounding rhythms and modal chanting of African music collided with the melodic and harmonic traditions of Celtic song and American music was born. Pure Americana like Ragtime, Bluegrass, Country and Western, barbershop quartets (a'capella song-form was straight out of Africa), Rhythm and Blues, Gospel and Jazz can be traced directly to these the collision of these groups of slaves encountering each other under the hot sun of British colonialism.

As history shows, the Scots-Irish/Irish/English slaves won freedom and eventually became the core of the Confederacy. The African slaves suffered greatly under the political system of their former comrades-in-misery, and the original musical revelation of the plantations went through countless variations, and eventually became Rock and Roll. And the midwife of this long and troubled birth was another uniquely American creation, the 'Holiness' Church.

The entire (and I mean entire) early generation of Rock and R&B stars sprung from the loins of the Pentecostal and Baptist 'Holiness' churches, both black and white. 'Holiness' churches ran the gamut from polite, if raucous, Gospel singing to entranced, near-Voodoo hoe-downs. Tearful shouting, speaking in tongues, witnessing, convulsions, snake-handling and countless other ecstatic rituals of these churches laid the foundations for the explosion of spiritual-sexual rites played out in stadiums and concert halls in the past 40 years.

However, the further we deviate from the original formula of Rock and Roll, the more boring concerts become. (I always cite the rote bore-fest I suffered through when Nirvana played the New York Coliseum to illustrate my argument that kids today are desensitized) In an age of 24-hour Media Overload, the eroto-spiritual liberation that Rock and Roll once provided seems now stale and rehearsed.

Back in 1980, when I first saw the Clash, there was no MTV. This was the only exposure you had to seeing your heroes in motion. At the crashing roar of 'Clash City Rockers' sounded, the entire crowd was on its feet, and the whole bloody hall shook. Primed by the slut rock of the B-Girls (Canadian slang for 'whore'), the ganja drenched mystical dub of Mikey Dread (joined onstage by a disguised Mick and Paul), and the old-time, gospel tinged R&B of Lee Perry, the crowd got a crash course in the essentials of the real Rock and Roll experience (in order: Sex, Drugs and R+B) and the Clash took the fucking ball, ran with it and blew up the hall. Although neither explicitly sexual or explicitly spiritual, the Clash left you with the impression that they understood both of these interlocked poles instinctually. The political silliness (which I never took seriously) seemed like a great way to act macho and still seem like you were on the side of the good guys.

But as the Clash made their way, they seemed to lose sight of the implied primacy of God and fucking (although neither were never high on their list of priorities), and the two less vital components of Rock and Roll, Politics and Drugs, took over. How did this happen? The Clash shied away from Sex and Mysticism, sacrificing them both to the altar of Political Correctness. Their bourgeois hang-ups were in direct contrast to their contemporary, Prince. Prince dove head first into the fertile wellsprings of God and Fucking, just as artists like Marvin Gaye and Jimi Hendrix (arguably his two biggest influences) had. The Clash were bashful about sex and religion and wrote about them only ironically, because they were typical awkward Englishmen. And they were also mired in the dreary, self-important milieu of the post Hippie Left. Johnny Rotten was vociferously anti-sex and anti religion and wasn't afraid to let you know it, but the Clash chose to ignore them. It's a shame because in doing so they closed themselves off from two of the building blocks of Rock and Roll and indeed the Reggae music they so admired.

HANDS UP FOR HOLLYWOOD
Originally posted 1/12/97

One of the most frequent criticisms of the Clash was that they were too obsessed with the movies. Marcus Gray got a lot of mileage out of this analysis, but he was certainly not the first. But this particular aspect of the Clash was squarely in line with what I believe they really were, namely multi-media performance artists.

It's long been a cliché that Rock and Roll and Television sprang from the same cradle. The post-War boom brought a relentless appetite for entertainment, and flamboyant stars like Elvis and Little Richard were manna from heaven for ambitious TV producers. Less obvious is the link between Rock and Roll and the movies, but the Rock hipster attitude revolutionized acting the late 50's, and many of the icons of the 50's cinema modeled themselves after Rockers. (Brando, James Dean, and Sal Mineo- to name just a few) And the wildness and spontaneity of Rock and R&B (as well as the improvisational spirit of Jazz) surely made a major impact on many of the decade's 'Method' actors.

The Beatles and Elvis were quick to exploit film's potential, and in the late Sixties with movies like *Gimme Shelter* and *Let it Be*, the concert film was born. Rock has contributed many classic films to Hollywood's canon including *Jailhouse Rock, Hard Day's Night, Woodstock, The Last Waltz* and *This is Spinal Tap*. In addition, many Rock stars have moved into feature films with varying levels of success. Elvis made a whole string of mediocrities, Mick Jagger starred in everything from the Nicolas Roeg classic *Performance* to garbage like *Freejack*. Roeg raided the music industry again to put Bowie in his classic *The Man Who Fell to Earth* (sidenote: points to Mick for celebrating Roeg in 'E=MC2'. For those of you unfamiliar with Roeg's work, rent Man Who Fell and Walkabout. Those movies will haunt you for a long, long time)

More recently, Stink , after some success in *Quadrophenia* and *Brimstone and Treacle*, tried to cross-market himself as a leading man in bomb after bomb, including the love-letter-to-himself, *Bring on the Night*.

Since 'Rock Around the Clock' was used as the opening theme for *Blackboard Jungle* , Rock has been ubiquitous in youth-themed movies.

One way you can tell a movie is a dud is when the TV ads play up the soundtrack over the contents of the film itself. *The Big Chill* spawned a cultural juggernaut by featuring Motown and British Invasion oldies in it, a juggernaut that soon led to the creation of Classic Rock radio. The *American Graffiti* soundtrack did the same for the nascent old-time Rock and Roll revival in the mid-Fifties. Hip-Hop was thrust in the public's consciousness with films like *Wild Style* and the spate of early Eighties break-dancing films. Bauhaus became notorious for their opening credits performance of 'Bela Lugosi's Dead' in the '83 lick-fest *The Hunger*.

Lastly, the movies have been lyrical fodder for great songs since Rock and Roll was young. ("I saw a film today, oh boy") British rockers, in particular, developed their vision of America in cinemas and acts as disparate as the Kinks and Queen have raided old-time Movie arcana for their records.

So, why the hell pick on the Clash? Perhaps because the critics had a vision of the Clash as hard-bitten social realists, a perception that says more about the critics than the Clash. Who the hell needs a rock group to face up to social reality? Do you think Bruce Springsteen, from the New Jersey Malllands, knows dick about the 'Badlands?' Rock and Roll is about escapism, about reinventing yourself. The dreary Nineties are full of whiny bores draining Rock and roll of all fun and fantasy, which is probably why KISS are raking in millions on their tour.

The Clash were in the movies from the get-go, first with Don Letts' *Punk Rock Movie*. Everyone on this board is familiar with *Rude Boy*, I'm sure. All I can say about that flick is that after I went to the Nickelodeon Cinema in Boston to see *Rude Boy* by myself after school one day in 1980, I felt like the King of the World. I've heard everyone bitch about that movie, and I think they are out of their minds. When I was a 13 year-old pissed off outcast, that movie made me feel like there was a world out there somewhere where I could reinvent myself to mirror these Rock gods. Growing up in redneck suburban Boston suddenly seemed less hopeless because there was this culture out there where skinny little losers could become heroes. And when it was re-released, I was lucky enough to fall in with a big clan of like-minded misfits, and we all traveled to see it like pilgrims traveling to Mecca.

My next Clash movie experience was in *DOA*. I saw this in a double feature in Harvard Square with the ska-flick *Dance Craze*. I was transfixed as the 'Police and Thieves' segment came on. As the song played, a montage of footage from a Brixton riot was shown from start to aftermath, synced perfectly to the dynamics of the song. It absolutely shredded the lame concert sequences (Pistols, XRay Spex, etc) that sandwiched it. The Clash were also tapped to star in Martin Scorcese's aborted period piece *Gangs of New York*, but were reduced to a split-second appearance in *King of Comedy*. Lest we forget, Paul also skipped the Electric Ladyland sessions in '80 to star with Cook and Jones and a pert, nubile, supple, young Diane Lane in *Ladies and Gentlemen, the Fabulous Stains*. (featuring countless playings of 'Join the Professionals')

Few, if any, Clash tunes were used for soundtracks while they were around. But, of course, Joe and Mick have completely immersed themselves in the big screen after the split. *Sid and Nancy, Straight to Hell, Walker, Permanent Record, Flashback, Among Friends, The Flinstones (!), When Pigs Fly* and *So I Hired a Contract Killer* feature Joe and Mick music, and *Straight to Hell, Mystery Train* and *Candy Mountain* feature Joe's somewhat amateurish acting. The grooves of Joe's and Mick's post Clash output feature countless Hollywood namecheck's and in BAD's case, sampled dialog. Clash fan Matt Dillon makes an appearance with Lawrence Fishbourne in the Joe-penned mini-movie at the end of "Dial-A-Hitman."

So in the end, it's foolish to expect a band as visually oriented as the Clash to have been able to resist Tinseltown's allure. And why should they? In twenty years no one will remember the best Rock critics, but kids will still be checking out *Rude Boy* to see what it was like in the old days.

HIPPIES, NOT PUNKS
Originally posted 2/4/98

You know, so much about the Clash has really gone under-analyzed. This may be hard to believe with all the books and magazine articles written about them. But still, if you spend as much time obsessing about them as I do, whole new layers of meaning reveal themselves. One of the main revelations I have had is that the Clash, in essence, were not a Punk band at all, but the last of the great Hippie bands.

I have been a life-long student of the history of Rock and Roll. There's nothing I like better than sitting down with a really good book about Rock History. Like few other art forms, Rock and Roll is about the tenor of the times. Rock and Roll has always closely mirrored the prevailing themes and attitudes of contemporary society. Which is also why the Clash remain interesting to me. They were such an anachronism. Even in their early Punk phase, the Clash stood apart from the mood of the times, which was essentially studied nihilism. The Clash were everything the rest of the Punk movement was not: earnest, optimistic, history-minded, critical, liberal. These attitudes were far more emblematic of a Hippie band. And that Hippie tendency only became more pronounced as the Clash left the Punk plantation. The Hippie bands were live acts, particularly the SF bands. They all got their start playing at all night raves at local clubs. They would play extended versions of all their tunes, adding in improvisations that would long outlast the original tune. When you hear the officially recorded evidence of the SF scene, you often wonder what all the fuss was about. One truly great record came from this scene, Jefferson Airplane's *Surrealistic Pillow*, followed by a host of less-great records and a lot of records that weren't really very good at all. The Hippie bands were really about playing for people, smelling the smoke and the sweat, feeling the lights and the pounding of the amps, grooving on the interaction of sound, light and humanity. Just like the Clash.

I don't think the Clash ever really understood what to do in the studio. None of them had the experience that you needed to really make a great record. By a great record, I mean something on the par of a *Who's Next*, a *Ziggy Stardust*, or an *Abbey Road*, or a *Led Zeppelin IV* or an *Are You Experienced*. *London Calling* often gets thrown in with that lot, but I don't think that will last. The Clash made very good records, records which I certainly listen to all the time, but they never made a definitive record. A record that is singular, that is complete, that is unshakable. *London Calling*'s sound is too uncertain, and there's too much filler. The first album is too crude and embryonic. This is why my motto is "The Only Good Clash is a Live Clash." Just like their hippie forebears, the Clash were only real and complete in front of people. The audience completed the circuit. Conversely, Led Zeppelin made great records, some of the greatest records of all time, but after their early punky days, they weren't very good live.

Just as the Hippies adopted the Blues as their spiritual source, the Clash adopted Reggae. Reggae informed the Clash's music from very early on. In fact, Mick stopped listening to Reggae for a few years after leaving the Clash because Paul and Joe "were so mad on it." Like their Hippie forebears, the Clash would bring black Roots artists on tour with them, like Lee Dorsey, Sam and Dave, and Bo Diddley. Like their Hippie forebears, the Clash would dress in a rag-tag military jumble. Just like their Hippie forebears, the Clash were obsessed with Viet Nam and 50's Rock and Roll. Just like their Hippie forebears, the Clash involved themselves with Third World guerilla movements.

If you ever get a chance to see old footage of the great bands of the Sixties you will see that the Hippie bands were nothing like what we stereotype Hippies as being. They were raw, aggressive, furious, and ecstatic. Even the Grateful Dead, in their early incarnation, were a kick ass Groove band. The Jefferson Airplane often resembled the MC5 in concert more than they resembled their mellower sounding studio records.(which after *Surrealistic Pillow* weren't very mellow, come to think of it) Big Brother and the Holding Company were a 'Rock the House' proto-Metal outfit. And little needs to be said about the ferocity of a Jimi Hendrix show. Contrast this with your average Damned or Sex Pistols performance. There, we just see a bunch of posing around like Alice Copper's grandmother. No fury, no catharsis, just mannerism. Or look at the Buzzcocks, just a bunch of schlubs standing there strumming away. There was plenty of volume and speed evident at the Punk bands' shows, but little real catharsis. A lot of this has to do with the relative lack of playing ability. Most of the Hippie bands were relatively more seasoned players and could cut loose live. Of course, a lot of these bands were hopeless in the recording studio. (Jerry Garcia - "We don't play so good for machines.") They would take massive amounts of drugs and twiddle around with this knob and that knob, grooving on the wacky sounds they made. What would often result was a pale and demented shadow of the band's live act. Sound familiar?

This is why the Clash remain interesting to me. The Hippie counterculture was a lot more positive and vital than the Punk culture was. They were not really all that different in many respects, but the Hippie Culture was a lot less marginal, and more engaged. There was also a broader range of expression in the Hippie movement. Punk will always fascinate me because I lived through it, but the 60's Counter-culture ultimately was more important and lasting. Unfortunately, much of that legacy has been poisoned and mutated, from the corporate Hippie scene of the Dave Matthews and Blues Traveler variety, and the deformed hateful Yippie god-children holding forth on today's campuses and the Group Resentment gripe movement, but this is what happens when you attach yourself to the externals of a movement and not the spirit.

Postscript: A lot of fans have criticized me for the Hippies, Not Punks dispatches, telling me how far off base I was. Let's get Mr. Strummer's take on this...

"Definitely! I was always a hippy. If you weren't a hippy then what the fuck were you, back in the day? Punks had a lot in common with hippies - like spliff, and booting authority around. Who else bloody invented rock festivals and getting down? All the serious things that go on in the counterculture of these islands are from hippies or ex-hippies. Lifelong dedication to the cause. I dare anyone to piss on that."
Joe Strummer NME *October 1999*

MYTHOLOGY REDUX
Originally posted 1/2/97

You know, as hard as Marcus Gray tried to deconstruct the myth of the Clash, the story remains. I don't think a myth is necessarily diminished once exposed, it is merely altered. A true myth has a self-contained veracity, that is, the story is its own truth. When one looks back at the march of events in the story of the Clash, one comes to the conclusion that the Clash ended because there was nowhere left for the story to go. I can't imagine the Clash just functioning as a pop band in the REM/U2 mode. The Clash were a cross between Don Quixote and the Knights of the Round Table, or the Unforgiven, coming out of retirement for one last kill. From the 101'ers and the London SS to the Punk media blitz to *London Calling* and international stardom to *Sandinista* and Bond's, to the *Combat Rock* breakthrough to the breakup to the busking tour to the *Cut the Crap* disaster to the '91 nostalgia explosion, the whole story has a tangibly literary feel.

Which probably explains why Joe, the most overtly myth obsessed of this crowd, has stayed out of the limelight. He probably just couldn't think of a new chapter to a finished story. And seeing his former comrade ride a downbound train to obscurity probably is not too heartening, either. I am sure he has plenty of songs tucked away, but the Clash were never just about songs, were they?

REVOLUTION ROCK?
Originally posted 2/3/97

"I'm into guns." - *Joe Strummer* , Boston Rock *interview June 1981*

Back in the day, the standard take on the Clash was that they were a 'political' band. They certainly used romantic visions of rebellion in their palette, but none of them were particularly rigorous in their ideology, especially when compared to Crass, Gang of Four, the Au Pairs, or Dead Kennedys, to name just a few of their more committed contemporaries. *CCS* followers will notice that I have written very few columns on their political beliefs, because for one thing, I don't think they really had any. The Clash's politics were very vague and impressionistic, though I think their anti-authoritarianism and anti-racism was sincere. In contrast to Rage Against the Machine, the Clash were practically apolitical. Interestingly enough, the Clash zestfully pursued intra-band politics with the constant one-upmanship and fisticuffs and power-playing that led to their dissolution, and Bernie Rhodes cannot be blamed for all of this by any means.

The Clash wanted to be rock stars. They idolized the canon of Classic Rock, and modeled themselves in many ways after the Beatles, the Who, the Stones and Bob Dylan. And since these artists did their best work in the mid-to-late Sixties, when the world was gripped in political upheaval, it was only natural for the Clash pick up those themes. Interestingly enough, Paul and Joe idolized Clint Eastwood, Robert DeNiro and other such anti-heroic action

movie stars, and leftism was fused with machismo in the Clash's *weltanshuang*. And since that blend was playing itself out in real life in Latin America and Africa, it became even more seductive to the Clash.

The other component in the Clash's outlook was the eternal verities of British class resentment. Much has been made of Joe's father's status as a Foreign Service bureaucrat, but this does not make Joe a hypocrite. There was probably a good deal of dysfunction in the Mellor household, given that his brother was heavily involved in the fascist National Front and eventually committed suicide. And lest we forget, insurrectionary movements have often been peopled by the children of privilege. One look no further than Che Guevera, the Weather Underground and the Baader-Meinholf gang for proof of this. The power structure in England is expert in divide and rule, and all the various classes and ethnicities in the UK have been well-conditioned to despise each other.

In conclusion, I think ultimately the Clash 's politics were a cool way to employ violence and machismo into their presentation and still seem counter-cultural.

MARRIED TO THE YOBS
Originally posted 12/19/97

I have always said a band is like a marriage. You have all the hassles and responsibilities of a marriage, only it's with three or four other people, and you usually don't have sex with them. In a deeper, more archetypal sense there is a symbolic marriage, a Tao-like synthesis. The great bands of British Rock can be seen as families, with a mother-father analog and children. Mick and Keef were wife and husband, and the rest of that pug-ugly lot were the kids. Mick's femininity was the muse and Keef's machismo was the structure. In other words, Keef built the house and Mick hung the drapes. The Mighty Zep were run in a similar but slightly different fashion. Former brick layer Bonzo and John Paul built the rock solid foundation, but Pagey was the architect, and Percy did the interior decorating.

The Who were different in their alchemical marriage as well. Daltrey wrote squat, but he gave the paternal authority to Townsend's fantasies. Townsend was like an Isek Dinesen, writing adventurous fantasies under a male pseudonym while Roger acted them out. It's interesting to note the contrast in voices here as well: Townsend's airy tenor vs. Daltrey's street fighting baritone. Mick's bluesy purr and flighty falsetto vs Keef's ten-pack -a-day rasp, Plant's orgasmic squealing vs. Pagey's roaring Les Paul. The Kinks buggered this whole continuum. Ray's squeaky music-hall yelping and Dave's raunchy barre chords fit quite nicely, but they were brudders. Perhaps that incestuous blurring of the roles can account for why the Kinks never really made it into the upper echelon. There are plenty of others you can plug into this Taoist analogy: Ziggy and Ronno, Ozzy and Tony, and if you want to go stateside, Steve and Joe (cast in the Stones mold) and Dave and Eddie (Zep paradigm). And in the true spirit of 70's Californian social experimentation, you can toss in Fleetwood Mac and see Lindsay, Stevie and Christine in some weird menage, or the whole bloody band as some hippie group marriage thing.

Then there's the Clash. Mick and Joe are almost the purest expression of this Yin-Yang continuum. In their roles, their voices, their appearances, The Clash were almost made to order in this regard. And in their solo careers, their yinnery and yangery has stood out in even starker relief. Picture 1978 - the Clash are barnstorming around on the heels of *Give 'Em Enough Rope*. Joe in military garb and brushcut, wields a pickaxe voice and jackhammer Tele. Mick willows about in satin and houndstooth, with curly shoulder-length locks and a willowy tenor, but in the classic British tradition of foppish violence, he wields a 20 megaton Les Paul-Marshall punch. Surly yobs Paul and Topper are the brats in the back seat who just won't shut up. Call Bernie what you will, but he put this amalgamation together, and that was pure genius. This was a brilliant pairing of Rock and Roll Yin-yang. The Clash were like some Jungian postulate of what a Rock and Roll band should be.

But all marriages end in some way. Zep's ended when Bonzo kicked, and that mighty foundation fell to the ground. The Who's did the same a couple years before, only they kept it going for the sake of the kids, and, oh yeah, their wallets   .

Mick's eggs went bad in '78 , but he and Keef kept procreating and their mongoloids have names like *Dirty Work, Steel Wheels, Voodoo Lounge* and *Bridges to Babylon*. Ozzy and Tony's union crashed after *Sabotage*, but they kept up appearances for a few years after, and then Ozzy went on to a number of fruitful liaisons like a Rock and Roll Ivana Trump. Mick and Joe split in '83, but things went bad in '81. That weird old hen Bernie, who set them up in the first place, came back because Mick never did the dishes and Joe was fed up with doing the housework while Mick went out discoing. They stuck it out for a one more album, but Joe took the Visa away from Mick and said, "There's gonna be some new rules around here."

They kept up appearances, but Topper was sent off to reform school and that polite neighbor boy Terry filled in. After their wallets got nice and fat, Joe decided he wanted to go out and raise hell with the boys, like in the old days, and Mick was doing just fine at the Disco Palace, thank you very much.

But, in a way a marriage transforms you. You can't help but internalize aspects of your partner. In Clash II and beyond, Joe has done plenty of ranting, but a soft edged melodicism has often crept in. Even on the Out of Control tour, more and more late period Clash numbers began to creep in as time went on, and Joe was given to write some ballads even before Bernie told him not to ("'Pouring Rain' can't be on the album, Joey, we need room for stellar tracks like 'Play to Win'"). And real Rock and Roll hasn't been a complete stranger to Mick, just an infrequent houseguest. And strangely enough, even though they will never get together professionally, Mick and Joe may get together in spirit. The first steps were abortive. Mick decided he wanted to try to make a Rock album, tried summoning the spirit of Joe, had second thoughts, and made *Cut the Crap* II (re-titled for release as *F-Punk*).

Joe had Mick on his mind and got together with Richard Norris, tried to make a BAD album, but was kind enough to spare us when it came out all screwy (I'm guessing, but educated-ly). But '97 has shown us that maybe the internal unions have taken hold. Mick has given us a very *No 10. Upping* sounding track called 'Sunday Best', that sounds like he isn't sorry for playing Rock guitar anymore, and Joe gave us 'Generations' a track that sounds uncannily like the song that was left off of *Combat Rock* because it was too energetic and made everything else look anemic. So, maybe if MCA stops dicking Mick, and Joe quits with the Hamlet routine, we will be blessed not with two half-Clash records, but with two records that have shown that even though they split, Mick and Joe still think about each other.

TECHNISONIC CINEMADELIA

Originally posted 1/24/97

The popular image of the Clash among non-believers is of a angry, rabble-rousing Rock/Punk band. While there is an element of truth in that description, it is ultimately limited. People like to categorize artists, as in "Oh yeah, Picasso, that guy with all the distorted faces and the Cubism and stuff," disregarding huge chunks of his career. For acts like the Clash who came from a specific musical genre, branching out was more painful and difficult than it was for British acts of the 60's. People wanted the Clash to be the Punk standard bearers, a desire that would have greatly limited the Clash's Technisonic Cinemadelic art. What was most befuddling about *Sandinista* to casual fans and critics like Nick Kent was the fact that it is inherently a Psychedelic record. Much like *Surrealistic Pillow*, or *Strange Days*, or *Revolver*, or *On Her Satanic Majesties Request*, *Sandinista* is about vast sonic landscapes and interior imagery. "Hearing the taste of purple", as it were. In everything but chronology, the Clash were not a Punk band at all, but the last of the great 60's British Invasion bands.

A lot of Rock groups will often gravitate towards two musical poles as they progress in their careers. The first is Dance or Funk, where the rhythm becomes paramount. Seasoned players will often play funk when they jam, since the layers of rhythmic possibility are more challenging than four-square rock. Of course, playing funky rhythms is often a way to disguise a dearth of melodic ideas, as The Pretenders' *Get Close* , the Talking Heads' *Naked* and the new U2 single display. The other pole is Psychedelia, where artists retreat into the studio and create sonic paintings. Pink Floyd is the prime example of this.

They will spend years in the studio constructing their records, whether the songs warrant it or not. U2, under the tutelage of Brian Eno, tried to pursue both dance and psychedelia simultaneously with *Achtung Baby* and *Zooropa*. They, of course, were doing what they have done their entire careers, namely aping what was going on in England at the time. Manchester and Acid House produced copious amounts of Psych/Dance rock in the early 90's, and the saga continues with Techno, Jungle, and Trip-Hop.

But none of that music is truly Psychedelic. As hard as it tries, modern dance music falls short of true Psychedelia because of it's emphasis on digital technology. Digital technology hinders two musical elements vital to true Psychedelia: Resonance and Improvisation. Digital musical instruments are simply simulators of sound. Nothing is struck, nothing vibrates, nothing resonates. When wood and metal and plastic are struck (all Rock instruments are percussive), they vibrate and the vibration causes atoms to move in the air. When fed through analog and vacuum tube amplification, heat affects the vibrations, creating deeper more resonant vibrations. When recorded through a tube-driven sound board onto magnetic tape, added heat and vibration further enrich the sound of the music. And these complex vibrations are what the expanded consciousness focus in on. This is why there is the mania for analog synths and guitar effects among today's musicians. Tom Scholz (guitarist/producer of Boston) is a electronics whiz who produces the Rockman line of electronics. He despises digital effects and digital recording. The first Boston album, which was made an astonishing 20 years ago, is still light years ahead of most records out today sound-wise, because Scholz understands the inherent superiority of analog technology and knows how to work with it.

When I pulled out my vinyl copy of *Sandinista!* , I was stunned by how much better it sounded than the CD. Not clearer, not more pristine, but just better. CDs operate on the principle that distortion is always bad and clarity is always good. But, when you see a glorious sunset in the summer, what you are seeing is distortion of light rays caused by heat and pollution. To take a recording made for vinyl and put it on CD usually means radical compression, squelching out huge chunks of mid-range, exactly the frequencies that excite the altered ear. The best 60's records are filthy, hiss-ridden, four-track wonders , but these records insinuate themselves into your subconscious in the way that grainy Viet Nam footage does. The distortion is part of the experience. This is why a million dollar industry exists to make guitars sound distorted and messy. This is why Brian Eno will often add tape hiss to CDs he's producing.

Improvisation is a corner stone of Rock and Roll. Many bands will compose tunes by jamming on a riff or three until something resembling a song is developed. When real live human beings play a song, they will deviate in subtle ways on the rhythm. A drummer will rarely hit the drum in exactly the same spot twice in a row, hence a slightly different tone is produced with every beat. These subtitles will often aid the writing process by producing suggestive 'triggers' to the musicians. Psychedelic bands like Pink Floyd, the Doors, Moby Grape and the Dead took improvisation as an article of faith. As stoned-out hippies staggered about, these bands would play a 'song ' often for twenty minutes or more.

Psychedelic improvisation got a new twist in the late 60's with

Jamaican dub, as DJs and producers improvised crude but effective electronic effects on instrumental tracks.

Sandinista incorporates both of these approaches, with an emphasis on the latter. Many of the songs on the record are vocal improvisations on funky vamps, and much of the material was written as it was recorded. Extended ragas were curtailed in keeping with the Punk ethos, but length was the only nod to those constraint.s (Gray implies that the song lengths were determined somewhat numerologically, in that the Clash were obsessed with having six sides with six songs each) The band's then current obsession with Reggae and Dub colored nearly every track on the album. Even the heavy rock tunes on the album make concessions towards Reggae Psychedelia. 'Somebody Got Murdered' starts with Mickey Dread toasting from the previous cut, and adds audio verite effects via Topper's dog. 'Up in Heaven' goes even further with this approach, adding a screeching subway train that nearly overpowers the tune at the fade. 'Police on My Back' adds scorching guitars over a rock-steady rhythm and 'Kingston Advice' adds its guitar fire over a more explicit Dub backing.

Dub/Psychedelia effects merge with Gospel, Jazz, Rockabilly, Calypso, Pop, and on and on. Rock critics usually hate Psychedelia, unfortunately, and this is why *Sandinista*! got so many pans. In addition , too many Punks only understand noise and subtler colors are to spat on. Marcus Gray understood how important *Sandinista* is, despite his other lapses in judgment. But even he dismissed the more extreme manifestations of the Psychedelic ethos, namely 'The Equalizer' and 'Mensforth Hill'. These tracks are pure psychedelia for it's own sake. The former track builds up a slow burn, and Strummer's moans and Dogg's fiddle gets sucked into the echo-box maelstrom, evoking a cold industrial wasteland with Strummer ranting hopelessly ("Prove me wrong!") beneath a gun-metal sky. The latter track revives that Acid Rock mainstay, the backward track. As 'Something About England' spins in reverse, random bits of dialogue and synth float above the din, creating a playful delirium.

But to my ears, the purest expression of the Psychedelic quest is a track buried at the end of side five, 'the Street Parade'. This track is pure dreamscape, almost like a Clash take on Wire's *154* album or the Beatles' 'Rain'. The track starts off like a dream of a Fifties urban serenade, with guitar and bongos echoing and panning, then picks up the pace as steel drums, guitar and sax float above the beat. The guitar riff towards the end sounds like it's a million miles away, and you picture a setting sun bleaching out smiling faces as the silhouettes of buildings loom in the background as if lending a sense of foreboding to the festivities. It all reminds me of a hazy memory of childhood I never had, riding on my father's shoulders straining to see girls spinning batons on the street before us. But if you try to assign specific images to the whirling sounds, the spell is broken. That is true Psychedelia.

WHY THE CLASH RULE!
Originally posted 7/10/95

The other night I was having a conversation with an old friend of mine, who was a fellow veteran of the Boston Punk Wars of the early 80's. We were discussing the Clash and why I am still obsessed by them. He asked me why I thought that was. Of course I supplied him with a pseudo intellectual bullshit answer, about this, that, and the other thing. I did so cause I did not have an answer at the time. But the answer is this: Because the Clash did it all.

Tonight I was listening to Blitz, one of my favorite Oi! bands, then Sweet, the great foot stomping glitter band, then some classic Cheap Trick. Last night, I was listening to some great old Reggae and some great new Trip Hop, then the latest Jah Wobble album. And I realized that all that music was related to the Clash. I could make a killer Oi! compilation, with Blitz, the 4 Skins, the Business, et al, and I could slip in some Clash cuts (anything off the first LP) and it would all blend it perfectly. Or if I was to make a killer classic Power Pop comp, I could put on some Cheap Trick, some Sweet, some Badfinger, 'Magic' by Pilot, etc. etc., I could put in 'Gates of the West' or 'Police on My Back' and not miss a beat. Or if I made a Trip-Hop comp with some Portishead, or Tricky or Massive Attack, 'If Music Could Talk' or 'Sean Flynn' or 'One More Dub' would go well. Or if I was to make a great Funk/Disco tape, I could put in "Mustapha Dance" or "The Cool Out" or "Overpowered by Funk." To stretch the issue: Rockabilly - Carl Perkins, Eddie Cochran, Stray Cats, Elvis-'the Leader', 'Midnight Log', 'Brand New Cadillac'. Reggae/Dub- Marley, Mighty Diamonds, Gregory Issacs, UB40 (pre 83 only) then 'Revolution Rock', 'Armagideon Time', 'Living in Fame'. Celtic -Tanahill Weavers, Capercaillae, Levellers (old) -"Lose This Skin', 'Rebel Waltz" Hard Rock - Zep, old Van Halen, Soundgarden- "Clampdown" or any number of live tracks.

By now you get the idea. What other band can you say this about? The Clash rule forever.

COWBOYS IN AFRICA
Originally posted Apr 14, 2000

In the late 19th century, Walt Whitman observed the musical interaction of Irish immigrants and freed black slaves on the streets of lower Manhattan and commented that he was witnessing the genesis of a uniquely American grand opera. These two groups, whose interlocked history has been characterized usually by hatred and enmity, had found common ground melding the sounds and rhythms of their ancestral homelands and set the framework for the music of the 20th century. These sounds weren't as incompatible as one might imagine, for the music of Ireland and the British Isles had been imported there by Phoenician traders who had brought it from the ports of Northern Africa to begin with. The pipes and whistles we associate with Celtic music are straight out of the Near East and Mediterranean basin. Only the caste and race consciousness of the Christian era had induced the cultural amnesia that caused the Irish to see their jigs and reels as indigenous in the first place.

When I was working in midtown Manhattan 100 years later, I was serenaded daily by the reverberating sounds of a break-dancing troupe that performed in Greely Square Park. The concrete canyons shook with the sounds of an ass-kicking drummer who played funky beats accompanied only by whistles, handclaps and shouts. This was a huge, almost incalculable influence on my own music and my musical thinking. The instruments might have been the familiar modern "traps", pioneered in Cuba in the earlier part of the century, but the vibe was as old as time. I was thinking of all this as I was listening to the first cassette of *the Story of the Clash*. Topper's playing on such tracks as 'Armagideon Time', 'Rock the Casbah' and 'Straight to Hell' is so authentic it borders on visionary.

If Joe brought the Beatnik vibe to the Clash, and Paul brought the style and vibe of South London and Mick brought the Glam and Pop, Topper brought the Africa. Spending as much time as I have listening to Topper's decline in '81 and '82 live recordings, I sometimes forget what he contributed to the sound, and how invaluable that contribution was. Topper was not an overwhelming technical powerhouse like Pete was, but he had assimilated the subtleties and polyrhythms of Black music in a way few white drummers have. Topper spent his teenage years immersed in Funk, Soul and Jazz and brought a complexity to the Clash's sound that Terry never managed. Sadly and ironically, Topper also adopted the addictive tendencies that many of his idols and forebears suffered from. Topper's decline and fall reminds me a lot of another diminutive English musical prodigy, Brian Jones.

I listen to a lot of 60's and 70's Funk and Soul and I am amazed to hear how many moves Topper picked up from these players. Topper in his prime was an extraordinarily tasteful player who understood the complex syncopations and polyrhythms of the music of the African Diaspora. The history of American and subsequently, Western Music, in the past century has been determined by the influence of Africa. The greatest popular musicians of the past 50 years have all been well-versed in this history. I don't think the Clash would have been as likely to explore the forms and styles they did had Topper not been in the band. Terry's four to the floor style helped the band recover as a live act following Topper's dismissal, but Terry's roots were in the hard Rock players of the late 60's and early 70's like Ian Paice, John Bonham and Simon Kirke, not in the big band and soul drummers who influenced those great musicians. Terry did tribal well but it his playing always sounded like it was drawn from very recent playing. Terry had very little Africa is his style.

Longtime Showdown readers know my most hated band is Metallica. Why? Well, one reason among many is that there isn't the barest shred of Africa in their music. Lars Ulrich makes Terry sound like Tony Williams. Metallica is the sound of the trailer park and the strip mall, and their roots go only as deep as the nauseating, crypto-fascist British Metal of the late 70's. Their music is the aural equivalent of tattoo art.

Contrast the suffocating deadness of the Metallica beat to Led Zeppelin or Aerosmith. Or for that matter, the chockablock fifths chording and finger-exercise lead playing of Metallica to the loose and clever playing of Joe Perry or Jimmy Page. Aerosmith, in their prime , wrote music drenched in the big city Blues of the 20's and 30's and simply added big Rock guitars over it. Led Zeppelin did the same to the oeuvre of Howling Wolf and Willie Dixon. John Bonham's style was straight out of the barrelhouses of the Deep South and the dance halls of Detroit. He just played so damn loudly that some people missed the connection. A casual look at Metallica shows they have all the looseness and vitality of department store mannequins or body-builders posing at a pageant.

In yesterday's dispatch, I mentioned the two-way pipeline between the US and the UK that really was as old as our country. In the suffocating con-formity of post-War Britain the Rhythm and Blues records that made their way to port cities in England were a revelation, an intoxicating blast of freedom in a repressed Nordic land. To some extent that exchange is still going on, but something is getting lost in the translation. The various drug-inspired dance scenes in the UK have produced a strange and inaccessible sound that deval-ues songs and performing and elevates the producer and the technician. It's almost like the technocratic impulse that has always lurked in the fabric in British society has taken over again and forced the spontaneity and humanity-the Africa- back underground.

This can be intermittently entertaining- Fatboy Slim comes to mind- but it seems old British habits die hard. England is a land of tinkerers and engineers, and the producer driven acts that dominate the charts don't translate too well here. It seems like the old musty professors have taken over again ("I say, I have a handle on this boogie-woogie business! Jolly good show!") and are giving us a hermetically sealed analog of Africa. Personality is washed away.

I keep harping on this because historically Britain has always lifted American music out of the quagmires it got stuck in. Now Rock is dead again, only this time the calvary isn't coming. Are there any young kids in basements in Islington or Manchester listening to their dad's Rolling Stones or Clash records and tracing the sounds back to Buddy Guy or Augustus Pablo and are preparing to bring the sound back? Black American music is as dead and cold as I've ever heard it and I'm hoping someone out there will bring back some Africa before it's too late.

Maybe the Japanese will help out...

ME AND THE CLASH COULDN'T BE PALS
Originally posted 3/26/97

Face it, me and the Clash could never be pals. It just wouldn't work. There is just too much water under the bridge. I mean, could you imagine me and Mick having a drink at some pub in New York? It would probably go something like this...

Mick: And the bloke goes, 'Right! that's my snorkel!'
Everyone at table (except See): Ha Ha Ha Ha Ha!
Mick: 'Ere, whatsa matter, See, you didn't like that one? Why are you staring at me like that, mate?
See: Help, help me out here, Mick. Alright, so Joe goes down to the beach on a bike and grovels for you to join the Clash. He'll sack Bernie, and you guys start from scratch.
Mick: Bloody hell, are we gonna start with this again?

See: No, no, give me a minute here. So, he completely humiliates himself and you shoot him down? I mean, what the fuck is that? Is Big Audio Dynamite that fucking important? Man, U2 would be opening up for you guys now. So, now you scrape around for cash to make records that no one wants to hear, for what? So, you could show Joe up? I mean, he said he was fucking sorry! What's the matter, you allergic to money?

It just wouldn't work, would it?

And with Joe, it would be a hell of a lot worse. OK, here's the scene, Slaughtered Lamb on W 3rd st., NYC. Cast- Joe and his entourage, including me...

Joe: So I'm just about to smack the bleeding wanker, when....right, See, what is it now?
See: Nothing.
Joe: C'mon, See, what is it this time?
See: Nothing.
Joe: See.
See: Well, it's just... I mean, OK, OK. Here's the deal: July '84, right? You go into the studio with Bill Price. If Bernie starts acting up, you have Nick and Vince kick his head in. He's your manager, OK? That means he's your employee.
Joe: Christ!
See: No, no... no. Listen, I mean, who cares if you didn't write the songs with Nick or some shit? Who cares? The songs are written, you've got enough for an album, OK? Two months, tops, start to finish. The album's out by Christmas, and Mick is still dicking around with his synthesizer. Boom. 'Pouring Rain' is the first single, and 'This is England' is the follow-up. I mean, is that so fucking hard? You tour for eight months before BAD even comes out. You rule the Eighties. I mean what is it? Do you like failure? What's your problem? Man, you ruined my entire year. Does that make you happy?
Joe: Aw, come on, See!
See: What? What? What? Does that make you happy? Don't you know how stupid I looked? I said to everyone, "The new Clash album will be their best." And what do you put out, a year and a half later I might add, Cut the fucking Crap! Yeah, thanks a lot, buddy, some hero you are!

None too pretty, huh? Well, how about me and Paul?

See: So, Paul, whaddya know?
Paul: Nothing.
See: OK.

(long awkward silence)

See: Well, gotta go!

Or heaven forbid, me and Topper?

See: Oh yeah, Topper fucking Headon. Friggin' snareboy! Hey Tops, what happened to your toms? I swear in that friggin Sun Plaza show, you don't use them once. Oh, yeah, and what happened on *Combat Rock*? What's the matter, your contract have a no-fill clause? Or did you just want to sound like that bitchin" drummer in the old Kraftwerk records? I got news for ya, Toppy, that was a god-damned DRUM MACHINE!
Topper: Oi, leave me alone, ok?

Well, at least me and Terry could hit it off.

Terry: What's the problem then?
See: Oh, Dr. Chimes, my back is going haywire. The pain is just shooting down the back of my leg!
Terry: Right. Well, let's have a look.

Oh, well, you know what they say. It's best never to meet your heroes.

LIVING IN THE PAST
Originally posted 12/27/96

I don't know how much any of you go in for Astrology, but I have always found I fit the entire Cancerian profile to a 'T'. (I also fit the profile for my birthday to a 'T', and if any of you out there wonder why I am so damn combative at times, let me just tell you that Mike Tyson and I were born literally hours apart). Anyhow, one of the prime aspects of a Cancerian is an obsession with memory and history.

Yesterday, I went to my local Rock and Roll emporium to replace my *Mutable Punks* CD because the Stockholm side is completely blank. I was hoping that if *MP* wasn't in stock, perhaps they would have *Out of Control*. I already have had *Five Alive* for years, and I have multiple copies of it on tape, but you can never have too much '84 Clash. I was disappointed to see that they had no Clash CD boots, probably on account of the FBI clampdown. So I started tooling through the vinyl and there they had 16 Tracks and the 12" interview picture disk. And what to my wondering eyes should appear but the Joe Strummer with the 101'ers and the Clash book. I strolled home with my booty and had an all-night nostalgia festival. I put the Interview disk on first, since I already have the *16 Tracks* show on tape. I listened to the Joe '84-style rant and I was transported in my mind back to those days. Boston, early Eighties, I'll tell you, the right place at the right time. It's impossible to put into words what that time was like, especially now in the negative, grunge-ridden 90's. Boston was Clash City, and my friends were all Clash-heads. We went in caravans to see the Clash. At a Clash show you would see punks, jocks, skins, burnouts, tons of pretty girls, hippies, new wavers, the whole gamut. Has there been a band with that wide an appeal since?

Of course, the curse of the Clash fan is to live in the past, which being a Cancer and all, suits me fine. But I wish I could explain the thrill of seeing and meeting the Clash in '84. I wish I could explain the mayhem and the energy that was unleashed in the hall that night, the pure frigging Joe-ness. Many of you know because you were there on a night just like them. I have friends who weren't there and they will never get it. I can't explain what it was like to take the subway to Newbury Comics after school, only to be greeted by *Paris '77/'78* , this strange forbidden artefact, in the Clash bin. Or what it was like to go into town during Christmas, and get *Sandinista* , just out on import. Or what it was like to get *Down at the Casbah Club* at that crummy stall at the Flea Market and hear the Clash blow away the weak taste *Combat Rock* left? How can I explain what it was like to see these strange ambassadors from an exotic world invade your dull, anemic suburban worldview, years before MTV? In the post-Modern sensory assault we are bombarded with, mystery and newness is deadened. Everything is just another blip on the screen. The Clash = Rancid, Buzzcocks = Green Day, The Specials =The Toasters, Missing Persons = No Doubt, hey, it's all the same, right?

I am so grateful to have been there when it all meant something.

GRRRLS VS. BOYZ

Originally posted 1/30/97

Clash fandom is pretty much a guy thing. Among the regular posters on this board, I see no women. Our sole female correspondent, Aya , was scared off a couple of years ago during the nasty flame wars that were going on at the time (of which I was a participant, I regret to say). The same held true in England, it would seem. Most reviews of Clash concerts I read in British papers often commented on the high proportion of football hooligans in the crowd, and the roughness up towards the stage. Of course, these reviews were written by English music journalists, a segment of that country's population not noted for their machismo. Some critics like Everett True have gone so far to slam the Clash for being a pack of male chauvinists.

But my memories of the glory days are different. I remember a high female turnout at Clash shows, even if they weren't in the pit. I met the girl whom I went out with for most of my High School career at a Clash show in '82, and not only was she a girl, but she was also a black girl. Even in the head-banging '84 tour, there were quite of few lasses in attendance, and I remember a high degree of them being quite attractive. But the Clash were exotic and fashionable back then, and perhaps many younger girls (as well as boys) went simply to see what all the fuss was about.

In addition, though the Clash didn't sing more than a handful of songs about sex or love or what have you, they also didn't sing songs about date rape or big tits like many of the Heavy Metal bands of the time did. So many of the girls who went to Clash shows were fairly intelligent, particularly in comparison to the bimbos hurling their tops off at Motley Crue shows.

I think the upshot of this is that Rock fandom is primarily a guy thing, particularly for a long-gone band of foot-stompers who liked to dress like GI Joe dolls. Women generally speaking tend to have different interests than men (duh), and guys are more likely to cling to interests they held as adolescents.

In closing, I think it's a shame that the Clash didn't stick together and learn how to play their instruments properly and mature into a soulful Rock and Roll dance band (a la J. Geils or 70's Stones). Girls like to dance more often than not, and if every Clash concert was a barn-storming hootenanny, there'd be plenty of lovely sheilas to shake a leg with. I think their instrumental limitations contributed to their demise because instinct only gets you so far when you are writing music. Sooner or later you need new places to go to keep fresh. Bernie is notorious for suggesting the Clash play New Orleans style soul, but his mistake was in overestimating their chops. Reggae came from Jamaicans trying to play the New Orleans R&B they heard coming over the short wave, missing the mark and in the process coming up with their own sound, so who knows what the Clash could have done with it. But you can bet it would have gotten the ladies dancing.

GET A LIFE
Originally posted 1/17/97

I took a break from my computer this morning to watch a bit of Comedy Central. They were showing a *Saturday Night Live* repeat from the '86 season featuring William Shatner. A soon as the show started, I knew what was coming: the classic Star Trek Convention skit. Those of you who have been to a collector's convention of any kind (whether Star Trek, comics, records, whatever) will relate to the brilliant accuracy of that sketch. As bespectacled losers bombard him with absurd questions dealing with Trek minutiae, Shatner pauses and then says: "Get a Life."

When I first saw that skit, I nearly died laughing. It was back in '86, when I was rocking around, pursuing my fantasies, but now it seems all too familiar. I laugh at Trekkers pondering the episode numbers and alien races of a TV show, and meanwhile I sit down every day and obsess about issues that are long since forgotten by Mick and Joe.

Fandom is a funny thing. People are usually fans of things they encountered in their youth, and only the seriously deranged become obsessive over things they encountered once they left adolescence. You see old men who still obsess over Roy Rogers or Bing Crosby, because that's what it hit them when they were young and impressionable. But the object of your fantasies is always elusive, which is the nature of fandom. When the object of your obsession is distant, you are able to project your own feelings onto it, and when you approach that fantasy head on, the illusion is most often shattered.

Another *SNL* skit came to my mind when I actually met Joe Strummer in '84. When I met Joe and he gave me his autograph, I remember asking him "Hey Joe, do you remember that song 'Stop the World?'" He paused for a minute, probably thinking "What is this kid, an idiot or something? He thinks I don't remember a song that came out three and a half years ago?" He then said, "Yeah, that's one of the forgotten Clash numbers." I don't know what I was expecting him to say, but I lamely replied, "I really like the lyrics to that song," and then felt like a moron. This reminded me of the 'Chris Farley Show,' where Chris would have on a someone like Paul McCartney and nervously ask him, "Hey do you remember that song 'Let it Be?'" McCartney would say, "Sure," in response and Farley would sit there bewildered, the wind taken out of his sails as if he actually expected McCartney not to remember it. Defeated, he then would say something like, "Yeah, that one was good. Heh."

One of the curses of being famous is to have fans. Being overwhelmed by uncritical zombies who seek to blindly idolize you must be one of the curses of being an idealistic rock star. This probably helped lead to the Clash's demise. (like, what didn't?) Joe said that the Clash was about seeing if you could go to number one and still have something important to say. He has since decided that that is an impossibility. Most people saw the Clash's lyrics in the same light as heavy metal or Yes lyrics, e.g.. an entertaining fantasyland for young kids to escape into. But maybe the Clash should know that some people took their message very seriously indeed, and it changed the course of their life.

DREAMTIME
Originally posted 1/12/97

I spend a lot of time bitching about Rock and Roll nowadays. There are precious few bands with any depth, vision, or staying power. But I think the real reason Rock and Roll is on life support these days is that you can't dream about it anymore. The fantasy is gone, and Rock and Roll was all about fantasy, not street credibility or harsh reality. The media explosion has taken most of the bloom off the bush. With MTV (M2 now) and VH1 and various Rock and Roll documentaries on TV, and thousands of video tapes available (it seems that every major band nowadays has at least one), one no longer has to wait months or years to see performances of their favorite bands. There has been a glut of Rock and Roll magazines in the past few years, so every band worth covering gets written to death. On top of all this, there is the Internet, with web pages and newsgroups (and *Clash City Showdown*, for that matter), so every last bit of information is wrung out of every artist of note. How is a kid supposed to fantasize about a group today?

When I was growing up (the same time as most of you reading this, I reckon), you had to imagine your favorite bands. They were never on TV for the most part, chances are good you were too young to go to their concerts, and there were only a handful of rock magazines. And if you were into left field groups, particularly Punk groups, you had to dream up your own vision of who they were. Led Zeppelin is a perfect example of this. After the second record, they never put their pictures on their record covers, they never talked to the press, and never made any videos. If you didn't see *Song Remains the Same* (which most Zep fans didn't), you were on your own. So you constructed an image in your mind of where these strange and wondrous sounds came from, and when your heroes came to town, chances are you went absolutely apeshit.

I often compare (unfavorably) the lame ass Nirvana concert I went to a few years back with this footage of an old Jerry Lee Lewis concert I saw on TV. When I saw Nirvana, there were loads of kids milling about listlessly and ignoring Nirvana as they played. There was the obligatory moshing, but it seemed half-hearted. Nirvana sounded fine, but they projected nothing from the stage and the show fell apart for the encores. Now switch to the Jerry Lee Lewis show. The stage was filled with kids, many of whom surrounded Jerry Lee at the piano. The kids were shaking their fists as Jerry pounded away, obviously out of their minds. Every note seemed to speak to them and they were going crazy to the music, just like they were supposed to. This strange music called Rock and Roll was so new to them, so foreign, that they couldn't help themselves. And the last band I've seen instill that kind of extreme reaction was the Clash.

Clash City Showdown (the fanzine and these dispatches) isn't necessarily about the Clash, it's about my dream of the Clash. It's about how I felt at twelve years old when I saw that Bob Gruen picture in *Rolling Stone* of these beings from another world, wielding their instruments like weapons, like nothing I had ever seen. It's about how I felt when I first put the needle down on *Give 'Em Enough Rope*, only to hear the most savage explosion I had ever heard back then. It's about seeing these alien rockers, dressed up as Jack the Ripper, Bruce Lee, Erwin Rommel and Napoleon in *Creem* magazine. It's about the rush I got when I heard 'Gates of the West', which sounded like every great glam and power pop record I loved in the 70's rolled up into one. Or when I was 13, staring down at these greaser beanpoles blowing the roof off of the Orpheum Theater. Or seeing them announce the death of the 70's with their *Fridays* appearance. And how it felt to hold *Sandinista!* on my hand on the subway, looking through the lyric sheet and wondering what on earth these 36 songs sounded like. It's about putting *Combat Rock* for the 600th time, listening to those helicopter guitars on 'Sean Flynn' pan through my headphones. It's about when these strangers calling themselves the Clash blasted through this weird song called 'Ammunition', sending people who never heard it into a frenzy. And most of all, it's about all the hidden corners of the Clash history, about the great songs left off albums, about live versions on hissy tapes that destroy every notion you ever had about the Clash, about Rock and Roll, about what it means to be alive.

I have a more specific dream of the Clash too. I had it almost every night for years and years, and I still have it from time to time. The details change, but it concerns going into a record store and finding a bin full of Clash bootlegs, chock full of songs I've never heard before. The songs are always composites of different Clash tunes, and I am always depressed when I wake up, because I want those damn records!

But, sometimes I really think the best thing the Clash did was to go away before the Information Age really took over. As much as I loved *Combat Rock*, I hated what it did: namely, make the Clash just another big time Rock band that no longer belonged to me. The Clash were so omnipresent in that year I could no longer dream about them. That's another reason why I went so hard for Clash II. Here was a band whose biographies I didn't know, whose idiosyncrasies I hadn't tired of, who seemed just as foreign and unknown as the original band did in the early days. And on top of that, they disintegrated before I got sick of them, which given the circumstances, probably wouldn't have taken long. Of course, on top of that, they played like demons on crack.

Anyway, this is my dream of the Clash. Marcus Gray is so possessed by his dream (namely the pre-USA Clash) that he wrote a 500-page book about it. Ralph Heibutzki is so possessed by his dream that he spent years researching his definitive articles in *Goldmine* and *Discoveries*. Tim Armstrong is so possessed by his dream that he formed a band patterned almost exactly after the early Clash.

And if you made it through this dispatch, chances are you have your own dream, too.

POST-CLASH DEPRESSION

WHAT'S WITH *CHRIS?*

HE'S DEPRESSED BECAUSE *THE CLASH* BROKE UP.

YOU MEAN BACK IN THE *EIGHTIES?*

No one took the Clash's breakup harder than me. I will never forget that day, when I was sitting around with my drug-addled roommates watching MTV when they announced the breakup. I was shocked. It was a slap in the face. I had spent nearly two years waiting for Joe's new Clash to rock the world and make Duran Duran and Ronald Reagan go away forever. I was left with nothing to obsess about. This was 1985, mind you, one of the worst god-damned years for music in history. Let's think about the musical landscape: College kids were all listening to dreary 'Indie' Rock like the Feelies, Sonic Youth, and Husker Du (even though all of those bands ended up on majors), as well as unplayable nonsense like the Butthole Surfers and Scratch Acid. Hitler was on the charts again as the Hardcore movement discovered Fascism. Satanic Death Metal was all the rage in the malls. The Top 40 was clotted with the most heinous artificial tripe known to man. Go West, Frankie Goes to Hollywood,

Animotion, Mr Mister, and A-ha had actual hits, and Huey Lewis was a super-star. And now, no Clash. What was I to do?

I was living in an area that was full of bad vibes. There were two biker pads on my block, two toxic chemical plants in my neighborhood, and a mall that was becoming notorious for parking lot murders. Two of my housemates dug up a grave and brought the headstone to the house, unleashing a torrent of bad vibes and violence. Two of my housemates were parolees, and two others had escalating drug problems. Dealers were in and out of the house, and we later found out that the FBI was in the house next door spying on one of the biker houses. (Thank God they didn't turn their attention next door) My land-lord decided he was tired of all these punks living in his house and showed up with a hired thug and an attack dog and kicked in the door to my bedroom. (luckily, I wasn't home - we ended up taking the guy to court) I would go to par-ties and listen to a bunch of skinheads prattle on about the virtues of Nazism. Over the course of a few short months, I watched my roommates turn into pot-addled couch potatoes. And to top it all off, the Clash had broken up.

I needed some new music to escape into. There wasn't much around. Everything was either plastic or tuneless. I started playing guitar more seri-ously and turned my attention backward, rediscovering stuff like Aerosmith, Eno, and King Crimson, thanks to the blessing of 'Nice Price' cassettes. Then the two bands that would define my haven in the post-Clash Dark Ages emerged in my consciousness...

I first got into the Smiths in 1983 with the 'Charming Man' single. Johnny Marr's quicksilver guitar took the top of my head off. But it wasn't until I heard 'Headmaster Ritual' off *Meat is Murder* that I really fell hard. In an torpid ocean of Van Halen clones, ham-fisted Hardcore morons and REM clones, that sound was like a revelation. A real guitar player in the mid-80's! Can you imagine? *Meat is Murder* just blew me away. A real band using real instruments playing real tunes. Go back sometime, listen to the absolute rub-bish that came out in the mid-80's and you realize how rare that was. The Smiths inspired me to take guitar more seriously as well. No longer content to settle for barre-chord blare, I discovered major sevenths, minor sevenths, sev-enth add nines, thirteenths, ninths, augmented Fourths, arpeggios, muting, double note leads - the whole nine yards. I was suitably amused by Morrisey's wry wit, but I must admit I was a bit uncomfortable with the homoeroticism. But that was probably the point.

I followed the Smiths closely up until *Louder than Bombs*. I loved that record, but somehow, I heard a page turning. Something told me that the story of the Smiths was almost over. That feeling was confirmed with *Strangeways, Here we Come*, a record I didn't even buy. They broke up soon after that, of course, and Morrisey soldiered on. I never bought one of his records. I was expecting Johnny to do something grand, but he wasted his time on crap like the Talking Heads, the The, and Electronic, and never did anything I found mildly interesting. Of course, in this post-Clash duality, the Smiths were the junior partner.

The center of my world was the Cocteau Twins. I first discovered them also in '83, when the legendary Bradley J played 'From the Flagstones' on *Nocturnal Emissions* on WBCN. I thought that someone had changed the channel and tuned into some alien frequency. I went out and bought the *Sunburst and Snowblind* EP and played it ceaselessly (there are few periods that were more musically exciting than the summer and fall of '83). I scooped up the 'Pearly Dewdrops Drop' single and was likewise enchanted. Then the Clash came around and I went into a long Punk/Metal period (anything loud and angry, just as long as it wasn't Thrash) and started hanging around the Boston Hardcore scene after a year's absence. Then came the dreadful events of '85-'86. After an ugly series of confrontations and a court case against my landlord, I moved from the hell-hole I was living in and moved out to a nice rural suburb. The Spring of '86 was gorgeous. Sunny, mild - it was like emerging from Hell and finding yourself in Heaven. It was time to stop the headbanging.

I hooked up with a singer from Queens. He was a big Siouxsie fan. He made these wacky demos with a Fostex four-track and an Electro-Harmonix 'Memory Man'. He also made me a 90-minute Cocteau Twins best of. It blew me away. That voice: it was like something from another planet. They say if Hell has a jukebox, it plays Heavy Metal. I always said if Heaven had a juke-box, then the Cocteau Twins would be in heavy rotation. I vibed on this cassette endlessly. It was like the music I heard in my favorite dreams had been committed to tape. This went on for some time.

*Those lips, those eyes, that voice....
I love you forever, Liz.*

Of course in '88, things picked up again and Jane's Addiction came along and suddenly there was a torrent of great music coming from everywhere. Suddenly, I didn't need the Twins anymore to redeem popular music for me. The Twins left their indie label 4AD and signed with Capitol and made pale, watered-down shadows of their best work. It's really a shame, because their influence is everywhere today. They totally changed the role of female vocals in a pop context. Sinead, the Cranberries, Sarah McLachlan, Alanis, Bjork, Paula Cole and many other acts I can't stand have made careers borrowing heavily from the Twins. (Of course uber-goddesses like Harriet Carter of the Sundays, and great bands like My Bloody Valentine and Bel Canto have also sprung from the Cocteaux fertile soil).

But this much is true, when Joe let me down hard, sweet little Liz Fraser was there to cushion the blow.

MARCUS GRAY AND THE LAST GANG IN TOWN

In 1995, a British journalist named Marcus Gray published the first edition of his Clash biography, entitled the *Last Gang in Town*. It was an exhaustive, 500 page work that focused primarily on the Clash's prehistory and time as a London-based phenomenon. To give you an idea of just how provincially biased the book was, 343 of the books 512 pages were focused on the time leading up to the band's first US tour. The remaining 16 years were crammed into a measly 169 pages.

The book is Anglocentric in the extreme. There is the usual BritCrit nonsense about how horrible *Give 'Em Enough Rope* was (I am always puzzled by critics who claim to love the Clash and dismiss every record they made aside from the debut and *London Calling*) and the general thesis of the book seems to be that the Clash were a bunch of phonies and hypocrites. There was a vaguely hostile reaction to the book in the fan community, but everyone seemed to appreciate the research Gray did on the bands pre-Clash lives (the chapters on the 101'ers would make a fine book in and of themselves). But the meat of the book was taken up with gossip and obsessive minutiae from the '76-'78 period.

Now, my feelings about the first edition of *Last Gang* are mixed. Gray did not write an exhaustive history on the Clash, he wrote a very biased and prejudicial book focusing on his personal view of the band. His sourcing isn't terribly impressive, especially compared to Ralph Heibutzki's work. There's little new information on the 80's Clash. In fact, most of that research into that era seems to be based on newspaper and magazine clippings. In all fairness, Gray has since revealed that he was rushed on the final chapters, but I think if he was interested in that era he wouldn't have saved it for last. And the supercilious tone might have played well in some quarters at home (actually it didn't, come to think of it), but it's hard for an American to stomach.

Now, I must admit I understand some of the hostility towards the Clash. They were an extremely enigmatic and frustrating band to follow. The band often seemed hellbent on dashing their fans' hopes and I can't think of any other band in Rock history that squandered more opportunities to make a real impact on modern culture. But their numerous faults were outweighed by their even more numerous virtues. But you wouldn't know that by reading the first edition of *Last Gang*.

Gray gives the impression of playing to the elitist intellectual milieu that has done so much damage to modern discourse and Western culture. The Clash are hopelessly déclassé to this poisonous lot of snobs and megalomaniacs. These are the types of people who were born into privilege, and spend their lives trashing everyone and everything in order to prove their own innate superiority. These 'Public School' types infested the *NME* and the *Melody Maker* like stinkbugs in the early 80's. The Clash were mildly amusing to them in the early days - that is, when Punk was an elitist, 'transgressive' fad. But once real working class kids (whom the Elitists are terrified of) started showing up, the knives came out. The Clash also committed the unforgivable sin of being popular in America without the Elite's permission. Gray himself documents how the constant press abuse in the early 80's nearly drove the band to give up on Britain.

It wasn't until the Clash took their case directly to the fans that they realized how distorted and meaningless the elitist sniping was.

Now the Elite's favorite hobby is the "revisionist biography'. There has been an avalanche of these unreadable 'texts' in the past two decades. The basic idea is that some over-privileged snot from Oxbridge or the Ivy League writes an "everything you thought you knew is wrong' screed on someone smarter, braver and more important than they can ever dream of being. ("my book will show you the real Buddha behind the pious facade") Now when I first read Gray's book , I was convinced that the cancer had turned its attention on the Clash. But I have since come to believe that Gray was simply being a revisionist poseur.

I am going to 'out' Marcus Gray, right here and now. Marcus, you are a hopeless Clash diehard. Gobba gobba, we accept you, you crazy bastard! Put 'er there! Have a beer on me! Hey, have you heard the soundboard upgrade on the Lyceum '78 shows? Fucking mint, man!

The thing is, no one writes a 500-page book and an equally lengthy revision (Gray is also reportedly working on a third edition) on the Clash simply to impress the under-achieving dipshits down in the faculty lounge. There's no real money or prestige in it and there are plenty of DWEM's to libel first. Gray also reveals his inner diehard throughout the books, and though he falls like a sucker for the dumb-ass, pre-fab lines on *Rope* and Clash II, he's far too careless about *Sandinista*. In other words, he foolishly lets on that he kind of likes it. Now, I know that some of the Public School dorks (now safely ensconced in UK papers like the *Guardian* and the *Daily Mirror*) have belatedly come to say nice things about the Clash, but it's always in a "political' context, not necessarily a musical or cultural one. In other words, they are simply trying to tie their political cart to the powerful horse of the Clash's enduring popularity. But again, Gray isn't one of them, he's one of us.

The second edition, entitled *Return of the Last Gang in Town* is a far better book. Some of the archaic 90's sneering is toned down and the sourcing is much more diverse. But a lot of the sniping remains, so here's hoping the third edition rectifies that. Now again, anyone who spends too much time researching the extremely fallible heroes of the Clash is prone to this type of thing. But one thing we all have to remember is that the Clash were musicians, not messiahs. One of the reasons I never pursued a career in music seriously was the unavoidable fact that musicians tend to be pretty fucked in the head. They are a pretty difficult lot to deal with and often the more talented they are, the more fucked in the head they can be. This is true of any creative types, but musicians are the worst.

The (understandable) UK bias is still prevalent in the second edition, and the Orthodox Rock Critic line is hewn throughout the book. Also, Joe's remarkable 1999 comeback is almost completely ignored. This is absurd to the point of being unforgivable, but again there's apparently another edition in the works.

In any event, both editions are must-reads for the true Clash diehard. If you can get past the silly revisionist sniping, there is a wealth of information in them. I look forward to the third edition. Hopefully, Gray will have made his peace with his 'orientation' and will let his inner diehard run riot.

THE LAST PILGRIMMAGE
Originally posted 12/27/02

      The first time I ever went to New York City was to look for '84 boots. It was October of '84 and some Art Punk friends and I took the bus into New York to scour all the shops. This was the days when kids could buy a can in a bag and we got drunk that day while walking the streets. My nutty skinhead friend, Buster, took it upon himself to piss wherever he pleased: on the sidewalk, in the park, in a doorway. I found a double cassette of one of the Academy shows at Bleecker Bob's, the one where Joe says "I will not play 'Train in Vain!'" So ever since that day, when I was all of 18, New York and the Clash have been intertwined. I cannot count how many boot crawls I've been on. Or during the Lost Years, how many magazine shops I would haunt, scouring for any news of Joe's activities, any little shred of information.

Greenwich Village is the setting for some of my craziest bacchanals, but that feeling of Clashitude is irrevocably interwoven in my mind. I have had literally thousands of dreams of scouring the streets of the Village in search of the Ultimate Bootleg- usually a bizarre dream-mix of *Black Market*, *Five Alive* and the *Studio Out-Takes* 7" with the Mick as Napoleon and Joe as Jack the Ripper pic on the cover.

So when previous plans fell through, I fought back the nearly stulti- fying Winter depression and dragged my shut-in ass for one last walkabout, and brought *From Here to Eternity*, *Give 'Em Enough Dope* and that crappy *Mutable Punks* transfer of *Five Alive* along with me (for sentimental reasons) and hit the streets. I blasted *GEED* in my car and was more convinced than ever that that stuff was pro-recorded and that a quickie Clash II live thing was being considered and then scrapped. It really kicks ass cruising down the highway too.

I hit Electric Lady first and looked at the little tribute. I forgot that Joe's bio page in the *Armagideon Times* had a comic book page in the back- ground, and eerily enough, it was some ghost story. I looked at the Futura hand-written track listing for *Rat Patrol* and it confirmed something I had been told earlier: 'Beautiful People' was really called 'Fulham Connection' and 'Kill Time' had the dreadful title of 'Idle in the Kangaroo Court W1'. I went over to Revolver Records and they had no Clash stuff, so I left. That place is a crusty old boomer-haven anyway. Went to Bleecker Bob's and was depressed: its a shell of its former glory. Lots of Satanist crap there- a sure omen of death and decay. The streets were nearly empty, since all the NYU kids were back at home counting their parents' money.

Walked over to Revolution Records - they had a lot of boots, but noth- ing I had to have. They were playing Joy Division, which I was listening to a lot of in '84, so I appreciated that. They had a vinyl thing of the *Rude Boy* stuff, but I didn't need that either. But Revolution has always flown the Clash flag, just like their immediate predecessor. Second Coming Records. The Clash never disappeared from the Village's collective consciousness.

I walked through the cold, grey streets to the East Village. New York can be the most miserable place in the world in the Winter. Or the most glori- ous, depending on the time of day and the company you're keeping. I was alone and I was feeling as cold and gray as the city seemed to be. Maybe it was in mourning, too.

I skipped Tower Records in favor of the Tower Flea Market and bought myself a nice warm scarf. I was reminded of the Portobello Road market stalls, and the vibe was enhanced by a stall pitching some vaguely Clash like gear—-with red and black star logos and all— to the teenie mar- ket. There was also a stall selling martial arts vids, which Joe would have found entertaining.

I made it to St. Mark's Place. Never a notable landmark in the Clash mythography, it is filled with a Clash-like spirit (and it was one of the settings for Joe's *Global Boombox* TV pilot). For those of you who've never been there, it is a short little block where the counter-culture still seems to exist, though increasingly as a museum/gift shop. All the t-shirt shops have always had lots of Clash goodies for the asking (and for the buying). Nothing to lift my spirits though. Went into the former Venus Records (once on the corner of 6th Ave and 8th st) now burdened with the dreary moniker, Bob's Records. I was severely depressed there. It was like walking into a nursing home.

Still, it was good to see the flag being flown from the store windows of old St. Marks. I skipped Kim's Underground and Trash and Vaudeville - I didn't want to get caught up in all that pop-culture ephemera. The only people on the streets seemed to be tourists. Joe would have been amused at the packs of fashionable kids speaking a host of tongues. I went in to the basement haven known as See Hear. This little hideaway was once entirely stocked with Rock rags and books- now it is a reading room dedicated to marginal culture- there are underground comics, occult stuff, fetish rags and the like vying for shelf space with your usual *MOJO*'s, *Maximum Rock and Roll*'s and the like. But as soon as I walked in I was confronted by the unlikely strains of 'Stay Free', which immediately segued into 'Junco Partner'. The owner was listening to Terry T. and Hova's Joe tribute on WFMU. The whispers and hints of Joe's restless ghost came out of the shadows. I was delighted to discover the *Return of the Last Gang in Town*, simply because I am a completist and didn't want to pay import prices for it. Gray did seem to fill in some gaps amid all the sneering and glaring errors.

I paid for it and then something else caught my eye- the Bob Gruen tome in all its glory. And at a non-assrape price too! Loathe as I am to continue my walkabout burdened with such baggage, I couldn't resist. It's a gorgeous book and if all of you don't have it, find it and buy it as soon as you done reading this.

So I glanced a bit at the female body hair fetish magazines in bemusement (who buys that crap - werewolves?) I hit the empty streets again on my way to Niagara. I was confronted with a sign for Happy Hour, which I didn't appreciate since I was wasn't very happy. I'm glad I brought the walkman, because the earphones were keeping the cold North Atlantic wind off of my ears. *FHTE* made me think one thought over and over: Hey Sony, open the vaults.

Niagara's Happy Hour wasn't very happy either. The place was nearly deserted and the place were I thought the tribute wall is was roped off. I sat down and ordered a Yeungling, in honor of my summit with Joe in Philly. It is a damn fine ale, criminally overlooked by quaffers. Yeungling is also America's oldest brewery, so it's your patriotic duty to partake. I didn't push the roped-off issue, since the whole thing had a Strawberry Fields vibe to me and the John Lennon parallels were already too strong.

I wasn't feeling Joe there. I was desperately sad. I couldn't take too much more.

On one hand, it was good to see the Clash still in the minds and stores of New York. A perverse thought entered my mind. The greatest Rock legends are all dead- Joe is now truly among the Olympians. And he has entered those august halls not as the has-been who oversaw the Clash's implosion, but as the elder statesman who triumphantly returned to the street-level Rock and Roll scene from whence he had sprung. He didn't exit as some wretched, addicted husk like Brian Jones or Elvis, or as some tragic misadventure like Hendrix or Jim Morrison, he died because his body had written the script since birth. And he went down with old debts paid.

I removed the phones and caught a cab uptown. I couldn't take any more melancholy. I hooked up with my boy Kenny K, who is a creative dynamo par excellence as well as a true bon vivant. If you cant be happy in Kenny K's company, it's time to punch your ticket. A true NYC rock god and a killer cartoonist and animator, as well as a dashing ladies man, Ken had been spinning the first three Clash disks to pay his respects. We hit Jackson Hole, home of the 7 oz. burger for a hearty meal and many laughs. The place is jam-packed with 50's and Cowboy memorabilia, which I know Joe would have loved.

WHY DID IT HAPPEN AND WHO WAS TO BLAME?

One of the reasons I have spent so much time obsessing on the Clash is because there were so many unanswered questions about their story that have plagued me. How could a band that seemed destined for immortality implode so early in their career? How could such a ferocious live band make such increasingly wimpy records? What exactly was happening in the relationship between Joe, Mick, and Bernie that made them behave as they did? What exactly was Bernie's role in the creation and dissolution of the band? What went on behind the scenes that the band only hinted at in interviews?

So many questions, so few answers. Most writing on the Clash, especially nowadays, tends to gloss over the really juicy bits in the band's history, in favor of a somewhat reductionist and hagiographic worshipfulness. That may be fine for some people, but not for an obsessive like myself, who knows more about the Clash than most of the people writing that crap. And now that Joe has left us, this tendency to sweep everything under the carpet will only get worse. I think the answers to some of these questions is too painful for those involved to ever have addressed, anyway. The answers are painful to me as well, but not having the benefit of knowing them was equally torturous. The Clash were well aware of what they had, and were well aware of how each of them were responsible for letting it slip away. And the sad part of it all is that they also realized that once broken, the Clash could never be put back together. From the moment of Topper's firing in May of 1982, an irreversible process had begun that could never be reversed. But as I learned, the process had actually begun 17 months before that.

THE BREAKING POINT

In early December of 1980, the Clash released the triple LP, *Sandinista*. To put it mildly, the album was not well received. Joe was given the task of talking to British journalists to promote it. Mick had returned with Ellen Foley to New York to produce Ian Hunter's new solo album and also to finish work on Ellen's second album. Joe reportedly deeply resented Mick's outside dabbling and now he had to defend what was essentially Mick's idea to extremely skeptical journalists alone. However exciting the recording experience must have been for the album, a triple album must have been a jarring proposition to a traditionalist like Joe. Joe later told Bill Holdship of *Creem* that there simply wasn't enough time "to give each track a good mix." But to have suggested such to Mick probably would have been by him as an unpardonable treason, given Mick's increasingly volatile disposition. Plus, it must be said the sheer chutzpah of a triple LP appealed to Joe's subversive side.

Joe much later defended *Sandinista* as a valuable document of a time and a place in the Clash story. This is certainly true. And the album is vastly under-rated and a favorite of hard core Clash nuts like myself. But let's be frank here: Mick Jones was a mediocre producer. He had neither the technical know-how or the experience to run a studio, and it is reasonable to assume that Bill Price probably did a lot of the heavy operational lifting. As Nick Kent pointed out in his *Melody Maker* review of *Sandinista*, Mick's instinct was to smooth everything in a soft-focus mush, and that's what keeps song after song on the album (and *Combat Rock* and most of the BAD albums as well) from asserting itself to full effect. This recording method had no real precedent in classic Rock and Roll, but, strangely, was de rigeur for middle-of-the-road Pop. Revealingly, it also made for a more pleasant listening experience for the seriously stoned. Any greatness Clash albums achieved was from the strength of the compositions and arrangements, certainly not the later performances and definitely not the production. A few extra weeks of mixing - with a real producer in charge - would have made for an astonishing, double-album *Sandinista*, one that would have put *London Calling* into the shade. The remasters do much to sharpen some of the blurriness of the original LPs, but even still it's frustrating to hear the albums' potential unrealized. Properly made, *Sandinista* could have been an earth shaker. Nick Kent was not the only critic to notice the Clash's (or Mick's) ineptitude at self-production. Roy Carr of the *NME* made this observation in his review of 'White Man in Hammersmith Palais' "as producers the Clash sell themselves far short of their obvious potential. There's absolutely nothing wrong with the Clash that a good producer couldn't rectify."

A good producer would also have been more diligent about getting the band to ratchet up their performances. Several tracks on *Sandinista* (and all of them on *Combat*) would have benefited greatly from a strong whip hand in the control booth coaxing more energetic performances from his charges. But the Clash wouldn't have stood for that. And then there was the problem of the Clash trying to tackle unfamiliar styles of music that taxed their limited range of skill.

Aside from Topper, none of the Clash were particularly adept musical craftsmen. I believe that they felt insecure about this, and in many ways felt they had something to prove. Their two main competitors, the Police and the Jam, were muso impostors pretending to be Punks, and there was no way the Clash could compete with their chops. All this heroic double and triple album stuff may have in part been a way to outdo their competitors. The Clash were prolific songwriters, but their need to show off prevented them from spending the necessary time carefully recording themselves. They also may have found the recording process boring - they certainly hated the *Give 'Em Enough Rope* sessions. But what saved their early records was the fact that the Clash had rehearsed the songs extensively, and what weakened their last two albums, aside from the ridiculous amount of drugs they were ingesting, was the fact that they were making material up as they went along in the studio. The Clash's heroic posture was masking short attention spans in this case.

That being said, It was generally assumed that *Sandinista* would be pared down to a single for US release, but that was not the case. It would have been a wise decision, -creatively and financially- for the band, but they responded to Epic's request to do so by threatening to break up. As a result of this gambit, *Sandinista* produced no hit singles in either the US or UK and the band would be denied touring funds by their US company. *Sandinista* was shaping up to be a major disaster for the Clash. So, if anyone doubts that Joe was in a desperate frame of mind following his experience promoting the album, or dismisses reports of serious friction with Mick as apocryphal, his first order of business once the junket was over puts any of that speculation to rest.

RHODES TO RUIN

Marcus Gray documents in chapter 15 of *Return of the Last Gang in Town* how Mick's blustery arrogance and cockiness had given way to withdrawal and self immersion in early 1981. There is little mystery as to why. Aside from a 5-star review in *Rolling Stone*, press reaction to his 3-record opus ranged from disappointment to outright hostility. The album was selling fairly well in America, but not nearly well enough to square the band's mammoth debt with CBS. Mick made it clear that he didn't care what the Punk contingent of the Clash's audience (or former audience) thought, but few of them seemed to be swayed that the Clash was not continuing to 'sell out'. The one-two punch of *Sandinista* and *Spirit of St. Louis* had scared all but the most committed original fans off. Ian Hunter's album met with little fanfare and Ellen's album was an unqualified bomb. Topper was on his own personal express train to junkie hell, and was becoming a serious liability to the band, creatively and otherwise. And to top it all off, Joe had gone and recruited Bernard Rhodes -Mick's sworn enemy - to return as the band's manager.

Any opinion a Clash fan is likely to hold of Bernie Rhodes is usually a negative one. Bernie is justly blamed for the *Cut the Crap* debacle, and his management style seemed to thrive on intra-band tension and antagonism. He also used the Clash as a cash-cow in his attempt to finance a Brian Epstein-styled stable in the late 70's, while the Clash themselves were penniless. And he certainly lost his nerve when it came time to making the new Clash the first true Punk band to break America. But what cannot be forgotten is that Bernie "imagined the Clash", as Joe Strummer put it, and developed many of the ideas that made the Clash so exciting. That he could take a wild-man Pub singer, a Glam band castoff, a underachieving Jazz drummer and a non-musician and mold them into one of the greatest Rock bands in history was an amazing accomplishment in and of itself.

Bernie also is responsible for the confrontational political element of the Clash. In truth, none of the players in the band had been political firebrands before the Clash and none would be so afterwards. This is why Bernie expressed disgust at the band's subsequent solo careers. He is famously quoted in a *Sounds* interview from 1988, "they're such squares, the Clash. They've gone back to how they really are." He also had memorably unkind words for them in the 1999 *MOJO* retrospective. But the Clash were his legacy and, in his own peculiar way, he cared very deeply about the band. He just always had a problem with Mick, however, and began trying to replace him as early as 1978. He also presented Mick with serious competition in the Clash power struggle. Which is probably why Joe recruited him to return. Despite some of his interview and onstage bluster, Joe Strummer was not by temperament a confrontationist. Saddled with feelings of insecurity and inadequacy, Joe would usually deal with intraband confrontations by taking off. For this, Bernie would later label Joe a coward.

Barry Miles wrote in *the Clash: An Illustrated Biography* that when Rhodes was re-hired, "The Clash have moved smoothly forward with fewer and fewer unnecessary diversions." Famous last words, but Rhodes' managerial genius was demonstrated in his decision to overcome the impasse the band faced in their two primary markets, the US and UK, by extensively touring Europe, and then booking week-long runs in New York, Paris, and London. He also sent the band to Asia and the Antipodes, and by the beginning of 1982, the Clash were an international band. They were also a band who had gotten themselves out of debt by creating new markets for their music. Aside from the Joe disappearance (which Rhodes turned into another Bonds-like publicity bonanza), the *Combat Rock* tour went almost too smoothly and the success of the *Combat Rock* combined with the Who dates filled the band's coffers for the first time in their careers.

Zig Zag writer Paul O Reilly described Bernie Rhodes in 1984 as " a very astute man, (who) has a devastating verbal manner, and there aren't many people I'd bet on against him in an argument. He has occasional flashes of pure brilliance, but against that you have to set an infuriatingly dogmatic side of his nature that can often reduce a situation to a stalemate." Rhodes came into a band that was entering a stalemate of its own, and he knew what he would do to break it.

In 1981, The Clash were struggling to establish themselves in a scene still dominated by 70's dinosaurs and the imitators. The New Wave movement had largely failed and the British wing would be revealed to be dominated by...

PUB SCHLUBS WHO LUST FOR THE GRUB

One of the crippling memes that was destroying the original Punk/New Wave scene was this absurd idea of musical 'progress'. As soon as the disappointing sales figures started trickling in, artists and critics began constantly droning on about "progress" and "relevancy" as if they were objective facts and not mere constructs, fed by drugs, cowardice, ambition and greed. The Pub Rock tagalongs who latched onto the Punk bandwagon were, predictably, the first to cash in their chips to the false god of "progress."

After an initial burst of success, Elvis Costello's record sales were slowing as the New Wave novelty wore off. Elvis obviously wanted to maintain his career trajectory, so a decision was apparently made to tailor his prodigious skills into recording an limpid string of easy listening records. There was a major obstacle to Elvis' wallet-stuffing campaign, though. The record company hype when he first burst onto the scene played up how he and others were bringing Rock and Roll back to its raw, primal roots and doing away with the singer-songwriter/Soft Rock mush of the 70's. So when he began to pollute the racks with his own Soft Rock mush, on albums like *Almost Blue, Imperial Bedroom, Punch the Clock* and *Goodbye Cruel World* (the latter boasting a Doobie Brothers soundalike called "Only Flame in Town" with Darryl Hall (!) on background vox), all of a sudden the story changed. We started to hear all this talk from Elvis and his partisans in the press about "growing as an artist" and "breaking new ground."

Of course, Elvis wasn't really growing as an artist. He was simply regressing to the MOR pabulum New Wave was supposed to have done away with. Elvis would later spend most of his time disavowing the aforementioned albums while promoting his 1988 release, *Spike*.

A&M's Elvis clone, Joe Jackson, was even more shameless about his selling out. After trying and failing to cash in on the Ska and Swing fads of the early 80's, Joe dropped any pretense of integrity and reinvented himself as a Barry Manilow clone with his toothless, geriatric *Night and Day* album, which was followed by the downright sleepy *Body and Soul* album. As soon as everyone got tired of that, Joe made a big noise about his 'return to Rock' on the 1986 bomb, *Big World*. The only problem was that Joe failed to realize that Rock wasn't waiting for him to return. Coincidentally, Elvis pulled the same move that year with his 'return to Rock', *Blood and Chocolate*. Since Elvis is actually talented (rather than simply facile), he was able to pull off his ass-covering move with somewhat more panache than Jackson. But just to hedge his bets, Elvis simultaneously released the sleepy-time *King of America* album. After Blood and Chocolate, Elvis soon pumped out another endless string of MOR, until he 'returned to Rock' again with 1994's *Brutal Youth*.

Another band of Pub Rock frauds who cashed in on the New Wave movement was Squeeze, who made Seals and Crofts sound like Motorhead with their wretched 'Black Coffee in Bed' single, off of their unlistenable *Sweets from a Stranger* LP. Difford and Tillbrook split Squeeze after *Sweets* bombed and went on to form a Hall and Oates knockoff duo. This ploy failed as well, and the pair immediately reformed Squeeze and 'returned to Rock.' The Stranglers, another Pub Rock castoff band, also went straight for the Soft Rock jugular with 1981's *La Folie* and proceeded downhill from there. If they ever 'returned to Rock', I missed it.

For the Clash, the inevitable selling-out by the Pub Rock bandwagon riders was probably nothing more than background noise, but the sheer number of acts sucking up to the status quo created an atmosphere of surrender that couldn't help but put pressure on the Clash to stay competitive. The Clash's main rivals at the time were the Jam - who were immensely more popular in England than the Clash- and the Police, who were immensely more popular everywhere else. The Clash would have been in a stronger position to compete with these bands had they been more judicious with their *Sandinista/Combat Rock* material (using a real producer would have been a nice place to start) but the turmoil within the band reduced Joe to bitterly (and impotently) complaining about their rivals in the press. Predictably, both Sting and Paul Weller- respective leaders of the Police and the Jam- broke up their bands in the early 80's and took the bullet train to Soft Rock City. Each spent the balance of the decade pumping out platters of corny schmaltz that made Air Supply sound like Discharge in comparison. As tempting as it is to brand them traitors, it's inaccurate. They and others like them were nothing more than muso carpetbaggers, so they betrayed no one but the gullible.

Interestingly, as the Muso and Pub Rock frauds abandoned ship, the Clash came to be seen as contemporary to Second Wave bands. There was a strong, new 'New Wave' in 1980, as bands like the Gang of Four, Stiff Little

Fingers and the Psychedelic Furs rose to prominence. These bands were far more abrasive than most of the 70's New Wavers, but sadly, they too would water down their music in attempts to gain acceptance.

Unfortunately, most of these bands only succeeded in alienating their core audience when they sold out. Most of them would later try and 'return to their roots' but not before disgust with they and their forebears' treason would give rise to the absolutist Hardcore movement.

A PUNK BAND, AS IMAGINED BY ORWELL

Gang of Four were biggest traitors of this second wave; in fact, they were probably the worst sell-outs in Punk history. Their story bears scrutiny because the Gang best illustrated what total hypocrites most of the British 'Political Rockers' were. Like the Clash, the Gang attempted to justify the abandonment of their original mandate as an attempt to better "put across their message." But Gang of Four marched straight into depths of cowardice and betrayal the Clash never even came close to succumbing to.

Gang of Four started as a standard Punk outfit at the University at Leeds. After a couple of indie singles, the Gang then incorporated feedback, hard Funk and Beefheartian dissonance into their attack. In their prime (a matter of mere months), the Gang were a ferocious, mutant, Punk-Funk machine, and their early gigs were brutal displays of naked aggression. They released two classic LPs, *Entertainment* and *Solid Gold*, both of which were packed with jittery rhythms, throbbing bass and raw guitar aggression. However, like their ridiculous Leeds 'comrades' Scritti Politti, the Gang soon decided that maybe all that Yankee cash wasn't so bad after all. After *Solid Gold*, the Gang lost their bass player, hired Sara Lee out of Robert Fripp's League of Gentlemen, and set their sights on stuffing their pockets with some US Disco dollars. 'Call Me Up' and 'I Love a Man in Uniform' were the single off of their 1982 sellout *Songs of the Free* and both tracks offered vague, soft boiled 'commentary' under an candy coating of slick Disco production.

Perhaps feeling that they had not yet plumbed the full depths of venality and fraudulence, the Gang then hired producers Ron and Howard Albert, best known for their work with Crosby, Stills & Nash and Firefall. (Think I'm kidding? look it up) This satanic aggregation spewed forth the sellout to end all sellouts, 1983's *Hard* (sic). *Hard* could only be short hand for the cold, hard cash the Gang were lusting after, because the album itself was a turgid, gelatinous mess of breathy female choruses, inaudible guitars and cloying string sections. For God's sake, don't track down this album, even out of morbid curiosity. *Hard* made *Combat Rock* sound like *This is Boston, Not LA*.

As was the established pattern, the Gang set out on a tour and drooled the usual "musical progression" propaganda to credulous journalists. But *Hard* was not only a sellout, it was a terminally inept sellout. The LP bombed and the Gang of Four broke up soon afterwards. Several years later, they did the return to Rock move, but no one cared.

The irony of all this is that there were bands who stuck to their guns and became successful anyhow. The Cure and Depeche Mode were almost completely ignored by the Industry and built huge followings anyway by constant touring and recording. Granted, these bands had a marked Pop slant to their music, but neither went around chasing trends to get attention, and the Cure always seemed to delight in following up Pop records with the doomiest dirges this side of Joy Division. Though Siouxsie and the Banshees took the treacle challenge in 1990 with their *Superstition*, they had previously wrote their own ticket.

The moral of this story no one respects a sellout and no one will stay loyal to a compromiser. People who stay loyal to artists do so because they want something to believe in.

CIRCLE THE WAGONS

This was the environment the Clash were faced with in the early 80's. Record companies had investments in the 'New Wave' bands and wanted to see returns. MTV wouldn't break nationwide until 1982 and even then, the new bands they did air were only those willing to play along. The 'Musical Progression' meme had taken root in Mick Jones' thinking, but Joe had already begun to resist it in 1981 interviews. In an interview with *International Musician and Recording World*, Joe stated Joe said his "idea of a 'great' record is 'Spanish Harlem' by Ben E. King or 'Jambalaya' by Professor Longhair" and offered that his vocal hero was Big Joe Turner. He also led the writer to not "be surprised if the next effort if the next effort from the Clash is recorded on an 8 track or a 16 track and is devoid of any additions except the band backbone." He then added that "I don't much like synthesizers. Maybe 'cause I'm not modern. But that ain't Rock and Roll." These retro sentiments plainly showed that, his earlier apologias aside, Joe was fed up with the direction Mick wanted to take the band in. An impasse was forming, and there was no one at hand to referee the oncoming battles. There was a potential middle ground in the early 80's, but the band's solipsistic competitiveness prevented them from seeing it.

INNOVATION VS. PHONY ' PROGRESS'

There were any number of bands in the early 80's that were moving forward in their art without betraying their original mandate, but one band bears special scrutiny.

The Talking Heads also were competing for dominance with the Clash, but until 1983's *Speaking in Tongues* album, the Heads made little effort to pursue the mainstream audience. They were concerned with musical innovation, meaning they were trying to expand their own sound by incorporating disparate elements into it, drawing on aggressive forms of African Rock, Hard Funk and Avant Garde Experimental music. Their 1980 classic, *Remain in Light*, was a work of true progression, in that it showed a clear and distinct curve of creative growth from the band's 1977 debut. But the basic elements of the band's identity remained intact, even with the presence of numerous studio musicians. *Remain in Light* sold quite well on the strength of the 'Once In a Lifetime' single (and video), but could never be construed as a sell out.

In fact, it was far less accessible than the band's earlier efforts. But the band's apparent refusal to compromise earned the respect of the curious and allowed to follow their own whims and not those of the record company. The Heads wouldn't cash in their chips until 1985's *Little Creatures*. But they were out of ideas by then anyways, so no harm done, really.

The Heads were also mature enough to realize that they were better served by a real producer, and their best work was produced by Brian Eno. They didn't even try to produce themselves until they all had several years experience in recording studios. The Heads all had strong personalities and musical ideas of their own, but were mature enough to sublimate their egos for the good of the band and then indulge themselves on their various solo projects. The Heads would compromise with each other, though not necessarily the record industry. This sort of compromise became impossible in the Clash by 1981, however. Paul told Richard Cook of the *NME* that with Mick "it was do it his way or sulk." And both Mick and Joe dealt with stalemates by proffering ultimatums, or in Joe's case, taking his ball and going to Paris.

COLLAPSING ONTO THE FINISH LINE

Pablo Guzman expressed bewilderment over the Clash's split in his old music column in the *New York Daily News*. He felt that "the Clash were just beginning to hit their stride" when they split. Many people felt the same shock. Wasn't *Combat Rock* the unqualified hit album that put the Clash into the big leagues once and for all?

No, *Combat Rock* was a disaster from the very start.

The story begins in the early Autumn of 1981. Fed up with the band's drift and stung by the underwhelming performance of *Sandinista*, Joe wanted to get back to the sound of the Clash, not the sound of an army of studio players. He also wanted to record the album with an 8-track studio. A compromise was reached and the Clash began recording at the Peoples' Hall in London, using a mobile studio on loan from the Rolling Stones. Most of the more conventional tunes from what was then known as the *Rat Patrol* sessions were recorded here: 'Should I Stay', 'Inoculated City', 'Know Your Rights', 'Ghetto Defendant', and the original 'Overpowered by Funk'. The initial idea was compromise. Joe told the *NME* that the Clash were " not trying to ignore anything we've heard before but we want to make it our own and all at once in every track." However, the band had to abandon the sessions for a string of concert dates and when they returned, Mick Jones had a very different idea of how he wanted to make the new record. "He said if we didn't produce *Combat Rock* in New York, he wouldn't be at the sessions, " Kosmo Vinyl recounted in 1984, "So we cart everything to New York and make the record there. One day there's an argument and that gets brought up and Mick goes 'Oh, I didn't mean it.' "

No, he certainly did 'mean it'. Mick chose New York in general and Electric Lady in particular for what he thought was a very good reason. To explain why, we need to put all of this into perspective.

POP STARS, LTD.

In 1984, when Joe accused Mick of wanting nothing more than to be a Pop star, Mick was probably confused. What else was there? Mick grew up idolizing Pop stars, and until the 'Year Zero' mentality of the Punk Revolution swept into town, there was nothing at all wrong with being a Pop star. In fact, quite the contrary - being a Pop star was an exalted dream for working class British kids. And why give yourself a cartoonish name like Johnny Rotten or Billy Idol or Joe Strummer unless you wanted to be a Pop star to begin with? However, the British Pop scene was one of relentless faddishness. Because the country is so small and the music scene was controlled by handful of media outlets like the *NME* and *Top of the Pops*, fashion obsessed British kids were quite efficiently catered to with an endless succession of prefab trends.

Glitter was the first, fully home-grown British fad and it was the first one that hit Mick square between the eyes. However, most people have forgotten how short lived the Glitter scene was, and few people today remember the terror British Pop stars once had of becoming unfashionable. "Progression" as understood by the British music Industry was not the Progressive Rock of King Crimson and Yes (shortened to 'Prog' in this case), it was the endless progression of ready-made fads and trends produced by Kings Row and Record Company tastemakers. Mick's 1984 fave-raves Frankie Goes to Hollywood were a perfect example of this. The members of that band had been kicking around Liverpool for years until they caught the fancy of ZTT honcho and former Buggle Trevor Horn. Luckily for them, Frankie had a couple tunes Horn felt were tailor made for manipulation by his vast array of brand new electronic gadgets. Stylists, fashion designers and journalists were then hired to help market this Frankie juggernaut, all based around a band no one had even heard of before. Predictably, the band's lack of talent was unable to withstand the daylight and they died, quickly and quietly, once the machine moved onto the next fad.

To feed the voracious star-making industry, British musicians were trained by the Press at an early age to stay on the fashion treadmill at any cost, or (at best) find themselves banished to the back pages of the *NME*. The Clash were the polar opposites of the pre-fab New Romantic movement (largely the creation of nightclub impresarios like Steven Strange), and hence, the *NME* and *Melody Maker* attacked them mercilessly in 1980 and '81. The Clash, who like most British kids were brainwashed into thinking that what the 'Inkies' said had any value, were stung by this and Joe bitterly raged against the sniping in interviews. Mick played his cards closer to the vest. If the press thought him retro and 'past it', they would soon eat crow when he took his secret weapon out of his quiver.

FAB FIVE FREDDY TOLD ME EVERYBODY'S FLY

At the same time the Clash were holed up in Electric Ladyland, the downtown NY art scene was exploding with energy. Painters like Keith Haring and Jean Michel Basquiat, performance artists like Anne Magnuson and Karen Finley and bands like Liquid Liquid and the South Bronx' ESG were creating a brand new aesthetic. Wall Street was beginning to boom and cocaine was flooding into the city from war-torn Latin America. Following ESG downtown from New York's ghettos was the nascent Hip Hop movement. This movement was multi media- encapsulating DJ's like Fab 5 Freddy and Afrika Bombatta, rappers like Kurtis Blow and Grandmaster Flash and the Furious 5 and graffiti artists like Futura 2000. And to any young hipster, the fact that New York had all the blow you could snort and all the freaky chicks you could fuck must have just been the icing on the cake.

Mick was totally enchanted by this collision of Bohemian smart alecks and inner city roughnecks. In fact, the rest of his career was set in stone during those few short weeks in the Spring of 1980. This new Urban Culture was in full bloom by the following year and accepted the Clash as conquering heroes when they returned in the Spring of 1981 to play at Bonds. The Clash recruited downtown faves like the Bush Tetras, Pulsallama and Grandmaster Flash as opening acts for the 17 dates, and various shows had any number of celebrities from Robert De Niro to Johnny Rotten in attendance. To Mick, the future must have seemed crystal clear. He had a large pool of new concepts to draw upon and some new bands to crib ideas from. There were two problems, however. The first was that, for all his enthusiasm, Mick had very little understanding of what exactly the new music was all about or how you went about making it. The second problem was that the rest of the band was putting on the brakes.

Mick was convinced this downtown scene was 'the new Punk' and he wanted to plug his stumbling band directly into it and give them a dose of the new electrical shockers. The fact that the Clash had no money to move their operation to New York didn't matter. By being right in the heart of the downtown scene, the Clash would transform all the tired, old Rock rehash from the Ear sessions into a new and exciting sound that incorporated the latest New York sounds. Once the Clash reached Electric Lady, the songs would be either drastically recast, or re-recorded altogether. New and old session hands would be called into help Mick realize this new masterpiece.

DRUGGY DRAG RAGTIME USA

Yet another problem sprang up: New York was not only the cultural capital of the world, it was also the drug capital of the world. And Greenwich Village was ground zero. Topper went off the deep end, and the others weren't far behind. Mick had declared himself to be the maestro in residence, but his own stultifying drug intake was erasing any potential he had as a producer. The songs got weirder and weirder as the weeks dragged on and the entire project was overdue and over budget. The Clash were off to Asia and Australasia for a very important tour, so the masters for what had been entitled *Rat Patrol* from Fort Bragg were brought with them.

That there was considerable turmoil in the Clash camp over the new album was revealed in an interview with Roz Reines of the *NME* in early 1982. When asked if the Clash were mixing the new album, Joe response was remarkably candid: "You won't get much out of me on that score. Don't forget you're talking to a man deliberately trying to forget all about it. In the last two weeks, I haven't thought about the tracks or listened to them." He added that he wasn't looking forward to hearing the recordings at a upcoming studio session in Sydney. Joe was also clearly wishing the album was something it definitely was not when he said "on this album it's R.O.C.K. and there's no getting away from it," and that the Clash were "trying to boil it down to one music." One wonders what album he was referring to here, because it certainly wasn't the one the Clash was recording. Joe was clearly extremely apprehensive about the new record, and had passed up the perfect chance to plug it in the *NME*, who were certainly not the Clash's friends at that point in time. Mick, by contrast, was effusive about what was then still known as *Rat Patrol from Fort Bragg*. After cheerily describing the individual tracks in detail to Reines, he added "altogether, it's a great record." In hindsight, it was clear that this album was Mick's baby, and that Joe was trying to wish it all away.

So, as the story goes, Mick did his version of a final mix for what would be a new double album. Kosmo Vinyl was uncharacteristically diplomatic when he described the bands reaction in 1984: "Another big problem was that he thought he should produce, but the rest of us didn't think he was ready. Maybe you've heard rumors about Mick being opposed to the commerciality of *Combat Rock*. Well, in fact, all that Mick was opposed to was Glyn Johns doing the final mix. Mick liked his own mix and when everyone else didn't, he took it really bad."

The album was mixed and handed into CBS/Epic. The label was obviously over the moon that the band had turned in a nice, simple single disk with a couple strong potential singles. The label pulled out the stops and showered the album with the kind of promotional cash the band had never seen before. What was remarkable, especially given its now agreed upon inferiority, was that usually hostile British reviewers fell over themselves praising *Combat Rock*. (What could have possibly possessed them?) American reviewers weren't nearly as kind. *Rolling Stone* damned it with faint praise, at least in comparison to its hysterical raves for *Sandinista*, but many others expressed either disappointment or outright contempt for it. The album charted at #2 in the UK, but sold sluggishly in America in the first few weeks of release. Then, the monster known as 'Rock the Casbah' was unleashed upon the earth, and the strange-filler-ridden shambles known as *Combat Rock* rode its coattails to platinum status.

But the albums' success was not convincing, certainly not in comparison to the sales figures that rivals like Police or Men at Work were racking up. Commenting on Mick's feelings of triumph over *Combat Rock*. Joe later said that "selling a million albums is not a big deal, it's a feeble deal." And *Combat Rock* was a feeble album.

The problem with many of the songs from the *Combat Rock* era is definition. What the hell are they supposed to be? 'Car Jamming', 'Inoculated City', 'Atom Tan', 'Midnight to Stevens' (which hadn't even made the first cut), 'Cool Confusion', 'Long Time Jerk', 'First Night Back in London' are not fast, not loud, not Reggae, not Rock, not Funk, not hard, not soft. They fall in between every possible gap without strong melodies or performances or even choruses to save them. Mick had told a horrified Joe that "verse and chorus as form are over," but the preponderance of the *CR* tracks had proven the inherent weakness of this concept. Mick was trying to appropriate the sounds of Hip Hop and Downtown Funk, but he had no idea how that music was even made. The only convincing Funk song on the album was 'Casbah', which was Topper's baby. All the disco production tricks on the re-recorded 'Overpowered by Funk' did nothing but bury a formerly standard Rock number with a funky bassline under a layer of cheesy crud. They had a good Funk song in 'Radio Clash,' but they left it off. And that song was lifted straight from 'Another One Bites the Dust' to begin with. Sadly, Mick didn't realize that his great strength was based in melody and chord progression. He didn't then had an ear for riffs or syncopations. Watt Roy had come up with the basslines that formed the foundation of the rap tracks on *Sandinista*. And he also didn't grow up with Funk, like all those New Yorkers did. It was all new to him, but he was too proud to admit it.

The success of *Combat Rock* was also tenuous. No one could guarantee that it could happen again. Used record bins were lousy with castoff copies of the album by the following summer. The band had more or less totally alienated their core audience with both the commerciality of the music and the conventionality of the tour and the album's promotion. It almost seemed that the Clash had stumbled over the finish line on their way to stardom. And the fact that Joe had gone missing prior to the tour, that Topper had been replaced, and that the band's live firepower was almost extinguished by tour's end did not bode well for the future. Things were happening very, very quickly on the music scene back then and the Clash were in serious danger of being left behind.

I don't really know what Mick thinks of the album today, but Joe was entirely dismissive of the album in his raving 1984 interviews. And his opinion of it didn't improve with age. In a 1996 interview in *Raygun* magazine he said , "*Combat Rock* is too weird to talk about. There's a few good cuts but most of them are really, really weird. It's a very druggy album." But with the commercial success of the *Combat Rock* salvage job, Joe may have begun to believe that he could unilaterally solve the band's problems. And as the perceived figure head of the Clash, Joe took most the blame for musical decisions that were usually made by Mick Jones and he was tired of it. Joe made it clear in 1984 that *Combat Rock* was his wake-up call.

The tensions that were reaching the breaking point were nothing new. They'd been there all along. Rumors had be leaking out since 1978 that the Clash were on the verge of splitting. For his part, Paul told *Creem* in early 1981 that "the great thing about the Clash is that we haven't broken up yet. Its a miracle"

The success of the album and tour had done little to improve relations in the band. In fact, it made them worse. By 1983, as Mick told *Rolling Stone* two years later that "we all knew that we were just doing it for the money. It was the worst." No one involved in the Clash was ever particularly motivated by money in and of itself, and the fact that *Combat Rock* had turned the Clash into a band lacking both in punch and conceptual integrity was obviously weighing heavily on everyone's mind. Joe and Paul felt that Clash had lost the power and spirit that had made them unique. Mick was tired of being a back-up man, and in fact was increasingly positioning himself onstage as co-lead singer of the Clash, sharing vocals on songs normally sung by Joe alone. He played less and less lead guitar onstage as well, and what little he did play was drenched in the latest electronic effects. This did not go unnoticed by the rest of the band. Joe bitterly complained in '84 that Mick "wouldn't play his damn guitar anymore." Paul weighed in on the issue in the 1999 *MOJO* retrospective: "I think he'd got bored of playing guitar by then. He had various shapes of equipment that would make it sound like a harpsichord or an orchestra." What Paul is referring to is the Roland Synth guitar that Mick had grown fond of. Most of the lead guitar work on *Combat Rock* is played through this instrument.

Mick may have lost interest in guitar playing because he was faced with a trend of competing bands with incredibly dexterous guitarists inspired by Eddie Van Halen. The Clash spent a lot of time worrying these bands - they said so in their interviews. They knew their primary market was America and they knew what American kids were listening to.

THE FINAL COUNTDOWN

Topper's firing had brought a change in approach to the Clash's stage attack. The free-wheeling dub jams of 1981 had given way to a straight-forward, 'just the facts ma'am' presentation of the Clash's best-loved tracks. "Terry was very matter of fact in his playing," as Paul told Bob Gruen. But whatever Terry lacked in finesse he made up in sheer force. Terry played the drums like they had said something bad about his mother. And Terry's primitive back-beat and perhaps the memories of the band's uncompromised early days it inspired cast a spell on Joe and Paul.

Contrary to popular mythology, there wasn't a preponderance of first album tracks in the *Combat Rock* tour setlists, the selections were actually very similar to the ones from the bands 1981 and early '82 tours. But Terry did play the new songs differently. Topper's playing was all over the map in his later days and his lighter gauge sticks and smaller drums gave his playing a lightweight, jazzy cast. Terry's playing was brutal and primitive in comparison. The simplicity and directness of his playing and the others' disenchantment with Mick's increasingly punch-less guitar may have done much to plan the seeds for the future direction of the band. And Pete's even more powerful drumming may have just reinforced those notions. Though Mick was certainly no Hendrix, Paul and Joe certainly may have felt disenfranchised by the band's musical direction, and the simplicity of Punk probably seemed refreshing after all the thorny syncopations Mick and Topper were toying with.

The *Combat Rock* tour ended with an anemic, early morning gig at the Bob Marley Center in Kingston, Jamaica. The band then returned to London to catch a breather. All was not well, by any means. Terry felt like a second-class member of the band and had keenly observed that Joe and Paul "couldn't work with (Mick) anymore." He would leave the band soon after tour's end. For his part, Mick had immersed himself totally in his 'New York environment.' Mick was having tapes of New York's WBLS sent to him so he could keep up on the very latest Hip Hop sounds. He said in 1986 that "In the last days of the Clash, they used to call me 'Whack Attack' because I used to listen to Hip Hop constantly, but only because it was the most happening music of the time." Inspired, he set about reinventing the Clash as a Hip Hop influenced band.

The others were having none of it. In an attempt to offer a compromise, Bernie proposed that the Clash delve into the sounds of New Orleans Funk and R&B. This was the kind of inspired suggestion that made Bernie so valuable to the Clash. The eerie Voodoo-Funk of Dr. John and the Meters drew upon the same roots that inspired both Reggae and Hip Hop and therefore offered a viable middle ground. Feeling this was an attempt to shut him down, Mick later excoriated this suggestion, commenting that the Clash "weren't from the bloody French Quarter." (The fact that they weren't from the South Bronx either escaped Mick's notice.) But the real problem was that New Orleans Funk was yet more retro music and Mick wanted to plug the Clash into the then-contemporary sounds of Hip Hop and Avant-Dance. The real story of the Clash reared its head again: Paul and Joe's love of Roots music vs. Mick's desire to plug into the latest fads. Realizing how foolish he must have seemed to his band mates, however, Mick was a little more contrite about his enthusiasms in 1999. He told *MOJO*'s Pat Gilbert, "I'd walk around with a beat box all the time and my hat on backwards they used to take the mickey out of me. I was always like that about whatever came along, sort of get excited for a while."

(Joe and Paul obviously took Bernie's New Orleans suggestion to heart for a while. One of the tracks Mick's prospective replacements were required to play along to was a New Orleans funk vamp, and 'Car Jamming' was recast as a Meters-styled funky jam when played live in 1983.)

Mick's love of fads caused him to lose interest in his original role in the band. And his behavior grew increasingly erratic. Joe, Paul and new drummer Pete Howard would wait for hours for Mick to show up for rehearsals, and oftentimes the guitarist wouldn't show up at all. In all likelihood, Mick's absence from rehearsals may have hastened his departure for reasons not immediately obvious. It's unlikely that Paul, Joe and Pete spent the hours smoking fags and flipping through comic books. It's more likely that they rehearsed on their own and laid the groundwork for the next chapter of the story of the Clash.

In *Westway to the World*, Joe quite famously referred to Mick's attitude as being like "Elizabeth Taylor in a filthy mood." There was a flash of genuine anger in his eyes when he said that, as if the memories of those days still angered him. Although Joe later expressed regret over the breakup, Paul did not. His reflection on the dilemma facing the band was unequivocal. "We're grown men," he recalled saying, "I cant take anymore of this. We were both in agreement that we were fed up, we wanted to get on with the job, rather than wait for Mick." He later states in the film that he had no regrets and wouldn't change anything, even if he could. His attitude was unchanged in a 2003 interview in *British GQ*, which is extraordinary given that the interview was done in the presence of Mick. Pete Howard, having had the benefit of playing with Mick and the new Clash, for his part had an interesting take on the breakup. He told Ralph Heibutzki "The real reason (for the split), I think, was a deterioration of the relationship between Joe and Mick. Suddenly they didn't like each other anymore. You know, best friend become worst enemies. Mick's relationship with (British model) Daisy had a lot to do with it, in my opinion."

Mick defended his behavior when Rhodes returned in a 1986 interview in *New York Talk* magazine: "I didn't get along with any of them (Rhodes and Vinyl). Every day they used to say 'Right we're going to fire everybody. We're firing Raymond, we're firing Barry Baker, we're firing all the people who work for us.' And everyday I had to go in and say 'No, you can't fire those people, those people are our family, you can't fire them.' For all those people it was like a megalomaniac situation from the people running it and I was the only one saying anything about it."

Amid all this bad feeling, it was Mick's reliance on his lawyer was the final straw: "He turned to me, supposedly his close buddy and said I don't mind what the band does as long as my lawyer checks it out first" Joe told *Rolling Stone*, "so I said you can go to your lawyer and write the bleeding songs with him. Because there wasn't any lawyer when we invented this spirit, this raging force." So, one late summer's day Mick showed up to a rehearsal in the late summer, only to be sent home, guitar and severance check in hand. Joe's and Mick's recountings of the breakup scene on the first of September 1983 conflicted wildly, with each casting themselves in a heroic role against a chastened adversary. The truth was most assuredly somewhere in-between.

AFTERMATH

A statement was released a week later, claiming that Mick "had drifted away from the original mission of the Clash." Mick fired off a rebuttal, claiming otherwise. Aside from the announcement that two new guitarists had taken Mick's place, little was heard from either camp until the new Clash premiered at California's Long Beach Arena in late January of 1984. Joe broke his silence, with a vengeance. All the resentments and slights and hurt feelings he had suffered came pouring out in an often-times nasty and vindictive manner, starting with some very nasty comments in *Rolling Stone*. Joe had a nasty side to be sure, and his verbal attacks against Mick were often as ugly and uncalled for as the beating he unleashed on Mick at Sheffield Top Rank four years earlier. But no one has ever argued that Mick was himself inoffensive. There had obviously been a situation were Mick had made Joe feel marginalized and inferior. Nothing is more hurtful than being snubbed, and the British, especially Londoners, are the Mozarts of snubbery. Mick was no exception - another ugly story would surface later where Mick had egregiously insulted Nick Sheppard and Vince White at a party when they had introduced themselves to him. In any event, Joe was hurt and pissed off and he wanted you to know it. As the tour dragged on, Joe would soften his line somewhat, but not before the damage was done.

Mick didn't return Joe's fire in the press. But he may have fewer grievances to air, other than the obvious one of being fired in the first place. But his reticence to badmouth his old mates didn't mean he was taking it all lying down. He immediately set to his lawyers to work in an attempt to cripple the new Clash. All of the band's assets were frozen, leaving road work the only way the Clash could pay for the most basic expenses. And according to Nick Sheppard, every hall they played was served an injunction forbidding the Clash to perform there.

None of the injunctions were heeded, but there was no doubt that the new Clash were not going to have an easy time of it.

The UK press reacted more negatively to the band's return to Punk Rock than it did to Mick Jones' dismissal. Predictably enough, the American press' response to Joe's complaints was to filter them through the knee-jerk response to anything involved with the Clash and politicize Strummer's gripes. The press party line became that Jones was tossed for being insufficiently radical and uncommitted to Socialism, a charge I have yet to read Joe hurl. Joe's litany that Mick didn't want to tour, didn't want to play guitar and was unwilling to compromise with the other members became an endless stream of Marxist namecalling placed in Joe's mouth. And it only got stupider and more inaccurate with every retelling. Keith Richards, whose insatiable appetite for heroin was only replaced for a vampiric lust for Yuppie cash , best exemplifies this game of retard telephone when he told Vic Garabini of *Musician* magazine "We've (the Rolling Stones) never kicked anybody out for ideological reasons. If that's what they think, they should go back to the Politiburo. I don't really listen to them because I cant stand that kind of pseudo -intellectualism. It's got nothing to do with essence." What 25 years of unlistenable albums and endless tours distinguished only by outrageously exorbitant ticket prices have to do with 'essence' has not yet been addressed by the Freddie Krueger in a fright-wig guitarist.

As late as 1995, the misinformation was still in circulation. Bill Flanagan, who really should know better, wrote in 1995 that "(Joe) vanished before one tour, came back for a while and then ousted his partner Mick Jones from the band for having become more interested in being a rock star than in staying true to the Utopian values of the Clash."

THAT OLD TIME GROOVE....

Though many people have claimed that Joe and Mick broke up because of Bernie's influence and not because of profound musical differences, this simply is not true. Mick himself confirmed in a 1986 *NME* piece there were serious musical differences between he and the band. "I was going 'C'mon, let's dance' and they were saying 'No, let's riot," he told Paolo Hewitt. There was also a serious and intractable difference of philosophy between Mick and Joe. Mick's attitude was that whatever music he produced was Clash music. If it wasn't Rock and Roll, or even if it wasn't played by the actual band, it didn't matter. The Clash was whatever he wanted it to be. If he wanted appropriate the myriad Dance Pop fads of the early 80's, that was okay: it was still the Clash as far as he was concerned. This type of thinking was reminiscent of the Beatles. They were profligate in their eclecticism as well, and there was plenty of room for what were essentially solo tracks with other Beatles playing or not playing along.

Joe saw things quite differently. He told Michael Goldberg of *Rolling Stone* in 1984 that Mick's 1983 demo "wasn't our music. He was playing with beat boxes and synthesizers. I was thinking 'It's time for us to stop ripping off the black people so much that they don't get on the radio anymore'." This statement is highly ironic in light of what Bernard Rhodes wrought on

Cut the Crap a year later, but even when Joe was playing nice in hopes of reuniting the band, he expressed similar feelings. In the March 19, 1988 issue of *Melody Maker* he said of 'Police and Thieves,' "It was Punk Reggae, not white Reggae. We were bringing some of our roots to it, not trying to mimic someone else's, I wish we really could have stayed that pure."

Joe's career, both before and after the Clash, showcased his philosophy of incorporating disparate influences in his own music. And in many ways, what Joe has done has always been based in the primal Roots-Rock of the 101'ers. The *Permanent Record* and *Earthquake Weather* projects were essentially 101'ers albums tarted up with Latin percussion and beat lyrics. And I have always seen *Rock Art and the X Ray Style* as Joe in some ways trying to simulate the integrationist album that *Combat Rock* should have been. *Global a Go Go* was promoted (somewhat foolishly in my opinion) as a 'World Music' album, but it was actually a fairly traditional Rock and Roll album with World-ish seasoning.

Joe and Mick both had totally different ideas of the Clash's importance as a phenomenon in and of itself. Jones was asked by *Musician* in 1981 if he saw the Clash together in five years time and he replied "No. Maybe. I really can't see it. Both Joe and I will be thirty and maybe in five years time we'll be completely somewhere else at that point in time." He told the same magazine the following year that he hoped to create a new Clash that had completely broken with the band's past legacy and call it "Clash Now." By contrast Joe told *Creem* in 1984, "I'd hope that if I started to act funny that I would be fired and the Clash would continue to roll on with out me."

IF I COULD TURN BACK TIME

And what would have Strummer done differently? He often said in 1999 interviews that the Clash should have taken 1983 off and reconvened after they were rested. But Topper's inactivity probably would have done nothing but aggravated his addiction and Mick would have continued to immerse himself further in Hip Hop and MIDI technology. And his own drug problems could well have worsened.

Looking back, one has to wonder what options Joe had in 1983, aside from sacking Mick. Mick's painful experiences in bands before the Clash, and his feeling that he was the band's sole driving force may have prevented him from quitting, but this is uncertain. One longtime band associate told Ralph Heibutzki that he was convinced that Mick was going to quit the band in 1983. After all, Mick was alone against Joe, Paul , Bernie and Kosmo and that may have become an intolerable situation for him. Unfortunately, his way of dealing with these odds was to become even more imperious and aloof. (I think that Mick's interpersonal issues were essentially borne of defensive mechanisms to mask insecurity.) But his hermit-like behavior following his firing proved how painful it was for him.

One other option was to wait for Mick to get his act together and then carry on with the original Clash. This is the option Strummer seems to imply in *Westway to the World* that he wish he exercised. But that would mean he would be making music that he didn't believe in.

Would Mick have moved closer to Joe and Paul's concept of the Clash had he a year off to think things over? Or would he have returned completely immersed in his enthusiasms? And personally, as much as I like the first BAD record, there is no way in hell I would have ever accepted that music as the Clash. That would have been the absolute last straw for me and thousands of other fans. To make matters worse, there were so many new bands coming out at the time that it's uncertain as to whether the Bubblegum audience would have filled the void left by disgusted Punks like myself. Finally, Joe's temperament would have not allowed him to carry on for long in a band that would for all intents and purposes would have been indistinguishable from INXS.

What other options were there? They could have ganged up on Mick and told him to go along with the program, but we don't know if they hadn't already tried that, and doing so would have probably made matters worse anyway. It certainly wouldn't have helped the Clash get an album out that year. Joe, Paul and the management team wanted to get back out on tour in early '83 to stay visible in the rapidly moving scene, but Mick resisted this and the bands nine-month vacation was broken up only by the May mini -tour and the Us Festival. That the Clash were in total disarray in 1983 is proven by the fact that the band wasn't even doing anything substantial in September when Mick was fired. No tour had been planned and no album was being recorded. And Joe, Paul, and Kosmo all claimed that if Mick hadn't been fired, this state of indolence would have continued. As it was, Mick didn't premiere his new group until over a year after he was fired and didn't get an album out until the end of the following year after that.

Joe was absolutely right in asserting that it was the chemistry of the classic four members that made the Clash what it was. No one can seriously argue against that. But what was he to do when half the band decided that their own personal interests were more important that the Clash itself? The events of the past two decades have shown that Topper's addiction was as serious and debilitating as anyone else's in Rock history, despite Joe's ludicrous and insincere assertions to Richard Cromelin of the *LA Times* in 1988 that they could have continued with the stricken drummer. Mick's drug problem wasn't nearly as serious as Topper's, but his standoff with everyone else created an equally serious problem.

And unfortunately, Mick's inability to work with others was not limited to the Clash. The entire lineup of the first BAD quit on him in 1990 (though Dan Donovan stuck around for a few months) and the lineup of BAD 2 also drifted off, albeit less dramatically. (meaning no one cared about them anyway) When three different groups of musicians decide that they cannot stand to work with Mick despite his prodigious skills, and despite the fact that he was in many ways their meal ticket, that speaks volumes about his behavior in those situations. Lay people may think that bands break up because musicians are simply too flaky to keep it together, but musicians at that level usually understand how difficult it is to create and sustain a career. Despite all the nonsense Joe spouted when trying to reassemble the original band, the fact remains that there was considerable tension in the Clash around the time of the release of *Sandinista*, most of it springing from Topper's addiction and Mick's boredom with Rock.

Joe believed in the idea of the Clash, far more than anyone else in the band. Hiring back Bernie was his way to get the band back on track after they squandered the momentum generated by the success of *London Calling*. Unfortunately, Bernie's presence made Mick's attitude problems even worse (lending credence to my theory that his arrogance was defensive). But even still, the band held it together for another two and half years. Joe understood how much he needed Mick and his reliance on his increasingly uncooperative partner prevented him from breaking up the band earlier. Joe said as much when he told Ethlie Van Vare in 1984, "I didn't just get up on the wrong side of the bed one morning and decide to fire Mick. I'd have done anything rather than get rid of him. But if he were still here, we wouldn't be touring. We wouldn't even be in rehearsal. Mick would be off on holiday somewhere." He told Richard Cook of the *NME* that "in order to keep the Clash going, I'd go around it, beg him to come to rehearsals and stuff." Really, how much longer could that have gone on?

The truth of the matter is that the Clash's split was tragic, but inevitable. The Clash had a unique chemistry, but it was dependent on each member to gave the Clash all he had. Topper was the weak link and he snapped. Mick was soon to follow. They say hindsight is 20/20, but in Joe's case it was myopic. And as we shall see, the Clash had almost twenty years to patch up their differences and reunite. There was certainly no shortage of big money offers to help induce wavering members. I would argue that the Clash made an honorable decision to put their friendships, such as they were, before cash and glory. I think they understood that a reunion would simply put them back in a situation that had become intolerable in the first place.

PUNK ROCK'S WHAT IT'S ALL ABOUT

"I keep going on about Punk because I always think about it. Because when a journalist asks me 'are you a Punk,' I say 'yes' because I like all the aggro that comes with that."
Joe Strummer, March 1982

For some observers, a return to Punk may have seemed like a strange choice for the Clash. Joe may not have spent a lot of time listening to Punk Rock, but he certainly loved playing it. Punk Rock gave Joe an adrenaline rush and a sense of power that the more compromised sounds of the later Clash failed to deliver. Punk also offered Joe the chance to experience the catharsis he so badly craved. "I'm looking for the ultimate wipeout," Joe said in 1984 "for the ultimate feeling out of every song." He also saw Punk Rock as the latest link in a chain of Rebel Culture that stretched back to the Delta Blues and included his beloved Reggae, Rockabilly and Beatnik poetry. The 101'ers were a Punk band in all but name, and Punk Rock informed almost every move Joe made in his career, until his dying day. He saw Punk as the white man's Rebel Culture and that identity and tradition were always very important to him. Up until his death, songs like 'London's Burning' and 'White Riot' were setlist staples, and his April 2002 gigs at St Anne's Warehouse in Brooklyn displayed an increasing drift towards the Punkier end of the spectrum.

Joe saw Punk Rock as integral to the Clash's identity and was horrified by Mick's cavalier dismissals of Punk in the press. Joe felt that Punk Rock
could accommodate an wide range of rhythms and styles and hence his plans
for Punk were not as cut and dried as Bernie may have liked. He told *Boston
Rock* that the new Clash's music would not be straight -up Punk, and that it
had to have other musical elements in it. And as the 'Out of Control 'tour made
its way across North America, late-period Clash songs like 'Broadway', 'Junco
Partner',' Jimmy Jazz' and 'Straight to Hell' crept into the setlists. The difference was that were played with more energy and aggression than the first lineups playings. Paradoxically, they were also played with more finesse and sub-
tlety. And two late tour numbers, 'In the Pouring, Pouring Rain' and 'North
And South' were much mellower and melodic than the earlier numbers,
though they too were played with plenty of energy. Joe obviously pictured the
new Clash to be just as eclectic and wide ranging as the original one, only the
new one would be sharper, edgier, more coherent and more aggressive.

REGRETS, I'VE HAD A FEW

But why did Joe later disavow a project he had staked his entire career
on? Joe would have had you believe that the whole thing was Bernie's doing
and he was just along for the ride. He claimed to have regretted the entire
episode. How much of this did he mean?

There were many reasons why Joe began to distance himself from the
Clash II project sometime in the summer of 1984, but none of them had to do
with any disagreement with the original concept. Any claims otherwise are
sheer foolishness. Though he later (and for good reason) came to regret the
entire episode, he also admitted sometime later to Sean O'Hagan that Bernie's
idea for a new Clash was "impressive." He also said in Q magazine in 2000
that the original idea for the Clash was "to be an oxyacetylene torch", something Mick had no interest in. But there were myriad problems with Bernie's
strategy and several outside factors were conspiring against the band. First
and foremost was Joe's mother coming down with cancer so shortly after Joe's
father died. Since his brother had committed suicide 13 years previous, Joe
was now faced with the prospect of having no family at all. I believe that this
fact alone sounded the death knell for the Clash. But, Joe was also not up to
the pressure of carrying the band on his own. By sacking Mick, Joe put the
enormous burden of the Clash on his own shoulders, particularly in the public's mind, and that was a burden he was unable to bear.

Joe's sheepish protests that he was just along for the ride are annihilated by his 1984 interviews (which he may have hoped people forgot) and by
his incendiary performances with that lineup. Even revisionist writers like
Barry Miles and Greil Marcus, who labored so hard to recast the 'Out of
Control' tour as a failure, could not fail to comment on Joe's shamanic stage
presence. Miles may have conjured up fans walking out in disgust from the
Academy gigs in his revised *The Clash: an Illustrated History* (a fact which
strangely escaped comment in contemporary reviews- in fact, critics derided

the audience for their vehemence) and described fans booing or sitting in stunned silence (strangely undocumented on bootleg recordings) and Marcus may have imagined that the Clash played to a "not-quite sold out crowd" (the show was described as being "overcrowded" in the *San Francisco Examiner*) and he may have recast the 10,000 seat San Francisco Civic Center as a "dumpy, medium sized hall" but neither tried to pretend that Joe's performances were not on a level of commitment unseen since 1977. But as we shall see, there may have been another agenda at work beneath the revisionism. Much has been made of Joe's exchange with Johnny Green (short version: Johnny told Joe the new Clash was crap, and Joe responded, "I know") at an Academy show, but those who met Joe knew what a people-pleaser he was and he may not have wanted to have a confrontation with a figure from the Clash's salad days. And Green's strange retelling of the to Ralph Heibutzki suddenly included a confrontation between Green and Bernie, followed by Joe threatening to punch Bernie, so I have no idea what to believe. Suffice it to say, that whatever Joe said or didn't say to Johnny Green was contradicted every night on the concert stage. And would Joe have written and continued to write new songs if he was such an unwilling participant? It's absurd. Again, this whole 'Joe wasn't into it' slant put forward by Marcus Gray (who never saw the new Clash to begin with) and others is nothing but pure revisionism. I met Joe backstage at Worcester in 1984 and he was quite cheerful and animated, not sullen or withdrawn. And given the fact that during the show he was climbing the scaffolding and leaping headfirst into the crowd kind of gives me the impression that gee, maybe -just maybe- he was enjoying himself and believed in what he was doing. Of course, what happened afterward is another story entirely.

Joe may have certainly longed for the chemistry and certainty of the Clash's glory days. An unnamed camp follower told Ralph Heibutzki that the "the band [would be] to the rear of the bus, having a good time [and] Joe would be somewhat separate, and detached from them, way up front. It was kind of sad, almost a loneliness I detected, I think he did [miss Jones] as early as that" Its also possible father's recent death was weighing heavily on him.

Lastly, Joe's entire feelings were colored by the way the entire affair ended up. He told Sean O'Hagan that he "didn't realize [Bernie's] motives until it was too late and the whole thing had gone too far." What Bernie's motives were certainly not had been heard on tour. But in light of train wreck at the end of the line, anything that had happened prior to the humiliation he suffered with *Cut the Crap* was surely seen as nothing but a prelude to it. But Joe also found himself outside of his comfort zone for another fundamental reason.

PLAYING WITH THE BAND

It's obvious, when you look carefully at Joe's career, that he wanted to be the frontman, never the leader of a band. Clive Timperley, Mole and Dan Kelleher were the musical directors of the 101'ers, even if Joe originated most of the songs. Mick was the leader of the Clash, Zander Schloss was the arranger and musical director of the work he did with Joe, Antony Genn led the first Mescaleros lineup and Scott Shields and Martin Slattery took his place when he was fired. Joe told *Select* magazine in 1991 that he was slumming with the wretched Pogues because he "needed to be be in a band, my ego wasn't happy when my own name was on a poster. I felt too exposed." There would be no place for Joe to hide in the new Clash. Even if Bernie was the puppet master behind the new lineup, any credit or blame would be Joe's alone.

Joe also like to collaborate and be part of a gang. Mick may have been the leader of the Clash, but it was more a case of first among equals, particularly when Bernie returned to the fold. Joe seemed comfortable with the Latino Rockabilly War, but far less so with the *Earthquake Weather* band, comprised solely of Zander Schloss and his friends.. And it wasn't until Tymon Dogg joined the Meskies that Joe really let loose onstage. Joe seemed at ease with the dismal Pogues because they were just a bunch of undistinguished Pub Rockers, and they were his drinking buddies to boot. With three new members several years his junior, and with Paul's participation tenuous, Joe had no one to play off of except Bernie. What the new Clash lacked for Joe was personal chemistry. But Joe's protests that he had nothing to do with the assembly of the new lineup are also to be taken with a grain of salt, especially when you consider the many parallels between the new Clash and the first Mescaleros lineup.

CRITICAL MASS

I am sure I am not alone in wondering exactly why were the critics often so hostile to the Clash's new direction. After all, this was a band whose original mandate after all was super-aggressive Punk Rock. But the extreme volume and aggressive stance of the band and the violent tendencies of the new crop of Punks may have been a turnoff to older, more cerebral Rock critics. The Clash had attracted a considerable following of journalists as their records became tamer and more emasculated, and the atavistic fury of the new Clash was a shock to many of them. Nothing on a Clash record could prepare someone for the sheer impact of the new lineup. It also must be said that the band was also hampered on the California mini-tour (when the press was paying particular attention) by the substandard equipment they were forced to use because of Mick's injunction. Nick was playing one of Mick's old Les Paul Jr.'s as late as San Francisco, a guitar notorious for its tuning problems. The band was reduced to borrowing equipment from opening act Los Lobos. As the money rolled in from the gigs, the band upgraded their gear and better performances followed. Ironically, the raunchy sound only seemed only seem to inspire the fans in San Francisco to greater heights of madness. At times the 10,000 strong crowd threatened to drown out the band with their screaming and hollering and carryin' on. I think it's no accident that the Punk Revival started just a few blocks away just few short years after this show. I am willing to bet that all of the late 80s Gilman Street movers and shakers were at this show.

The extreme responses the new Clash inspired did not escape comment by reviewers. Phillip Elwood commented in his *San Francisco Examiner* review of the bands mediocre but wildly received SF show that, "I seldom get fearful and claustrophobic in jammed arenas, but I was on this occasion." Later in Britain, Lola Borg of *Smash Hits* had the misfortune of attending a concert when Joe stopped 'Know Your Rights' and threatened to kill a couple gobbers in the front row. She watched in horror as Joe plucked "a spiky haired youth from the front row, gave him brutal verbal abuse" and had him ejected. (Joe's rant from that show is a must-hear) She wrote that "a Clash concert isn't a suitable place for those of a nervous disposition" and complained about that the fans "total hero worship reminded me all too much of Heavy Metal." This was not your older brother's Clash.

But the standard line taken by reviewers was that yes, the new Clash were a great show and all, but they no longer mattered because... well, we say so. Jim Reid neatly encapsulated this sentiment when he commented in *Record Mirror* that the new Clash "hadn't lost any of the kinetic energy that had always made them such an exciting rock spectacle" and that for "spectacle and dynamism the Clash still leave the likes of U2 and Big Country out there on guitar solo number nine." But perhaps feeling he had been too enthusiastic about the show he added that "the Clash have lost meaning." *NME* hitman Gavin Martin claimed to have gone to see the new Clash with an "open mind" (please) but dismissed the band on the usual bizarre theoretical grounds, saying the new band was "no big departure" and that the show was 'heaviest and most orthodox I've ever seen the Clash play." Tellingly, he also whined about the Clash's use of confrontational imagery, which was anathema to the sunny, Pop image the record industry was taking to the bank and that the *NME* was, by sheer coincidence, favoring. Anthony De Curtis was initially unambiguous about the Clash's performance at Atlanta's Fox Theatre in his *Musician* review. He stated that "the Clash are back with a ruthless vengeance. Their nearly two hour, twenty four song onslaught made for an urgent, intense performance." But he too apparently felt obliged to end the review on a down note, and made a series of confusing and inconclusive observations about why the band (whose performance he just raved about) had not given "us" a "reason to believe."

Doug Simmons wrote in the *Boston Phoenix* that the "at the (Worcester) Centrum, the Clash looked healthy and sounded mighty." But he then prefaced a long, confusing and meandering rant by saying that "as thrilling as they were, the concert was less than a triumph." Aside from saying he didn't like the new songs, Simmons failed to explain exactly why the show wasn't a triumph. Having been at that show, I can tell you the 10,000 kids there didn't share Simmon's sentiment in any way, shape, or form. *Boston Herald* reviewer Larry Katz also contradicted Simmons' baseless claim when he wrote that "as soon as the revamped Clash hit the stage at the Worcester Centrum Friday night and crashed into 'London Calling', everyone in the audience stood up. No one sat down until the show ended 90 minutes and 24 songs later. That's excitement."

Like Simmons, Bill Holdship prefaced his interview in *Creem* with a long editorial cataloguing the Clash's failures, and like Simmons, he strangely seemed to imply that the new Clash were somehow saddled with responsibility for the old lineup's failures. And like Simmons, Holdship admitted the new Clash put on a great show, but he didn't like the new songs either. How anyone can make a definitive judgment on songs played at ear-splitting volume at a chaotic Punk Rock show is beyond me, but then, I'm not a Rock critic.

What the hell was going on here? How could critics alternately praise the new lineup's performances and then proceed to trash them on vague and confusing theoretical grounds? It didn't make any sense. And for some strange reason, reviews written by staff writers on newspapers and by the independent press tended to be more favorable towards the new Clash than the standard (ie., reliant on record company advertising) Rock magazines. To be sure, Rock critics are particularly prone to Groupthink, but one can't help but wonder if there another agenda at work here.

PAYING THE PIPER

Nick Sheppard told Ralph Heibutzki that CBS was "extremely upset" about Mick's sacking and that "offers of money were made" for the two camps to patch up their differences. One is almost given to idle speculation about whether some of that CBS money was diverted in ways that might facilitate a reconciliation between Joe and Mick. Now we all know such things as 'bribery' or 'payola' are out of the realm of possibility, but there is an interesting precedent for undue record company influence on the press. In their book, *Stardust: the David Bowie Biography*, Henry Edwards and Tony Zanetta wrote about how publicist Lou Siegel arranged for Bowie to get some much needed coverage in *Rolling Stone* magazine:

"Siegel was friendly with John Mendelssohn, who wrote for *Rolling Stone*. In exchange for an all expenses paid trip to San Francisco, a city Mendelssohn loved, Siegel extracted a promise from the critic to review *the Man Who Sold the World* and do a feature about David for *Rolling Stone*. This is not an uncommon practice. Freelance Rock writers usually augment their small incomes with free lunches, trips, receptions and the like from record companies. In the process, *the writer often tacitly becomes one of the media arms of the record company publicity process.*" Edwards and Zanetta went on to say that Mendelssohn's subsequent review was "perfect fodder for (publicity house) Mercury to give credibility to this unknown English artist." Later, Mendelssohn would "rush into print with a *Rolling Stone* review t*hat could be used as record company propaganda.*" (italics mine)

Rolling Stone would later cover the new Clash's concert in Santa Barbara as a straight news story written by Michael Goldberg. Other that declaring the new lineup was raw and visceral, Goldberg made no qualitative comment on the new Clash's performance per se, but managed to add that "something was missing, and that something was the dynamic chemistry, a certain electricity that once existed between Jones and Strummer." Certainly, it was strange that such a subjective observation wold be inserted in what was clearly presented as a news story and not a review. In any event, *Rolling Stone* was packaging itself as a lifestyle magazine and in-depth music coverage had been shifted to its short-lived glossy spinoff, *Record.* Having recently named Joe Strummer 'chump of the year' (1983) for firing Mick Jones (a sentiment coincidentally seconded by CBS suits), *Record* proceeded to launch a full-scale assault on Joe Strummer and his new Clash. In an egregious hit-piece entitled

'The Mouth that Roared,' Joe was trashed as the "most shrilly, self-righteous boor in Pop History." and 'the least rhythmic rhythm guitarist in Pop History.' It was obvious Joe and Kosmo had no idea what was coming for them, because their attitude in the interviews was cheery and expansive. The interviewer had clearly approached them in a friendly manner, given the fact that Joe and Kosmo were not shy in confronting journalists they perceived as being hostile. 'The Mouth that Roared' was pure 'gotcha' journalism and Joe's quotes were presented in a way to make him sound foolish. They were also framed by sneering commentary, just in case the reader didn't catch on to the idea that Joe was an idiot and an asshole. That the new Clash were being humiliated in such a prominent forum would surely discourage them, and perhaps convince Joe and Bernie that on top of all the other negative press the band was receiving that maybe the new lineup wasn't so great an idea after all.

In an amazing stroke of fate, 'The Mouth that Roared' was written by none other than *John Mendelssohn.*

WILL WONDERS NEVER CEASE?

By sheer coincidence, the press' take on the new lineup (which suddenly contradicted previously widespread press sentiments that the Clash should stop dabbling and go back to playing Rock and Roll) was perfectly in line with what the Clash's paymasters at CBS thought. This was not entirely surprising to longtime Clash watchers. The British press reception was mixed to the double-album *London Calling* and downright hostile to the triple-album *Sandinista*. It was surely coincidental that unprofitable and hard to market (especially in recession ravaged Britain) mutli-disc sets by the Clash were trashed, and that the potentially profitable single record *Combat Rock* was praised to the skies. It was surely coincidental that BAD's sunny Pop records enjoyed extensive promotional and advertising coverage while *Cut the Crap* and Joe's subsequent solo releases received practically none. It was surely coincidence that the Clash in general and Joe Strummer in particular were the whipping boys of the press following the band's initial split and continued to be so until Sony bought CBS and decided that the Clash's back catalogue was ripe for exploitation via an extensive reissue program. One can only wonder just what Joe Strummer could have possibly been referring to when he complained onstage at show in St Louis about "999,000 cynical journalists" who were "only in it for the kickbacks"

TALE OF THE TAPE

Strangely enough, Joe Strummer announced at the 12/7 Scargill gig that the Clash "had a record" that would be "out in the New Year" as soon as "some things by." Considering the fact that the band wouldn't even enter a recording studio until later that month (according to Marcus Gray) or January '85 (according to Ralph Heibutzki) to record *Cut the Crap*, this claim was puzzling. But reports had circulated in the summer that the Clash were in Paris working on an album, and even Clash intimate Lisa Robinson had announced

in her syndicated column in October of 1984 that the Clash were busy recording their new album. Two possibilities exist here: either the rumors (as well as
Joe's startling announcement) were made of whole cloth, which is difficult to
imagine in Robinson's case, or perhaps the mystery of the *Give 'Em Enough
Dope* tracks has been solved. (though a third possibility exists- Joe may have
been referring to the album that was *about* to be recorded, but that doesn't
explain the news items)

      In 1988, three bootleg EP's appeared in collector's shops which con-
tained twelve Clash 2 performances from gigs in Chicago, Portland, OR and
Seattle. What was remarkable about these tracks was not that they were
soundboard recordings (fans were used to Clash 2 soundboards by then) but
that they sounded not only professionally recorded, but professionally mixed
as well. The drums and vocals are soaked in reverb, the background vocals
(which were always too loud on soundboard tapes) are way back in the mix
and Paul's bass is deep and sonorous, rather than rubbery. Rumors later circulated that guitarist Nick Sheppard leaked these tracks, which is possible, but
given the way he and the others were treated by management, highly unlikely. (Also, one of the EPs included 'Three Card Trick', a tune Sheppard told
Ralph Heibutzki that he didn't like) What may be possible is that Joe was right
at Brixton: the Clash did have an album - a live album.
      Strummer has never talked about this, but perhaps he wasn't involved.
He spent the second half of 1984 with his terminally ill mother, but the previously announced plan was to enter the studio in late summer and get a new
album in the stores before Christmas. The hirelings spent the balance of 1984
numbly staring at each other in a rehearsal room, so obviously Bernie and
Kosmo were doing something. And there was a precedent for a project like this.

      Following Randy Rhoads' death in 1982, Ozzy Osbourne shelved live
tapes for what later became his *Tribute* album. Since most acts were contractually obliged to release one album a year in those days, Ozzy plugged the gap
caused by Rhoads' death by assembling a pickup band and recording a live
album at the Ritz in New York. At the time, there was some squabbling in the
press between Ozzy and his former band, Black Sabbath, so Ozzy recorded a
set of Black Sabbath covers and released them under his own name. This over-
shadowed Black Sabbath's own live competing live album, *Live Evil*, and
helped Ozzy maintain his career momentum after the loss of his guitarist and
collaborator. Perhaps not coincidentally, *Speak of the Devil* was released on Epic,
home of course, of the Clash.
      Releasing a live album while a band was in turmoil was a standard
fallback for bands in the 70's and 80's. The aforementioned *Live Evil* was
released while Black Sabbath were shedding their singer Ronnie James Dio.
Van Halen released a live album while they were in the process of figuring out
how best to destroy their careers and get dropped by their label. The Clash had
announced a live set recorded at Shea (a sickening ploy since they were an
largely unwelcome opening act at that gig) the previous year, which was
scrapped when Mick was fired. Since Mick Jones had all the bands prior assets
impounded by his lawyers, a live album would circumvent the expensive

recording process and get product in the shops before Mick had even played out live with his new band.

So if this was the plan, what happened to the record? Well, rumors were rife that Mick's lawyers had so effectively crippled the new Clash that they were unable to release anything. Items followed in the papers that Mick had the Clash forbidden by the courts to even play out under the name "the Clash" in 1985. Lenny Kaye wrote in his BAD cover story in *Spin* that Epic were so exasperated by the legal wrangling between Mick and the Clash that they put *Cut the Crap* out anyway and let the parties fight amongst themselves in court.

If Mick was trying to destroy the new band, incessant badgering by his lawyers would have been a sure way to do it. But Mick later claimed that his idea for the 'Medicine Show' video was a OK corral shootout between BAD and the new Clash, so he may have just wanted the Clash album delayed until he was ready to release his own album. The competition between the two albums would ensure added publicity for his own fledgling group, publicity it may well not receive on its own. Mick was in "Howard Hughes mode," as an intimate of the band put it to Ralph Heibutzki, while the Clash were playing a concert every night in the US, and didn't even premiere his new band until the end of 1984, so he may well have followed this strategy.

SECOND VERSE, SAME AS THE FIRST

The problem with the original concept behind Clash II was that neither Joe nor Bernie seemed willing or prepared to face the horrible reality of the mid-80's Pop scene. Joe made a lot of noise that the new Clash were going to be the biggest band in the world, but that was an utterly impossible achievement for a band as uncompromising as the 1984-model Clash. What most likely happened was that while Joe was out of the picture, Bernie had time to think things over and in doing so, lost his nerve. Johnny Green had noticed Bernie's mercurial nature as early as 1978. He told Heibutzki that Rhodes' alleged master plan for the Clash "changed so often, that you soon lost faith in it on a day-to-day basis." Not much had changed since then, it would seem.

The original plan was to break the Clash as a 'real' Punk Rock (or 'Rebel Rock' as Punk had been rechristened by the Clash camp) band. What was being bandied about was nothing less than a revolution. But the Clash found themselves shoveling against the tide. The entire industry had invested itself in the New Pop movement, and the go-go mood of the mid-80's was an eternity removed from the malaise and pessimism of the late 70's. It's likely that Bernie and Joe realized this, because the next batch of songs to be written were totally removed from the brutalist political fury of songs like 'Ammunition' and 'Sex Mad War'.

New songs like 'Dirty Punk', 'Fingerpoppin' and 'Cool Under Heat' were vague, inoffensive ditties about Joe's fantasyland vision of the Punk life. At some point in time, 'Three Card Trick' went from being a blistering, Punk Rock face-puncher to becoming a cozy, *Combat Rock*-styled Ska ditty, and the lyrics to 'We Are the Clash' were re-written to be a matey anthem and not a scorching political manifesto like the original. Only 'North and South' had any political implications and they were, at best, vague. It was clear that before the year was over, the plot was lost entirely and Bernie's original plan was scrapped. This is why the new boys were sidelined and Watt-Roy and Gallagher were summoned to rehearse with Joe and Pete. The Clash were getting ready to play by the rules. Yet again.

The new plan was to make the Clash a listener-friendly, Punk-flavored Pop band, ready made for the mid-80's charts. Record companies were then insisting that their acts used drum-machines, whether or not the technology was appropriate to the bands sound or not. Hence, we heard absurd synthetic monstrosities by hoary and hairy old veterans like Bob Dylan. Tom Petty and Jethro Tull in 1985. Despite all of Joe's complaints about Mick and his electronics, the basic tracks of *Cut the Crap* were all built on drum machines and synthesizers. According to Nick Sheppard, the new plan to rationalize away this obvious surrender was recast as "recreating Punk for the 80's." The result of this was that the Clash would be doing almost exactly what BAD were doing, only with louder guitars. Despite the uninformed dismissals by critics, *Cut the Crap* was not a Punk throwback in any sense (if only!). In fact, it was as conceptually 'progressive' as Mick's album, it just was a lot more poorly made. Joe later told his former inquisitor Gavin Martin that Bernie indeed had a more abstract and theoretical aim with this new 'new Clash'. "All he became interested in," said Joe of Bernie, " was could you take elements like songwriting, rock and roll- that strange thing we call creativity- and package it like it was canned tomatoes?"

COULD IT EVER HAVE WORKED?

It's certain that Joe hated *Cut the Crap*, even while it was being made and the busking tour was his reaction against it. Joe and Bernie then parted ways for months and the way Bernie was making the album played a large part in this split. Joe would be faced with even more sniping and accusation from the press when he re-emerged to promote this very synthetic album, and that prospect was probably instrumental in causing him to breakup the band weeks before the albums' release. The band was contractually bound to release something and Joe in no way could afford to fight both Bernie and Mick in court. Given the choice between the devil and the deep blue sea, he opted to throw himself at Mick's feet and try to get him to rejoin the Clash. This, however, would result only in humiliation.

There was only one way the new Clash could have succeeded and that was to enter the studio immediately following the end of the 'Out of Control' tour (like they said they would) and readied an album for a Christmas-time release. This way they would have recorded the songs as they had been developed while the band was still hot. The seven month layoff between the end of the tour and the beginning of the Crap sessions gave Bernie all to much time to scheme and Joe all too much time to equivocate.

The irony here is that *Cut the Crap* makes the same mistakes the Clash were making on *Sandinista* and *Combat Rock*. Like it's predecessors, *CTC* tries to incorporate trends and fads that the Clash did not fully understand. Like its predecessors, *CTC* is a studio concoction played mostly by studio musicians, not the record of a well-rehearsed batch of songs by a legitimate band. In the end result, Jones and Rhodes were the true Janus twins of the Clash. It was, after all, Mick and Bernie who created the Clash in the first place. And both of them labored under the same delusion in the mid 80's: namely that English intellectuals were able to understand and interpret fast moving, American urban musical fads. Mick was able to create a marketable product with BAD, but its actual connection to the Hip Hop which so inspired it is tenuous, if not nonexistent. Neither Mick nor Bernie understood that Hip Hop's flavor and character was vernacular, and so was inseparable from the musicians who made it and the environment it sprung from. It would not be until Eminem that the core Hip Hop audience would accept a white interloper, and neither *Cut the Crap* nor BAD had a prayer of appealing to the Hip Hop audience in 1985. Neither noticed that it was the *instrumental* version of 'Magnificent 7' that was being played on WBLS, which was par for the course for Hip Hop. After all, Rap tracks had already been based on jams from ultra-white bands like Blondie and Liquid Liquid.

Another problem Bernie had in common with Mick was his succeptibility to the 'Reinventing the Wheel' syndrome. None of the *Crap* versions improve upon the originals and the same holds true for Mick's strange, druggy revisions of the *Rat Patrol* songs. In fact, many of the tracks were remixed for *Combat Rock* by Joe and Glyn Johns to more closely resemble the versions heard on the previous tour.

Cut the Crap and *Rat Patrol* share a lot in common in other ways as well: inept mixing, annoying sound effects, bad vocals, anemic beats and so on. The parallels become even more eerie when Mick released his inexplicable *Cut the Crap* analog, *F-Punk*. One has to wonder what strange issues Mick and Bernie must have had between them. Much is made of Joe's relationship with Bernie, but what about Mick's? It almost seems that Bernie was waiting for Mick to make his move with BAD, in order that Bernie could steal ideas for the Clash.

Joe did certainly regret the whole episode, not because of the idea of a 'new Clash' (which one could argue the Mescaleros were as well) or the new songs or because of their performances, but because of how it all ended up. Joe may have felt that the new Clash had a chance when they were on tour, but the hard brick wall of reality was there to greet him once the band was off the road and Bernie's agenda came to the fore. Joe's response to Bernie's horrible record and treatment of the new players was to round up the band and take them upon a flatbed truck to the depressed northern Britain with no Bernie and a handful of acoustic guitars. This was Joe's response to what had transpired over the past 10 months. It was a brilliant, heroic last gesture for the band's last stand. Joe knew the jig was up by then but wanted to go out with his boys for one last crusade, one last tilt against the windmills. Of course, some journalists dismissed it as a publicity stunt, but they never understood what Joe Strummer was about. They still don't.

Whatever his motivations, Strummer played *Cut the Crap* all wrong. Two possible courses of action might have saved his reputation. Firstly, he could have announced the split when it actually happened (ie; well before the release of the album) and disavow *Cut the Crap* and put the blame on Rhodes. The second option was to do a *Combat Rock*- style salvage job on the masters. *Cut the Crap* has a lot of fundamental flaws, but the most glaring problem is its atrocious mix. There are several courses of action that a professional engineer could take. The first is to bring the drum machine tracks up in the mix and treat them with "room" reverb so they don't so canned and phony. '85-vintage drum machines were cheesy to be sure, but they didn't have to sound as lousy as they do on *Crap*. Next, bring up the lead vocals and mix down the backups. Joe is buried on most tracks, often beneath all the synth bleats and sampled voices. The album was made in a 48-track studio, and Rhodes felt that most of those tracks had to filled up with raunchy sounding Punk guitars. The layering made the guitars sound like mud. Half of them could have been scrapped, and the scattered, often inaudible lead guitars could be brought up. The mix is so absurd that Joe's vocals are often drowned out by the bongoes, for Christ's sake.

But all Joe did was run off to Spain and let the shit hit the fans. And aside from the disappointment of the album itself, the biggest heartbreak for his fans was that Joe did nothing to prove his worst critics wrong. A real Clash II album would have been a fork in the eye of all the nay-sayers, but if Joe decided to at least stand and fight for *Cut the Crap*, he could have also saved himself a lot of humiliation. Don't forget that *Cut the Crap* charted at number 16 in Britain, and there was a Japanese and Australian tour booked for December.

He may not have liked *Cut the Crap* and may not have believed in it, but he felt the same way about *Combat Rock*. There is no doubt in my mind the album would have sold if the Clash toured it, no matter what the reviews were. *This is BAD* got a lot of lousy reviews, too. But then again, his mother was in her last months at that time, and the combined heartache of the album and her impending death may have been to much for him. Despite the hype and imagery, Joe was not a roughneck or a thug. He was a sensitive, complex and thoughtful man.

Joe then re-emerged from his self-imposed exile in 1986 and gave a number of humiliating interviews where he blamed himself entirely for Mick and Topper's dismissal (going so far as to claim that Topper's addiction wasn't really a problem in one ridiculous *LA Times* piece) and blamed Rhodes for *Cut the Crap*. Journalists picked up on the former and almost completely ignored the latter. The Rock Intelligentsia had a new agenda- to humiliate Joe Strummer and make him the scapegoat for the Clash's squandered potential and to some extent, the failure of Punk. And Joe played right along. He hoped that if he supplicated himself and stroked Mick's ego enough, Mick would scrap Big Audio Dynamite and return to the Clash. Joe would take odd jobs, mostly in the movie business, while he waited for Mick to come around. He would wait a very long time indeed.

REUNITED AND IT FEELS SO GOOD

Joe went out of his way to smooth out things between himself and Mick in 1986. He was desperate to reunite the Clash and undo the past three years. He said as much to the *Melody Maker*: "The Clash were a good group, but we fell to ego. To be honest, I wish we still together today." To make this wish a reality would require Joe to smooth some very ruffled feathers. Mick was devastated by his firing, and Joe went almost too far in the press to put things right. In light of the fact that the quasi-reunion of the 'Love Kills' single and *No. 10 Upping St* was very short-lived, there is a definite whiff of insincerity (or perhaps wishful thinking) in some of his interviews. He told the *LA Times*: "I did him wrong. I stabbed him in the back. Really, it's through his good grace we got back together and we're going to write together in the future. We cover completely different areas so we're not (cramping) each other's style. That's a good thing, a rare thing and in the last two years I've learned just how good and rare that is."

Perhaps sensing he was overplaying his hand, Joe then did backflips to preserve some sense of dignity with this quote: "Mick and Bernie had never got on... and Bernie sort of coerced me into thinking that Mick was what was wrong with the scene. That wasn't hard because, as Mick will admit now... he (Jones) was being pretty awkward. Plus my ego... was definitely telling me, 'Go on, get rid of him.'"

Joe had taken his fans from the nasty litany of complaints in 1984 to the extremely diplomatic "he was being pretty awkward." Joe was working very hard to undo the damage his prior attacks on Mick's own egotism had done to their relationship. This is understandable. Joe went way over the top in making his case for the firing, and it's almost certain he would have more persuasive about his motivation for such a drastic move had he not been so nasty and vindictive in the papers. However, Mick's view of himself of the sole creative force behind the Clash had not waned in 1986. He referred to his firing from the Clash in a November 1986 interview with *New York Talk* as "We've got a high speed express train and we just throw off the driver."

Joe's new subservient attitude wasn't limited to interviews. He put up the old bravado when he told Chris Salewicz in *Musician* that in coproducing *No. 10* he was "getting them to roughen up the sound and lose that Radio 2 tendency Mick has," and that "Mick isn't going to know what happened when this record gets going in the mix," but he also made sure didn't let himself get too carried away. He told Michael Kaplan in *International Musician and Recording World* that when push came to shove Joe would "step back every once in a while," and tell Mick, "its your album, man." It's likely that both Mick and Joe saw *Upping St.* as a test-run for a possible reunion, and it's equally like that neither of them thought this trial reconciliation was successful, for reasons they themselves might not have consciously understood at the time.

HE DOESN'T WANT A GUITARIST THAT TASTES GOOD...

One reason the reunion was short-lived is that Mick may not have forgotten Joe's reaction to his initial exposure to the 'Sound of the BAD'. Upon hearing mixes of the first album after he flew down to search for Mick in the Bahamas, Joe told Mick that *This is Big Audio Dynamite* was " the worst load of shit I've ever heard in my life." Just in case Mick didn't get his drift, Joe added, "don't put it out, man, do yourself a favor." In light of this appraisal, Mick would have been correct in assuming that Joe had an ulterior motive in all of his supplications.

Joe told Salewicz that he and Mick had started work on songs for an album called *Throwdown*, which they would produce together as Joe's first solo album. Of course, this album never materialized, and was in fact just one of an endless string of projects that Joe had announced that would never material-ize. After his work on *No. 10*, Joe flew to Spain to work on the Alex Cox stinker *Straight to Hell* and went from that to composing his brilliant soundtrack for Cox' next film, *Walker*. By the time he was finished with that, he had appar-ently already lost contact with Mick, and didn't even know that BAD had a new album out when interviewed by *Cut* magazine in 1988. There was a some-what revealing undercurrent of cheekiness in his response when told of the release of BAD's *Tighten Up vol. 88*, "Is it Rock and Roll? Is there a lot of guitar playing? I like it when he plays guitar."

We can only speculate on the interpersonal reasons why Mick and Joe would never collaborate with other again, but the projects they immersed themselves in might better tell the story. Joe's *Walker* soundtrack was a retro melange of Country ballads and Latin Jazz, while *Tighten Up vol. 88* continued in the up to the minute, samples-and-sequencing vein BAD had established. Joe's nearly simultaneous release to that was the soundtrack to *Permanent Record*, where he inexplicably scored a 80's teen weepie with a soundtrack filled with raunchy 50's trashcan Rockabilly spiced with Tex-Mex seasoning (reportedly infuriating the film's producers in the process). Their next simul-taneous releases were BAD's uber-synthesized, Acid House-derived *Megatop Phoenix* and Joe's Pub/Punk Fender-fest *Earthquake Weather*. What really had changed since 1983?

Joe's self-flaggelating demeanor was in short supply when he responded to the inevitable Clash-breakup inquiries in *East Coast Rocker* in 1988. "You go on for ten years and it gets to a point where the other guys taste is so far from yours that you think it stinks," he told interviewer Harold DeMuir. If you need an explanation as to why Mick and Joe stayed Splitsville, there it is.

WHY DID THE REUNIONS NEVER PAN OUT?

Ironically, riches could have been Strummer's for the taking if he had agree to reform the Clash which, around this time, Mick Jones was now suggesting to him: "It was when the first Big Audio Dynamite had left Mick, maybe about that time." The pro-posal foundered over Strummer's (some might say astonishing) insistence that Rhodes be brought back as manager: "I'm terribly loyal in a stupid way and I knew that the best combination was Strummer-Headon-Simonon-Jones on the floor and Bernie Rhodes managing it. I'd got Bernie back in when we were faltering somewhere in the middle period to manage us for the final two years of glory. I didn't really want Mick's manager to manage the Clash."

RECORD COLLECTOR, Jan 2000

Contrary to popular opinion, there were a number of abortive reunion attempts in the talking stages from the mid 80's to the mid 90's. Aside from the episode the above passage referred to, Strummer also told the *NME* in late 1991 that the Clash were mulling a tour for 1992. This was squashed, in part because of the success BAD II had with their album *the Globe*, but also because Paul reportedly wanted nothing to do with it. Bernie had also gotten CBS to bankroll a lucrative reunion deal for Joe and Paul in 1987 (which they didn't even consider) and there was also the well publicized offers to reform for Lollapalooza '95 and Woodstock. Despite the millions of dollars offered to them at one time or another, the bait was never taken. They also passed up a personal request from the Beastie Boys to appear at the first Tibetan Freedom show.

What was going on between the ex-Clash members that prevented them from capitalizing on their legacy and reforming? To answer this, you have to look at the complex and difficult relationship they shared. Mick, Joe, and Paul would make reference to the fact that they would see one another on holidays, which leads one to believe that they didn't really socialize much during the rest of the year. And Joe gave the impression in his 1996 *Raygun* interview that he and Mick's get-togethers were not entirely pleasant experiences:

"I get on with him, but if we meet up and have a session about five in the morning he'll say (putting on distraught voice) 'You cunt, you fucking sacked me' while I'm sitting on the sofa, rolling my eyes to the ceiling."

The churlish tone of this quote leaves you with the impression that the mea culpas of 1986 were well forgotten. But it also tells you that Mick and Joe still had many unresolved issues between them. And when you add up these lingering conflicts, Mick's success with BAD, the yawning musical chasm between Joe and Mick, Paul's customary dislike of the spotlight, Topper's continuing addiction and the entire band's reticence to tamper with their legacy, it becomes clear that money alone would not motivate the Clash to saddle up once again. Unlike many of their contemporaries who took the reunion plunge, the Clash were still enjoying a healthy income from royalties from their back catalogs. And Mick was riding high with BAD up until 1992 or so, which was not only made him money, but offered him the creative control he needed and the vindication his wounded ego craved after his sacking. If BAD never hit the heights the Clash did, at least he didn't have to share the glory. And he would be forgiven for relishing the fact that BAD was a lot more successful than anything Joe was involved with. And after all is said and done, BAD *was* Mick Jones. Why would he go back to playing second fiddle to Joe Strummer?

Though Mick expressed gratitude for his "second chance" with BAD in 1986, he may not yet have realized how far back he had been knocked in the Pop star pecking order. He may once have believed that his climb back to Clash-like heights was inevitable, but he would in time be disabused of any such illusions. BAD was treated as a flash in the pan in the UK, and none of their records would do well there after 1986. Even *No. 10 Upping St* made little noise in Britain, and in Europe the situation was even worse. As he bluntly stated in *ID* magazine, "BAD records have done horribly in Europe." Mick blamed the record company for this, but as the years progressed BAD's success would be mostly limited to America and Australia.

And even then, none of BAD's albums ever cracked the top 40 in the US. BAD played the balance of their career in the club circuit in the US, despite the huge promotional push they got from Columbia. And In 1991, Mick blamed BAD's failure in the UK on CBS, claiming they secretly wanted him to reform the Clash. But he failed to take into account that by presenting himself as lightweight pop star, he suffered the exact same fate that lightweight pop stars suffer in fad-crazy Britain.

But despite all this, Mick had a viable band with a huge promotional machine behind it to help heal any wounds he felt from being fired by the Clash. But if BAD's success had allowed Mick to rebuff Joe's pleas for a reunion, BAD would later cause both Joe and Paul to return the favor.

CHANGE OF ATMOSPHERE

Mick may have done much to alienate himself from the rest of the band by putting future BAD hit 'Rush' on the B-side of the 1991 re-release of 'Should I Stay.' This ploy deprived the other members of additional royalties (the single hit #1 in the UK) and did nothing but give fans the impression that Mick was trying to exploit the Clash's success for his own benefit. And the ploy failed; neither 'Rush' nor Big Audio Dynamite II enjoyed any success in the UK.

There may have been another old wound that the B-side reopened. Many of you may have scoffed when I mentioned before that Mick's belief that Clash music was any music that he made, but the 'Rush' B-side may actually be an illustration of this. Many decried Mick's chutzpah and opportunism for putting his new bands single on the B-side of a Clash record, but Mick may have seen it as entirely appropriate. His feeling may well have been that BAD II is what the Clash were, namely a vehicle for the music of Mick Jones.

But the fact that Mick had done so much to cripple Clash II may have made the inclusion of BAD *Two* song on a Clash single especially insulting to Joe and Paul. Indeed, Paul made it clear in a public statement that this move had "added insult to injury." For whatever reason the song was included, it really was a extremely dubious move by Mick, and may have been the last straw for any reunion. After all, most subsequent reunion efforts were largely efforts shepherded by Mick and his manager Gary Kurfirst, and were scuppered by either Joe or Paul (reportedly usually Paul). And as recounted previously, Joe went so far as to insist that Bernie would have to be the manager if the Clash reunited, a situation he knew Mick would never, ever agree to. And if the reunion bid Joe was referring to in *Record Collector* was in fact the one that he had announced in late '91, the Bernie ultimatum may have been Joe's little bit of payback for Mick's power play seven months prior. Ca plus change...

What's more, it's been reported that Joe nixed both the Lollapalooza and Woodstock deals. And there was a nearly three-year window of opportunity for a Clash reunion following the simultaneous collapses of BAD and Joe's project with Richard Norris and no reunion was even in the talking stage. A recent conversation I had with an old friend of Joe's at a tribute concert in New York revealed that Joe's true feelings about reuniting for the Rock and

Roll Hall of Fame were less than enthusiastic because Joe held lingering resentments over Mick refusing Joe's offer to return in 1985, and Paul has made it clear he had no intention whatsoever of ever playing there. It's entirely possible that the 'Rush' B-side was the last insult Joe and Paul were willing to stand. They could be Mick's friend, but never again would they be his bandmates.

AND WE JUST DISAGREE

Strummer stated on *the History of Rock and Roll* documentary series that the struggle to achieve stardom kept them together. So it follows once they had achieved it, they no longer had much in common. Joe expanded on this theme in his final interview when asked by *Rolling Stone* why the Clash broke up:

"Everybody wanted to take over... When you think about groups like the Red Hot Chili Peppers, they were boyhood friends. But we met when we were already grown up. Some groups might last longer if they played basketball together when they were eight."

One thing they did have in common was a desire to preserve the myth and legacy of the Clash. They were nearly successful in totally expunging *Cut the Crap* from the ledger, and Sony's promotional department worked overtime in creating a marketable image for a band whose image had become so tarnished and whose identity had become so confused. Joe cited the disappointment the Velvet Underground's extremely underwhelming victory lap engendered as reason enough to not risk doing the same with the Clash.

By the mid 90's the Clash's reputation had been restored, and the scorn heaped upon the Sex Pistols 1996 cash-in may have well justified the band's decision to leave well enough alone. Joe would never say never, but his attitude by 1999 is that he'd do it if his kids were starving and maybe- just maybe- if they made it into the Hall of Fame.

Despite their contrasting natures and tastes, in a strange way, Mick and Joe can best be understood as brothers. When their solidarity was strongest- around the time of *London Calling* - they even dressed and did their hair alike. Both of them grew up fully steeped in the Rock and Roll myth, but both of them focused on opposite poles of it. Trapped in horrid English boarding schools, Joe focused on the raw, earthy mythology of the rebel Bluesman, the Beats and American outlaws roaming vast frontiers. Trapped in the downwardly mobile squalor of tower block London, Mick focused on the glamour and style elements and the urban arts-chool sensibility which gave rise to Bowie and the Glitter Rock movement. Joe believed in going back to the Roots and Mick believed in 'progression', and this is what tore them apart. Mick put it this way in 1985: "I kept movin' and they wanted to go backward." While Paul and Joe were having their all night record parties, soaking up the most obscure old Rockabilly and Dub platters they could dig up, Mick was hitting the discos and having WBLS taped so he could immerse himself in the nascent New York Hip Hop scene. When Joe and his new Clash were touring as a near-hardcore Punk outfit, Mick was studying Frankie Goes to Hollywood records.

As the Eighties progressed and popular music continued to splinter and dissolve into ever more specialized sub-genres, it was inevitable that these

Janus twins would be pulled apart. And as the years rolled by, they even less in common musically.

And the reason their relationship was able to be torn apart was that, like brothers, they traveled in their own social circles from very early on, but unlike brothers, had no common upbringing to relate to each other through. Mick was living with his grandmother traveling in the post-Glam circles of the London music scene while Joe was squatting and playing with the least glamorous band in London, the 101'ers. Both of them spent some time in art school, but neither were terribly enthusiastic about art, and Mick admitted he went there to meet wannabe Rockers. Both had an interest in underground pop culture, but again they focused on different aspects of it.

The projects that each had involved themselves in just prior to Joe's death speak volumes about the fundamental difference between them. Joe's last tour was called the 'Bringing It All Back Home' tour, named after the old Bob Dylan song. The setlists were more retro than ever, with the Stooges' '1969' filling the proto-Punk classic slot previously occupied by 'Blitzkrieg Bop' and 'Walk on the Wild Side'. The new tracks were Rootsy in the extreme, drawing upon 60's Garage ('Coma Girl'), Surf ('Guitar Slinger Man'), Fela Kuti-style Afro Pop ('Dakar Meantime'), and Wailers-type Reggae ('Get Down Moses'). The very last songs Joe recorded were an eerie Country lament called 'Long Shadow' (which he recorded as a demo for Johnny Cash) and a cover of Bob Marley's 'Redemption Song.' By contrast, Mick had recently produced the debut album by Britpop sensations, the Libertines, and was working with Tony James on some tracks in the latest Brit-Dance style, Mash-Up. These were two entirely different men, up to the very end.

The shame of it is that what made the Clash so rich and exciting in their prime was the harmonization of these opposites. Joe's salt and Mick's sugar gave the Clash depth that none of their rivals could emulate. Joe was the roots and Mick was the branches.

But there was no precedent or roadmap for the Clash to follow. And since most of their '77 contemporaries had either broken up or sold out, they had no real support system to draw upon. It's hard to imagine now, but there was no guarantee in the early 80's that Punk, New Wave, or whatever you wanted to call it would last. There was every reason to believe it would be seen as just another fad once the excitement died down.

Because of this, Mick felt that the Clash needed to build their music around a "new skeleton," as he put it, to stay viable. Joe felt that Clash had a sound and an identity that could accommodate a number of different shadings and flavors but still remain Clash. Joe was enamored of the raw, unvarnished energy of Roots music but Mick was fascinated by the new technology that was streaming out of Japan, so fascinated he wrote a song about it for his first BAD album.

The shame of it is that if the Clash could have swallowed their pride and hired a professional producer to referee their disputes and help synthesize the Joe's thesis and Mick's antithesis, they may well have created a new sound that would make them both happy. Joe and Mick were great singers and song-writers and Bernie was a great manager and conceptualist, but none of them were anything near a competent, big-league producer. At all.

I vacillate all the time over whether they should have tired to make it work or whether it was all well and good the way it ended up. I was getting really sick of them in their *Combat Rock* mode, and I'm already sick of the corporate propaganda that follows them around today. I can't say I totally regret that Clash II never went anywhere. I'm angered by the consant outright lying and revisionism, and I would have loved to get an well-produced album out of them, but there are so many great live recordings that capture the band in their prime. And given the incredible sickness behind the scenes, maybe there was nowhere to go but down, particularly in the musical black hole of the 80's. They disappeared before it all got too predictable and familiar and I got sick of them too. But their biggest problem was that they were way ahead of their time. The self-styled sophisticates and coffeehouse heroes who came aboard for *London Calling* and the like wanted the Clash to continue in their 'progression'- that is, to become a completely impotent stoner band. And when the new Clash didn't go along with this program and instead went back to the original idea of the band, Mick's partisans and lame-brain critics accused them (in a positively Stalinesque fashion) of crimes against the almighty virtue of 'progression.' But had that lineup come along in 1994 or today, they would have set the world on fire. Mick had the right idea for the mid-80's, it would seem, but his career might have benefited from a longer view.

But when I compare the Clash to U2, another band I was a huge fan of back in the day, I really appreciate that the Clash exited the stage leaving everyone hungry for more. The media machine created in the 80's by MTV and the like is truly sickening to me, and it sucks out any of the mystery and excitement that real Rock and Roll needs to stay vital. It's not like Joe and Mick disappeared after the Clash, and both *Combat Rock* and *Cut the Crap* showed that the band had reached a metaphysical cul de sac that could not, and perhaps should not, have been overcome.

As I write this, I am listening to *Earthquake Weather*, an album that I've had severely mixed feelings about in the past. But my disappointment in it was that it struck me as being an unlikely vehicle to return Joe back to the top of the heap. But now the strange, abstract lyrics that bothered me so much before just sort of seep back into the mix. It gets me to thinking: We expected so much of the Clash that maybe our expectations became a fictional construct that had put Joe and Mick into a straightjacket that they could escape only by breaking up. They just couldn't do so consciously. And I am glad they never did reunite. They were just too far apart to ever make it work again.

AFTERWORD

As I write this, I am listening to *Streetcore*, the final studio album from Joe Strummer. It is, in many ways, the final chapter of the Clash story. Though I've heard that Mick Jones is putting together a new band with former Generation X bassist Tony James, it seems unlikely that Mick is either willing or able to shoulder the burden of the Clash's legacy. Joe Strummer was to the Clash was Jim Morrison was to the Doors- it's personification. A lot of people don't realize that it was actually Robbie Krieger who penned the Door's big hits. But once Jim was gone the book was closed, at least as far as most folks were concerned. I always felt that the Clash would become the new generation's Doors, but I had no idea that the metaphor would extend so far as to losing Joe.

As I wrote in this book, the Clash were in many ways the last of the great Classic Rock bands. The Clash rest comfortably in the canon with the second line of the Rock and Roll echelon- with the Kinks, the Doors, Jefferson Airplane and the Who. But they also share many eerie parallels with the Beatles. John Lennon and Paul McCartney both grew up without their mothers, and Mick was raised by his grandmother when his mother emigrated to the US. And Joe spent most of his life in miserable boarding schools, away from his parents. Joe was very much the Lennon figure in the Beatles- idealistic, poetic, thorny and contentious. Mick was the McCartney- romantic, melodic, untroubled. Neither Joe nor Mick possessed the talent of their archetypal forebears, but they played the roles well enough. After the Beatles split John released a string of difficult records until he 'retired' ostensibly to care for his son Sean. In reality, he was about to be dropped by Capitol and his retirement was a strange hermitage marked by drug abuse and emotional turbulence. Paul hit the ground running, and formed the uber-Pop Wings, and continued on pumping out the hits, without missing a beat. John re-emerged from his sabbatical and hit the charts with the *Double Fantasy* album, only to be cut down by a assassin's bullet. After the Clash, Joe soon found himself in a cul de sac and was told by Epic in 1991 not to bother recording a new album, because they wouldn't release it. Mick formed the uber Alt-Pop Big Audio Dynamite, and mined much the same audience the Clash did. Joe re-emerged for a marathon 3 and half year binge of recording and touring, only to be cut down by a genetic fluke. Again, Mick and Joe's success was nowhere the level that Paul and John enjoyed, but the parallels remain.

Sony has done a remarkable job in marketing the Clash as a legendary band, which is ironic since the Clash's legendary status was earned on stage, not in the recording studio. Another parallel is brought to mind- the Grateful Dead. The Dead were the first to admit they were never able to put across their music to full effect in a studio, since their music was part of a real time experience. Real Dead fans ignore the studio albums and concentrate on the live material. The Clash made some great records, and left more than enough great tracks amongst all the filler on their last studio sets, but this pales before their best concert performances. I bought my tickets to see Clash II the same day tickets went on sale for the Dead and there must be some meaning there. I saw the Mescaleros are the new Dead, a parallel that was reinforced by their two-drummer first lineup (and was driven home on the tracks that Slatto played keys on). If you think Joe didn't listen to the Grateful Dead, you're wrong. Joe listened to everything. Brian May of Queen recounted a story where he sat next to Joe on a trans-Atlantic flight and was stunned to find out that Joe had an almost encyclopedic familiarity with their catalog. Like the Dead, the Mescaleros served up a gumbo of Roots Rock styles and proffered a taste of the experience of the Clash and old school Punk culture to fans too young to have been there.

I was struck by how reminiscent of *London Calling*-era Clash the Mescaleros were in the '01 and '02 shows I saw. The Ska, Reggae and Punk-heavy setlists brought me back, and you younger fans who saw those gigs consider yourselves lucky. You definitely caught a glimpse of the old spirit.

The Mescaleros were getting away from that spirit on this new record, however. Only two tracks on the record feel like Joe Strummer music. One is the leadoff 'Coma Girl', written in tribute to his daughter Jazzy's wanton ways. This track is pure Joe and sounds like the only track on the record Joe wrote in its entirety. The mighty 'Get Down Moses' (first aired at the April 2002 Saint Anne's gigs in Brooklyn) appears, but is several steps removed from the savage punch of the original. Joe's vocal is resigned where it was once assaultive. The album is somewhat of a salvage job, given the fact that many of the songs were without vocals at the time of Joe's death and thus remain unreleased (some demos and leftovers were used to fill in the gaps).

The Mescaleros seemed to be taking control of the music and Joe seemed to be retreating, as he had with Bernie and Mick. Lacking the soulful contributions of Tymon Dogg and the earthy vibe of Joe's guidance, the finished tracks sound like Joe singing on someone else's record. The direction the music was going in was far removed from Joe's usual obsessions, making the album a strange parting shot for Joe's career.

And the lyrics are yet more dispatches from that strange and abstract interior world that Joe had been inhabiting since 'Love Kills'. Obtuse references and non-linear musings on post-war Americana abound. Obviously, Joe's way of dealing with the boredom and misery of his adolescence was to immerse himself in the dreams of Hollywood, Rock and Roll and the American dreamscape of Jack Kerouac, Ken Kesey and Raymond Chandler. And once the fires of the Clash had cooled, Joe retreated back into that world in his lyrics, adding touches of globalist idealism as seasoning with the Meskies.

However, his performances are spirited enough, leading one to believe he was happily along for this new ride. I was somewhat taken aback by the music the first few times I played it, but I've made my peace with it. Joe is gone and the album is what he left behind. And on repeated playings, the album is taking on a strange, dreamlike quality. It's almost like a Joe Strummer record from a parallel universe. Joe was always striving to do something new and in that light, *Streetcore* is a fitting final farewell.

But Joe himself was never my focus. My focus was always Joe as the heart of the Clash, but Joe himself was not the Clash. Nor was Mick, nor Bernie. The Clash was not Joe, Paul, Mick and Topper. Nor was it they and

Bernie. The Clash was more than that. The Clash was a story of a point in time, and it was the story of a band of not-especially skilled musicians guided by a mad genius and thrust into a time when everything was up for grabs. The Clash was also the fans and writers who invested so much of their hopes and dreams in the band. The Clash was also the Cold War and Mutually Assured Destruction, the Shah of Iran, Fidel Castro, Thatcher, Carter, Reagan, the National Front, the Socialist Workers Party, Rock Against Racism, Nick Kent, Garry Bushell, Johnny Lydon, Jimmy Pursey, the Specials, the IRA, the UDA, the Baader Meinholf gang, Jonestown, the Gong Show, MASH, Elvis Presley's death, Kurtis Blow, Andy Warhol and on and on and on. The Clash were a time and a place and an idea, as much as they were musicians and songs. They were the great white hopes and the whipping boys. They were the focus of the Alternative music world, and every smart kid at the time at least had an informed opinion of them. They burned bright, kicked against the pricks and fucked up whenever they possibly could. They offered something onstage that hadn't been seen since the late 60's- pure catharsis and ecstatic release. But times changed, selfish agendas set in and the world no longer wanted them, so they went away.

The world may no longer have wanted them, but it needed them and it still does. I don't believe another Clash will ever appear. But I think people should start to think seriously about what they represented. The Clash personified many important ideals, one being the ideal of sheer possibility. The Clash believed they could and should try anything, because anything was possible. It turned out that not everything was probable, but you can't blame them for trying. The Clash, like the Pistols, were created to self-destruct. But unlike the Pistols, the Clash had many more seeds to sow before they did themselves in. Some of the seeds failed to take root, but many others have born fruit.

I have always thought of the Clash as their own genre. I once dubbed this genre 'Mongrel Groove', borrowing a phrase from a old review in Q magazine, but I think 'Clash' is even better. My dream is to see a whole movement, an entire sub-culture of Clash. A movement that grapples with the themes and memes the Clash did, and strives to reconcile the future and the past as the Clash had attempted. A movement that wants to take it all and throw it all in the blender and have it come out all saw-toothed and vital and colorful. A movement that takes the sounds and sights of yesterday and tomorrow and shows you that it's all the same thing, dammit, because yesterday can make tomorrow seem like today and vice versa, whatever that means. A movement that delves into the rich musical troves of the Third World, but makes those sounds their own. A movement that eschews the whiny navel-gazing of the new Punk and replaces it with engagement and awareness, but keeps a sense of humor amid the outrage. Seeing Joe all those times has shown me that I haven't gotten enough of that feeling, nor do I want to. Kids throughout history have delved into earlier movements to create their own, and I humbly submit the Clash as a movement unto themselves that you can take inspiration from.

You'd better act fast, though. In the 90's I thought Rock and Roll was just sleeping, but now I realize it's in a coma and is on the 'guarded condition' bulletin. Kids today aren't stupid, and they realize that video games are offering them more bang for their buck that the fake Rock and Punk bands out there. No one seems to be saying anything, and every damn song I'm hearing is some vague and pointless tantrum towards someone who doesn't "feel that way" because "something has changed" and they just "turned and walked away" or they are now "so far away" and all the rest of those cheesy clichés that we've been hearing for the past 15 years. I'll hear a band like Linkin Park or Evanescence scream and whine and have no idea what they are so angry about when the song is over. There is plenty to be angry about out there, perhaps more than there ever was in the Clash's day. But no one seems to have anything to say about things that are making real people angry. Sadly, not even Joe bothered to address the mess the world is in on the new *Streetcore* tracks.

I think one of the great things about the Clash is the deeper you dig, the more you find. There are tons of great shows out there on tape, tons of videos, and tons of great pictures and interviews, all of which are just a click of the mouse away. The official version that Sony peddles is just a drop in the bucket. And when you add in all the pre-Clash and post-Clash material, there is a true treasure trove waiting for you. It's kept me busy for a quarter-century now. It hasn't always been easy or fun, but it's been incredibly rewarding.

The Clash has been more than a short-lived band, it's been a way to look at the world and a way to synthesize disparate and contradictory ideas and concepts. Almost by accident, the Clash produced an exegesis of their times- a dialectic- and their basic concepts and approach are still valid today. The externals have changed but human nature has not. And there has been precious little true musical innovation out there since they left the stage. In closing, my hope and dream is that the Clash could become a movement, a genre unto itself that transcends the band that inspired it. My fantasy is that 'Clash' could displace what now passes for Punk, and provide young people with a positive and constructive way to engage themselves in the world they live in.

The completion of this book marks the end of a quarter century of my life. By writing this book, I have now purged myself of the Clash. Perhaps in some ways I was meant to write it, simply to offer another vision of a phenomenon that has been constantly reduced into a easily digestible (and marketable) pabulum, or simply to relieve myself of the burden I took on when I chose to be one of the Clash's young footsoldiers. There may be more to say, but I will leave that to fresher troops. If there is one thing I want the Clash to be remembered for, it's their incendiary, revelatory and life-changing live performances. The Clash to me were modern shamans of the highest order, even if they never realized it. Compared to that, everything else about them is completely trivial. I don't understand some of their younger fans- they seem to have a completely different vision of the band than I do. Perhaps because they never had the chance to be bathed in the sweat and fire of the Clash on stage.

I was blessed enough to be there, in the pit or cheering in the wings when that awesome power was let loose. The purity and the intensity of it will never leave me- it will always be in my blood. Sadly, nearly everything else will be found lacking in constrast. I certainly got a taste of it at three of the eight Mescaleros shows I had the good fortune to witness, but the best Mescalero show I saw was roughly equivalent with the worst Clash show, at least when it comes to that pure cartharsis.

Whether or not I can understand or relate to some of these fans is irrelevant, though. The story of the Clash ended on December 22, 2002 and everything since has been post-script. There is nothing really left to fight for or about when it comes to that story. It's time to move on, especially as the pillars of the Earth shake and tremble before our eyes. Joe was unable to see the writing on the wall, or was unwilling to translate it for us, and Mick has never made it his business to man the ramparts. The Clash story ended as the Age they emerged from vanished from the stage. Storm clouds more ominous than anything the Clash witnessed darken the horizon. The veneer of law and international order wilts under the brutal exercise of realpolitik and soon smoke may be rising yet again from the charnel houses of the world. But if the story has ended, maybe it's time for a new one to rise from its ashes.

THE END

Printed in the United States
32074LVS00003B/65